BEST SPORTS STORIES 1983

Edited and Published by
The Sporting News

President and Chief Executive Officer
RICHARD WATERS

Editor
DICK KAEGEL

Director of Books and Periodicals
RON SMITH

Published in the United States by The Sporting News Publishing Co., 1212
North Lindbergh Boulevard, St. Louis, Missouri 63132.

Library of Congress Catalog Card Number: 45-35124

ISSN 0067-6292
ISBN: 0-89204-133-1
10 9 8 7 6 5 4 3 2 1

First Edition

Table of Contents

The Prize-Winning Stories

Other Stories

ON THE COVER: The first-place color prize goes to photographer Jay Hector, whose picture of Ferrari team driver Didier Pironi in his 126 C2 during Formula 1 competition in the Detroit Grand Prix originally appeared in *Road & Track* magazine. While capturing a true sense of the race's speed in a still photo, Hector's picture creates its own beauty. The fire engine-red paint on the car's body pops out from the gray road to produce an arresting graphic appeal. Although the human eye never sees motion as depicted in the photograph, the picture uses the camera's unique ability to distill onto film the essence of racing—speed.

PREFACE

When attempting to chronicle and portray the top events and personalities that make up a year in sports, what better tools are available than the eyes, words and cameras of the men and women who were there? That's the premise upon which *Best Sports Stories* was founded in 1944 and that foundation remains solid through the publication of the anthology's 39th edition in 1983.

Best Sports Stories, which annually honors a year's top writers and photographers, owes its rich tradition to the foresight, dedication and hard work put forth for the better part of four decades by its founding fathers, Irving Marsh and Edward Ehre, and its publisher, E.P. Dutton of New York. Mr. Marsh died in 1982 after an illness that prevented his involvement with the 1982 edition. It was a major loss for the journalistic community. Mr. Ehre, who shouldered the massive judging responsibilities alone in 1982, and E.P. Dutton have turned over the publishing rights for the anthology to *The Sporting News.*

The Sporting News, indeed, has a difficult act to follow. With that in mind, here's a preview of *Best Sports Stories 1983.*

The prize-winning writing categories have been expanded from two to four with the winning entries receiving $500 each. That allows the newspaper features, commentary and reporting entries, all lumped into one massive category in 1982, to be judged within their specific frameworks. The fourth category honors the writer of the best magazine story.

The photo sequence of the contest remains the same—with one exception. The winners of the black and white action and feature categories will receive $500 each. But this year's contest also honors the top color photo entry, which runs on the cover. That winner will receive $500.

To select one winner from among the hundreds of quality entries in each category is, of course, a difficult task. The selection of the other top stories and photographs that fill out the book is only slightly less agonizing. To find a qualified panel of judges with knowledge of the subject matter and the ability to recognize and analyze good writing, *The Sporting News* turned to the University of Missouri School of Journalism, long recognized as one of the best journalism institutions in the world. The result was a five-man panel of judges. Each member of the panel has impeccable credentials and a strong interest in sports. Here are brief profiles (more in-depth profiles can be found at the end of the biographical section at the back of the book) of the judges:

George Kennedy, an associate professor and chairman of the editorial department of the *Columbia Missourian,* the student and faculty-run daily newspaper that serves the city of Columbia, Mo.

Daryl Moen, a professor and managing editor of the *Columbia Missourian.*

Brian Brooks, an associate professor and news editor of the *Columbia Missourian.*

George Pica, an instructor and city editor of the *Columbia Missourian.*

Ken Kobre, an associate professor and the head of the photojournalism sequence at the university.

After poring over the hundreds of stories and pictures submitted from all over the country, the judges selected the following winners.

WRITING

Reporting	Thomas Boswell	Washington Post
Features	Armen Keteyian	San Diego Union
Commentary	John Schulian	Chicago Sun-Times
Magazine	John Underwood	Sports Illustrated

PHOTOGRAPHY

Color	Jay Hector	Road & Track
B&W Action	Robert B. Stinnett	Oakland Tribune
B&W Feature	Glenn S. Capers	Tucson Citizen

These stories, writers and photographers are merely the cream of a very rich crop. The all-star lineup featured in this book is outstanding and covers a wide range of 1982 sporting events that, in retrospect, made up an interesting year in sports.

As seen through the eyes, words and cameras of those who were there.

Best Action Photo
Cal Beats the Band

by Robert Stinnett of the *Oakland Tribune.* The power of this exclusive photograph is the combination of jubilation, shock and confusion it captures during one of the most extraordinary, unforgettable finishes to a college football game ever. The game was between California and Stanford Universities and ended in confusion when Kevin Moen (26) danced triumphantly into the end zone, through startled members of the Stanford band who thought the game was over, to complete a five-lateral play that gave Cal its memorable 25-20 victory. Copyright © 1982, Oakland Tribune.

Best Feature Photo
Envy in Stride

by Glenn Capers of the *Tucson Citizen.* This powerful, provocative photograph of legless swimmer Keith Moore elicits a human reaction in the viewer through its contrast with the bodyless legs passing by. The friendly, upbeat expression on the swimmer's face keeps the picture from becoming maudlin. Copyright © 1982, Glenn S. Capers.

Best Reporting Story

Orioles: On the Threshold of a Dream

BASEBALL

By *THOMAS BOSWELL*

From the Washington Post
Copyright © 1982, Washington Post

Perfection.

The sky above Memorial Stadium was pale blue and utterly empty today. Not even a cloud could get in free. The air was an ideal, invigorating autumnal 70 degrees. Scientists might call such conditions "standard temperature and pressure." Baseball fans, however, would call this fervid pennant-race afternoon one of raging high fever and almost unbearable pressure.

Occasionally, what should happen does happen.

Today in Memorial Stadium, it did.

On the penultimate day of a gloriously improbable pennant race, the Baltimore Orioles, baseball's symbol of intelligence and economy, finally caught the mighty Milwaukee Brewers, symbol of numbing slugging power.

Now, after this day's 11-3 Oriole victory over Milwaukee, the two teams with the best records in baseball, the two clubs that have battled each other for six months, find themselves breathlessly deadlocked after 161 games at 94-67. These Orioles and Brewers will meet one more time here on Sunday at 3:05 p.m.

The starting pitchers will be two gentleman with serious claims on bronze busts in Cooperstown: Baltimore's 263-game winner Jim Palmer, who's won 13 of his last 14 decisions, and Milwaukee's Don Sutton, winner of 257 games. All this in the final regular-season game of the final season of the Orioles' manager, Earl Weaver.

To the winner goes the American League East Division championship.

If that winner be Baltimore, then the Orioles will also find a splendid place in baseball history. No club since the professional game first breathed in 1869 has ever swept a season-ending, four-game series to win a championship by one game.

To stretch the point still further, Baltimore would have gained five games in the standings in the final five contests of the season; that, too, would be a first in baseball annals.

"We've gone from extinction to a tie for first place in less than 48 hours," said a stunned Hank Peters, Baltimore's general manager, recalling how bleak the team's chances looked before they scored four last-gasp runs in the ninth inning to beat the Tigers in Detroit, 6-5, Thursday night.

More than that. When the final Brewer out this afternoon was recorded at 5:25 p.m., it meant that Baltimore had beaten Milwaukee *three* times in just a few minutes less than 24 hours.

To Sunday's loser will go a winter of the bitterest grief.

If that loser be the Brewers, then this exceptional team—the club with the most staggering offensive statistics since the '52 Brooklyn Dodger Boys of Summer—will run the risk of being remembered, and reminded forever, for having the worst late-season collapse on record.

It would be a spurious infamy—simply the sort of star-crossed, uptight, five-game losing streak which any team can have, but one which, in this case, would come at the least propitious time imaginable. What has happened to the Brewers here has been so sudden, more like a series of natural disasters than baseball games, that somehow they hardly seem culpable.

As the Brewers left Memorial Stadium this evening, they had the look of 25 Androcles looking for the face of a friendly lion in this dizzy, deafening den.

"SWEEP, SWEEP, SWEEP," bellowed this standing crowd of 47,235 as the Brewers trudged to their quarters. Then, as usual, the chants of "O-R-I-O-L-E-S."

To say that the Brewers now face a colossal bit of soul-searching would be an understatement of the first order.

In these 24 Hours of The Oriole, the Baltimoreans have won, 8-3, 7-1 and, now, 11-3. Every time the Brewers have shown the least sign of resistance or will, the Orioles have redoubled their pummeling of the Brewers' suspect pitchers in their next at bat.

The most staggering statistics from these three games is that the Orioles have had 46 hits—18 of them today—and 58 men on base in just 24 innings. Every time the Brewers look up, the bases are drunk with fowl. Sooner or later, somebody's got to score. Keep enough pressure on and accidents will happen.

Those who think such abnormalities cannot continue were not present in Fenway Park in September 1978 when, with similar stakes on the table, the New York Yankees humiliated Boston by a total score of 42-9 over four days. That was the Boston Massacre. This might be the Baltimore Bushwack.

Several unique psychological burdens hang over the Brewers'

heads.

First, all evidence says that they simply play miserably against Baltimore. The Orioles have won nine of 12 meetings. Baltimore has hit .325 for the year against the Brewers while Milwaukee has batted just .238 against the Orioles. These Brewers, who dominate the lists of major league leaders in almost every statistical category, have 51 *fewer* base hits than Baltimore in their dozen meetings. The top five men in the Brewer order were two for 18 today.

Given all this, the Brewers, who've been in first place for the last 60 days, must ask themselves the gravest of all athletic questions between two fine teams: Given what has happened, do we really deserve to win?

At the moment, the Orioles—who have gone 33-10, including 17 come-from-behind wins, since they began a sprint August 20—now have the sort of statistical aura that might bespeak superiority.

Next, the Brewers have been trying desperately to put on the skids ever since they arrived here.

"This has gone far enough," said Gorman Thomas before the game today.

"If there's such a thing as overconfidence," said Brewer General Manager Harry Dalton, "then we've pushed them to the brink."

The Brewers seem caught by the first baseball Law of Motion: over the long haul, the sport is a game of statistical norms, but, over the intense short haul of a pennant race, it's largely adrenaline, luck, momentum, unpredictability. In other words, this is the time of year for streaks, collapses, heroism. Ask the world champion Los Angeles Dodgers, who appeared to have the N.L. West wrapped up until they lost eight straight.

At one level, this weekend has been, and will be, just a jubilant gathering of the baseball fans and clans.

However, to the participants, it's a form of pastoral torture. Baltimore Manager Weaver, whose imminent retirement may be serving as an inspiration to his team, is so tight that you could play "Dueling Banjos" on the lines on his forehead.

Underneath all these major chords, this symphony of a final showdown has one tantalizingly bizarre *leitmotif.*

None of this should ever have happened.

Back in June, Milwaukee catcher Ted Simmons thought that a John Lowenstein strikeout had ended an inning, so, he casually rolled the ball back toward the mound. Before Simmons realized there were only two outs, a pair of Baltimore runners had advanced a base. The next man singled home two runs, instead of just one. The game ended in a 2-2 tie instead of a 2-1 Milwaukee victory, when rains arrived after nine innings.

But for that tie, which was replayed here as part of Friday's doubleheader, the Brewers would already be A.L. East champions.

Baseball historians will instantly note the similarity of the famous Merkle Boner of 1908 when Fred Merkle cost the New York

Giants a midseason victory over the Chicago Cubs when he neglected to touch first base after an apparent game-winning hit. Instead of a victory, the game went down as a tie and the Giants, forced to replay the contest at season's end, lost the pennant to the Cubs by a single game.

Perhaps such plays, such baseball miracles, come along once in a lifetime.

Judge's Comments

This story belies the notion—popular in some quarters—that good writing is found only in the domain of feature writing. Superb imagery, subtle transitions and clear, concise writing allow the author to tell today's story, that the Orioles have caught the Brewers in the standings, while setting the stage for the next day's drama—the game that will decide it all.

This article obviously ran as a color sidebar to a game story that contained an inning-by-inning account of the action. Our guess is that the game story was superflous in most respects because so much of the audience watched the event in person or on television. Mr. Boswell's article set the stage perfectly for Earl Weaver's farewell. We find ourselves thinking seriously about digging through microfilm of the Washington Post to find the author's account of *that* one. One delightful aspect of the piece is the author's selective use of quotes. There are few of them, but they effectively complement the author's prose and the pace of the story. There is a clear reason for using every one of them and a clear reason for placing them where they are placed. There is no quotation for the sake of quotation, a malady all too common in much of today's writing.

All of this is accomplished in a story of reasonable length. The author writes what must be written, then stops. That, too, is a marvelous trait seldom found in today's writers.

In every respect, this piece is a winner.

Best Feature Story

Julie Moss Found Ecstasy After Losing to Agony

TRIATHLON

By *ARMEN KETEYIAN*

From the San Diego Union
Copyright © 1982, San Diego Union

All you could think was, "Oh God, she's going to fall again. She's 15 feet from the finish line, 15 lousy feet from all the glory she deserves, and she's going to fall again. Dammit, she's not going to make it."

For nearly 12 hours, she had given everything the human spirit can ask of the human body. The race, this 140.6-mile torture test called the triathlon, had been hers since five miles into the marathon. She had passed the previous tests—the 2.4-mile swim in the Pacific, the 112-mile bike ride. Now, with 15 feet to go in the 26.2-mile run, her world was falling apart. The finish line was almost close enough to touch, but she looked as if she couldn't possibly get there.

Her legs, so rubbery they looked like jelly, shook and then surrendered.

She had fallen the first time 440 yards from the finish and sat there, dazed and staring at the street, unable to rise for nearly three minutes. Finally, she struggled to her feet and forged on.

With less than 100 yards left and her nearest competitor closing fast, she collapsed again. And got up. With less than 50 feet left, her legs gave way once more. Some race officials tried to help her to her feet so she could finish. Somehow, she picked herself up again.

Now, for the fourth time, she was down—a frail, crumpled heap on the ground, 15 pathetic feet from a dream.

The streets of Kona, on the Big Island of Hawaii, had been packed with partiers—"It looked like the Rose Parade," she would say later—but they had fallen silent. No celebration now. The surrealistic side of sport had taken over. The revelers could do nothing more than bear witness. A courageous Raggedy Ann look-alike seemed to be struggling for her life at dusk.

This happened February 6. Thirteen days later, in living rooms across America, millions of people watching ABC's "Wide World of Sports" saw the tapes of this utterly compelling spectacle and sat stunned, collectively thinking the only possible thought: "If anything is fair in this world, let Julie Moss get up right now. Let her walk, stagger or crawl those last 15 feet. Let her finish. Let her be the women's winner in the World Ironman Championships. Please."

In the background, a haunting, beautiful instrumental tune played on.

Commentators Diana Nyad and Jim Lampley said nothing. Minutes earlier, after the second fall, Nyad had delicately explained a substance on Moss' shorts, saying, "In situations of extreme stress you sometimes lose control over bodily functions."

There was nothing left to say now. It was only Moss and that mysterious music. All the crowd could do was hope.

"I couldn't see their faces," Moss said recently, drawing lines in the sand at Cardiff Beach near her home in Carlsbad as she thought back to the scenes that gripped a national television audience. "All I could feel was arms actually trying to lift me up and carry me along. The energy was unbelievable.

"Then I looked up and saw Kathleen cross the finish line."

The race was over. Kathleen McCartney of Costa Mesa had won. Moss could have quit. Instead, she started to crawl. Slowly, agonizingly—red head down, one thin arm in front of the other—she crawled.

No one can describe the sight of an athlete such as this, beyond the limits of exhaustion, crawling to a finish line. Nobody tried. Only the music played on.

One minute later, the odyssey ended. Julie Moss wobbled and fell once more. When she did, her left hand felt the finish line. No matter that she was second. Incredibly, she had made it.

You wanted to cry. Many did.

"Have you ever seen pictures of dead people?" she says now, her freckled face very much alive. "When I saw the picture of the finish line, I thought: 'That's what dead people look like.' But you know what? My eyes were closed, but I was smiling. I knew, finally, it was all over."

No it wasn't. The story of 23-year-old Julie Moss, who grew up loving the beach in Carlsbad, was only beginning. From that moment Moss, even more than winner McCartney, became to many viewers an instant and authentic heroine, an unforgettable inspiration.

Ever since February 21, when host Jim McKay closed the telecast by calling the 20-minute sequence "perhaps the most dramatic moment in the history of Wide World," and ABC News and Sports President Roone Arledge went immediately to the phone to offer rare congratulations to the crew, the reaction had been astonishing.

Top-level executives of other networks, 40th-floor ivory tower types who usually don't get excited about anything except Neilsen ratings, called ABC, moved and envious. A touched public called, too.

"We've had more calls on that show than any in recent memory," an ABC spokesman said. "I can't remember anything like it. It was an amazing thing . . . It gave people the impetus to go on with their own lives."

Add this: Every week for 12 years, a shot of Yugoslav ski jumper Vinko Bogatej crashing horribly has epitomized "the agony of defeat" in the opening montage of "Wide World." Suddenly, for the first time, there is talk around ABC of footage dramatic enough to compare with it.

In the last 34 days, Julie Moss has flown back to New York with McCartney, at ABC's expense, for a live, in-studio update with McKay on February 28; accepted an invitation to NBC's upcoming "Survival of the Fittest" competition with men's Ironman champion Scott Tinley (also of San Diego) in New Zealand this month; and turned down a guest spot on David Letterman's TV show. She was contacted about joining ProServ, a Washington, D.C., firm that represents athletes as diverse as Moses Malone, Tracy Austin and Tai Babilonia, and has been interviewed by dozens of newspapers around the country. She is making a motivational speech at a June IBM convention in Hawaii and picking clothes for magazine cover shots. *People* magazine thinks she is a celebrity.

She's just Julie now, sitting in gray blouse and jeans on the beach in Cardiff, not far from the house where she lives with her parents. She is 5 feet 5, skinny, and very cute in an athletic, outdoorsy way. Like many before her, she could be playing it cuter in order to magnify her moment, maneuvering to promote what might be shortlived star status. She hasn't done that. It just wouldn't be the Julie who has lived in San Diego County since fourth grade and majored in physical education at Cal Poly San Luis Obispo. She leaves tomorrow, at NBC's expense, for New Zealand and the "Survival of the Fittest" show, and will stay for a month's bicycle tour. This summer she will work as a life guard and train for another go at the Ironman Triathlon in the fall.

She says the Letterman appearance was accepted, then turned down because, after watching the late-night show, she didn't like Letterman, or his act.

"I have a special feeling about that tape," she says. "I just thought it deserved better than late-night television."

McCartney has met with the William Morris agency, but Moss intentionally avoided a New York meeting with ProServ, the sports marketeers.

"Basically that's not what I'm into," she says. "Do I promote and go while the going's good? I asked myself what's my goal. I know it's to do well in October (the next Ironman competition). I kind of had to draw the line."

The need to draw the line arose the day after the Ironman, in two time zones. At an awards dinner in Hawaii her name was called, honoring her second place time of 11 hours and 50 minutes. Suddenly, spontaneously, some 2,000 people stood and cheered. Five hours east, the fire was beginning to burn at ABC.

As soon as Moss returned to Carlsbad, Nyad called and said the show was being moved up from an original April air date, that people were working around the clock to get it out.

ABC Production Assistant Jimmy Roberts, 25, was part of a hardened Hawaii film crew. "We don't get excited about too many things," he says. "But even before we edited the tape, Bryce (producer Bryce Weisman) knew we had something very special. All of us felt the same way. This was a story we were all very attached to."

Roberts worked six days, 10 a.m. to midnight, editing the tape. He found the mysterious background music, a Tim Weisberg song entitled "Dion Blue."

"I went to the ABC Music Library. Fifteen minutes after I got there, I found Weisberg's greatest hits album. I knew as soon as the needle hit that that was the song," he says. "Usually, you wait to see how it takes with the video. Not this time. There was no doubt about it."

A couple of days later Roberts was in putting sound to tape, working in a large audio screening room. "People had heard about the screening," he says. "It was packed. There were network executives . . . A whole other show in production at the time stopped and watched. There was nothing but silence. People were dumbfounded."

The New York trip with McCartney has been Moss's biggest thrill to date. Originally, in-studio interviews in Los Angeles were proposed. Arledge said the reaction was already too great. He wanted both women back in New York with McKay.

So a couple of California girls took to New York for a three-day freebie: Limousines, rooms at the Plaza ("Every woman in a full-length fur coat"), sightseeing at the World Trade Center, Tiffany's and The Metropolitan Museum of Art, lunch at the Russian Tea Room. Moss loved the city. And the city, as doesn't often happen in New York, loved her back.

A man in Macy's was the first to notice. A short time later, a businessman stopped Moss on the street. "Both men said, 'Saw you on TV and just wanted to tell you how wonderful you are and to welcome you to New York."

Four years ago, the year after the Ironman was created, Julie Moss couldn't run two miles without stopping. It was only last summer that she competed in a triathlon of any distance. Her best previous finish was third at the 23-mile Del Mar Days Triathlon in September.

It was after Del Mar that she decided to try Hawaii. Christmas killed any idea of December workouts. She surfed instead. In January she began cycling 100 miles a week, swimming five miles in a pool and running 40 miles. Good mileage, but hardly worth consideration at Kona.

She arrived in Hawaii on January 21, 17 days before the Ironman. A transformation took place. Captivated by the other Kona crazies, she increased her weekly mileage dramatically: 300 miles on the bike, 10 miles in the water, another 50-60 on foot. "The energy level was incredible," she says. "Everywhere you went, someone was saying 'Let's go on a run or bike.' We worked out from 6 a.m. to 6 p.m.

"Psychologically, that's what separated me from those who were just trying to finish. I was ready to go."

In the swim, she ignored warnings and went out fast. At the halfway point she found herself all alone—a unique feat, considering there were 580 competitors. "I must have found a pocket between the real fast swimmers and the rest of the pack," she says. "I swam the last mile with no one around me."

Her time was 71 minutes, strong enough to nearly tie men's winner Tinley. She knew her time was well into the top 10, but how far, nobody knew. Later she realized she was third.

Halfway into the 112-mile ride along Kona's striking lava fields, Moss caught a tiring Shawn Wilson, pushing after leader Pat Hine, who was hindered by a stress fracture in her foot. Hine was barely walking when Moss passed her on an uphill grade, five miles into the marathon.

"It was weird," Moss remembers. "I never imagined I would be leading."

The ABC crew immediately made friends. "We're with you the rest of the way, Julie," one said.

About this time, Moss met Rowen Phillips, an Australian triathlete who was in Hawaii, alone to compete in the Ironman. "His accent was so thick I couldn't understand him. He kept talking. Finally I said, 'Look, I have trouble talking in a race. You talk, I'll listen.'

"It's funny, one of the things he said to me was, 'I'll just hang around you to get my picture in the paper.' "

Phillips never left Moss' side for the rest of the race. As the drama wore on, he became the only constant in a sea of uncertainty. He gave her inspiration as she inspired millions.

"People have told me how we were working for each other," Moss says. "I guess we were. I know I could have run with someone else, a friend. But they may not have been as gallant, or whatever the word is, as Rowen. I guess I didn't want to disappoint him."

Experience is the unseen edge in any sport. It means more in the Ironman, where one must gauge personal time and distance, the ability to spring and relax, in relation to unseen leaders and followers.

Moss said she made her first mistake 16 miles into the marathon. Word came out McCartney was eight minutes behind. "I felt a need to keep pushing, to stay ahead," she says. "In retrospect, eight minutes might as well have been an hour. After that much time, there's no way you can gain on a person."

At 20 miles, after four miles of increased pace, Julie Moss' body broke down. "I hit the wall plain and simple," she says. "I realized right then I hadn't eaten enough. With the excitement and everything I was cutting down on food. I should have been eating more. You learn that with experience. But by then it was too late."

She began to feel lightheaded. She drank an electrolyte replacement fluid, watered-down Cokes, then full cans. Anything. "I was looking for any kind of buzz to keep me going," she says.

Nothing worked. Her legs stopped functioning. Phillips kept her walking, trotting, until there were only 440 yards to go.

"The first time I fell, I could see the finish," she says. She could also see the end. "I felt like I had nothing left. In my head, I wanted to get up and sprint out. My legs said, 'You're done for the day.' "

So she sat for almost three minutes. The ABC cameras, sensing the impending drama, closed in. Time and again, Moss struggled to rise, only to plop back to the pavement. "I kept trying to figure out different ways to get up. I was trying to get my legs underneath, to throw my weight forward."

Upright at last, she says she mistakenly "ran out a little too hard." She fell again.

The third time, 50 feet from the finish, the awful truth became inevitable. ABC flashed the fresh-faced McCartney onto the screen. She was less than 100 yards away. Race officials ran to Moss' side, attempting to lift her to her feet.

"They wanted to help me up, and I didn't want them to. But then I lost my balance and had to reach back for them. It killed me to do that. By reaching back I was saying, 'I need your help.' "

Somehow she lurched forward. A young Hawaiian woman tried to hand her a flower. A hand unconsciously brushed it away. "I knew I couldn't accept it until I crossed the finish line," she says.

Seconds later, she was down for the final time.

Would she crawl? From the corner of the screen came McCartney. She went past, to the finish line. It didn't matter anymore. Yet to Julie, it did.

"It was really easy to crawl," she says. "I thought, 'It's only 15 feet. I didn't know where the next girl was, but I didn't want to finish third. Not now. I didn't care if it was embarrassing. A lot of what happened was embarrassing. I didn't care what people thought. I wanted to finish that race."

The future for Julie Moss? It is hard to say. She does not want to be overwhelmed by celebrity. Her boyfriend, Reed Gregerson, who finished fifth in the Ironman, will accompany her. They had broken up during intense triathlon training, only to reunite that awards night in Hawaii.

How much does she want to win the next Ironman? Listen to her: "You know the neatest thing? An athlete rarely has a chance to take him or herself to the limit, and then go on. I know if I ever have to, I can do it. I can take it to the very end. Not many people can say that. And it's a feeling I can hang on to forever."

Judge's Comments

Strip away the hoopla of the Super Bowl, the flowing drinks and tasty hors d'oeuvres of the Kentucky Derby, the bigger-than-life aura of the World Series and the essential element of sports is revealed. The moment of truth, one person against himself or herself. When Julie Moss reached deep within herself at the World Ironman Championships, the drama was genuine. Had it not been for television's insatiable appetite for sports, this drama might have been frozen only in the minds of the relative handful of spectators.

Thanks to Armen Keteyian, we, too, are privy to Julie Moss' agony. The writing compels us to extend her a hand, just as the spectators wanted to do. We, like those privileged to be there, must only watch: "The revelers could do nothing more than bear witness. A courageous Raggedy Ann look-alike seemed to be struggling for her life at dusk."

We are uplifted by her spirit: "Moss could have quit. Instead, she started to crawl. Slowly, agonizingly—red head down, one thin arm in front of the other—she crawled."

We are buoyed by the response: "At an awards dinner in Hawaii, her name was called, honoring her second-place time of 11 hours and 50 minutes. Suddenly, spontaneously, some 2,000 people stood and cheered."

We could ask for more; we could get to know Julie Moss better. But let's be thankful for this feast of athletic courage. Keteyian seized on a story about the essential challenge in sports. He recreated the drama in such a way that even those among us who saw the ABC film can still appreciate it. Even more, we can savor it. We can reread it and let the images linger in our minds. On television, it's gone. That's the power of the written word, and Keteyian harnessed it for us all to enjoy.

Julie Moss starred in her own "Chariots of Fire," and no script writer had to embellish the details. This is real, right down to the second-place finish. She placed first in courage. The story places first because it permits us to share the moment.

Best Commentary Story

Dailey Is a Sorry Character In Deed

BASKETBALL

By *JOHN SCHULIAN*

From the Chicago Sun-Times
Copyright © 1982, Chicago Sun-Times

Quintin Dailey never said he was sorry. In the middle of his second day on the verge of a multimillion-dollar career, contrition didn't even seem to occur to him. You could throw the possibility up to the rotten plum the Bulls picked first in the NBA draft, but he kept responding as though he cut out his soul on the same dark night he cursed a woman with a lifetime of savage dreams.

He flirted with rape and he faced three felony charges and he avoided jail only by getting down on his knees and pleading guilty to a crime that didn't smack of sex. He came within inches of being scorned as an animal and yet Quintin Dailey, child of the Baltimore playgrounds and grim proof of how sports distort reality, was more concerned about telling the Chicago press that he is starting life over at 21. For a moment Wednesday, you wondered why Paul Westhead, his scholarly new coach, didn't tell him what Shakespeare said about the evil men do living after them. But in the end, your only choice was to think it best that Quintin Dailey was shown for what he is.

When you asked if he realized how close he came to doing time in a stinking cell, he offered exactly the response you would expect from an All-America who rode the University of San Francisco's gravy train as far and hard as he could: "Either you're there or you're not there. I'm not there. You have to do things to keep from going there."

When you asked if he ever thinks about the woman he assaulted, ever wishes he could somehow erase that long cruel night for her, his answer splattered across his image like a bird dropping on an already soiled sheet: "Basically, I don't. I had to go through the situation by myself, so I don't concern myself."

And when you walked away from him as quickly as you might a bad accident, you couldn't suppress the wish that some day Quintin Dailey will feel the same terror he so casually inflicted on his victim.

There are only two people who know how bad it really was that night in USF's Phelan Hall, but even the sketchy details provided in police records are enough to fill you with revulsion. On Dec. 21 of last year, at 3:45 in the morning, the star guard of the school's basketball team entered the room of a 21-year-old student nurse and held her captive until dawn was breaking three hours later. He wanted her to fellate him and he made her masturbate him and, on at least one of the occasions she reached for the phone to call the police, he wrapped his spidery fingers around her throat.

No matter how many cheap thrills his acts provided, it was not a performance Quintin Dailey wanted recounted in the newspapers. Better they should praise him for his long-range shooting, the kind that kept his scoring average at 25 points a game regardless of what his conscience should have been doing to his insides. But there was no hiding for him after his victim overcame her reluctance to press charges and USF's spineless officials decided to quit harboring a criminal, glamorous though he was. Then came the deluge.

At first the papers and the public bought his pleas of innocence, for in America athletes are still regarded as virtue's last pillars. Gradually, though, word began to circulate that he had taken two lie detector tests and that he had admitted his guilt to the San Francisco policeman administering them.

Quintin Dailey was trapped by his own deceit, even though he was still trying to make a game of it Wednesday. "You didn't hear my side of the story," he said, "but I'm not going to tell you my side of the story." Maybe he felt smug because, thanks to the lawyer his friend Reggie Jackson bought for him, he was spared the ignominy of being nicknamed San Quintin Dailey. He was saved by plea bargaining and God knows what else, put on three years' probation by pleading guilty to nothing worse than a non-felony assault charge. But even so, he will spend the rest of his days in a prison without bars.

There will be none of the sympathy that John Lucas gets in his battle with cocaine, none of the disbelieving smiles that greeted Marvin Barnes' fly-by-night eccentricity, none of the tears that fell when Reggie Harding, the hapless 7-foot stickup artist, got himself shot to death. What Quintin Dailey did was rob another human being of her dignity and scar her psyche. If he doesn't think it's necessary to ask forgiveness after that, he can rest assured he will get no forgiveness.

The people who call newspaper sports departments have made that abundantly clear, and the people who buy tickets to the Bulls' games are sure to echo them. "I didn't think we had a problem 24 hours ago," Jonathan Kovler, the team's managing general partner said Wednesday. "Now I do."

The Bulls have offended their female customers and angered male customers who have the least bit of humanity. They have wedged Paul Westhead between a rock and a hard place, although their latest coach apparently wasn't smart enough to let sin cancel talent, and they have displayed an appalling lack of salesmanship. By the time Westhead and general manager Rod Thorn decided to counsel Quintin Dailey on common decency, he had already proved he is no longer the gifted innocent who endured his parents' deaths, dated Reggie Jackson's niece and worked with handicapped children.

Something snapped inside Quintin Dailey that December night and the loose wires continued to short-circuit whatever charm he possesses Wednesday. He was as remorseless and unrepentant as you ever could have imagined, and he didn't seem to care. "When you're a superstar, people are going to think whatever they want about you," he said with a shrug.

He should know, however, that those people he takes so lightly can do more than refuse to watch him play basketball. They can hate him. And well they should.

Judge's Comments

Few newspaper columns attracted as much attention during 1982 as the winner of the commentary category. John Schulian's attack on Quintin Dailey, written in anger, stirred outrage directed at both writer and subject. Commentary should generate reaction, but the reaction is not the reason Schulian was picked as a winner.

He won because he crafted a clear and compelling essay on an important topic. Writers of commentary are essayists. The form demands that each essay, no matter what the subject or the length, make a point and support it convincingly. Schulian, from indicting introduction to condemnatory conclusion, leaves no doubt about how he feels or why. You don't have to agree. Many don't. But you do have to think about what Schulian says. That's effective commentary.

To be effective, commentary doesn't have to be angry. In fact, only two of the other columns included in the book have anger in them. All, though, have emotion. Blackie Sherrod writes in humor, Ray Didinger in sorrow, Bill Lyon in celebration. All write of the human spirit.

Best Magazine Story

"I'm Not Worth a Damn"

PRO FOOTBALL

By *DON REESE* with *JOHN UNDERWOOD*

From Sports Illustrated
The following article, "I'm Not Worth a Damn" by John Underwood,
is reprinted courtesy of Sports Illustrated © June 14, 1982.

*(The following story is written in the words of former professional
football player Don Reese as told to John Underwood.)*

Cocaine arrived in my life with my first-round draft into the
National Football League in 1974. It has dominated my life, one way
or another, almost every minute since. Eventually, it took control
and almost killed me. It may yet. Cocaine can be found in quantity
throughout the NFL. It's pushed on players, often from the edge of
the practice field. Sometimes it's pushed by players. Prominent
players. Just as it controlled me, it now controls and corrupts the
game, because so many players are on it. To ignore this fact is to be
short-sighted and stupid. To turn away from it the way the NFL
does—the way the NFL turned its back on me when I cried for help
two years ago—is a crime . . . Users call cocaine "the lady." The lady
has a widespread acceptance in the best of circles. However, those of
us who are—or were—hooked can tell you it's no lady. And until I am
cured, I consider myself hooked. Even now, talking about it makes
me want it. I can feel the familiar signals going through my body,
making my heart beat faster.

I am 30 years old, and desperate. A 6'6", 280-pound desperate
man who should have known better. Who *knew* better, because I was
raised better. Six weeks ago I took myself out of society (and out of
football, which I don't intend to play again) to a rehabilitation hospital where help was available, and I think, I *pray,* I've seen the light.
But to see it, I had to see a lot more.

I had to see myself depicted in the press and on television and
everywhere else as a drug dealer, even if my dealing was a silly
one-shot kind of deal that was more naive than evil.

I had to see the jailhouse door slammed shut, and know I

wouldn't walk free again for a year. As bad as that was, it still didn't cure me. I got worse *after* I was freed.

I had to see my family shy from me, the wife I doubt I could live without grow disgusted, the mother and father I love and respect grow ashamed. I had to see players I considered close friends go through the same deterioration, their lives messed up, their talent blowing away.

I saw my own fortune wasted—thousands and thousands of dollars, down the drain. I now know the embarrassment of hiding from creditors, of having checks bounce and cars repossessed. I was like a man at his own funeral as my career as a defensive lineman went from what I thought was the brink of All-Pro in 1979 to the edge of oblivion in 1981.

And I saw more. I saw the dark side of the drug world, from a frightening perspective. Twice I looked down the barrel of a loaded gun, held by men who said they would kill me if I didn't pay the debts I owed. Debts for cocaine. At this writing, I owe drug dealers $30,000, and there's a bullet scar in my home in New Orleans because one dealer tried to scare me into paying. I couldn't pay.

I now see myself as a miserable human being, not worth a damn. I reached the point where I really *wanted* to die. To kill myself. One night in Miami I went into the streets looking for enough heroin to do the job. Other times I put the barrel of my own gun into my mouth, and practiced pulling the trigger.

Here's what it's like to be a big-time football player in America and screwed up: In New Orleans, where the drugs got to be so bad in 1980, I began getting blackouts in my thinking. Like climbing a ladder with rungs missing. I couldn't hold conversations without my mind going off somewhere. I thought I was losing it. I was in a stupor much of the time. I had no conception of day and night. My little boys, Myron Paul, 7, and Philip Charles, 2, are crazy about me. Every morning they would come and jump on me in bed, playing on me like little deer. I would remember them doing that, and I wouldn't be aware of anything else until they came and jumped on me again at four in the afternoon.

I hate football. I hate the NFL. I know those feelings aren't completely rational, that *I* am responsible for my actions before anyone else. But I feel them just the same. I wish now I'd never made the decision to play the game beyond high school. I wish I'd never accepted a college scholarship. I wish I'd stuck to my word when I said I didn't want to play pro ball. I think I would be a better person, whole, today.

Football—the environment, not the game itself—as good as wrecked my life. I should have been smarter. I should have been stronger. I know that. But drugs dominate the game, and I got caught up in them, and before I knew it I was freebasing cocaine. And then I was a zombie.

The lady is a monster, a home wrecker and a life wrecker. In the body of a skilled athlete, she's a destroyer of talent. Right this minute she's spoiling the careers of great athletes you pay to watch on Sunday afternoon. Even the super ones like Chuck Muncie, who I think potentially is the greatest player in the game. Muncie has to be a superman to do what he does on the field and use coke the way he does off it. I single Chuck out because I love him like a brother, and if he ever got off this stuff he would be like *two* Jim Browns. Somebody has to shock hell out of the players of this game and scare the league. I hope I do that. I'm scared myself. Scared to death it won't happen. The NFL is heading for catastrophe. Drugs are causing it.

But even if you don't give a damn about the players, if you care about the game you have to be alarmed. What you see on the tube on Sunday afternoon is often a lie. When players are messed up, the game is messed up. The outcome of games is dishonest when playing ability is impaired. You can forget about point spreads or anything else in that kind of atmosphere. All else being equal, you line up 11 guys who don't use drugs against 11 who do—and the guys who don't will win every time.

If you're a team on drugs, you'll never play up to your potential, at least not for more than a quarter or so. Then it's downhill fast. I've known times on the field when the whole stadium blacked out on me. Plays I should have made easily I couldn't make at all. I was too strung out from the cocaine. It was like playing in a dream. I didn't think anybody else was out there.

Pittsburgh has always been a clean team, and look how long the Steelers stayed on top. Miami was clean until it started winning Super Bowls, then it changed. I was there when it was changing. New Orleans lost 14 games in a row in 1980, when freebasing became a popular pastime in the NFL. New Orleans was a horror show. Players snorted coke in the locker room before games and again at halftime, and stayed up all hours of the night roaming the streets to get more stuff. I know. I was one of them. San Diego is a team that should have won the Super Bowl twice by now, as talented as it is. San Diego has a big drug problem. For a short time, I was part of it. I played my last football in San Diego in 1981.

Ask the people who are using and they'll tell you that a cocaine cloud covers the entire league. I think most coaches know this or have a good idea. Except the dumb ones. Dick Nolan must have suspected that we were on the stuff in New Orleans, because he asked me about it a couple of times. Don Shula was too sharp to let it go by unnoticed in Miami, and we had to be extra careful around him. Don Coryell must have known in San Diego.

I have to think the owners know. Or at least have heard. I know John Mecom Jr. found out in New Orleans, because we talked about it later. He systematically broke up the Saints team during that time, and I think for that reason. I know that Mr. Mecom loved Chuck Muncie, and he got rid of him just the same.

Cocaine is a .38 at the head of every player in the game. And it's getting easier to put your finger on the trigger all the time. I had 15 different sources for cocaine in New Orleans. Dealers even had a "beeper" system in operation there, just like doctors. Ring up your friendly coke supplier, wait for the beep, leave your order and in minutes get a delivery at your front door.

I've seen dealers literally standing on the practice fields of the NFL, guys everybody knew. They're not there to make the game better. What they do, and what they know about the players, can't possibly be good for the game.

You know all this if you're a player. You might not know for sure who's really hooked, but the heavy users are easily spotted—the big heaving chests, the sweat pouring down, the nervous energy, and most of all the decline in effectiveness. You see a player coming off the field complaining about phantom injuries and you know he's probably messed up. He's coming out of the game because he *needs* to come off. I asked to be demoted in New Orleans in 1980. I didn't want to be first team anymore, considering the condition I'd let myself get into by then.

And in the privacy of locker rooms, players talk about it. And argue.

In San Diego, Fred Dean, the defensive lineman, used to yell at us. Dean was clean. He didn't even drink beer. None of the Chargers I freebased with would do anything around Dean. But the Chargers had Dean so screwed up over his contract he was always up tight, and he'd yell at the players in the locker room: "Why don't you free-basing bastards get the hell outta here! You're killing us!" Fred got lucky. The Chargers got so tired of listening to his tirades that they traded him to the San Francisco 49ers last season. And what happened when Fred got to San Francisco? The 49ers won the Super Bowl, with Fred playing a big role—the biggest role, in fact—on the defensive line.

The reality of how contagious it has become hit me a year ago in New Orleans just before I got released by the Saints and picked up by the Chargers. The Saints had come off the misery of 1980 without much hope of anything better. My own life was a mess. I was high half the time, and wishing I was the other half. But for a while I got myself straight, and a few of us started working out, getting ready for a new start. Then this rookie running back showed up at mini-camp.

I'd never met the kid. Never even seen him play. But we were in the dressing room, and he and another dude came over to where I was standing. He said, "Hey, man, I understand you're the one can put us on to a little coke." I couldn't believe it. I said, "Get you ass away from me." He disgusted me. He hadn't played a lick in the league, and here he was talking like Captain Cocaine. Then I realized what I was looking at: *me* seven years before. Just as eager to screw up my life then as he was now.

Two months ago I got a letter from my mother in Prichard, Alabama. My mother is a beautiful person, in every way. Very compassionate, very perceptive. I hate myself for ever causing her a moment's pain. All this time I had thought I had kept most of my disgrace from her. I was kidding myself. In the letter, she told me *exactly* what I had been doing. From A to Z. And why it was wrong, from every standpoint. She begged me to see a doctor. She said if anything happened again like what happened in Miami, when I got arrested and sent to jail, it would kill her.

It was like a fist in the face. All along she had known. When I look back on all of it now and realize what it did to my family, I'm amazed they stuck by me. But if they hadn't, I'd probably be dead.

I take shelter in none of the standard excuses for being where I am. I wasn't raised in a ghetto, scratching for bread or fighting for turf. I knew no poverty or hunger. I came from a strong, loving, God-fearing family that taught the responsibilities and joys of hard work. I learned those things early. And later on, I married the best woman a man could have. *That* sure didn't hurt me. So Don Reese can't blame his downfall on anybody but Don Reese. My progress down the ladder of success is Horatio Alger in reverse.

There were 11 children born to Albert and Osie Dean Reese, and I was the fourth, the third of eight boys. My father was no respecter of sex. He treated us *all* like daughters. I wasn't allowed to go out until I was 17 or so. I didn't smoke or drink, either, and a marijuana cigarette was something I only heard about. Education, not pot, was pushed on all of us. Albert Jr. and my oldest sister, Gladys, both went to college. My brother Eddie played football at Grambling.

I really didn't want to go to college to play football myself. I'd have been content to stay in Prichard forever. I got a letter from Alabama asking if I'd be interested in being one of the Bear's first black players, and I certainly didn't want that. But there were a number of scholarship offers, and my father very skillfully changed my mind about playing football in college. I know how strongly he felt, because I was going to sit out one game in high school due to an injury, and when I asked him if I could use the car to take a girl, he said, "Hell, no. If you don't play, you don't use the car." He had started a vault (grave digging) company when I was 15 or 16, and four days a week he had me up at 6 a.m. and on the road digging graves. Sometimes I'd dig four or five a day, with a pick and shovel. Sometimes the funeral procession would be coming down the road and I'd still be digging. And if the work made me bigger and stronger, it also made me realize I didn't want to do *that* the rest of my life, either. College football seemed like a good place to hide.

I wound up at Jackson State, a mostly black college in Mississippi, partly because I had an uncle who played there and partly because it was only 180 miles away. My father supplied me with wheels—a 1967 Chevrolet Impala SS 396, the slickest car on campus —and I became a college boy, with a diamond in one pierced ear and the hair piled high on my head, looking every bit the punk a lot of people probably thought I was. I always say I *eased* out of Jackson State, but that's not quite right. There was nothing easy about it. Jackson was the best of times, and the beginning of the worst.

I met my wife, Paulette, at Jackson. And I was a football hero. My play as a defensive end got me an invitation to both the Senior Bowl and the Coaches All-America Game, and eventually got me drafted in the first round—number 26 overall—by the Dolphins.

But I was in trouble all through college. Little things, mainly. Breaking curfew, jumping the wall to visit Paulette off campus. But drugs were never a problem until the very end, and then only marginally. My junior year, I smoked my first reefer. They were plentiful on the Jackson State campus by that time, and I was curious. Paulette and I and three other couples took some rooms at a hotel in Jackson for a party, and the Greeks—the fraternity guys—brought in some marijuana. It seemed like they always seemed to have it.

Actually, we were more into drinking then. We drank Ripple wine, or that Mogen David 20/20 everybody calls "Mad Dog" because it's 20 percent alcohol and looks like blood and can knock you on your tail. But I tried a reefer with the others at the hotel. And like everything else I try for the first time, wine included, it made me sick.

A couple of weeks later I tried one again, with some players in the football dorm. This time I kind of liked it. We all got a little buzz on, and we sat around listening to music, and it was cool. I smoked it fairly often after that, usually after games at parties, and then in the off-season. But if I said I used it more than once every couple of weeks, it's probably an exaggeration. I know I never paid for it. The guys just had it, and they passed it around.

My career at Jackson State ended on Thanksgiving night of my senior season, after we had beaten Alcorn State in our last game. We were celebrating, and one of the guys sneaked a couple of majorettes into the dorm, and a group of us went up to my room to smoke some reefers. We had barely lit up when there was a banging on the door: "Reese!" It was Coach Bob Hill. "I know what's going on in there, Reese. Just pack your bags and get the hell out of here. We don't want you here anymore." I left school right away.

Then came the day Don Shula called to tell me Miami had drafted me. I was all pumped up. The Dolphins sent a scout to bring me to Miami to negotiate. We were the only two in first class out of Mobile. "You're in the big time now, baby," he said. "Order anything you like." I ordered a vodka and orange juice. Then a gin and orange juice. Then a *bourbon* and orange juice. I was flying high.

Joe Robbie, the owner of the Dolphins, gave me a $45,000 bonus to sign, and a three-year contract calling for $28,000 the first year, then $30,000, then $30,000 again. That's important to remember. Abner Haynes, a former player, was my agent. He took his cut off the top of the bonus, and they took some more for taxes, and I wound up with $9,000 to buy myself a new car. That was about all I saw of my signing bonus.

Then Haynes took me back to his place in Dallas "to celebrate." If I knew then what I know now, I'd have skipped Dallas and gotten my rear end back to Prichard. But I was going to be a big shot. In a Dallas Holiday Inn, downtown, I sat in a room and watched some people take out these little brown vials of white powder, pour it on a glass, cut shares with a razor blade, and then sniff it up their noses. My first look at cocaine.

I didn't do any. I *wanted* to, just to try it, but I didn't. The next night they snorted again, at an apartment, with some of the other players Abner had under contract, but I passed again. I left the party early and went back to my room, still a virgin.

While I was in Dallas I got a call from Jackson State asking me to come back to the campus—the same campus I had been kicked off— to be honored. The frog had become a prince. I never got my degree, but I have pictures of me shaking hands with the governor.

I was still clean when I went to Miami's training camp. I remember how impressed I was seeing the big names of the Dolphins in the locker room—Larry Csonka and Mercury Morris and Larry Little. Little had gold all over him, and those two Super Bowl rings, and I thought, "Damn, wait'll I get me one of those suckers."

I tried coke for the first time that week, right there in a room at Biscayne College in North Miami. Lloyd Mumphord brought some to the room. Mumphord had played for Texas Southern in the same league I'd been in at Jackson, and he was a regular defensive back for the Dolphins. We divided it up, and he and I tooted it through a straw. It seemed natural enough. I heard a lot of the guys were doing it, and if they were doing it, why shouldn't I? The only regret I had was that it burned my nose. But I got a terrific tingling sensation, and then a sudden and powerful need to go to the bathroom. I remember sitting there and thinking, "Dang, this is the best s—— I ever had."

The next week I tried it again, a little heavier. This time I *really* felt it—wiinnnnnngggg, opening up my nostrils and going right to my toes and back up again. From then on, I was available whenever *it* was available. By the time the season started, I was snorting at least once a week.

I never paid for it. Not then. I'd guess half the players on the Dolphins—whites as well as blacks—were using it in small amounts, as "recreational" doses, you could say.

After a while I realized I would have to find it on my own occasionally, so Mumphord put me on to a Cuban dealer named Juan, and he was my principal source. Juan had a place in Little Havana. I'd call and he'd say, "Come on by," and I'd go get it. I only had to pay $40 a gram at that point. The players always got it cheap, if they paid at all, which should tell you something. I didn't give it much thought one way or another. It was fun. It was "sociable." I liked it. I wanted it.

And my want grew just like a cancer. I went up to two grams and then to what people called "eighths"— three and a half grams. An eighth is a "big snorter." Later on, tragically for me, I learned it's also a "small baser" or freebaser. You really can't freebase with less than an eighth. The going rate for that now is around $325. But I didn't know what freebasing was then. That piece of carnal knowledge came much later.

By 1976, my third season at Miami, I was riding the crest—a starter at defensive tackle, with a lot of good publicity. My coke use was expanding, too. I had about 12 sources; some I paid, some I didn't have to. You get lulled into believing the bargain rates will last forever. And it was still a well-hidden exercise. I didn't think so at the time, but the best thing we had going for us at Miami was Don Shula. He's smart, and he's been around players too long not to see things. Everybody always had to be on their toes. That kept the lid on. Mercury Morris said Shula asked him once if he was on anything. Merc said no.

I didn't use it before games at Miami, and I don't think many Dolphins did. We sure as hell didn't use it in the locker room. If you're only snorting, you can do without coke before a game. It's *after* a game that you want it bad. The only real chances we took at Miami were on plane rides back from road games. The coaches always sat up front, and we'd be in the back where it was dark, with our little brown bottles that held about a gram, and we'd sit and sniff right out of the bottle. Or if we were being extra cautious, we'd slip into the bathroom and sniff it there. It's almost impossible to tell when you're doing that little, especially under circumstances where you're *supposed* to look strung out.

A Dolphin assistant coach would come back and see me dead in my seat, all sprawled out, and say to me, "You tired, Don?"

And I'd say, "You know it, man." What I was feeling was no pain. Coked out.

Nobody really checks like they should, of course. The league could attack the drug problem in a minute with urine tests, but they steer off that land mine because the Players Association objects so strenuously. It's crazy, really. You object to something that will prove you're doing wrong, and you get *carte blanche* to keep on doing it. In sports involving dogs and horses, they take tests all the time. And Olympic athletes have to be tested. But they don't dare test the players in the NFL. It's crazy.

After a while, I began snorting it at our home in Hialeah. I'd stay up, waiting for Paulette to put Myron Paul to bed, and then I'd take some cocaine out and toot it. One night I even got Paulette to try it, but one sniff and she said, "Unh-unh. That ain't me."

On May 4, 1977, the bubble burst. It was bizarre, and it was dumb, and when I look back I still can't believe I did it. For a lousy 500 bucks, I threw my career into the toilet.

Randy Crowder and I were never drug "dealers." The first time we tried "dealing" was the only time, and like the amateurs we were, we screwed it up every way possible. I don't think Randy would have done it at all if I hadn't talked him into it. He was a good person, a starting defensive lineman for the Dolphins, and when the "opportunity" first came up he was dead against it.

Here's what happened. One night Randy and I went down to Mercury Morris' house to play some basketball and drink some beer, and when we dropped back by Randy's place—he wasn't married then; he lived alone—an airlines stewardess named Camille Richardson called. She said she wanted to buy some coke. Camille had tooted with us before. She said she had a problem and needed to get some to sell. Randy said, "Girl, you must be crazy. No way."

But Camille persisted. She said her mother was sick in the hospital, and the bill was running close to 5,000 bucks, and that's what she figured she could make on a coke deal, selling it "to a couple guys from Philadelphia." If we got it for her. Dumb Don Reese fell for it like a ton of bricks. The little professor in my mind said, "Hey, you can make something on this transaction without even getting involved."

I talked to a dealer the next day. He said there was a "lot of good stuff in town, at a good price." I called Randy and told him we should go along. Just pass it from one hand to the other and take a middleman's cut. He was still reluctant.

This went on for eight or nine days. Camille changed her story. She said the Philadelphia guys wanted to come in and get it that week, but now they needed a pound and they'd pay $18,000 or $19,000 for it. I was still willing. I figured if we bought a pound for $13,000, we could cover Camille's mother's expenses and still split a thousand bucks between us. Just to make the switch. Finally, everyone agreed.

It rained hard all morning on May 4, a bad omen. Randy and I drove to Camille's place in Randy's baby-blue Lincoln Continental, and the cars were flooding out all around us. We were unlucky. We got through. I should have known something was wrong immediately because Camille's apartment was practically cleaned out. I said, "Camille, you didn't tell me you were moving." She said, "Oh, yeah, I have a new place."

We tooted a little on the way over to meet the "buyers" and got lost, but we finally met them at the Green Dolphin restaurant in Miamarina. After she introduced us, Camille left . . . "to make a flight." Randy and I took the two guys outside to the Lincoln to talk. One of them said, "We can only pay $15,000." I said, "Man, that's not near enough." We dickered, and they agreed to pay $18,000. I pulled out a half ounce for one of them to sample. I was watching in the rearview mirror and it looked like he faked sniffing it, but he said, "Hey, man, this is good," so I let it pass.

"You want it then?"

"We want it."

We arranged to meet at the Holiday Inn on Brickell Avenue in Miami to make the switch. But when Randy and I left to get the stuff, I began to get antsy. I told him we ought to meet at the Ramada Inn on LeJeune Road instead. I could get adjoining rooms, and we could check them out before we made the final commitment. I got my car and went to Little Havana and bought the stuff from the dealer, and when I walked into the Ramada Inn there was a call waiting for me at the desk. It was Randy. He said the Philadelphia guys wouldn't come way over there in the rain, they were "afraid they'd get lost," and for me to bring it to the Holiday Inn as originally planned. I didn't know it then, but the Ramada Inn is outside the jurisdiction of the Miami police.

By this time I was so nervous I couldn't sit still. Scared stiff, actually. I drove around the Holiday Inn six times before I went inside. I had two bags in the car with me—the bag of coke and a bag of bread. I took the bread inside. As I walked through the lobby I began getting really bad vibes. But I kept on walking and went to the room, and they were there drinking beer.

"Where you been, man?"

"It's still raining outside," I said.

"Where's the stuff?"

"Right here."

And I handed them the bread. If I hadn't said another word, we might never have been arrested. But I got a pang of conscience, or an attack of ignorance, or something, and I said, "Wait a minute. This isn't it. The stuff's in the car." And I went back down and got the coke.

When I walked through the door again and they checked it out, the room exploded with cops. One hit me on the head and another put a gun down my throat. Randy panicked and tried to back off the bed where he was sitting, and they jumped on him and beat hell out of him. It was a nightmare. In the wink of an eye we had turned from prominent big league athletes to common criminals.

I said, "Oh, my God, what have we done?"

One of the detectives took me into the other room and said, "O.K., Don, we'll make you a deal. You tell us which players are messing with this stuff and where you're getting it, and we'll let you go. Shula won't know, Robbie won't know." I said, "I don't know where it came from. I'd tell you, but I don't know." They tried the same thing on Randy, and they took us to jail, to a holding cell, where the magnitude of our predicament really hit Randy. He went wild, yelling and beating on the wall. He was sick that his parents would find out. I knew it would break my mother's heart, and I thought it would probably end my marriage.

We got busted about 7:30 p.m. We were in jail until almost 1 a.m., and then we got out on bail. When I got home, Paulette met me at the door, sobbing. It had been on the late news. We were both numb. I prayed all night that night. I saw the sun come up. The next three months were pure hell. Our trial had been announced, and nobody would touch us. My parents were mad. Our friends were scared to come around. Joe Robbie said the only way we'd ever play for the Dolphins again was if it proved to be a case of mistaken identity. Some players asked Shula if we could still come to mini-camp, but Shula said no.

Randy stayed at our house most of the time, and we just sat there, soaking in our own sweat. Our money was running out. Two days after we got arrested, the credit company sent a couple of guys around to repossess my Continental; at the time I was a month behind on the payments. They weren't taking any chances. I don't seek sympathy when I tell all this, because I deserved what I got. But I won't pretend it was easy. Paulette had a job teaching school, and four or five days a week Randy and I got up at dawn, rented a rowboat at six dollars a day, and fished the Everglades for bass and bream. Sometimes we paddled over a mile to get to a pond. I mean we went *fishing*, Jack, and everything we caught, we took home and cooked and ate.

Despite having every reason to believe we'd been set up, we pled guilty to the charge, hoping to get a light sentence. We took lie detector tests before the court of Judge Joseph Durant Jr. to make sure we'd never been involved in any other drug deals, and when we passed he got all the lawyers together and agreed to the punishment: a year in the Dade County Stockade. Light if you don't have to serve it, heavy if you do.

I had a seed with me when I went in. I put it in a flowerpot and watered it every day, and when I came out 12 months later, it was a full-grown plant and so pretty that Paulette hung it on a wall. But *I* came out more stunted and fouled up than ever. There were as many drugs inside the jail as out. We used marijuana freely. Coke I snorted there once; I could have had as much as I wanted, but I was wary.

The question at that point wasn't so much who Randy and I would play for, but if we would ever play again. Shula had been encouraging. He said we "should not be condemned for all time." The Miami papers didn't like that a bit. One writer jumped all over him for being such a flaming liberal. Then Robbie said we would "never play for the Dolphins again," ending the debate. Robbie tried to get the league to ban us, too, but Pete Rozelle decreed that we could play ... if anybody still wanted us.

The Toronto Argonauts sent their general manager down while we were in prison to offer us contracts. Good ones, too—$60,000 a year. But they were contingent on our getting out early to play, and Judge Durant said no. He had taken a lot of heat for going "soft" with our sentence, and when our attorneys tried to get him to cut it to nine months, he wouldn't hear of it. I didn't really blame him.

As it turned our, it probably wouldn't have mattered. Canadian immigration authorities let it be known that we wouldn't be allowed into Canada to play football.

We were released from the stockade in August of 1978, not knowing what to expect. But within eight days we had signed to play again—Randy with Tampa Bay, me with New Orleans.

Mr. Mecom made me an offer I couldn't refuse. First he said he would clear all my debts. Then he gave me a $40,000 bonus and a $70,000-a-year salary. Then he hugged me and said, "I don't care what's happened before, you're a Saint now, and I'm glad we have you." I really like Mr. Mecom. He was like a little boy over the signing. I thought I'd died and gone to Heaven.

For two seasons, I did my best to repay him. I was the closest thing I could be to a changed man. I had my best year as a pro in 1979. I led the team in sacks and was named Most Valuable Player on defense. I felt I should have made the Pro Bowl. Mr. Mecom renegotiated my contract to $150,000 a year, and gave me another bonus. My troubles, at last, seemed all behind me. Then something happened that even now I hesitate to bring up, but I know it affected me deeply. How much it screwed up my mind I'll never know.

Our second son, Philip Charles, was born right after the 1979 season, two months premature. He weighed only four pounds, 12 ounces. He contracted so many diseases at birth, the doctors said it was almost as if he didn't want to live. Right away I felt a closeness to Philip that I'd never felt for anyone before. I sat with him 48 hours straight in the hospital, and it was so sad, watching him struggle to live. His main problem was hypospadias, a malformation of the penis. He is still far from cured. Already he has had one operation and needs another.

I felt so helpless and depressed I couldn't stand it. Here I was, always so big and healthy, and there he was, so small and sick and vulnerable. It didn't seem fair. Deep down I think I blamed myself. I thought he was being punished because of me. I *know* I began feeling sorry for myself again, something Paulette hates in me. She thinks self-pity is for losers, and totally unproductive, and she's probably right. In any case, for whatever reason, I was on the verge of the next fateful step down in my life.

The popularity of cocaine got a dramatic boost in early 1980. Who knows why, but everywhere you went, people were talking about it. And the big new item was freebasing: cooking a large amount of coke down to a gummy rock, "freeing up" the base, then scraping off a little at a time, putting a hot flame to it and pulling the fumes right into your lungs through a glass pipe. Freebasing is what nearly ruined Richard Pryor.

Except for a few reefers, I had stayed away from drugs in New Orleans. Partly because I was afraid, and partly because the players were afraid of me. Elex Price, a defensive tackle, said a lot of the Saints thought I might be an undercover narcotics agent. He said, "Man, you got off light in Miami. We better not be fooling with you." I said, "Listen, man, I'm not looking for stuff. I just want to be friends."

Then one night a bunch of players went over to Bob Pollard's house—Pollard, a defensive end, himself was clean; he was out of town, having been traded—to toot some coke, and I went along. And I got that old familiar zing. We sat around snorting, and the subject turned to freebasing. I'd only heard about it that year, but Chuck Muncie said, "Man, that's not new." I said I wanted to try it. So Chuck and I got together at his house and he cooked some up and brought out the pipe. And I took one pull and threw up. I got sick as a dog. It tasted like raw chemicals.

But if I am consistent about anything in life, I am consistent about being a glutton for punishment. Two weeks later, Lloyd Mumphord came through town, and he was into freebasing. He still had a house in Miami and he made periodic stops in New Orleans on his way home to Opelousas, Louisiana. Mumphord had the stuff, and I tried freebasing with him. This time I liked it. It had a different taste—sweeter, actually. And it gave me the best high I ever had with drugs.

I inhaled it, and when I blew it out I got that ringing in my ears—*wiinnnnnngggg,* real high. One of the popular drug songs calls it "ringing your bell." I call it getting a ringer. When people ask me to describe the total experience of freebasing, I say it's like enjoying an all-league climax. The funny thing is that it makes you *want* to fornicate, too, but you can't. You usually can't get an erection.

Muncie got me in on the freebasing after he'd processed it, and I wanted to learn myself, so Mumphord showed me how. Paulette was working, the kids weren't home, and whenever Mumphord came to town I got the pot out and lit up the stove and we cooked. Mumphord always wanted Muncie to join us, but Chuck did it with us only once. There were others who didn't hesitate to join in. We got a regular little circle going, at one place or another, and we started basing every chance we got—Clarence Chapman (a defensive back) and Mike Strachan (a running back), and even some of the white guys on the team. I freebased with Guy Benjamin (a quarterback) one night. Another time Strachan and I sat there and smoked nearly an entire eighth.

After a while, I stopped snorting altogether. All I wanted to do was freebase. And that meant an ever-increasing expense. I suddenly realized I wasn't getting as much free stuff as I used to. I began making regular withdrawals from the bank, and when I stopped to figure it out, I had a habit that was costing me $1,500 to $1,800 a month.

The 1980 training camp started, and instead of tapering off, we accelerated. The dealers scurried around Vero Beach, where we trained at Dodgertown, to answer our needs. We had pots and little stoves and hot plates in our rooms at camp, and every night was fun night. We were so bold with it, it got to be ridiculous. One time Chuck and I cooked all night long for three nights in a row. I just about went nuts one day when I got back to the room and found that someone had run off with my hot plate.

More than once I came right out of freebasing into team meetings. A coach would be talking, and I'd sit there in a daze, all messed up, breathing hard, my chest swollen, my heart pounding, just dying for another hit and unable to get it. Finally I said screw the meetings. I started skipping. And every time I missed, I got fined $250. Which meant that I was spending $400 a day for coke in order to screw myself out of another $250.

If anybody on the team didn't know what was going on, they were deaf, dumb and blind. Players would come into the dressing room after being up all night, and they'd brag about it. "Boy, I got me some good stuff last night. I couldn't stop, man. I had a rock this big." Or, "Boy, the s———— I had last night was awful. Like to made me throw up." They'd be in the meetings with their chests all puffed out, and sweating, and unable to sit still, and you'd have to be in another state not to recognize the symptoms.

Finally, Dick Nolan asked me what was going on: "Are you on drugs?"

I said, "Coach, I'd be a fool to be on drugs."

He said, "O.K.," and that was all.

About that time the NFL sent Charles Jackson around for his annual pep talk. Jackson is an ex-narcotics officer, and he has a regular routine about drugs that he uses to lecture players with. Nobody seems to take him seriously, but you listen because he's entertaining. I supposed the league office thinks he identifies because he's black, but it boils down mainly to appearances. He makes an appearance, and nobody sees or hears from him again for a year or so.

I knew Jackson from before. He called me one of his "special" people because of my Miami troubles. He came to me in the locker room and said, "Hey, baby, what's happening?" and slapped my hands. "You all right?"

"Yeah, I'm all right," I said. I was messed up as I could be.

"You staying clean?"

"Yeah, I'm clean." I was dirty as I could be.

"O.K., man, anytime you have any problems, anything at all, you just give me a call."

I said O.K.

He gave me his card. I already had one.

Despite everything, we thought we were going to have a good season in 1980. But we got upset by the 49ers opening day, and then we lost again, and the rout was on. When we got to 0 and 4, I realized we needed help. The players were in the streets at night, going from house to house, getting stuff. I got out Jackson's card. I called his number in New York and his secretary said he wasn't available at the moment, "but he'll call you right back."

He never did.

And I didn't call him back, either. I was too frustrated and too discouraged. I felt like I was in the water with a bunch of drowning men. But instead of doing something positive, I did something foolish. I told Tom Pratt, the Saints' defensive line coach, that I didn't want to start anymore. I said I was hurt—my right knee was bothering me—and I didn't want the pressure as long as I couldn't contribute. He and Nolan agreed to play Tommy Hart in my place, but each week they'd only leave Hart in for about a quarter, then I'd go in.

We lost 12 straight, and right after a Monday night game with the Rams, the Saints fired Nolan. We had stunk up the joint against the Rams, losing 27-7. I especially hated that because it's embarrassing to lose on Monday night with all those people watching on television. At our next practice I blew up. Actually, blew up is an understatement.

I'd hurt my knee in the game, and I was standing on the sidelines talking to one of the writers when Pratt saw me and ordered me to "come over here." I didn't care much for his tone, and I took my time walking over. As I passed some of the other players, I made a comment—"You sorry bastards," or words to that effect—and (Defensive Tackle) Derland Moore said, "*You're* the one who quit, not us." I knew then that they'd been looking for me for leadership, and I hadn't provided it. And I went blank.

I jumped Moore, and we fought. And when they tried to pull us apart, I fought everybody in sight. They had to gang up on me to hold me down. And when they let me up, I fought all the way to the dressing room. I was hysterical. I couldn't stop fighting. I *wanted* to stop, but I couldn't. I don't know what I did or who I did it to, but when we got inside I jumped Moore again. At that moment I hated him. I wanted to kill him. It was my messed-up mind doing it, because I actually liked Derland Moore.

Dick Stanfel, the interim Saints coach, suspended me for the last four games of the season. But now I knew how far gone I was. I went to Fred Williams, Mr. Mecom's righthand man. I told him a little of what was going on, mainly about my own problems. He said he would get Mr. Mecom to agree not to advance me any more of my deferred money until I was satisfied I was straightened out. He said, "Hang in there." And that's all. He didn't tell Mr. Mecom. Mr. Mecom knows *now*, but he didn't know then.

In June of 1981, Bum Phillips, the new Saints coach, told me they had put me on waivers. He said they were "going with young players." My heart sank. But a few days later, he called and said San Diego had picked me up.

I was elated, to say the least. Muncie had been traded to San Diego during the 1980 season, and I knew enough about the Chargers to think there might be a Super Bowl in my future after all. I wasn't sure why they wanted me, but I had sacked Dan Fouts three times in 1979, and I figured the memory was there. But there was no Super Bowl in San Diego for Don Reese. There was no future at all. Not even a season's worth. I was about to make my final flame-out.

The only difference between the drug abuse in San Diego and the drug abuse in New Orleans was that in San Diego more and bigger names were involved, including Chuck Muncie, and the action was a lot more cautious. Chuck and I took the same flight out of New Orleans to training camp. We were picked up at the San Diego airport and taken directly to the University of California at San Diego, where the Chargers train. Before nightfall, I was freebasing again.

One of the Chargers wide receivers met me at the college almost the minute we arrived. He was riding a bicycle, and we got to talking about coke and how to cook it, like housewives discussing recipes. My nerve endings began to jangle.

We were due to take the team physical the next morning, but when my mind got on freebasing, nothing else mattered. I pressed him. He said, "Let me make a few calls."

A little later he came to our room and said, "Let's go."

I tried to get Chuck to join us, but he said no. We had gotten an eighth of coke for $275, a good price, and we went over to a girl's room and cooked until two in the morning. When we ran out, we called somebody else and got some more, and we smoked until eight, right there on campus.

Then we went to the training room and took our physicals. And I passed. I said, "Oh man, this is ridiculous. All this crap in me, and I still pass a physical?"

I had a two-year guaranteed contract with the Chargers, for $185,000 the first year and $210,000 the second. But I had suffered an injury and couldn't play after the fourth game. They kept shooting it with novocaine and playing me, but I finally had to have surgery. They waived me with two games left in the season.

I went back to New Orleans and wallowed in as much pity as I could find for myself. Paulette tried to carry the load, teaching school. Our debts piled up. What little money I had I used for drugs, and what I couldn't pay for I charged. I had already run up a big debt with dealers, and one of them was of a type you don't run up debts on. I'd escaped to San Diego right after writing him two worthless $1,000 checks. He called my wife a few times while I was on the coast, telling her she "better get in touch with Don." I finally called him back. "Can't you wait?"

"Yeah," he said, "we can wait."

When I showed up in New Orleans, he *was* waiting. Only instead of cutting me off, he got me to use even more, and my debt and my habit got heavier and heavier. One night he got me up in his apartment in the inner city. With five of his guys surrounding us, he pulled out his magnum and put a pipe in front of me and *made* me freebase. He said, "You know you like this s----, *smoke* it." I said. "Hey man. I don't want it under this kind of pressure."

He said, "Smoke the s----, nigger," and jammed the gun against my neck.

He did that to me twice. Each time he added the cost of the coke to my bill. Finally he came to my house and demanded payment, and took out his gun to convince me. He was no stranger there. He had often brought stuff to me late at night, and even joined me a few times in my kitchen, cooking it up. Eventually he started coming earlier, and I had to make Paulette and the kids go in the back. By that time, Paulette was a basket case. It didn't help her frame of mind any the day when he fired a bullet, trying to scare me.

I was scared, all right. But not just of him. My whole world was coming apart. When it was either kill myself or run, I ran. With nothing but the clothes on my back, I sneaked out of New Orleans like a thief in the night. And for once I did the right thing. I checked into a hospital and finally got the help I needed. I know I *wanted* to be helped, and they told me that's the first big step.

I'm out now, after a stay of almost five weeks, but I don't see my life getting better quickly. I know I've got to work at it. But I want to change, to be productive, to be a good person and a good father. I want to be. . . . O.K. I'll tell you exactly what I want to be. I want to be like my wife. With her morals, and her sense of responsibility. To Paulette, marriage meant giving herself to me and the family, in every way. She had kids just because I wanted them. *I'm* the one who hasn't lived up to the bargain.

Paulette's a unique individual. Very deep. She always makes the right decision, always does the right thing. I think sometimes her standards are too high, but since I know mine are too low, I'm hardly the one to judge. She told me she didn't want me back until I straightened out. It's a goal worth striving for, because I have no doubt she'll be there if I make it.

As for what is happening in the NFL with drugs, I don't see it changing until enough people who care are made aware of how bad the situation is. How destructive it is for the game. Sending comedians around to tell stories about drugs won't turn the problem around. And the Players Association loves to quibble over salary percentages and television cuts, and while it bargains for the membership, the membership is being eaten alive by a cancer. As for the owners, while they enjoy the high life, their most valuable asset—the players—is wasting away.

But I don't have any illusions. Rather than reform, what is more likely to happen is that the NFL will say I've exaggerated everything here. That you shouldn't pay attention to a guy who admits he took drugs, and dealt drugs, and did all the wrong and stupid things I've done. And it will try to discredit the diagnosis instead of curing the patient. And the players who don't deny it completely will say it's not nearly as bad as I've made it out.

But I know better. And what I've had to say is something that needed to be said.

The sad part is that it wasn't said a lot sooner.

Judge's Comments

The magazine article chosen the best of 1982 proved one of the most controversial of the year. But the fact that 'I'm Not Worth a Damn' created a furor when published in Sports Illustrated in June is the least of the reasons for its selection for top honors. Publication of 'I'm Not Worth a Damn' was followed by a flurry of articles and broadcasts on the subject. That has a tendency to make the material seem stale six months later. But in rereading the article, I was struck once more by its power and poignancy.

Admittedly, it is self-serving. But there is an innocence about it as well. Don Reese's mea culpas are aimed more at his family than society in general.

Among the article's greatest strengths is the fact that it is frank rather than flowery. It is simple, conversational, direct. Yet it is a finely told tale. Few writers with years of experience shaping emotions and images into words could have better said what has been said here.

Much of the credit must go to John Underwood for having the seemingly good sense to restrain himself from forcing his vocabulary into Reese's prose. Underwood appears to have done what too few writers are willing to do—allow the subject to speak for himself when he can do so with eloquence.

Those who examine the winner in this category and the other magazine selections in this book will notice a trend toward expose. This is less by design on the part of the judge than the result of changes occurring within the field of sports journalism. Writers are becoming less awe-stricken, more willing to look realistically at their subjects.

Just Plain Red

GENERAL

By *FURMAN BISHER*

From the Atlanta Journal
Copyright © 1982, Atlanta Journal-Constitution

The Atlanta Falcons had played the Dallas Cowboys in the play-offs about a year ago, and lost, and I was driving Red Smith back to his hotel. The weather was cold and bitter, and we talked of all those long days that had run into years in the press box.

"Days like this make it tough on an old man," he said, "but I know of no better way to go than in a press box." As he started to leave the car, he put a hand on my shoulder and said, with hoarse passion, "And the hell of it is, I love it."

He was 75 then, and my God, a gallant old thoroughbred who couldn't give up the race. Here was a man who was more than a sports writer, he was a literarian with a classic name, Walter Wellesley Smith, yet happily content to go through life with the handy title of a bullpen catcher. Here was a talent worthy of "Somerset Bosworth Smith" or "Farnsworth Emerson Smith," but he was plain American "Red."

He was 76 when he died Friday. The shock wave the news spread through our industry was akin to the dull emptiness felt across the country when Bing Crosby died. Any younger sports writer who didn't have Red Smith as his ideal was on a primrose course. Evidence is that there'll hardly be a columnist across the U.S. who won't put his own reverent epitaph to his name.

He was showing disturbing traces of age at the World Series, but each day, and night, he made his route faithfully in the discomfort that baseball inflicts on even one of his stature. Crossing the country on physically draining night flights, cramped in an assigned space in jerry-built "press boxes," delivering his day's work to the New York Times under no kind of conditions for such an artist to perform.

When I last heard his voice, sometime in November, coming from his study in Connecticut, he said, "I'm sitting here groping."

The column was his life and breath down to the very Monday of the week he died, and that beautiful mind of his never lost any wattage.

Red Smith started life in Green Bay, started newspapering in Milwaukee, then to the St. Louis Star-Times, to the Philadelphia Record, the New York Herald-Tribune, the World-Tribune-Journal, and—if you can believe it—Women's Wear Daily before the ultimate marriage to The Times. Indictment of the Pulitzer Prize process is that his work wasn't recognized properly until he reached The Times. If ever there was a star of a more brilliant show in sports journalism than Red Smith when he played the lead on the old Herald-Tribune, I've never known it.

Coming from Green Bay and educated at Notre Dame, he grew up in the football atmosphere. He waited tables in the players' dining hall at Notre Dame, another brick in his sports foundation. He began newspapering, though, as a city reporter. In maturing years he moved to sports and his affection switched to the more healthful surroundings of horse racing and the outdoors. He fished the world. Those were his two loves at the end, I think, baseball having long since lost him through its over-developed imbecilism.

His closest friend was Frank Graham Sr., the Journal-American columnist, and one of the same gentle nature. They traveled so many miles together they became known by the horsey designation of "1" and "1A." After Graham died, Red took up with Jack Murphy of San Diego, drawn together as they were by fishing and horses. He outlasted them both, for Jack died of cancer before his time.

What Red Smith did most impressively was make a reader feel the scene he was writing from, delicately selecting only those relevancies that transmitted the mood of the event. And on deadline. Some of his choicest lines linger in my mind, such as his description of Cookie Lavagetto in the coaching box: "He clapped his hands intelligently," Red wrote from spring training.

Harry Truman came through in this humanizing vignette from an Army-Navy game: "A slight four-eyed man stood teetering on his tiptoes near the 40-yard line."

And when the British had to give back the only gold medal won in the Olympics of 1948, a track victory repealed by committee, he wrote: "The Royal Air Force band must now return to the desolate, forsaken field of Wembley and unplay 'God Save the King.' "

He wrote with elegance, but could just as swiftly jerk you up by the seats of the pants. As lovely and gentle a man as he was, he could sting the ball. No one has felt it more than Bowie Kuhn, and the rapacious owners who have violated baseball in his eyes. He came along in a time when the game was a mistress to be cared for and adored. He unhappily saw it turned prostitute. It grieved him.

He lived good. He had his high times, sang many a night into the dawning hours harmonizing with misguided tenors, encouraged by strong potion. He had a taste for aged Scotch.

Red Smith was the last of the heavy hitters, all gone now. Grantland Rice, Bill Corum, John Kieran, Dan Parker, Joe Williams, Jimmy Cannon, Frank Graham, Arthur Daley, all who lived through their columns. Red Smith was the newspaperman's columnist, the consummate craftsman, a loss our trade can ill afford.

Handy Man

by Eric Mencher of the *St. Petersburg Times.* The Tampa Bay Rowdies' Luis Fernando raises his hands, only two of which are his, in jubilation after a Tampa Bay goal during a North American Soccer League game in Tampa, Fla. Copyright © 1982, St. Petersburg Times.

Super Block

by Terry Bochatey of *UPI Newspictures*. San Francisco running back Bill Ring (30) was forced to use his head, literally, to keep Cincinnati linebacker Reggie Williams away from quarterback Joe Montana during Super Bowl XVI in Detroit. Copyright © 1982, United Press International.

Gritty Connors a Two-Timer

TENNIS

By *JOE GERGEN*

From Newsday
Copyright © 1982, Newsday, Inc.

A Wimbledon tournament begun amid controversy and conducted under ominous clouds ended in conciliation yesterday. To the winner of the men's singles championship went the respect of his peers and the cheers of the people. To the loser went the honor denied him last year. Hip, hip, hooray.

If Jimmy Connors' 3-6, 6-3, 6-7 (2-7), 7-6 (7-5), 6-4 victory over defending champion John McEnroe didn't bear the stamp of greatness, perhaps that was due to the thin men's field that challenged neither man. Or perhaps it was just an aftereffect of all the rain that descended on the All England Lawn Tennis Club in the course of the tournament, the trickle-down theory, so to speak. Or perhaps, and this seems most likely, it was men attaining the level they have achieved in the past.

What Connors and McEnroe produced before a capacity crowd at Centre Court yesterday was quantity rather than quality, perspiration rather than inspiration. They gave 4 hours and 14 minutes of themselves—in the longest men's final since the tiebreaker was introduced in 1971—until there was no more to give. It was the fault of neither that the play lacked the distinction of the last three finals, all of which featured Bjorn Borg.

Certainly, the 29-year-old Connors was not about to turn down the championship trophy, not after hungering after it for eight years since his victory over Ken Rosewall in the 1974 final. He said over the course of the tournament that he no longer had anything to prove, that he wanted to win a second Wimbledon just for the self-satisfaction. But he contradicted that notion in the postmatch press conference.

"I'm not a one-timer," he said, "someone to be forgotten. I've had chances (in finals) three times since then. And I was going to do anything not to let the chance slip by today."

He deserved commendation for his grit, especially on a day when his brave new serve almost blew up in his face. Connors double-faulted 13 times, six times in the third set alone, and fought back from a point down in the fourth-set tiebreaker to claim his first Grand Slam tournament victory since the 1978 U.S. Open. Connors and McEnroe are not the best of friends, but the effort was commendable, and McEnroe patted him on the back at the end and told him so.

"We went out there and played and had no disagreements among ourselves," said McEnroe, referring to the screaming match in the semifinals here two years ago and other rancorous run-ins. "I'm glad. He won fair and square, which is important."

Although McEnroe did not behave impeccably (he slammed a few balls into the net and berated himself, as usual), he was not chastised by umpire Bob Jenkins. There was only one fine imposed against McEnroe during the fortnight, $500 for verbal abuse in the semifinal victory over Tim Mayotte on Saturday. For this or reasons the club chose not to reveal, McEnroe was granted the honorary membership he did not receive after winning the singles championship in 1981. He was so advised between the singles final and the doubles final, which he and Peter Fleming lost to Peter McNamara and Paul McNamee of Australia, 6-3, 6-2, relinquishing the title they won last year.

"I guess I'm happy about that," McEnroe said of the club's gesture. "I think they made an effort to be nicer this year. I don't agree with what happened last year, but I think they tried this time."

McEnroe tried, too. He held his emotions reasonably in check. But his play never approached the level of last year's final against Borg. He was inconsistent throughout the tournament, although his march to the final was an easy one, and his play yesterday was throughly erratic.

The man served 19 aces, which was 19 more than Connors mustered. But he also had 10 double faults, including one in the third game of the fifth set in which his service was broken by Connors and the match decided. And he and Connors both used the net for target practice with their ground strokes and volleys through the first three sets. After one exchange, Connors walked to the net and measured it with his racket. It must have seemed too tall for much of the match, just as the sidelines appeared too narrow.

Such was the tenor of the early play that Connors won one service game despite three double faults. "It's a poorly played match," decided U.S. Davis Cup captain Arthur Ashe, the conqueror of Connors in the 1975 final, after two sets. Ann Haydon Jones, the 1969 women's champion, watched three sets and called the match "interesting, but not very good."

It was in the third set when Connors' generosity got out of hand. Not since Alphonse met Gaston on Centre Court in ought-something-or-other had two players staged such a giveaway in the famous old amphitheatre: "You take it. No, you take it." And then Connors, serving for the third set, completely lost his Wilson T-2000.

At 0-30, he had received two presents from McEnroe in the form of a wide forehand return (McEnroe fell to his knees) and a shoddy forehand return into the net (McEnroe grasped his throat in the familiar choke sign). Connors repaid McEnroe by promptly firing off two double faults. That squared the set at 5-5 and Connors blew whatever chance he had in a nervous tiebreaker with a double fault at 1-4. "I almost double-faulted the match away in the third set," he said later with accuracy.

Connors staggered through a 16-point service game at the outset of the fourth set, overcoming his 11th double fault with the help of two McEnroe errors, then suddenly righted himself. "After the third set, I regrouped," he said. "My serve came back. My serve actually brought me through the fourth-set tiebreaker and it was good in the fifth. I had lost my rhythm and my toss was off. But I got it back."

Just in time. McEnroe, needing one set to win, never had an opportunity for a break after that first game of the fourth set. And Connors made his three best serves of the day in the tiebreaker, the first two at 3-4 and 4-4 and the last at set point. All three serves were hard and flat and down the middle of the court.

The key break occurred in the third game of the fifth set. After McEnroe double-faulted at 15-0, he hit a wide backhand volley and then failed to lift a little half-volley over the net, leaving Connors with two break points. On the first, Connors netted a cross-court backhand return with half the court to shoot for. Then he nailed a lovely backhand return down the line and did a little strut.

"When he gets the scent of victory or the opportunity," Jenkins said, "you can see the way the man reacts." Connors started pumping the air after each successful shot. When he closed out the eighth game with a deft backhand down the line, he turned toward the crowd, held aloft one finger and shouted, "One more." The last game was easy, McEnroe merely waving at three deep serves. The only point he gained in the 10th game was on Connors' 13th double fault.

McEnroe credited Connors' strong serves, the erratic bounces and the changing weather conditions (the rain held off, but the wind didn't) with hindering his return game. But Jenkins thought there was more to it. "I wonder if the heavy schedule over the last four days might have exacted a toll," the umpire said. "He's a great competitor, but he does tend to push himself to the limit of his availability."

Because of the problems caused by the rain (interruptions in play were recorded in 10 of the 13 scheduled days), McEnroe played two doubles matches on Thursday and both singles and doubles matches on Friday and Saturday. McEnroe declined to use fatigue as an excuse.

Jenkins issued only one warning during the match, and that was to Connors for abuse of a linesman. Connors said he merely was questioning the judgment of the service-line machine ("a piece of tin") and not the man, but, according to Jenkins, "He gave a 'Harvey Smith' sign behind his back to the line judge." A Harvey Smith, it was explained, was a proper British expression for what Americans know as the finger.

Nevertheless, Connors became the people's choice at the club he had offended by boycotting the Centenary Celebration in 1977. He walked away with what he came for, the 1982 championship trophies. And McEnroe left not only with the trophies from last year which the All England Club finally managed to deliver, but also a bloody club tie of mauve and green. For the second year in a row, he declined to attend the champions' dinner, but this time he had an excellent reason. "I think the champions should be there," he said.

Why Suicide?

PRO BASKETBALL

By *STEVE MARANTZ*

From the Boston Globe
Copyright © 1982, Boston Globe Co.

Nobody knew what was in Bill Robinzine's mind September 15, the day he killed himself. The people closest to the seven-year NBA veteran think he may have been distraught about his struggling career, his marriage, or his financial situation. They aren't sure. When Robinzine, 29, left his car motor running in a storage unit in southeast Kansas City and went to sleep in the back seat, nothing was sure except one thing. He wasn't going to wake up.

Giving up was something Robinzine never did on the basketball court. He was a hacking power forward who set an NBA record for personal fouls (367) in a season, a player who led his teams in floor burns and body-banging rebounds. Last season, with the Utah Jazz, he played with an injured knee. The Jazz were heading toward a last-place finish when they visited Chicago in November. Chicago was Robinzine's hometown. "Bill had a brace on his knee," recalled his mother, Betty Robinzine. "He could barely run. But when he got in the game, he was scuffling harder than any of them. He always had the will to keep going. That's why I can't understand his suicide."

Robinzine did not seem the type—depressive and/or melancholic —to commit suicide. "You could name a 100 players, and Bill would have been the last one I would figure for suicide," said Joe Axelson, general manager of the Kansas City Kings, Robinzine's team his first five seasons. "He was an upbeat, effervescent guy, one of the most positive guys I ever knew."

He is described as an extrovert, self-assured and well-spoken. "He met people well," said Lloyd DeGraffenreid Sr., father of Claudia Robinzine, Bill's widow. "He wasn't like a lot of athletes. He could shake hands and socialize with all types of people." Robinzine made a good appearance in his expensive tailored suits, and public relations people found him a willing volunteer for speaking engagements and media requests. He was particularly fond of children and gave freely of his time to the 43rd Street Boys Club in Kansas City.

If anything was suspect, it was that Robinzine may have been too upbeat and jovial.

"He always joked and clowned around," said Ollie Johnson, a teammate in Kansas City. "He had fun to excess. It seemed to me he was always working at it, not letting it flow."

Robinzine didn't need a crowd to be entertained. And those who knew him say he didn't drink heavily or use drugs. He enjoyed music, chess, cooking, photography and reading. In high school, he was good enough on the trumpet to earn a trip to South America as a first-chair player with the All-America Youth Orchestra. He was also a good enough sandlot basketball player, and big enough at 6 feet 7 and 228 pounds, that when he went to DePaul University, he made the varsity as a walk-on sophomore. DePaul coach Ray Meyer recalled: "I remember him for coming so far. He came on like gang-busters. He was a great kid to coach, who did everything I asked of him. He played with a broken hand. They should all be Bill Robin-zines."

He started at DePaul for three years, was graduated with a degree in physical education and, on the basis of an MVP performance in the Pizza Hut Classic, was taken by Kansas City in the first round of the 1975 amateur draft. He gave DePaul a $5000 gift off his first contract, a four-year deal worth $500,000.

Having money was a new experience. Robinzine became accustomed to its touch. In 1979, he signed a three-year deal worth $600,000. The gravy train seemed to be a luxury express with no schedule and no destination.

The easiest explanation for the suicide was that Robinzine was distressed about his career. His second contract ran out after last season, and a summer of waiting had not brought forth another offer. Three years ago, Robinzine was a starter on Kansas City's division champion. He was traded to Cleveland, Dallas and finally Utah, where he got little playing time. Robinzine may have felt his NBA career was over at an age at which more players hit their prime. He may have felt this despite the possibility of going to some team's camp as a free agent.

"Bill was a very proud person," said Arlene Lacey, wife of Sam Lacey, a teammate of Robinzine in Kansas City. "Players have big egos. They have to, because playing well depends on having self-confidence. You have to think you're better than anybody else out there. Bill had gone down and down until he couldn't go down any further. He couldn't call somebody up and ask for an invitation to camp. Not unless it meant the difference between eating and not eating."

Some felt Robinzine had a blind spot about his basketball ability. He understood his strong points. "Bill was tough on the offensive boards, good at setting picks and shooting in close," said Larry Sta-verman, a former coach and assistant general manager in Kansas

City.

But Robinzine was stubborn about his weaknesses. "Bill would put the ball on the floor in the middle of the court and invariably get picked clean," said Axelson. "He would irritate his coaches by turning the ball over."

"Bill never accepted what ability he had," said Staverman. "He wanted to be Dr. J, and he couldn't be, with his frame and physical tools."

Late last season, Robinzine talked with Staverman, now the stadium manager for the Cleveland Browns.

"He asked me about the Cavaliers," said Staverman. "I said I might be able to recommend him as a role player. I don't think Bill accepted that. He shrugged and said, 'Maybe you've got a point, but I think I can do more than that.' I told him it was no knock on him, but that's what I thought he could do."

Robinzine had an offer to play in Italy where he might have earned $65,000. But his pride, and a marriage too fragile to withstand the move, made that impossible.

According to a source who has seen it, Robinzine's two-page note listed his various assets and the observation that his wife would need all of them to pay his debts; asked that his car be left to his father, his jewelry to one brother and clothes to another brother; and bid his goodbye to his sisters and parents.

The note also included the lament, "I always did love you, but you never believed it."

Bill and Claudia Robinzine were a striking couple. Bill wore linen suits, silk ties, gold chains and diamond stickpins. Claudia was fresh-faced and slim, with fine features and large liquid eyes. She wore furs as if she had been swaddled in them. She hadn't. Her father was a homicide detective in the Kansas City police department.

There are indications that it was not the happiest of marriages. Rick Novorr, a clothing salesman at a store where Robinzine shopped and a friend of Robinzine's, remembered the quarrels Robinzine spoke of.

"They had fought like cats and dogs from the time they met," said Novorr. "The day before the wedding, they had a big fight.

"Bill had a bad temper and she did, too. They were both stubborn. Several nights he would spend out because he was too stubborn to go home and say he was sorry. He knew that when he went home, he had to go home with a gift. He spent a lot on Claudia. He bought her jewelry and nice clothes and furs. He enjoyed her looking good."

Claudia, 10 years older than Bill, was divorced and the mother of a 12-year-old son when they met. She had supported herself and her son as a clerk at an accounting agency.

Bill's parents opposed the marriage, and he agonized over the decision.

"One night, I couldn't sleep, and I was walking to the icemaker," said Ollie Johnson. "It was real late, and Bill was still awake, and he called me into his room. He said he was going to marry her and that it was a big decision, and he talked a long time about it. It was something my mind jumped back to when I heard he killed himself. He was weighing it (the marriage) so hard. It seemed like there was an urgency to it, like he wanted to do it right now."

Claudia quit her job after they were married. They moved into a $115,000 house in southeast Kansas City. Robinzine grew close to her son, Steve.

"Bill loved Steve more than if he was his natural son," said Novorr. "Bill advised him and worried about him. When they moved into an all-white neighborhood, he worried about Steve being accepted. He wanted him to be accepted on his own and not as Bill Robinzine's son. So he stayed around the house a lot and set up a lot of things for Steve to have friends over."

If there were problems in the Robinzine marriage, they apparently emanated from three sources. Two of them did not involve money.

The first—and there is no delicate way of putting it—was Robinzine's womanizing. It apparently increased during his last two years.

"He'd have a woman come to watch practice," remembered Clarence Kea, a Dallas teammate. "And he'd ask me to say the woman was with me, if anybody asked.

"He was with a lot of women. They flew in to see him, but he wasn't paying for them. These were well-dressed women who had a little clout themselves."

At Utah, Robinzine brought a date to two team functions and upset his teammates' wives. Some of them told a team official that they couldn't be friendly to Claudia when she visited because they felt they couldn't be honest with her.

At the time of the suicide, there was speculation that Robinzine was being blackmailed by a girlfriend. The idea was quickly dropped.

"Bill didn't do anything people didn't know about," said DeGraffenreid. "If somebody had said, 'I'll tell your wife,' he would have laughed about that."

The second problem was Robinzine's being traded to Cleveland, Dallas and Utah within a two-year period. Claudia spent time shuttling between their Kansas City home and Robinzine's apartments, while Steve stayed with Claudia's parents. During the summer of 1981 Robinzine bought an option to a townhouse in Dallas and was frustrated by being traded to Utah a month later. Claudia flew down to sign the papers when Bill left for Utah.

"Two years of being uprooted creates unbelievable tension in a family," said Arlene Lacey. "It's financially and emotionally devastating trying to keep up two households. They were all set to move to Dallas and enroll Steve in high school when Bill was traded to Utah. That was a blow. They weren't excited about Utah because it's not the place for a black family.

"When this chance to play in Italy came up, Claudia said, 'We just can't do this again.' Steve had one more year in high school. It was a bad time for him to be moving."

Robinzine's mother, who is separated from Robinzine's father, speculated about why Robinzine didn't divorce Claudia.

"He wanted to keep his name out of gossip columns," she said. "He thought it was shameful. And then, (it) could be he loved his wife, so he stayed. He said he loved her in the note."

Financial problems may have dragged Robinzine down, although evidence pointing to this is sketchy. Robinzine's note said, in effect, that he thought his assets would almost cover his debts.

The Kansas City Kings say that, last year, Robinzine borrowed against the four years of deferred payments (worth $164,000) from his first contract.

He had also lapsed on the premiums for $200,000 worth of whole life insurance and $200,000 of term insurance at the Sanford L. Cohn Insurance Agency. The $4000 annual premiums had been paid for three years from the issuance of the policy in 1975, but Robinzine had subsequently borrowed on the policy's cash value. At his death, both policies had lapsed, but one of them still carried cash value worth $194,389 to Claudia, the beneficiary.

"About four hours after they found Bill, Claudia's agent walked in and said he needed the claim forms right away," said Sanford Cohn. "They went right to the company (Guardian Life) and got paid. Bang bang. I told somebody it seemed like they were in here before the body was cold."

The standard NBA life insurance policy worth $75,000 is also believed to have been collected by Claudia. William Fears, Utah Jazz comptroller, said Robinzine's premium was paid through the end of September. The expiration date of the NBA policy may have prodded Robinzine to act when he did.

Since Robinzine died apparently without leaving a will, his estate is being probated intestate (without a will), and it was felt that large claims against him might surface in probate court. In the first two weeks after filing, the only claim was $172.10 by Sears. The administrator of his estate estimated the value of his personal property at $200,000 and his real (land, buildings) property at zero.

But his real property apparently belonged to his corporation—of which he was the sole stockholder and officer—and will be valued in an impending inventory of the corporation's assets. The corporation owns the Kansas City house worth about $140,000, which had been purchased with an $87,000 loan in 1978. Robert Mann, Robinzine's attorney who negotiated his second contract (worth $600,000), has concluded that Robinzine was not experiencing serious financial problems. Mann thinks Robinzine inflated the amount of his indebtedness in his last note.

"His debts are not excessive in my opinion," said Mann. "It's true that Bill made it apparent that he had funds and liked to buy things.

But he didn't have 14 cars or extra houses to my knowledge. He bought a lot of extra items like jewelry, and he was wise enough to insure his jewelry."

Robinzine's jewelry warranted insurance. In Utah, he walked into a store and ordered a cross studded in diamonds. His two-page note indicated the location of a safety deposit box containing jewelry.

Laura Herlovich, the Jazz' relations assistant, thinks Robinzine was troubled by financial rather than marital problems.

"He didn't seem to have a lot of guilt," she said. "I don't think the marital thing was a big factor. I think he took his financial situation much more seriously. He told me about his investments one day. He was very interested in what was being done with his money and how his contract was written. He knew all the bonus clauses."

Robinzine was unusually kind-hearted and generous, by all accounts. In Dallas, he befriended Kea, a marginal player. He took Kea to clothing stores and told him what to buy and how to wear it. "He had me over to his apartment, and he'd cook dinner for the two of us," said Kea. "He treated me like a younger brother."

One day, one of Claudia's sisters couldn't take her 7-year-old son to the movies. "Bill came over and took him," recalled Claudia's father. Robinzine's fondness for children led to his involvement with the 43rd Street Boys Club. Bob Cohen, a former Kansas City public relations man, recalled Robinzine as saying, "if you get anything (appearance requests) with kids, count on me."

Robinzine donated a pew to the church of Tom Jones, a dentist and one of his closest friends. "Bill and I were a lot alike in that we both tended to do for others," said Jones. "We were as close as brothers."

He was sending money regularly to his mother and younger sisters, ages 17 and 13.

"Bill was a soft touch," said his mother, Betty. "One of Bill's best friends told me at the funeral that Bill lent money to everybody who touched him and never asked to be paid back."

The coolness between Robinzine's mother and wife bothered him. Betty's visit to Claudia's house in Kansas City after the funeral was only her second. Claudia's only visit to her mother-in-law's apartment in Chicago was last November, when Utah was playing in Chicago.

"It was something that had been on Bill's mind for a long time," said Kea.

Robinzine's mother is frankly bitter. "He had a happy life his first 25 years," she says. "Then in four short years (of marriage), he was gone."

Betty recalls twice loaning her son money on his trips through Chicago, once in the amount of $500. He promised to have Claudia repay her with a check in the mail.

"Two times she sent me checks that bounced," Betty said. "I told Bill, and he said, 'I don't know why. I've been putting enough money in the account.' It cost me $15 to handle the bad checks."

Claudia's feelings toward Betty were evident when the mother requested a copy of Bill's two-page note. According to the mother, the copy presented her has certain passages blackened out. Those passages allegedly contain the numbers and locations of Bill's safety deposit boxes.

At the funeral, Betty asked the toughest questions. She believes Claudia held the two-page note for a day before alerting Bill's father, whom Claudia telephoned in Chicago.

"It's quite likely that William did not spend Tuesday night at home, since one of his friends told me he had been spending many nights out," Betty said. "The coroner told William's father that it was likely that William was dead 24 hours when he was found. In that case, he left the note on Tuesday afternoon (instead of the reported Wednesday morning). You tell me why his wife didn't call anybody for a whole day."

Claudia has not granted an interview since the suicide and rebuffed The Globe's efforts to talk to her at her home in Kansas City.

The psychology of suicide includes the "death trend" phenomenon. A high percentage of suicide victims have experienced during childhood a painful or traumatic death of someone dear to them.

When Robinzine was in high school, his band was scheduled to fly out of O'Hare Airport on a tour. He missed his train and arrived late at the airport. As the bus that Robinzine was in approached the hangar, an airplane crashed into it, and the hangar went up in flames.

"Bill's friend, Frank Pappas, was in there," Betty said. "He had 70 percent burns over his body. Bill was extremely upset when he (Frank) died. If he hadn't missed that train, he would have been in there."

The weekend before Robinzine killed himself, he attended the NBA Players Association meeting in Chicago as the Utah Jazz players' representative. He visited his family and his childhood and college-days friends, including Meyer. Everybody thought Bill was in good spirits. "He seemed as clear-headed as anyone I have ever seen," said Meyer.

In retrospect, the trip to Chicago may have catalyzed a depression so black that Robinzine lost hope.

"Being around his former peers and knowing that he was no longer part of it," said the Jazz' Herlovich, "and also being around the people he grew up with and played college ball with, all that must have depressed him. He was a symbol of success to these people. Maybe he felt he let them down.

"Another player made the observation that Bill was so self-assured, maybe he couldn't say just once, 'I'm a loser,' no matter how close he was to somebody."

When Robinzine returned to Kansas City, he telephoned his friend, Tom Jones, twice on Tuesday. They made small talk, but

Jones realized Robinzine was distressed during the second call. "All my life, I'll remember his voice on the phone," said Jones. "He didn't tell me anything, but he was trying to say something."

That night, Robinzine drove to the Kansas City Fitness Center and sat in the hot tub. Larry Drew, a Kansas City Kings guard, chatted with him. "He said he really enjoyed himself in Chicago," said Drew. "He showed no signs of being disturbed."

Robinzine's attorney believes his behavior his final two weeks indicate he was planning his suicide.

"The family thinks Bill was planning it, and I am inclined to agree," said Mann, the attorney. "He was fairly high. The books say that is characteristic of people who have made the decision. That's my assumption about his trip to Chicago. He spent all of his time with his family and other people important to him. When he came back, he had two telephone conversations with Tom Jones."

Friends noticed a gallows humor coloring Robinzine's disposition. A couple of weeks before the suicide, Robinzine was with Lacey and Ernie Grunfeld, another Kansas City teammate. At the time, none had contracts for this season, although Grunfeld has since signed with the New York Knicks.

"We'll have to get some tin cups and stand around on street corners," Grunfeld had said.

"I hope you guys like peanut butter," Robinzine had answered. "We're going to be eating plenty of it this winter."

The Masochists' Marathon

RUNNING

By *LEE GREEN*

From Playboy
Originally Appeared in Playboy Magazine
Copyright © 1982, Lee Green

The murky high Sierra dawn was lightening to pigeon gray as the army of runners pressed intently toward the top of the first climb. Like most of the others, Doug Latimer was silent, listening to footfalls and labored breathing as he measured his strides on the steep dirt road. This year it would be different, he assured himself. When the grade steepened, he fell to a brisk walk; less cautious runners streamed past on either side. Latimer clenched his teeth, fighting the compulsion to move faster. He was determined to restrain himself this time, a strategy born at the pain and futility he had endured in this race the previous two years. When the course abandoned the road and the pitch became steeper yet, he began pausing every two or three strides to rest his legs. At 8000 feet, oxygen has a hard time making its way to muscles, a deficiency that takes a cumulative toll. Only a fool will push it those first five miles, with another 95 beckoning.

How could the race have gone so wrong the year before? Latimer had turned it over in his mind a thousand times. When you pour that much of yourself into something, you can't afford to fail. "I've never worked as hard for anything or had this kind of obsession," he admitted the day before that 1980 ordeal. "And that's a little scary, because if it doesn't go well. . . . I *think* I can deal with it, but I'm not sure."

Latimer had left himself open to an emotional plummet. But if you don't take chances. . . . What was it he said? His worst psychological defeat? Yes, that was it exactly. *The worst psychological defeat or trauma that I've had in my entire life.*

The more he thought about that race, the more it depressed him, because as the truth became clear, he felt stupid. He had violated his own precepts, running too hard too early, not drinking enough along the way. So utterly ravaged were his lean, freckled legs as he lay on the front seat of his brother's pickup—out there on Highway 49 near No Hands Bridge—that his friend Jim Santy had to hold them outstretched by the ankles so Latimer's quadriceps wouldn't clench. And every time Santy accidently moved them a hairbreadth, Latimer would go absolutely nuts, writhing and screaming. At the motel that night, it took Santy an hour and 20 minutes to hand-feed Latimer a steak in bed. Jesus. How could such severe bodily harm be self-inflicted?

"Until you've run 100 miles in this kind of country," Latimer said, "you can't comprehend what it does to you." Of course, most of us, even if we are functioning just barely inside sanity's out-of-bounds markers, are never going to run 100 miles in that kind of country. Or any *other* kind of country, for that matter.

The object of the Western States Endurance Run, a.k.a. the Western States 100, is to run westward across the Sierra Nevada mountains from 1960 winter Olympics site Squaw Valley, California —near Lake Tahoe—to the foothill province of Auburn, California, once a prosperous mining town, now a three-off-ramp community of 8000 perched alongside Interstate 80 between San Francisco and Reno. One hundred miles, predominantly on historical Indian and mining trails and logging roads in the Tahoe and El Dorado National Forests—much of it so remote that it is accessible only by foot, horse or helicopter—with elevations varying from a timberless 8750 feet atop Emigrant Pass, near the start, to 570 feet at an antiquated train trestle called No Hands Bridge, near the finish. Temperatures vary from as low as the 30s in the high country to more than 100 in the lower canyon bellies. It is a route that, when graphed, looks like a seismograph's representation of heavy aftershocks. There are 17,040 feet of altitude gain, 21,970 feet of altitude loss. In a bad year, there might be 20 or 30 miles of snow in the upper reaches. Even under the best conditions, the footing is treacherous in some tortuous stretches where boulders, roots, ruts and loose rocks abound. The bears and the rattlesnakes are the least of it.

The first four and a half miles constitute a grueling climb of 2550 feet, beginning at an elevation of well over a mile. There are two rugged canyons between the 49th and the 60th miles, back to back. At mile 79, there is a river to ford. Most runners don't reach it until well after nightfall, when they have been grinding along for 18, 20, 22 hours.

A lot can go wrong out there. When the human body is so severely traumatized, hundreds of biological complications occur. Significant maladies aggrieving runners each year include heat exhaustion, hypothermia, hypoglycemia, dehydration and acute fatigue, any one or combination of which can cause disorientation or hallucination. As a precaution, entrants are permitted to have "pacers" accompany them the final 40 miles. Each runner is required to wear a plastic hospital wristband bearing his or her name, blood pressure, resting pulse, weight and allergies, an adornment that gives the field the appearance of a roving horde of escaped inpatients. As Dr. Gilbert Lang of the race's medical staff says casually, "The most serious risk you take is death." The ultimate finish line.

Some run just to see if they can make it. Most run to see if they can make it in a single day and take home the coveted silver belt buckle etched with the figure of Hermes, the Greek messenger of the gods. And a few run to win. Latimer, a 43-year-old publisher, husband and father, runs to win.

"When he talks about the race," says his 38-year-old brother, John, who cherishes his annual role as Doug's support-crew chief, "it's THE RACE in capital letters with flames coming out the back."

Doug has convinced himself that winning wasn't his top priority for the 1981 race, but he hadn't convinced anyone else. "I'm not going up there to win," he would say nonchalantly. "I just want to enjoy myself and finish the race within 24 hours."

"I laugh in his face when he says things like that," scoffs John. "He's never approached anything halfheartedly in his life. He *always* goes out to win."

After Latimer's wrenching loss in 1979, when Mike Catlin overtook him at mile 94, though he had led for more than 11 hours, and after the devastating defeat the next year, when Catlin—Catlin *again!*—waltzed past a crippled and prostrate Latimer at mile 82, though he had led for 30 miles . . . after those bitter, festering defeats, Latimer couldn't dredge up winning as an avowal again. Not this time. The emotional ante was too high.

Latimer is a lean man, just under six feet, with a clean-shaven, freckled face and neatly trimmed ruddy hair. His leanness is accentuated by his erect posture, his countenance rescued from terminal boyishness by metal-framed glasses and an astute, gracious bearing derived from the cosmopolitan upbringing that comes of being the son of a Foreign Service diplomat. From Deerfield Academy to Princeton to the publishing world. By the time he was 30, he was a vice-president of Harper & Row and the youngest-ever member of the company's board of directors. Now he lives on the San Francisco peninsula with his wife, Karen, and their three young children and publishes a national magazine—*Women's Sports*—and two provincial entertainment guides.

The main thing, though, is the race. Latimer awoke the morning after his traumatic loss in 1979 obsessed with winning in 1980. Not a day passed that he didn't dwell on it. A White House Inauguration could not be planned more meticulously than Latimer planned for that race. He carefully logged his workouts and monitored his fluctuating weight loss under varying weather conditions, calculating how much he needed to drink at a given temperature over a given distance. He timed how long it took to urinate (30 seconds to a minute) and then perfected the art of taking a leak while moving.

The time commitment was phenomenal. Latimer averaged 145

miles of running per week during peak training. On four occasions, he made the eight-hour round-trip drive from his home to the Western States trail for workouts. He logged 14 training runs of 40 miles or more, including a 67-miler lasting nine and a half hours and a 74-miler that took 11 hours.

"I could put up with the time," said Karen, "but his mind was somewhere else. He was constantly preoccupied with the race."

When the big day arrived, Latimer went out with his spring wound too tight and ran himself into the ground. He wasn't about to make himself vulnerable to a letdown like *that* again. Not this time. Yet the thought of winning kept lurking in the recesses of his mind the way the thought of escaping lurks in the mind of a lifer.

Running easily, almost gliding, feral instincts aroused, Latimer descended the sylvan trail into El Dorado Canyon. Mile 55 and leading, just like the past two years. Suddenly, he grasped the reality. He was leading and they—Catlin, Jim Howard and Buffalo Bill McDermott—were chasing. Predators and prey. My God, he thought, it's all going to happen again. Two paroxysmal sobs escaped, tears welling, a visage of self-pity.

Howard, on a roll of victories, including the tough American River 50-miler in April, was about a minute behind, running second. Howard is a 27-year-old part-time physical-education instructor at Sacramento State, a diffident young man who is quietly into born-againism. His Lincolnesque face, with red beard, pale-blue eyes and aquiline nose, is often the first to appear at finish lines, though this race has confounded him for three straight years. At 5'9" and 138 pounds, Howard is probably the most talented runner on the course.

McDermott, 30, was holding third, a minute behind Howard. He had achieved that position after starting dead last in the 251-runner field due to an ill-timed, hasty retreat to a bathroom at Squaw Valley Lodge, a contretemps magnified when he slipped off an embankment and landed on his ass before he could take his first step across the starting line.

Catlin, 29, was fifth, ten minutes behind McDermott and 12 minutes off Latimer's pace. Although he had been victorious the past two years, it was never Catlin's style to lead at this point.

Latimer recovered quickly from his emotional purge as he plunged into El Dorado Canyon. No one runs the downhills like Latimer, graceful as a deer, his stride smooth and ethereal. He had caught all three of them—Howard, Catlin and McDermott—in the previous canyon. When he came down upon Howard, he found him planted in the middle of the trail, taking a leak. Howard politely moved aside when he saw him approach.

To Latimer's amazement, Catlin was just around the next switchback. "Hi, Mike," he called as he closed the gap. "How's it goin'?"

Catlin wasn't interested in divulging his problems—nausea, diarrhea, kidney complications—so he contrived a dissembled response.

"I don't know," he said. "I'm just running along. I can't figure out what to do."

Passing, Latimer said wryly, "I've gotta run these downhills fast or I won't destroy my quads before the end of the race. And it wouldn't be a typical Western States if I didn't do that."

At the next switchback, Latimer passed Jim Pellon, a 30-year-old structural engineer from Mission Hills, California, who was as surprised as anyone that he had led earlier and, even now, was running near the front. A few minutes later, as Latimer started climbing the verdurous canyon's far side at mile 50, he spotted the leader, McDermott. He caught him quickly.

"How's it goin', Bill?"

"Gee," McDermott said softly, "this canyon always gets me. It's just so *hot* down here! The sweat's just drippin' off me!"

"Yeah, well, it's runnin' off me, too," Latimer consoled.

McDermott had no sooner been passed by Latimer than Howard passed him, too. Let 'em go, McDermott told himself. I'd be a fool to chase two guys known for going out too fast and blowing up. As McDermott contemplated that wisdom, he was at almost the exact spot where Howard had collapsed in 1978, after leading the race at a feckless pace. After resting in a stupor for some three hours, Howard had managed to tough out the final 40 miles and finish sixth, but in both 1979 and 1980, he had run himself into nauseated debilitation and had dropped out. This time, he was determined to do things differently.

Earlier, Latimer and Howard had been running together on Red Star Ridge, with its pristine, forested watershed. Nearly 20 miles into the race and well behind the leaders, both runners were using every form of discipline they knew to throttle themselves, kindred spirits hoping to atone for their previous transgressions on a course that demands deference.

"Jim, do you think we're hanging too far back?" Latimer had asked apprehensively. "Maybe we'll never ever come close to the leaders—they're getting so far ahead."

"No, we're doing just the right thing," Howard said confidently. "This is perfect strategy. We're gonna be fresh—they're gonna tire. We'll let them run themselves out."

The pair ran in silence for a minute or two. Then it was Howard who had doubts. "Doug?"

"Yeah?"

"Do you think we're hanging too far back? Think we're lettin' 'em get away from us?"

"No, Jim, this is perfect strategy," Latimer replied. "They're burning themselves up. We'll catch 'em at the end."

Two and half hours later, after crossing densely timbered and shadowed Duncan Canyon and arriving at the meadowy 32-mile check point called Robinson Flat, they learned they were only five minutes behind the front runners. Howard grinned broadly and slapped Latimer on the back. "We're in it, man!"

Now, having overtaken McDermott, Latimer and Howard were running one-two. The field of ectomorphic marvels was strung out for miles. It was obvious that the soaring temperatures forecast had materialized. As three o'clock neared and the race approached the ten-hour mark, the canyons were absolute kilns, baking at over 102 degrees in the shade, stagnant. It would get hotter yet for another two hours. Runners were stalled at various of the first nine of the course's 20 check points, getting treated by their support crews or by the race's volunteer medical staff for blisters, bruises, sprains, cramps, abrasions, fractures and heat afflictions.

In general, though, this field was the best prepared ever. Fully 161 entrants had run the race before, most in 1980. Only 19 would withdraw before reaching the halfway mark; 146 would finish, 82 within 24 hours.

Conventional curiosity leads expeditiously to the question of why anyone would submit to this flagellation in the first place. To most outsiders, the rationale is utterly elusive. The runners themselves find the rewards ineffable.

"I just enjoy it immensely. It's strictly self-satisfaction," says one.

Larry King, husband of Billie Jean and three-time participant in the Western States race, echoes the feelings of many of the runners in his assessment of the experience: "It is the most memorable thing I've ever done for myself."

Even those who haven't run the race but have witnessed it are seemingly awed. Dr. Lang, who has seen two Olympiads and numerous world-record performances, including Jim Ryun's first mile record and Bob Beamon's 29-foot long jump, says the Western States Endurance Run is "the most amazing and inspirational" athletic event he has ever seen.

The 1981 runners, ranging in age from 21 to 65, hailed from 28 states, plus the Netherlands, New Zealand, Israel, Canada and Peru. They convened at Squaw Valley's Olympic House on a Friday in June, the day before the race, for the traditional orientation.

"If you die out there or get lost," warned run president Curt Sproul with mock solemnity, "I don't care what your excuse is—you don't get a belt buckle." This elicited a big laugh, so Sproul played it for more. "If you don't finish, it'll help our financial statement." Another big laugh. Sproul then turned serious and apologetically explained that someone had surreptitiously removed some of the yellow ribbons of surveyor's tape that serve as trail markers.

The specter of getting lost hangs thick at this event. Invariably, some runners become disoriented, especially in the wee hours of the morning—the *second* morning—when they're stumbling along in the dark, powers of rationality diminished by fatigue, orienteering with a prayer and a dimming flashlight and a pacer who doesn't know where the hell he is, either. Complicating matters is the ubiquity of misleading yellow ribbons belonging to surveyors and loggers in the area. "You've got to look for the *new* yellow ribbons," advised one wily race veteran.

In 1980, McDermott was in third place and running strongly at about the 85-mile mark when he missed a yellow ribbon indicating a turn and ended up rooting around the scrub oak and manzanita at nightfall for an hour or two without ever finding his way again. Eventually, he flushed onto a paved highway and hitched a ride to the finish.

Hoary and wizened Wendell T. Robie, the 87-year-old race patriarch, invariably has a few carefully considered words for the entrants at the orientation. He decided to allay apprehensions. "We've never lost anyone out there more than one or two days," he bellowed sepulchrally.

Robie is one of Auburn's most enduring landmarks—a wealthy banker, land-owner and patrician. A Placer County kingpin. Twenty-seven years ago, he got it in his head to ride a horse 100 miles, from Squaw Valley to Auburn, within a day's time—this at the age of 60—to prove to friends that central California horses were still as durable as when they were bred for the pony express. His feat inspired the Tevis Cup ride, an annual endurance test for horses and riders that follows virtually the same 100-mile route Robie traveled in 1955. The Western States Endurance Run is a Tevis Cup spin-off.

It was in 1974 that Gordy Ainsleigh, then 27, distinguished himself by participating in the Tevis Cup ride without the full complement of accounterments normally associated with the event. He had, for instance, no horse. Ainsleigh is a 6'3", 205-pound blond, bearded karate brown belt, whose physical presence commands attention. It is his manner, though, an alluring affability, that ingratiates him. He inspires confidence. Once, during a 50-mile endurance horse ride, he convinced a flagging, sodium-depleted female rider that her salvation lay in the licking of salty sweat from her horse's hindquarters. Clearly, any man who can persuade a woman to lick a horse's ass is unique.

People go through life yearning to make a difference, to start something, end something, leave some mark or at least score a prefect 20 on a *Reader's Digest* word-power quiz. Ainsleigh had no such aims when he ran the Tevis. The adventure was purely a lark. Yet, in finishing the course in 23 hours and 42 minutes—a performance superior to those of many of the horses—he unwittingly propagated the annual frenzy that has burgeoned into the *ne plus ultra* of endurance trail races in America.

Invention being the mother of emulation, 27-year-old California rancher Ron Kelley ran with the Tevis horses the following year. He made it to within four miles of the finish before running out of reasons for continuing. The event might have died then and there but for an affable, if bizarre, construction worker known and, in fact, once listed in the Tahoe City, California, telephone directory as "Cowman." Cowman, 37, is a large, full-bearded, perenially disheveled individual with a proclivity for emitting strange howling sounds without warning. He also enjoys competing in endurance events wearing his patented furred, cowhorned helmet. In 1976, he ran in the Tevis and completed it in slightly more than 24 hours. The race committee decided to sanction the run as an event in its own right; in 1978, it began to conduct the ride and the run separately.

And now it's got a hit on its hands, with aspirants greatly exceeding the number of runners—250 or so—the committee feels the trail can reasonably accommodate. A lottery entry procedure has been implemented to enforce the quota and to prevent the race from becoming a tree-leveling stampede.

Already there are imitators, 100-mile trail races having bloomed in Virginia, Utah and Nevada. Three similar events have emerged in run-crazed California. But the Western States 100 Hermes belt buckle is the preeminent cachet for the swelling ranks of fitness addicts perpetually in search of a crucible. If you want to test your endurance, it is said, compete in Hawaii's Ironman World Triathlon. If you want to go beyond endurance and have a glimpse at your soul, try the Western States 100.

Michigan Bluff, elevation 3500 feet, is a jerkwater town, a gold-rush remnant perched above El Dorado Canyon. It features a narrow, tree-lined asphalt road that shimmers in the June heat. Each year, on the occasion of the Western States race (this year, the race starts June 26), the hamlet swells from maybe a dozen families to several hundred cooler-toting, solicitous support-crew people, numerous race officials and a radio-communications contingent from the search-and-rescue component of the Placer County sheriff's department. Automobiles line both sides of the street for half a mile. This is a favorite check point for runner's crews, owing to its accessibility and to runners' need for them here after negotiating two deadly canyons.

Latimer was the first to arrive, floating in at 2:50 p.m. with that fluid stride of his that is so admired, lifted by applause and encouragement from awed spectators. The 145-pound runner was an image of incongruity. It was inconceivable that he could appear so strong, seemingly unfazed, after 60 miles—almost ten hours—in Sierra back country. When Ainsleigh made his precursory run in 1974, one of the Tevis Cup horses never saw this check point. It died in El Dorado Canyon.

Thirty-six competitors will not see this check point today. Another 18 will manage to get here but will go no farther, several receiving intravenous fluids from the medical staffers. Six more will stop for the mandatory medical check, rest, head out again, think better of it, return and quit.

Latimer stopped to allow doctors to check his pulse, weight and blood pressure, a routine administered at the start, at the finish and six times along the way. If you don't pass the physical, you're pulled from the race.

The leader hastened up the road, where his handlers provided—as per his detailed written instructions rendered several days before the race—a Bodabelt (a plastic canteen worn about the waist) filled with E.R.G. (electrolyte replacement with glucose). Latimer surrendered an empty Bodabelt in exchange. His crew also gave him—per instructions—a fresh sockful of ice, which he placed atop his head, beneath his Moosehead Beer cap. The temperature on the bluff was in the 90s, at least 30 degrees above optimal running weather but cooler than in the canyons.

Latimer's crew padded along with him for 75 yards as he left the check point, having stopped for only three minutes. Howard, who had checked in two minutes behind Latimer, was already on his way out, too, 50 yards back.

"I don't think I'm gonna win," Latimer said evenly. One of his handlers reminded him that he wasn't out to win, anyway. Just an enjoyable run, Doug. Another belt buckle.

"Howard is gonna get away," Latimer insisted. "He's looking awfully good."

"Still a lot to go, Doug," said Santy, Latimer's close friend and business associate. "Remember what happened last year."

"Yeah, I'm just trying to take it real slow," Latimer said reassuringly. "I'm not even thinking about racing."

McDermott, clad in a truncated Buffalo Bill T-shirt, white nylon shorts, running shoes, a white rain hat and dark sunglasses rolled into Michigan Bluff ten minutes after Latimer and Howard had departed. Complaining about the heat and his waning blood sugar, he drank a Coke, treated a blister, changed shoes, grabbed a banana for the road and was gone within nine minutes. Catlin had recovered from his earlier afflictions and was in and out in three minutes, 30 minutes off the pace and fifth behind Pellon. Pellon was happy with his day so far and figured anything thereafter was icing.

White Oak Flat, elevation 2000 feet, is a dusty, sparsely oaked foothill locale in the middle of nowhere that serves as the 75-mile check point. Latimer arrived two minutes behind Howard, who had taken the lead and was setting a remarkable pace. Howard in a ridiculous-looking visor with white toweling hanging down the back of his neck. McDermott had looked at him earlier in the race and said, "Where's your camel, Jim?"

After his medical check, Latimer conferred briefly with his brother. About to leave, he searched for Howard. "Where's Jim?"

"Oh, gee," John said. "He already left—about a minute ago. He's out of sight."

As Latimer left the check point on a winding dirt road that leads into the river canyon, he was nagged by the fear that Howard had thought better of their agreement. Howard was the one who had suggested it, seven miles back in the hamlet of Foresthill, after erasing Latimer's negligible lead. "How would you feel about running in together?" Actually, Howard and Catlin, who are roommates, had discussed the notion of tying one night during an all-purpose bull session. Obviously, allowed Howard, they would both be in the hunt near the end, so how would Catlin feel about running in together, sharing the victory?

Catlin just about shit: "No way will I run 100 miles to tie! Hell, I'd rather take second than tie! I'd sprint the last 100 yards to beat you if I had to!"

Latimer's reaction was the opposite. When Howard made the proposal as they ran through Foresthill, he agreed unhesitatingly. "There's nothing I'd like better. It'd be terrific if you really want to."

Such an accedence was uncharacteristic for a man of Latimer's competitive bent. But this circumstance was unique. Latimer and Howard had been within shouting distance all day. Indeed, they had run much of the race in tandem. And for three years, they had tacitly commiserated over their mutual misfortunes in the Western States race, misfortunes that had probed the contest's furthest outposts of physical and mental evisceration. So Latimer understood the spirit in which Howard, who is doggedly competitive himself, had made the offer, and he accepted in the same spirit.

At the time, Latimer had felt that Howard was the stronger runner, though he was sure he could hold his pace to Auburn. The leaders agreed that they couldn't afford to let up, not with McDermott and Catlin just a couple of miles back. So when Latimer stopped at the edge of Foresthill to collect a fresh Bodabelt from his brother, Howard kept going. "I'll just keep this pace," he said, "and we'll see how it's going at White Oak." But Howard hadn't waited at White Oak, and now, as Latimer arrived at the bouldered bank of the middle fork of the American River, it was obvious he hadn't waited here, either. There would be no catching him now.

After fording the river, Latimer was joined by his pacer, Ed Wehan, who had been a top finisher in the 1979 race and was intimately aware of Latimer's abilities. Latimer expressed pessimism about his chances. "Hey," enthused Wehan, "you're only a minute or two behind. At this pace, Howard can't be going much faster. Let's just see what happens." And they pressed on, unaware that Howard had been leaving messages at check points indicating that he still wanted to tie.

What neither Howard nor Latimer knew, had any way of knowing, was that Catlin had made it only a mile out of White Oak before turning back and withdrawing at the check point with knee problems. McDermott was way off the pace—an hour back—and Pellon was even farther back.

On a sandy riverbank somewhere around the 89th mile and into the 15th hour, Latimer and Wehan noticed footprints. Howard's and his pacer's footprints. The strides were uncharacteristically short. Howard must be slowing. All competitors walk the steep hills in this race, but this was flat. It appeared that Howard was walking or barely running where he should have been moving much faster.

This was exactly where Catlin had used the same technique to deduce that Latimer was fading in the 1979 race. The irony wasn't lost on Latimer. He quickened his pace.

On an uphill stretch that leads to the 92-mile check point, Latimer came around a bend, and suddenly, there was Howard just ahead, moving slowly with his pacer. Latimer shouted. The pacer turned and frowned. Latimer caught up easily and asked Howard how he was feeling.

"I'm having a hard time," Howard admitted weakly. "I'm really dehydrated."

Latimer moved past. "Do you still want to tie?" he asked earnestly.

"I'd still like to if you want to," Howard said, forcing the words from a mouth that was so dry, his tongue cleaved to it.

★　　★　　★

Highway 49 check point. Ninety-two miles and daylight on the wane. When the runners arrived, striding abreast, their crews set upon them immediately. John approached his brother. "Go for it, Doug! He's dying! He's dying!" Howard was getting much the same from a crew that was certain its 27-year-old stallion could put away a 43-year-old man in these last eight miles. Howard gulped Coca-Cola to slake his thirst and get sugar into his enervated body. Both runners shook off the admonitions with laconic replies. "We're going to run in together." And off they went, side by side, through a golden field, pacers in tow.

Catlin was among the bystanders. Someone asked if he was going to head over to No Hands Bridge, the 96.5-mile check point. Catlin replied tightly, "Why rush over to the bridge to see two guys who are gonna tie?"

John Latimer, who had suffered with his brother in the emotional flotsam of the 1979 and 1980 losses, was still disappointed about the tie months later. "It may have hit me harder because I didn't have a voice in the decision," he explained. Which is not to say his eyes weren't misty, along with everyone else's, when he saw the two runners emerge from the dusk and enter the illuminated Placer High School track stadium at 9:02 p.m. Some 150 spectators in the infield and the bleachers applauded and cheered as the pair rounded the final turn, hands clasped and upraised as they marked the last 40 yards of their ordeal.

The time, 16:02:37, was a new record, breaking Catlin's old mark of 16:11:56, which was set before race officials took a careful measurement of the route and then lengthened it 4.8 miles to make it precisely 100 miles. Latimer and Howard stopped for no more than a total of 15 minutes during the entire race and ran the final eight miles at a pace faster than they had run the previous 92.

Howard, looking moribund, eyes glassy, was asked by a race official if he wanted something to eat. "No," he whispered, "but I would like to go home." Fifteen minutes later, he was slumped in a patio chair on the track infield, dry heaving. His crew surrounded him and fended off press photographers, then led him to a cot and covered him with jackets.

Latimer, meanwhile, was wrapped Indian style in a blanket, blithely talking with friends and reporters and showing little evidence of the physical toll. When he spotted Howard on the cot, he jested, "Jim, if I'd known you were going to be sick, I would have pushed harder." Two hours later, Latimer's blood pressure plummeted and he, too, was on a cot. He later calculated that he had consumed 46 pounds of fluids during the race, while his body weight dropped two pounds—a 48-pound liquid displacement. Latimer is certain his patented moving urinations saved crucial minutes and enabled him to share in the victory. What he is uncertain of is whether or not he could have beaten Howard if they had raced to the stadium. Neither athlete has any regrets, but both will always wonder.

For 14 hours, runners straggled home. An infield cot was occupied by a pacer McDermott had run to exhaustion. McDermott finished strongly in third, an hour and 37 minutes behind the winners. Bill Weigle, a 1972 Olympic race walker, picked his way through the ranks—mainly running—for 18 hours and 16 minutes to place fourth, 37 minutes behind McDermott. After having his blood pressure recorded, he tried to rise from a chair but collapsed and lost consciousness, an inane grin on his face as he went down. Pellon placed fifth, his weight down from 141 to 127.

⋆   ⋆   ⋆

The day had come and gone, as had the night, and the next day was heating up as the last finishers under the 30-hour cutoff struggled in and made no pretense of their emotions. Cowman, who had rolled in with Ainsleigh shortly before four a.m., watched contentedly, looking more disheveled than ever for having run 100 miles. Before the race, he had announced his intention to turn around in Auburn and run the 100 miles back to Squaw Valley.

"Hey, Cowman! How come you didn't do the second 100?" inquired an admirer.

Cowman offered a lazy smile. "Aw, just wasn't up for it, I guess."

"Savin' it for another day, huh?"

"Yeah," Cowman said, his smile broadening behind his bushy beard. "A *hotter* day."

He Didn't Ask to Be a Hero

HOCKEY

By *ALAN GREENBERG*

From the Los Angeles Times
Copyright © 1982, Los Angeles Times
Reprinted by permission.

The trees stand like glowing sentries along Route 38 south of Boston, their leaves fiery hues—reds, yellows, oranges—more brilliant than the brightest palace guard. Autumn in New England.

The breeze stiffens and the fallen leaves dance you down the scarred, two-lane road. Past the Unity Church. Past the Steadfast Rubber Co., its short, blackened chimneys poking at the sky like a child's dirty fingers. Past the cemetery, its headstones topped with American flags.

And leaves, everywhere the leaves. Blowing, flowing. Dancing, prancing. Across the roads, the lawns, the graves. Dancing until the winter snows come to bury them. For everything, there is a season.

Turn right on North Main and the sign on the black lawn-post in front of a two-story, four-bedroom frame house tells you that you have arrived: "Craigsville Pop. 10."

But that's an old census. Cancer took the mother six years ago. And the eight children, though frequent visitors, have grown up and moved away.

Leaving the father, 63 and retired, as curator of a place that is virtually a museum. He sits in the living room, surrounded by dozens of trophies, plaques and pictures commemorating his second-youngest son's athletic feats.

But the son's ultimate accolade is nowhere in sight. It sits atop the dining room grandfather clock, nestled in a blue felt case, the lid shut.

"Any time you get a little blue," Don Craig says, opening it to show a visitor son Jim's Olympic gold medal, "you might take a little peek at it."

Sometimes, Don Craig likes more than just a peek, At night, one of his favorite pastimes is turning on the video recorder and watching the tapes of every game his son and his U.S. teammates played en route to stunning the world and winning the ice hockey gold medal at the 1980 Winter Olympics in Lake Placid.

"I sit and watch them by the hour," Don Craig said. "I've watched each game about 20 times."

Jim, the Olympic goalie and certified American hero, has never watched them, even though he too has them on tape at home. Nor, in all his visits, has he reached atop the grandfather clock to look at his gold medal.

"One of these nights, I want to read what really happened, see what really happened in the Olympics," Jim Craig said. "I haven't had a moment's rest yet where I can sit back and reflect on it."

Many people relish reflecting on this: Craig beating the Russians. Craig beating Finland for the gold medal. The U.S. team going crazy while Craig, a man apart in both the good and bad sense of the word, skated the ice with Old Glory on his shoulders and concern in his eyes as he searched the stands for his father. The TV cameras were on him. When they found each other, America's sporting heart skipped a beat.

"I went from being a kid without a bankbook to an overnight hero," Craig said. "I never wanted that role."

But it was thrust on him anyway, and he seemed to revel in it. Then, he was unique.

Now, James Downey Craig, 25, has something in common with 10.4 percent of American adults. He is unemployed, released Oct. 6 by the National Hockey League's Boston Bruins one day before the 1982-83 season opener. It was a long time coming: Craig had last played for the Bruins February 4, 1981. Injured most of last season, he got into just 13 games for the Erie (Pa.) Blades, a Bruins' minor league affiliate.

When the 6-1, 195-pound Craig was released, New York Rangers Coach Herb Brooks, his Olympic coach, and Minnesota North Stars' General Manager Lou Nanne were quoted in a Boston paper as saying they would have been interested in signing Craig had they not been already contractually committed to other goalies.

But the bottom line is any NHL team could have picked up Craig for $100 when he was put on waivers this—or last—September. None did.

Today, Craig has a wildly enthusiastic, well-connected agent—Boston's Bob Woolf—but only a vague notion of what the future holds. He has mortgages on two homes, one on Cape Cod and another in the Boston suburb of Milton, limited savings and no income. Whenever possible, he takes the Boston trolleys rather than his car to save money.

Woolf is busy trying to arrange national interviews and TV cameos for Craig, hoping the exposure might help him land a job with a quality firm.

"I believe you can fool some of the people some of the time,"

Woolf said, laughing, "and turn a neat profit."

Craig, who hasn't turned much of a profit since he got $35,000 to do a soft-drink commercial his rookie year in the NHL, seems somewhat dazed by whirlwind Woolf and the realization that he's being remarketed, albeit on a lesser scale. He's also dazed that when he's seen in public with other Woolf clients like Larry Bird and John Havlicek, people think he's got it made.

"Every time I go anywhere, everyone thinks I'm making a million dollars," Craig said. "I've got nothing. Running around with John Havlicek and people like that, it doesn't matter to me. You go out and everyone thinks you're a star. What a joke. And then you still go home alone."

But most people will always consider Craig a star. More than a star. A hero. And doesn't a hero's bread always land butter side up? Aren't our heroes forever young? Sure they are, because we keep them that way in our mind's eye as we go about our life's business. Let them be mortal on someone else's time.

One of Craig's problems is he's mortal, and acts it. He was being interviewed recently by a Los Angeles reporter at Woolf's downtown Boston office when Woolf interrupted to introduce Craig to Jack Kirby, a superpermed 30ish TV news producer.

Kirby came on like a 21-gun salute extolling Craig's virtues while the ex-Olympian nodded weakly.

"So you're doing well, aren't you?" Kirby said, enthusiastically.

"I guess," Craig said, half-heartedly.

"We see you all over the place," Kirby said.

Craig said nothing. Most of the publicity he's gotten lately, he could have done without. The problem with being a certified American hero is that whenever you mess up, or there's even a rumor that you might have messed up, you're in the headlines. Mainly because the only thing some people seem to like as much as heroes is heroes who mess up. Proves they weren't better than the rest of us to begin with.

"When somebody figures out a (right) way for an Olympic hero to act," Craig said, "I wish they'd let me know."

One thing not to do is get charged with vehicular homicide, as Craig was after his white BMW collided with a car driven by a Westport, Mass., woman near Mattapoisett, Mass., on a rain-slick highway just before midnight May 29. A 29-year-old woman passenger in the Westport woman's car was killed and another was critically injured. Craig was acquitted after a trial, but the dead woman's sister is suing him for $850,000.

"If it was my fault at all, I'd be a mental case," Craig said. "I don't have any guilt. It was just a terrible tragedy."

Far less serious, but nearly as disturbing to Craig, was the media attention he got from a May 7 incident. Craig and five other men, two of them his brothers, were charged with disorderly conduct for allegedly breaking the glass in a public telephone booth and general rowdy behavior in Cuttyhunk, an island off Cape Cod with only 47 year-round residents.

Charges against Craig, whose "crimes" were taking the players for a ride in his boat after their Lowell (Mass.) team won the NCAA Division II hockey championships and having the poor judgment to drop them at so sedate a place, were dropped.

"All that," Craig said, "over an $11.25 pane of glass."

But ability, injuries and attitude, not brushes with the police, are what ended Craig's NHL career.

After the Olympics, Craig joined the ailing Atlanta Flames, who'd chosen him on the fourth round of the 1977 amateur draft. Both were on the verge of collapse: The Flames' woes were financial, Craig's emotional and physical.

More than 2,000 people showed up at Craig's first press conference. He was hailed as the savior of pro hockey in Atlanta. And so he saved. Just six days after winning the gold medal, Craig turned back 24 shots in his NHL debut as the Flames beat the Colorado Rockies, 4-1, at Atlanta before 15,156 fans. It was the Flames' first—and only —home sellout of the season.

He was America's most interviewed, and exhausted, athlete.

"It wasn't me the hockey player they wanted," Craig said. "It was me to sell the team. I didn't want to do the interviews, any of them. I did it for the organization. Anybody that does five, six interviews a day, it's got to affect them."

Craig played three more games and did 3,000 more interviews for the 1979-80 Flames, but it didn't save them for Atlanta. With the franchise set to move to Calgary, Canada, where the drawing power of an American Olympic star would be negligible, the Flames traded Craig to his hometown Bruins for a couple of draft choices.

Craig played 23 games for the 1980-81 Bruins (with a 3.68 goals-against average), including a win over the Montreal Canadiens, whom the Bruins haven't beaten since.

"To play a good game against Montreal, that buoys your hopes for a month," Bruins General Manager Harry Sinden said.

But not forever. In February, the Bruins decided to send Craig to the minors so he could play every day and sharpen his skills.

Craig refused to go. He had a two-way contract that allowed the organization to cut him from $80,000 to $18,000 while he was in the minors. Craig said the Bruins' motives for sending him down were financial.

"That's bull," Bruins Coach Gerry Cheevers said.

"It had nothing to do with being too good to go down," Craig said. "(Mike) Eruzione was picking up on everything. It was a financial decision."

To Craig, the minors meant lost luster, not to mention endorsement and appearance money which he reasoned would then almost surely go to Olympic team captain Eruzione, a fellow Bostonian and teammate at Boston University. At the time, Eruzione and Craig had the same agent, Bob Murray, formerly an assistant coach at BU.

Eruzione chose a different path than Craig. Rather than tarnish his post-Olympic marketability by bidding for what he reckoned would be at best a journeyman NHL career, Eruzione retired and tried to capitalize on his Olympic glory. He's a professional celebrity, and a happy and successful one.

Those who know him say that Eruzione, who was elected captain by his Olympic teammates, is the kind of guy everybody likes and vice versa.

"Nobody wants to knock Jimmy because of all the bad stuff that's happened to him lately," Eruzione said. "But I think Jimmy made a mistake not going to the minors. Either you're going to be a hockey player or a personality. Maybe Jimmy couldn't decide which he was. I feel badly for him, but I had a feeling things weren't going to work out for him. He rubbed people the wrong way sometimes."

Aside from his family with whom he's always been extremely close, Craig admits to being a loner. When the Olympic hockey team was picked and began training, the players roomed together. Except Craig. He lived with the team doctor.

"That didn't help him with the guys," Eruzione said.

Nor did the fact that teammates thought that Craig, a sensitive, emotional sort who wears his heart on his sleeve, talked too much. When the Olympians exchanged Christmas gifts, they gave Craig a jawbreaker.

"Everybody got a joke gift," Eruzione recalled. "Except that Jimmy's wasn't really a joke."

Craig: "If I started worrying about what I did, I'd become paranoid. I was me."

Which didn't make him a favorite with his Bruin teammates. Despite recent American inroads, Canadians and Canadian methods still dominate the National Hockey League. In general, Canadians are far more reserved than Americans. Reggie Jackson types are tolerated in American professional sports. They do not exist in the NHL.

Craig suggested that some of his problems as a pro may have been due to the fact that he was that rarity of rarities—a U.S.-born goaltender—and that he did not come up through the Canadian junior ranks as most NHL players do.

Bruin defenseman Mike Milbury, a native of the Boston suburb of Walpole and a graduate of Colgate (N.Y.), says that Craig's problem was personality, not geography. Milbury said rookie Craig talked more than many of the veterans, critizing Bruins talent and strategy, even going so far as to diagram the Olympians' power play for the disbelieving Canadians.

Later, Craig committed the cardinal sin. He gave an interview to a reporter for an "underground" Boston tabloid which was headlined "Jim Craig: Sex and the Single Goalie." In it, Craig discussed his teammates' sexual proclivities. Craig claimed he thought the conversation was off the record. The Bruins seethed.

"He was kind of cocky, difficult," Milbury said. "I found him honest, too honest for his own good. Someone like that, totally lacking in tact . . . is very difficult to take. It just doesn't wash. To do that immediately upon entering the locker room was not looked on fondly . . . He wanted to make a contribution. He was brash about it. He didn't take time to learn.

"He should have kept quiet and gone to the minors and worked hard. He wasn't ready to do that. It was always, 'Why are they picking on me.' It was a case of self instead of team. Guys tried to tip him off. He listened, he digested what was offered. But he found it very difficult to change. I thought he had a lot of potential. He was pretty quick, pretty strong, but he didn't improve as much as he could have."

General Manager Sinden, head down, doodles furiously on an envelope while talking about Craig. It is clearly not his favorite subject.

"I don't think . . . he played reasonably well for us," Sinden said. If reasonably well is '5', he played '4'.

Sinden admits that it was tough on Craig, with all the media attention on the hometown hero. But, hell, the Bruins desperately needed goaltending when they acquired Craig. Cheevers had retired, Rogie Vachon's skills had greatly diminished. The job was there for the taking.

"I was given too much of a chance at the beginning and not enough of a chance when I deserved one," Craig said. "I haven't played long enough to say my talent was great quality. If I'd have been brought along slowly, I might have worked out better.

"I'd not even be playing and the media would be all over me. It was embarrassing. Before the Olympics, nothing I said was important. Suddenly, I was like E. F. Hutton talking . . . Now I feel like the cow that's been banged up against the electric fence so many times that, when I see a reporter coming, I wait to get shocked again. I don't care what people think anymore."

But he does. He's warm, open and cooperative. He says if he can't have an NHL career, all he wants is a good 9-to-5 job and to spend time with friends and family. He seems like a regular guy.

It's not easy being a regular guy when you've lived Craig's post-Olympic life. Once he unlocked his Chicago hotel room to find a naked woman sprawled on the bed. ("Please leave," Craig says he said). Another time in Chicago (are women brassier there?), he awoke with the feeling someone was watching him. Four female hotel employees were peering around the door. Once in Atlanta, a girl told Craig she'd been speaking to God about him, kissed him passionately on the cheek—and passed out.

Before the Olympics, Craig was never regarded as a great goaltender. He split the goaltending chores as a junior at BU, and didn't make All-America until his senior year.

"At BU," Sinden said, "we thought he was average."

But he was brilliant at the 1979 World Games, which got him to the Olympics, and immortality.

And, some believe, loss perspective of his own abilities.

"Everyone was telling him how good he was for so long," a Bruins official said. "Maybe he finally believed it. Life is not a fantasy. The Olympics were fantasy."

Even Craig's father says, "Just because you beat the Russians one night doesn't mean you're a proven goalie. . . . If I had to do it all over again, I'd have advised him not to go into (pro) hockey after the Olympics."

After his disappointing rookie season, and the acrimony he caused by refusing to go to the minors, Craig was determined to prove his worth during the 1981-82 NHL season.

He played summer hockey for the first time in five years and went to the Team USA training camp for the Canada Cup in great shape. But a shot deflected under his stick glove and broke his right index finger. He missed most of Bruins training camp and was sent to the minors. This time he went.

Shortly after his recovery, he had a shoulder operation to remove bone spurs. He was beginning to skate again in December when he fell 11 feet from a hayloft and broke an ankle and tore ligaments. Then he hurt his back when a player fell on him while Craig was diving for the puck. He was in traction 12 days. It was during this period that his grandmother and favorite uncle died.

Then came Cuttyhunk, the car accident, the lawsuit, and unemployment. And lately? Well, a few weeks ago Craig was building a doghouse when his brother accidently hit him above the upper lip with a two-by-four. It took four stitches to close the gash.

Because of that, Craig grew a mustache. He's also had his sister perm his hair. He's confident there are better times ahead "because my mother always told me, 'If you're good and you're honest and you care, things are going to turn out OK.' "

Sometimes, Craig said, he wonders if he'd have been better off not being an Olympic hero. The most rewarding thing that's happened to him since the Olympics, he said, was when he took some autograph-seeking kids at Boston Garden out of a cold winter rain and over to McDonald's for burgers and fries.

"They'll remember that as long as they live," Craig said.

Craig's immediate plans are to play for Team USA when it opens practice after Thanksgiving in Colorado Springs. And get this: If the IAAF, which governs the Olympics, amends its rules to allow anybody not under professional contract to participate in the upcoming Games, Craig wants to try out for the United States 1984 Olympic team. And not as a ski jumper.

Woolf, who sees Craig trying to match his 1980 perfection as a no-win situation, advises against it.

"But to win for my country . . . ." Craig said, pausing. He liked the sound of it. "That's an obligation, the way I look at it. . . . Anyway, there have been so many situations in the last two and a half years where I can't win. What difference does one more make?"

Henderson's Joke on Us

PRO FOOTBALL

By *JOE FITZGERALD*

From the Boston Herald-American
Copyright © 1982, The Hearst Corporation

Did you ever pick up a paper and read a line that seemed to capture everything you felt in your guts?

Well that happened to me once, back in 1968 when funeral arrangements were being made for the gunned-down Bobby Kennedy.

Jim Murray, the L.A. Times' gifted columnist, was at Lake Tahoe when that killing occurred, and whatever he planned to write was quickly scrapped because as he put it, the time had come for anyone with a podium to take a stand against madness.

In a piece entitled America The Beautiful Is Sick, he lashed out at what he saw as a society gone soft, and contemptuously suggested, *"Love is handing a flower to a naked young man with vermin in his hair while your mother sits home with a broken heart."*

That line—exploding with indignation—has come back to me so many times during the intervening years, just as it came back last week while the Patriots were splitting their sides over that Snow Plow Caper perpetrated by a felon named Mark Henderson.

Henderson, a thief by trade, escapes the shackles of incarceration by participating in a work-release program at Schaefer Stadium—which in itself raises a disturbing question: Aren't there any unemployed family guys who'd love to make those few extra bucks Henderson gets for tidying up the Sullivans' joint? Then again, this is not a story about common sense.

Henderson became an instant hero by obeying Ron Meyer's command to clear a path for John Smith's game-winning field goal here against the Dolphins. The players then invited him into their locker room where he was cheered for his dubious deed. Billy Sullivan embraced him as shutterbugs clicked. Talk shows jumped on his band wagon, not only here, but as far away as San Francisco. The New York Times sought a moment with him, as did NBC's Today Show. Reporters flocked around the lad, as if he were Lindbergh touching down in France. And Henderson played it for all it was worth, especially when someone suggested his actions might have been illegal. "What are they gonna do?" he laughed. "Put me in jail?"

Au contraire, Le Miserable. If they—being the Patriots, the media, the John Deere manufacturers, the ambulance chasers who masquerade as agents—have their way, they'll probably turn you into an NFL version of J.R. Ewing, and then wait for the money to roll in.

And that's the part of the story that bugs me, for what are we doing here? We're laughing over the irony of a confessed thief getting away with another heist. We're congratulating ourselves for having successfully pulled a fast one. We're telling Don Shula and anyone else who cares, "Yeah, we suckered you—so whaddya gonna do about it?"

Well now, at the risk of looking like a Neanderthal, I've got to confess I just don't see the humor.

More than that, I wish some of those cameras, notebooks and microphones that engulfed Mr. Henderson had, instead, been held in front of a 63-year-old lady who would have no trouble playing the part of Jim Murray's "mother with a broken heart."

Her name is not important, nor is the name of the nearby town she lives in. All you've got to know is that she and her husband did a marvelous job of raising 15 kids who now range in age from 22 to 41.

Theirs was a home rich in things that money can't buy, which was fortunate, given the fact there was seldom extra dough to toss around.

But this mother had one prized possession: 17 settings of sterling silver.

"My husband and I started the collection after he got out of the service in 1946," she said. "Next to the education we were able to provide for the kids, this was the only inheritance we were going to be able to leave them."

It was more than a collection, however. It was almost like a diary.

"Mother's Day, Christmas, birthdays, you name it," she said. "We added to it on every occasion over the years, because the kids knew how much I loved it. That's why we used it all the time, rather than storing it. I wanted them to remember using it as a family."

Then came that awful morning in March, 1979.

"I was up very early," she recalled. "The dining room door was open as I walked into the kitchen, and from the corner of my eye I could see some things on the floor. So I looked in—and I got sick. The drawers were missing and a window was open. I knew right away it was gone."

Her insurance company gave her $1,000, but the replacement value is $14,000 or more.

"That's what they tell me," she says, "but I could never put a price tag on it. Every piece meant something special. You know, I'll still go over to the buffet and reach for something that's no longer there. And it hurts so much. This was our legacy to the kids. This was something I wanted them to have, because I knew it would always remind them of what we shared together. And I'm sure come Christmas Day, when they're all here with their husbands, boyfriends and girlfriends, I'll reach for something once more, and it will hurt all over again."

That's where Mark Henderson's story begins, when he stole those gifts of love.

And now it ends up in cheers for the "job" he pulled at Schaefer Stadium.

A joke? No question about it. The only problem is, I've got a hunch the joke's on us.

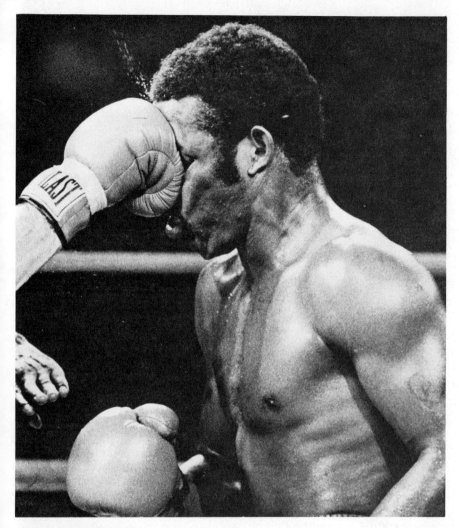

Hard Right

by William Serne of the *St. Petersburg Times.* The gloved hand of Mark Frazie seems to come out of nowhere to the bewilderment of Wilford Scypion. Despite the temporary setback, Scypion gained a unanimous decision in the middleweight bout held in Tampa, Fla. Copyright © 1982, St. Petersburg Times.

Horsing Around

by Curtis Chatelain, a free-lance photographer out of Ogden, Utah. Pete Cornia of Randolph, Utah, found himself in a precarious position when his mount, Rio Blanco, got a bit carried away before the gate opened during competition in the Wilderness Circuit Finals Rodeo in Elco, Nev. Cornia broke his neck, but has since returned to action. Copyright © 1982, Curtis Chatelain.

Sue Stadler: Alone Through Tears, Triumph

GOLF

By *KEN DENLINGER*

From the Washington Post
Copyright © 1982, Washington Post

She was standing on a bench 50 yards away, high enough to peek over hundreds of heads for the last dash of drama today, and when her husband finally won the Masters, Sue Stadler leaped and let loose a wild, nonsensical wail of emotion.

"Unfortunately," she recalled later, "I was standing with Dan Pohl's wife."

Mitzi's man had missed the four-foot putt that gave Craig Stadler victory. Sue apologized for the outburst to her close friend; Mitzi understood. It had been a wringer of an experience, part frenzy and fantasy, cruel and wonderfully ironic. She had cried twice, once in agony when it seemed as though Stadler was about to let another chance to win slip away and later in playoff ecstasy, when somebody else couldn't get up and down.

"We've been the underdog for so long," she said. "(During the final three holes of regulation) it was the Crosby (collapse) all over again, and I couldn't handle it. He's never been in command like he was today (six shots up at the turn), and I could see it falling apart."

Golfers play out their fate; wives suffer.

There never will be a more touching tableau in sports than Sue Stadler just off the 14th fairway as her husband was lining up a four-foot par putt. He had bogeyed 12 and gotten a lucky par at 13. A dreamy stroll into history was getting sticky.

As Craig lined up his putt, Sue leaned against a pine 100 yards away, her hands in her pink jacket and her eyes closed tightly.

She was alone, but her lips told everyone nearby what was in her heart: "Please. Make it. Make it. Make it."

He missed.

The round had started so well. Stadler had birdied three of the first seven holes and no one had made any sort of move. On the 10th fairway, humor filled the air around Sue and Craig's parents.

"Stadler chokes," somebody in a red sweater yelled as he walked by.

Sue smiled. No stranger jokes about that in front of her and gets away without at least 20 lashes from her tart tongue. But that was no stranger. It was Stadler's tour caddie, Judd Silverman, unable to work the Masters but here to help in any way he could.

"Still want your job?" she cooed.

Three years ago, two holes deeper into "Amen Corner," Stadler had all but blown any chance of winning the Masters with a double bogey. Sue vividly remembers something even more bitter:

"A man near me by the ropes yelled, 'All right, fat boy, bogey 'em all.' I really laid into him. It was emotional as it was, and Craig was a bunch over (par). I proceeded to the next fairway and had a good cry by myself."

Today, seconds apart, Sue was both cautious and greedy.

"Three more birdies will do it," Craig's mother said after a gritty par at 10.

"Eight more pars," his wife corrected.

Then she said, "I want some goblets. I want an eagle."

She talked about the family having an Easter egg hunt this morning with their 2-year-old son Kevin, how Craig and Kevin had played hide-and-seek before Sunday's round. Smoke from a fan's cigarette reminded her of the morning sickness of late and she moved away.

"Haven't been to (my) doctor yet," she said, "but I had some tests at Hilton Head. It's due in October, probably. Imagine! Two of them on tour."

Suddenly, the Masters machine was sputtering, and Sue's smile grew harder. And then disappeared.

Crowds here are so enormous that only those who stake out seats hours before the golfing parade begins or scurry for mounds see every shot. So Sue followed Craig, but rarely saw him. Often, her ears told her what her eyes couldn't see over five-deep galleries.

Twice, her senses failed her.

On the 16th tee, a ball was struck and shouting greeted it: "Go in the hole." Clearly, it was a gorgeous shot. Sue Stadler jumped for joy and clapped.

It was Jerry Pate's ball.

Stadler's shot found sand; his wedge shot barked at the hole but wouldn't bite the green. A three-foot par putt became a 30-footer. He missed. Another bogey. The Stadlers had gone from golfing paradise to purgatory in less than an hour.

As Sue was walking toward the 17th hole, numb or however one feels with the chance of a lifetime melting, an unknowing person in her path said, "Oh, he's going to do it again."

Another was more graphic: "He's too much walrus for me."

Came a splendid par at 17 and Stadler came to the point of his career he and every other golfer want more than any other: the 18th tee at Augusta National in the final twosome with a one-shot lead. Still shaken, his wife walked up the left side of the fairway. She saw none of the shots, had no idea where Stadler's ball was on the green until a television aide in a tower above the green gave her two okay signs.

He had a makeable two-putt.

Sue pushed through the crowd and sat in a golf cart behind the scorer's tent, letting her ears describe Stadler's fate. Loud applause. Great lag putt. She shot out of the cart with anticipation.

It was for Pate again.

She sat back down. When groans greeted Craig's timid lag and missed six-footer for par, she looked ill. Then she gathered herself, tried to pep up her husband as he stalked toward the 10th hole and the playoff with Pohl.

The ironic 10th.

The last time down that fairway had been so pleasant. The major thoughts had not been whether Craig would win but by how much. This trip was torture, and she couldn't get any closer than a bench near the 15th tee box. Near the wife of the man who could make Craig Stadler a humiliated loser again. One of her good friends.

Sue never looks at Craig's short putts; she did see Pohl's limp by. Masters green coats whisked Stadler off the 10th green and back uphill for a television presentation before his wife could get to him. So she walked back up the long hill by herself, alone again but so happy.

In about 20 minutes, Stadler was slipping into a green jacket. They had one large enough to fit after all. One of Jack Nicklaus' from his hefty days, somebody said. Sue Stadler could be seen sipping water from a Masters goblet. Her husband hadn't made that eagle, but nobody seemed to care.

They seem a good-natured couple, unpretentious. When somebody asked Sue Stadler what she thought would be an appropriate endorsement for her Craig she said, "Probably light beer." That crowd would like him.

Going Nowhere, FAST

BASEBALL

By *PAT JORDAN*

From Inside Sports
Copyright © 1982, Active Markets, Inc.

Steven Louis Dalkowski, a pitcher from New Britain (Connecticut), signed a baseball contract with the Baltimore Orioles and then was assigned to Kingsport (Tennessee) of the Appalachian League shortly after his 18th birthday in 1957. He was given his unconditional release by San Jose of the California League shortly before his 27th birthday in 1966. In nine years of professional baseball, mostly in Class D and C towns like Kingsport and San Jose and Pensacola and Aberdeen, Dalkowski won a total of 46 games, lost 80 and had a lifetime earned-run average of 5.57. Throughout much of his career, which covered 11 teams and 9 leagues, Dalkowski managed records like 1-8 with an 8.13 ERA at Kingsport, 0-4 with a 12.96 ERA at Pensacola, 7-15 with a 5.14 ERA at Stockton, and 3-12 with an 8.39 ERA at Kennewick. Dalkowski never pitched an inning in the major leagues, and pitched only 24 innings as high as Triple A, where his record was 2-3 with a 7.12 ERA.

On May 7, 1966, shortly after his release from baseball, *The Sporting News* carried a blurred, seven-year-old photograph of Dalkowski along with a brief story. The headline above that story read: LIVING LEGEND RELEASED.

"I can answer a lot of questions," said the old woman in the rocking chair. "But then again, what's the answer?"

"It's over" said her 35-year-old daughter, seated at the dining room table. "Everyone knows Steve's an alcoholic."

"He called me up," said the old woman, "and said, 'Mom, I'm all done.'"

"Is he coping? Is he surviving?" said the daughter. "People ask me. His high school coach. I tell them I don't know him anymore."

"It was the adults started him drinking," said the old woman. "New Britain was a town for all sports. The old-timers would grab a kid who was good in sports and buy him shots and beers. Whether a kid was good or not, he turned out to be an alcoholic."

"There are a lot of hard-drinking Polacks here," said the daughter. "It was a very, very exciting time."

"Oh, my, yes," said the old woman. "There were 15 big league clubs in our house the day Stevie graduated from high school. They were wonderful fellows. Their cars were lined up all the way down Governor Street. Big, beautiful cars. One came with a chauffeur. I couldn't even concentrate. And oh, how they dressed! Rubies and diamonds! They were big shots."

"It was all very exciting," said the daughter. "It's all gone."

"He calls every once in a while," said the old woman. "I tell him, 'I think of you when I go to bed, and when I get up.' We talked all the time when he was growing up. About girls, anything. But you couldn't go deep with him. He didn't question."

"He was a follower," said the daughter. "Like a puppy dog. He'd follow anyone."

"And do anything they said," said the old woman.

"The best time was when we went to spring training one year," said the daughter, brightly.

"Oh, my, yes," said the old woman. "I sat in the bleachers with all those rich women. Ha! Sports was our life." She pulled her sweater tight to her chest, and began to rock back and forth in her chair. She smiled upward, toward a vision of the past, and said, without looking down, "How far is Hollywood from Bakersfield?"

It was four o'clock in the morning at the corner of Baker and Sumner streets, and, as always in Bakersfield in January, there was the fog. It obscured the railroad tracks and the Arizona Cafe and the approaching cars that could be heard and not seen until their greenish-tinted headlights appeared out of the dark fog only a few feet away.

Three shadowy figures stood under the blinking lights of the closed Metropole Liquor store. Their shoulders were hunched up and they swayed left and right on their feet to keep warm. They carried paper bags with their lunch in them. One of them lit a cigarette. Their breath hovered before them in the fog. There was the sound of footsteps, and then another figure appeared out of the fog and took its place in line with the other three. A flatbed truck appeared out of the fog. A woman with a kerchief around her head got out and talked to the men. Each, in turn, hopped up onto the bed of the flatbed truck, and waited. They sat facing each other without speaking. The bed of the truck smelled of urine and vomit and dried sweet wine from the day before. Other men appeared and hopped on. When the truck was full, it moved off into the fog toward the fields where the men would pick cotton or oranges or potatoes or whatever the crop of the day was. The truck would stop once before it got to the fields, so that the men could buy wine to get them through the cold, damp day, and, at the end of the day, the truck would stop again so that the men could buy more wine to get them through the night.

It was 4:30 in the morning, and Steve Dalkowski, dressed in construction clothes but no longer healthy enough to work the fields, stood in the living room of his tiny apartment in a suburb of Bakersfield, trying to recall his pitching motion. He was 42 and had not thrown a baseball since 1966. His wife, Virginia, seven years older, sat on the edge of the chair, watching him. His stepdaughter, Kelly, 15, sat on the sofa, simultaneously watching *La Cage Aux Folles* on television and her stepfather.

Dalkowski began his imaginary motion, tottered backward, almost fell and stopped. "Damn, we're going to get it right!" he said, and left the room. He moved lightly, on the balls of his feet, as if walking over spring grass. He went into the bathroom where a bottle of wine was balanced on the sink. He sipped from the wine and returned to the living room.

"Just a little to keep me going," he said. "It calms me down. Stops the shakes." He began his imaginary motion again. This time he did not totter. His right leg rose, made a quick curl to his left, then shot out toward the imaginary batter. His left arm flicked out from the side of his body like an attacking cobra.

He was never a particularly big man. He stood about 5-10 and weighed less than 185 pounds. His pitching motion was small and compact. He flipped the ball toward the plate using mostly his arm and little of his body. The Orioles, who signed him, were convinced that the secret to his speed lay in his thin wrists, but they had no way to prove this. There was no rational reason to explain why Steve Dalkowski could throw a baseball so hard, except that he, an ordinary man, was given a superhuman gift. He always seemed bewildered by this gift. He did not ask for it, nor did he have the faintest idea how to tame it.

"All them walks used to kill me," he says. "I'd throw the ball to hit the plate and it would just start rising. Sometimes it would rise to a batter's chest. Sometimes it would go over his head."

Ray Youngdahl, a former teammate, describes what it was like to face him at bat. "The ball would leave his hand the size of an aspirin. Then you would lose sight of it along the way. Then it seemed to be on you as big as a balloon. It just got bigger and bigger as it got close to you, and you either dove out of the way or you'd swing way above it, where you thought it would end up."

There are many theories as to why Dalkowski could never throw strikes consistently. Some people say his drinking and late-night carousing affected his career. Others say it was his fear of hurting someone with his fastball. Others say he was nervous, disinterested, too easily led. Maybe it was just that the Orioles made too much of a fuss over him with all their experiments. They put batters on either side of the plate, and he threw the ball down the middle. They put Harry Brecheen behind the mound to talk to him, and he threw strikes. The minute one of those batters left the plate, the minute Brecheen walked off the mound, Dalkowski was as wild as ever.

All of these things may be true, or some of them, or maybe none of them. Maybe simply, Steve Dalkowski, a mere mortal, was given a god-like gift no one could be expected to tame.

Steve Dalkowski pitched his first baseball game in his sophomore year of high school. "I threw faster than anyone," he says. "And every year I just got faster." He often struck out 17 and 18 batters a game. He also regularly walked about the same number. In his senior year he pitched a no-hitter in which he struck out 18 batters and walked the same number. He also pitched one game, with dozens of scouts watching, in which he struck out a Connecticut record 24 batters and walked only four.

Dalkowski also began drinking alcohol in his junior year, although he had been around liquor for as long as he could remember. His father drank heavily and, when Dalkowski was barely a teenager, would take him with him to bars. One night, when his father was drunk, Dalkowski drove their car home and hit a telephone pole. "The fact that Steve Dalkowski drank," says an acquaintance, "is not unusual. It would have been unusual if he never drank coming from New Britain."

"My father worked hard every day," says Dalkowski. "He never said nothing. He just worked and gambled and drank. Some days we never had nothing and some days we opened the ice box and something would be in there. My mother always had to work. We lived in a three-bedroom house. I lived in my own room, my father lived in his own room, and my mother and sister lived in one together. I was just a kid, but I couldn't understand why my mother and sister lived together and my father was alone. Finally my mother left my father. He died in 1979 in an empty room. My mother said he was dead in that room for five days before anyone found him. It was a closed coffin, you know."

On the night of Dalkowski's graduation from high school, every major league team except the Indians sent a scout to his home to try to sign him. In those days it was a major league rule that teams could not sign a player for more than a $4,000 bonus or else he would have to play in the big leagues for two years. To circumvent this rule, many teams got in the habit of offering players money under the table to sign. Dalkowski claims he was offered money under the table by a host of teams, including Baltimore.

"The Orioles gave me a car and about $40,000," says Dalkowski. "Still, they was taking a chance on me, I was so wild. But I guess they thought I was worth it. Harry Brecheen (the Oriole pitching coach) came to my house and just shook his head. 'How do you do it?' he said."

	G	GS	CG	W	L	IP	H	R	ER	BB	SO	ERA
1957 Kingsport	15	10	2	1	8	62	22	68	56	129	121	8.13

He was 18 and scared to death to leave home. "I didn't know where I was going and I had to take this train," he says. "Everything looked so different, the color of the dirt, you know. Before I left, I asked the Orioles, 'If I throw so hard, how come I got to go to Kingsport and not Baltimore?' "

At Kingsport, Dalkowski learned how to chew tobacco. And since Kingsport was a dry town, he had to go to West Virginia to drink beer. "I didn't drink that much then," he says. "But I just couldn't win. I'd strike out 19 batters and lose. I walked a lot. I led the league in wild pitches with 39. One morning I picked up a paper in Bluefield, West Virginia, and see where I walked 22 guys. That night a man and a boy came up to me and said, 'Mister, who taught you how to throw that hard?' I say, 'You don't get taught to throw that hard.' "

At Kingsport, an incident occurred that would color Dalkowski's career, and from it would spring the beginnings of his legend. He was pitching against a team in the Dodger organization. The batter was crowding the plate. Dalkowski threw a fastball that sailed in and hit the batter on the side of the head. It tore part of the boy's ear off and sent him to the hospital with a concussion. According to Dalkowski, that boy was never quite right again, and he never again played baseball.

"I just walked off the mound, went into the clubhouse and threw my glove through the window," says Dalkowski. "I visited him in the hospital. I said I was sorry, but he never played again. I don't even remember the guy's name."

	G	GS	CG	W	L	IP	H	R	ER	BB	SO	ERA
1958 Knoxville	11	10	0	1	4	42	17	41	37	95	82	7.93
Wilson	8	0	0	0	1	14	7	19	19	38	29	12.21
Aberdeen	11	10	3	3	5	62	29	50	44	112	121	6.39

He began 1958 at Knoxville, a town he remembers as perpetually covered by fog and populated by men with spade beards and corncob pipes, men who sat stoically in the stands when he pitched. As usual, he was fast and wild.

In one game he fired three successive fastballs through the home-plate screen, scattering the fans behind it. The next night, a father with small son in tow asked if he was pitching. "If you are," said the man, "I'm taking my son home." In another game, he fired a fastball so close to a batter's head that the batter had to return to the clubhouse to change his pants. "I threw so hard that night," says Dalkowski, "that I scared the entire town."

One afternoon at Knoxville, his manager set up a wooden target, gave Dalkowski a bucket of baseballs and told him to keep throwing until he could get those baseballs inside the wooden square over the plate. Dalkowski threw for hours, and when he returned to the park for that night's game, he found a small crowd of opposing players around that target that had been splintered into bits and pieces.

He finished the season at Aberdeen, South Dakota. One morning, the Orioles sent him to the Aberdeen Proving Grounds in Maryland to time his fastball. He threw from a level surface the day after he pitched a game. It took him 40 minutes to throw a ball within range of the radar's measuring device. Finally, when he did, he was timed at 93.5 mph. If he had not pitched the night before, if he had been throwing from a high mound and if he had not exhausted himself before he got the ball in radar range, it is estimated that his fastball would have been timed at more than 110 mph.

	G	GS	CG	W	L	IP	H	R	ER	BB	SO	ERA
1959 Aberdeen	12	10	3	4	3	59	30	43	37	110	99	5.64
Pensacola	7	6	0	0	4	25	11	38	36	80	43	12.96

At Aberdeen, Dalkowski pitched a no-hit, no-run game in which he set a Northern League record with 21 strikeouts. He walked only five. He set the record against Grand Forks, among whose players was Gene Michael. "I never saw anyone throw like that," says Michael, manager of the Yankees. "Later I faced Sandy Koufax, but Steve Dalkowski was the hardest thrower I ever saw."

"He struck me out five times in one game," says Joe Pepitone, now a roving batting instructor in the Yankee minor league system. "He threw harder than anybody who ever lived. The ball started low and rose above your chest. It was ridiculous. The umpire called a strike and I said, 'That's no strike, the ball sounded low.' The ump said, 'It sounded like a strike to me.' I was scared to death. Here I was with a chance to make some progress in the minor leagues and I had to face this guy who could kill me."

After his no-hitter, however, Dalkowski suffered the worst streak of wildness of his career. The next game he walked the first eight batters he faced, and for four games after that he seemed unable to throw a strike. The Orioles reassigned him and another pitcher, Bo Belinsky, to Pensacola of the Alabama-Florida League. But first they wanted Dalkowski to go to Baltimore to work with Paul Richards, then the manager.

"The manager at Aberdeen told me to stay away from Bo," says Dalkowski. "Bo liked women. He was always knocking on my door and I would tell him to get away. 'You're not supposed to be here,' I'd say. 'I'm trying to sleep.' Bo never slept. He smoked them funny cigarettes, you know. Marijuana. I had never heard of it before, I'd be asleep at 5 a.m., and I'd hear Bo walking back and forth, fully dressed. He never slept. He said marijuana was better than drinking. I said, 'I'd rather drink.' Bo said it didn't matter anyway. 'Everything's going to catch up to everybody,' he said. He's with Alcoholics Anonymous now, you know. He sent me a tape the other day. Bo got sent down with me because he fielded a bunt in Aberdeen and flipped the ball to first base behind his back. The manager took him out of the game and said, 'Get your ass outtahere.' It took us five days in Bo's car to get to Baltimore. We stopped in Chicago and went to all the strip joints. Somebody stole Bo's clothes out of his car and we spent the night going to every whorehouse looking for his clothes. I never seen Bo so mad. We never did find his clothes.

"When I got to Baltimore, I threw for Richards. He was a funny guy. He wore a cowboy hat in the dugout and his belt was always turned sideways. He'd pull out a cigarette and four guys would be there with their lighters. Richards would tell Harry Brecheen to tell this guy to tell that guy to tell the other guy to tell me to begin throwing."

Dalkowski and Belinsky ended the season at Pensacola with another fast, wild-throwing, wild-living lefthander named Steve Barber. Between the three of them, the manager had a heart attack. He never knew from day to day when some sheriff might call to tell him one of his pitchers was in jail.

"Bo and me was roommates in Pensacola," says Dalkowski. "He was going out with a girl at the time. One day, he went on a road trip with the team—I stayed behind with a cold—and there was this knock on the door. It was the sheriff and the girl's mother, looking for Bo. He never came back from the road trip. They didn't find him for two years. You know what I always wonder? Bo made the big leagues and he didn't throw hard. How come? It blows my mind sometimes."

	G	GS	CG	W	L	IP	H	R	ER	BB	SO	ERA
1960 Stockton	32	31	7	7	15	170	105	120	97	262	262	5.14

In the middle of the 1960 season, Dalkowski was featured in *Time* as the fastest, wildest pitcher who ever lived. He was barely 21 years old, and already he was a legend. Opposing batters would walk up to him after a game, and ask if he would give them his autograph. One such player sheepishly asked, "Can I touch your arm? I want to be able to tell my grandchildren."

"Sometimes the ball took off, sometimes I threw strikes," says Dalkowski. "One day I got so frustrated I threw my glove into the stands and walked off the mound. I told the clubhouse kid to pack my stuff, I was going home. The manager, Billy DeMars, says, 'Don't go home, Steve.' I said, 'Take my glove and shove it.' But he talked me into staying. I loved Billy DeMars. He almost made me a big leaguer. He'd sit on the bench beside me during a game and talk to me. One day he said, 'Steve, I'm going to have to fine you. You go out every night screwing around. I'm going to have to stay with you all night before you pitch.' One time I got drunk in Stockton, and I was playing around with this tractor we had in center field. I drove the thing right through the clubhouse. Billy was in the office in the back and I almost got him, too. He fined me $175. That night I struck out a lot of guys, maybe 17, and only walked two."

Finally, DeMars took Dalkowski to a psychiatrist who used hypnotism for behavior modification. "The psychiatrist sat me down for one-half hour and made me look at a picture. It had a waterfall in it, and lots of trees. He says, 'What do you see?' I say, 'I don't see nuthin'.' He says again, 'What do you see?' I say, 'I don't see nuthin' movin'.' The psychiatrist says, 'Wouldn't you like to be in that nice, peaceful place?' I say, 'Screw you, man, this ain't workin'.' The psychiatrist says to Billy, 'Give me my $50 and get this SOB out of here.' "

	G	GS	CG	W	L	IP	H	R	ER	BB	SO	ERA
1961 Kennewick............	31	22	1	3	12	103	75	117	96	196	150	8.39

In 1961, as he had in 1960, Dalkowski set a record for most walks in the league. He also began to drink more heavily. One night he came to his hotel room, drunk, at 3 a.m., to find DeMars waiting for him. "I open the door really slow," says Dalkowski, "and I see Billy sitting there. I say, 'Oh, damn. . . .' Billy was really getting pissed by then. He would make me go out real early in the morning with him when he knew I had been drinking, and he'd work me hard. He tried everything. Sometimes the plate looked real close, like I could just hand the ball to the catcher. Then the next time, I couldn't get the damn ball over. I had some good games over there for Billy. Ha! I had a lot of bad ones, too."

	G	GS	CG	W	L	IP	H	R	ER	BB	SO	ERA
1962 Elmira	31	19	8	7	10	160	117	61	54	114	192	3.04

In 1962, for the first time in his career, Dalkowski began to throw strikes. During one stretch he recalls pitching 53 innings, fanning 111 and walking only 11. He pitched 11 innings without giving up a hit or a walk. He led the league in shutouts with six. Yet, neither he nor his manager, Earl Weaver, could understand why. Dalkowski was doing nothing different from any other year, either in his pitching or social life. In fact, he was probably drinking even more heavily. A friend says, "It didn't matter whether Steve had a bad game or a great game, he used both as an excuse to go out drinking after the game."

"I hated Earl the first time I met him," says Dalkowski. "He was an SOB. But he was honest. And smart. And he wins wherever he goes. I've got his picture in my bedroom. I wake up to it every morning. They say that I threw strikes that year because Earl left me alone. But I don't understand how that could happen. Maybe it was the slider. I began throwing a lot of sliders that year. I threw it as hard as my fastball and I could throw it for strikes. I'd just hit the black part of the plate with it when I was right. I struck out Ken Harrelson five times one game and he says to me, 'I don't believe it! I just don't believe it!' "

One night in Elmira, Andy Etchebarren, the team catcher, bet Dalkowski he couldn't throw a ball through the wooden outfield fence. "How much you got?" said Dalkowski, who already owed Etchebarren $20, which he had used to get drunk. Dalkowski took 10 steps back from the fence and, after warming up, fired the ball through the wall. Etchebarren claimed Dalkowski must have hit a knot. "You find it," Dalkowski said. When Etchebarren did the same thing, the ball bounced off the wall back to him.

Another night, Etchebarren, Dalkowski, Youngdahl and a fourth player were walking home after a night of drinking when they began to bend over STOP signs as a lark. The police caught three of them at a diner—Dalkowski avoided arrest by going to sleep "early" for a change—and they spent a night in jail. The local headlines read, THREE BASEBALL PLAYERS SLIDE INTO WRONG BASE. That night the fans at the stadium began to chant, "What kind of birds don't fly? Jail birds."

"The worst thing that ever happened to me," says Youngdahl, who is now a probation officer in the San Francisco area, "was running into Steve Dalkowski. I was going down the drain with him. I remember one night, about a month after the STOP sign incident, I fanned four times in a row with men on base. I went out to a bar with Steve, and after awhile I went to my car and fell asleep in the back seat while Steve kept drinking. Anyway, it seems Steve, who can't see good even when he's sober, gets in the car while I'm sleeping and starts to drive home. He's driving down the middle of a two-lane highway, in the fog, and he couldn't find the windshield wipers. A cop pulls us over. Steve has no driver's license, so the cop tells him to follow him into town. Steve puts the car into reverse and backs into the police car. They arrested him and drove me home."

"Steve was a good kid at heart," says Weaver, "but nobody could handle him. I tried to leave him alone as much as I could. In 1962, he was right there, mechanically. He still drank the same, but he always did, whether he was winning or losing. You know, he was tested on the Stanford-Binet Intelligence test, and he finished in the last one percentile. That means if you had something to teach 100 people, Steve would be the last to learn."

	G	GS	CG	W	L	IP	H	R	ER	BB	SO	ERA
1963 Rochester	12	0	0	0	2	12	7	8	8	14	8	6.00
Elmira....................	13	2	0	2	2	29	20	10	9	26	28	2.79

In 1963, Dalkowski went to spring training in Miami with the Orioles. He had the best spring of his career. After 7⅔ innings against major league batters, he had fanned 11, walked five, and surrendered only one hit and no earned runs. Harry Dalton, the Oriole farm director, told him the Orioles were going to take him to Baltimore as their short reliever. Manager Billy Hitchcock, upon seeing Dalkowski throw, said that of the pitchers who ever lived, if he had to choose one pitcher to get out one batter, be it Mickey Mantle or Babe Ruth, he would choose Dalkowski. "I don't know why, but it was easy to strike out major leaguers," says Dalkowski. "I just got faster and faster every year, and I could do nothing to stop it."

One day, Dalkowski pitched three innings against the Dodgers and, as he put it, "I blew them away. The next day, Sandy Koufax was asked about me. He said I needed a better curveball." Dalkowski's last sustained appearance that spring came against the Yankees. In his first inning he struck out Roger Maris on three pitches.

Later, on a throw to first after a bunt, he felt something snap in his arm. He tried to pitch to Bobby Richardson but the pain was too intense. He was taken out of the game and examined by a doctor who told him the injury was not serious. A few days later Dalkowski tried to warm up in Vero Beach but the pain was unbearable. He would never again be the kind of overpowering pitcher he had once been. He began the season at Rochester, could not win a game there, then returned to Elmira, where he managed to win two games. He pitched only 41 innings the entire season.

"Damn, I can't believe that day in Miami. Why then, after all those years? I never had a sore arm. I think I know why. The night before I pitched against the Yankees I went out drinking. I met this broad and took her back to my room. Maybe that's where I lost it. She had a half-pint of vodka in her purse. The next morning I got up, and I was hung over. I don't know. I threw that first pitch to Richardson and the ball just took off and hit the screen.

"I think a higher power took it away from me when I had it all together. I'm not mad. It was my own fault."

	G	GS	CG	W	L	IP	H	R	ER	BB	SO	ERA
1964 Elmira	8	2	1	0	1	15	17	12	10	19	16	6.00
Stockton	20	13	7	8	4	108	91	40	34	62	141	2.83
Columbus..............	3	2	0	2	1	12	15	11	11	11	9	8.25

Although Dalkowski had only his second winning record ever in the minor leagues in 1964, he was not throwing like the Dalkowski of old. "I wasn't so wild anymore," he says. "And I was getting guys out. But my arm really hurt, and my fastball was straight now. I couldn't throw fastballs by guys when I wanted to."

	G	GS	CG	W	L	IP	H	R	ER	BB	SO	ERA
1965 Tri-Cities..............	16	15	4	6	5	84	84	60	48	52	62	5.14
San Jose	6	6	2	2	3	38	35	25	20	34	33	4.74

In 1965, for the second time in Dalkowski's nine-year minor league career, he was unable to average at least one strikeout per inning, playing in leagues where years before he had struck out 150 in 103 innings and 262 in 170 innings.

"Baltimore sent me to Tri-Cities, and I was doing good at first. I don't know what the hell happened. I think I screwed up somewhere in a bar. It was off-limits. The manager, Cal Ripken, released me. I signed on with the California Angels and they sent me to San Jose.

"The San Jose manager says to me, 'I know you're no Santa Claus, but leave the kids alone. If you want to go drinking, go with me.' I roomed with nobody."

"I was the one who released him," says Ripken, now a coach with the Orioles. "Yet there's not a soul in the world who didn't like him, including me. He just didn't give himself a chance. Why, in the spring of 1965, he was sent from the Triple A camp in Daytona to the minor league camp in Thomasville, Georgia, and it took him seven days to make a few-hour trip. Harry Dalton got pissed off, and was going to release him, but I told him I'd take Steve with me to Tri-Cities. I told him he had to be in bed early the night before he pitched. That lasted about two weeks and then he drifted the other way.

"He still threw hard then, maybe 90 mph, but not like he used to throw. Steve Dalkowski threw harder than anyone in baseball. I saw Nolan Ryan and Dalkowski from the third-base coaching box, and Nolan Ryan didn't compare with Dalkowski. I caught Steve, too. His ball was light as a feather. He was wild high, not in and out. You never worried about a ball in the dirt with him, only over your head. His ball took off two feet. If he didn't throw it at your shoe tops, you couldn't catch it. I remember once, in Pensacola in 1959, I gave him a curveball sign, and then I crouch down and in to the batter. Steve didn't see the sign and he throws a fastball. He hit the umpire on the mask, broke the mask and gave the umpire a concussion. He was in the hospital for three days. The ball never touched my glove. It's funny, but Steve's ball got bigger as it rose. You always saw it plain but it was always high. I never saw a ball hit well off him. I truly think that Steve Dalkowski, if he had pitched in the big leagues, would have been a legend. He was capable of striking out 21 batters in the big leagues."

The Angels sent Dalkowski to Mazatlan of the Mexican League in the winter of 1965. He was the only non-Mexican on the team. Although he claims he hated the experience, he also says that the Mexican people treated him "like a king. And look at the way we treat them when they come here." It was this experience that prompted him a few years later to begin work in the fields where most of the migrant workers were Mexican.

When he was told, in the spring of 1966, that he was being sent back to the Mexican League, Dalkowski quit baseball. He went to Stockton, took a job in a foundry and then, for all intents and purposes, vanished from sight. His friends and family lost track of him, except late at night, when he was drinking and he would call from odd places throughout California. There were rumors. He was in jail. He was dead. He was a member of the Oakland chapter of the Hell's Angels. He was still pitching somewhere, under an assumed name, and he could still throw 90 mph. All of the rumors were untrue. What he was doing was drifting from one California Valley town to another—Lodi, Fresno, Stockton, Bakersfield—working at odd jobs. Finally, one day in 1969, he began to pick peaches in Stockton.

"I used to drink beer after work," he says. "That's all I ever drank in the minor leagues. Then one day on the bus back to town from the fields, I see this Mexican guy drinking wine. He felt happy, see. He says, 'Try it!' So I tried it. Like a friend of mine says, 'It's a killer. There ain't no grape ever saw that wine. It's all chemicals.' But I like it."

Along the way, Dalkowski got married and then divorced after he left his wife, a schoolteacher, one day under the pretext of getting a pack of cigarettes. He drove off in her mother's Thunderbird, and they never saw him again. Shortly afterward, he began accumulating a long series of arrests for public drunkenness, many of which resulted in his being sent to road camps to dry out. After each stay, he would return to the fields and his wine. "I had a dog with me in the fields," he says, "and my bottle of wine. I was happy. Nobody bothers nobody. You just work."

It was about this time, in 1969, that Dalkowski met Virginia Greenwood, who was working at the St. Francis Hotel in Bakersfield. They began going together and in 1975 they were married. She became the cornerstone of his life, and he of hers. Whenever he felt his drinking was going to cause her to leave him, he signed himself into a detoxification center, and, as always, she stayed. "I don't know why," he says, "but I love that girl so damn much. I just can't tell her."

During the 1970s, Dalkowski was arrested, by his own estimation, at least 20 times for common drunkenness, served at least five stretches in road camps, and signed himself into detox centers at least five times. Finally, in 1978, even Virginia had had enough. He left their apartment and moved into a transient hotel near the Metropole Liquor store. He no longer was eating, and at best could hold in his stomach only a few drops of sweet brandy each day. He was near death when Ray Youngdahl found him.

"I had lost track of Steve for 10 years," says Youngdahl. "But it wasn't hard to figure he was headed for skid row. I think he drank because, like most ball players, he was geared to an easy life. Getting paid to play baseball is a God-given gift. It's not work. Some can't handle it. When I found him in 1978, he was about ready to die. He smelled so bad. I put him in my car and drove him to my home in San Mateo, where I got him in a detox program. They had to strap him down for four-and-a-half days. He vomited, got the shakes, all symptoms of alcohol withdrawal. When he finally got out of detox, I got him into a landscaping school. He lived with us for a time. He was sober for 110 days, and then we began to find wine bottles around the house. Then he went on a bus to Bakersfield to see Virginia, and somehow he got off at San Jose and started drinking again. Somebody's always going to try to save Steve. He looks for others to save him. Steve always falls in love with people and they love him."

Charles Garrett is a small, white-haired man with a ruddy complexion. He is a senior counselor for the recovery program at the Bakersfield detox center, a low brick building that looks like an inexpensive motel. There is an orange tree in the front yard, and one day a few months earlier, Steve Dalkowski showed a visitor just how he used to pick those oranges with a particular twist of his wrist, just as when he was trying to throw a curveball.

A long hall divides the detox building in half. On either side of the hall there are rooms. There are wooden railings, like those ballerinas use when practicing in front of a mirror, on either side of the hall. The railings and the tile floors are polished smooth by the hands of those alcoholics holding on for dear life and their slippered feet sliding across those floors because their possessors are too sick to raise them and take normal steps. "I walked them halls more times than I can count," Dalkowski says.

"It is not uncommon," says Garrett, "for an alcoholic to go through detox five times." Garrett, who once was an elementary school teacher, is also an alcoholic. He met Dalkowski when they were both serving 90 days for common drunkenness on the road camp in 1973. "Steve is a helluva likable person," says Garrett. "He's slow to release anger, which is why he drinks. Most alcoholics have a low opinion of themselves, and a low frustration level. They generate anger over the slightest insult, but they can't release that anger. So they drink. Steve came here voluntarily. He was confused, and he was having marital problems. We got him physically sober in 72 hours. During all the times he's been here, he never mentioned his baseball failure as a cause for drinking. A lot of migrant workers drink. Maybe because it's not a very self-fulfilling job. They drink a wine called white port. There's ether in all wines, even imported wines, but the cheaper the wine, the more ether. That's why alcoholics turn to white port. We have very rich alcoholics in this town who take a cab to the poor sections of town so they can buy white port. It's a lot worse than whiskey. Whiskey, once it leaves your system, the effect is gone. Wine stays with you longer. Why white port? No wino will ever drink red port, because when he throws up, he won't be able to tell if he's throwing up blood like he can with white port. That's the sign with winos. By then they've already stopped eating, their body is breaking down. We call it vitaminosis, vitamin deficiency. The next step is incurable insanity and then death."

Ken Cullum is a short, dapper man with curly blond hair, piercing blue eyes and a soft voice. He is 44, a businessman, who plays weekend games of softball and who was a bonus baby with the Milwaukee Braves in 1959. He played minor league baseball for four years and, by his own admission, was probably an excessive drinker ever since he was in high school with Steve Dalkowski. They ran together in their teens and early 20s, though they have not seen one another in almost 10 years.

Cullum sat at a bar near his home in New Britain. He was drinking Perrier water and lime. "I started to stop drinking seven years ago," he said. "It took me two-and-a-half years to stop. Six months later I had withdrawal symptoms. The shakes. I was tired, couldn't think, in a constant state of depression. One morning I woke up and it was all gone. Now, saying no to liquor is the easiest thing in the world. I have no need for it. When we were younger, Steve *had* to have a drink. I drank because it was part of a good time. Steve and I would work out at the park for two hours every day, and then he had to have 30 beers. Someone always knew him in these shot-and-beer bars and bought him drinks. When the bar closed, they would get a bottle and go someplace else.

"Some people say he drank because he had a screwed-up father. Ha! Who didn't? Steve was insecure. He hung around with unstable guys. Drinkers. They were much older than him. He felt confident being with this kind. Steve is funny. He couldn't handle good feelings, you know what I mean? When he pitched his best game, he had to get the drunkest he ever got. He didn't get so drunk after a bad game. Also, he had no long-term goals. Just passing ones. A game. Girls. These things he could only handle when drinking. He was ultra-sensitive. Childlike in his aspirations and enthusiasms."

Cullum got up to leave. "Steve Dalkowski was the natural athlete deluxe," he said. "He could throw a football more than 60 yards on target, and yet he couldn't throw a baseball over the plate from 60 feet, six inches away. Now, he's going to kill himself. It's in the cards."

Steve Dalkowski and his family live in an apartment complex in Oildale, California, a suburb of Bakersfield. It is the kind of housing project punctuated at odd hours by screams and random violence. Two men with pickup trucks square off in the parking lot over a right-of-way, while their women scream encouragement. The police come.

On this particular morning, Dalkowski awoke at four. His cat sat in front of the cage, staring at the hamster. Virginia Dalkowski, a lean, weathered-looking woman, was seated on the edge of a chair at the dining room table. She was born on a farm (cotton, cantaloupe, spinach) near Keota, Oklahoma, about 100 miles from Tulsa. She moved with her family to Bakersfield when she was 15 and at 16 she began working the fields. Even after she was married for the first time—and had five children—she continued to work the fields while her husband occasionally slept in a car nearby. She finally got up the nerve to leave him, taking a job as night clerk in a hotel—where she met Dalkowski—near the Metropole Liquor store.

"I used to leave my key over the door," said Dalkowski. "When I'd come back from working in the fields for 12 hours, I'd reach for the key and find these little notes. I didn't even know where the notes came from."

"God, when you first came to Bakersfield, I guess you didn't have very many clothes," she said. "Your T-shirts and shorts was so dirty. Black. I had to soak them in Purex. I'd just take so much pains with them clothes, you know. Fold them. Take them to him in his room."

"I didn't care about nothing," he said. "I'd just go to work in the darkness, the fog didn't bother me, and work my ass off in the fields. I'd put a bottle of wine at each end of the rows I was picking and just work my way back and forth to each bottle. I'd come back to the hotel and have my bottle of wine and chiliburger. Sometimes I wouldn't even eat, just lock myself in my room and go to sleep."

"He wouldn't come out for days. His room had no windows."

"But I was happy. I'd forget."

"He never told me anything about his baseball. Then we found an article about him in a magazine. He told me sooner or later somebody would be finding him. In a way, I guess he was hiding. He don't hardly talk about it when he's sober. It's weird, he's so quiet. But when he's drinking, he hardly ever shuts up."

"Virginia began to work in the fields with me after that. She'd stand with me under the Metropole sign waiting for the truck."

"We'd get up at 4 a.m.," she said. "Sometimes we'd pick potatoes. Sometimes grapes. It gets nasty under them vines with the heat and the gnats. I hated prunes. You had to crawl on the ground dragging a bucket. Boy, they were heavy. In those days, there was 30-50 men and women in the fields. Families, too. Now it's mostly men."

"Sometimes I chopped cotton with the short-handled hoe. They outlawed it now. I was the only white guy chopping cotton. I once did it for 35 straight days in more than 100-degree heat."

"It was really hard work. I worked as hard as I could with him, too, you know. I wanted to show him so he'd be proud of me. He'd work real fast just for meanness, and he'd say, 'You're just sitting around and don't ever know how to work.' I actually cried. But I worked that much harder. I cried because I thought he didn't think I was doing good."

"Yeah, but she always beat me picking potatoes," he said. "I couldn't even have a cigarette."

"Sometimes we'd make as much as $40 a day each."

"It was hard work, but I loved it. I'd drink a little wine and get mellow and then I'd be picking faster until I got ahead of all the Mexicans. It was like a game for me. I was the only white guy and I was working faster than them."

Dalkowski took his first sip of wine from the bottle on the bathroom sink to combat his morning sickness and then dressed and went into the living room to watch TV. He sipped from the wine until seven, when a friend arrived to take him to work. Dalkowski doesn't drive when he is drinking.

Dalkowski worked for the town maintenance department then, raking and cleaning public parks and fields throughout the day. He was no longer strong enough to work the fields, after recently having been released from the Bakersfield detoxification center again.

Often, after leaving work at 4 p.m., Dalkowski would drink more wine at home while waiting for his wife to return from one of her two jobs—babysitter in a bowling alley and clerk in a bakery—to prepare supper. Dalkowski would rarely eat supper. Instead, he would drink wine until he would fall asleep at about 7 p.m.

"The thing about the drinking is, I can't find it. Why the hell do we ball players drink so much? I had it all together once and then I forgot. It starts out, you know, after the game you get a pizza, a beer, and then hit the broads. The first time I really drank heavily was in Modesto in 1964. I fell asleep in the clubhouse before a game I was supposed to pitch because I was so hung over. But it started before that even. I used to hang around with the older guys. Guys that already had their World Series rings. One year in spring training in Miami, Gene Woodling taught me how to drink beer through a straw to get higher. In 1959, I met Stan Musial in Miami and me and him and Billy Loes used to go to all the strip joints. That was the year Boog Powell and I got so drunk one night, when we got back to the hotel, Boog just picked me up and carried me under his arm like a piece of luggage through the lobby of the hotel. Earl Weaver used to say I'd never make it past 33 years old. When I did, I called him in Baltimore to tell him. 'I got it licked,' I said, and I believed it.''

Mark Alcorn

COLLEGE BASKETBALL

By *DAVE DORR*

From the St. Louis Post-Dispatch
Copyright © 1982, St. Louis Post-Dispatch

"Do not go gentle
Into that good night.
Rage, rage against
The dying of the light."
—Dylan Thomas

He did, with all the fibers in his body. He had felt a concentration of will, a surge of strength, very quickly after those awful moments on a December day 14 months ago when he and his parents were told by a physician that he had a rare form of cancer.

The prognosis then was chilling. He was told he had 90 days to live. If he felt cheated, he did not say so. If he was angered by his helplessness, he kept it to himself.

He promised himself he would maintain his dignity and his self-esteem. He would not back off from a fight; he never had before. He was confident he could master this disease and he would do it quietly —privately—because that was his way.

Each day became a bonus and in his eyes and in his smile you could guess what he was thinking: "Who knows what's going to happen to me? I might make it and I might not. But I've got today, this day, and I'm going to make it count."

An athlete, he knew his body. The fight that he was fighting made him and those around him acutely aware of the joy of living, of how precious life is.

Mark Alcorn stretched himself and his capacity to endure, particularly so in the last months when there was little respite from the pain.

His world, once a widening dream with limitless boundaries for one so young, had shrunk to either a hospital room with its antiseptic smells or the couch in his living room. He preferred the couch. At home he was more comfortable and he was surrounded by a warmth he could find nowhere else. But the days were passing by, existing as little more than blurs.

"Death belongs to life
As in the birth
As in the raising of the foot
And the putting of it down."
—Rabindranath Tagore

In the quiet of a September Sunday evening, in the 10th month of his illness and not long before he was to go to Houston for a final, all-out assault on the malignant cells that were multiplying rapidly in his body, Mark Alcorn wrote a four-page letter to his God.

In it, he expressed his faith, his fear of the unknown, his mental anguish, his hope, his trust. He prayed for wisdom and asked that his family be together as one.

He finished by writing, "I know You are there. I know You love me. Lord, I am a strong person. You made me that way. I won't quit because I know You won't quit."

Mark's father, Harold Alcorn, only recently saw the letter.

"The strongest one through all of this was our son," he said. "We had some pretty good talks about death; the whole family did. Mark knew we were doing everything possible to keep it from happening. But he was prepared for it."

Still, there were questions, the only questions that mattered. The parents who were watching their 23-year-old son suffer so felt what most people in similar circumstances feel: a deep, aching sense of unfairness.

Mark questioned, also. "Why are You doing this to me?" he asked.

If one's death serves a greater purpose, why is it not one's privilege to know?

"When we were told it was terminal, we would not accept that," said Harold Alcorn. "In my own mind I never thought he'd die. Now I'm proud of the fact that there is a reason and purpose for it. If we were chosen, we are honored."

Mark adjusted. He fought. In March, the former DeSmet High School star was able to join his Louisiana State University teammates for the National Collegiate Athletic Association basketball championship at Philadelphia.

He was recognized there by the U.S. Basketball Writers Association, which gave to him its Most Courageous Athlete Award. He was on the LSU bench when Landon Turner and Indiana defeated the Tigers in the semifinals. How could Alcorn have known then his life would be intertwined with that of Turner that summer?

In April, former UCLA coach John Wooden, long one of Alcorn's idols, visited St. Louis. The first thing he did upon arriving at the motel where he was speaking was to phone Mark.

"He talked to me like I had been his old friend," Alcorn would say later, his voice filled with wonder.

In midsummer, his fight appeared to be turning. When X-rays showed no active tumor in his chest, "I was jumping for joy," said his mother, Sheila. Mark talked cautiously about returning to his studies at LSU in January.

The news of a car crash on a twisting Indiana highway that left Turner paralyzed from the chest down jolted Mark. Again, he took pen in hand. He wrote Turner a letter, sharing encouragement. When Turner—who did not lose the use of his arms—was able, he returned a letter, sharing his encouragement. The two basketball players were tied by a common bond.

Mark returned to Baton Rouge, La., for a visit. A friend let him use his car and he picked up an LSU teammate, Andy Campbell, at his apartment. They drove to the apartment of another LSU player, Brian Kistler, for a party.

"We let loose," said Campbell. "It was just like the Friday afternoons when a bunch of us would go to the White Horse (a campus tavern) and talk and talk for hours. That night at Brian's place Mark laughed so much he said it was the best time he'd had in 12 months. We left together at 1:30 in the morning. It was probably too late for him to be out, but he didn't want to leave."

The fates were cruel. In late autumn the tide changed. Just when recovery seemed very real, it began to ebb. Alcorn was hospitalized at the reowned Anderson Cancer and Tumor Institute in Houston, where the dosage of medicine he had been receiving was stepped up six times.

The massive size of the treatments was too much for his weakened lungs. He fell gravely ill but then, almost miraculously, he bounced back beyond anyone's expectations. The family's hopes soared.

"One day we packed some sandwiches and took a blanket and went to Galveston, about an hour from Houston," said Harold Alcorn. "Mark sat on the beach and listened to his radio. I suppose it doesn't sound like a big deal to some, but to him and to us it was."

I am a part of all that I have met.—Tennyson

The attention given Mark Alcorn's battle by both the local and national media embarrassed him on occasion. Why was he singled out? he asked. What about the cancer victims whose stories are known only to their families?

His father explained to him that as an athlete he had a unique capability of reaching many. Letters and cards poured in from everywhere after his brave fight was made known to the country during those Final Four days in Philadelphia.

"A lot of people were touched by him," said his father. "If it takes a Mark Alcorn or the next Mark Alcorn to make this a better world in which to live, to make people stop and think about their own lives, then the suffering we have done will be worth something."

In December, Mark returned home and was hospitalized because of a virus. His many friends who had watched his ordeal closely realized the days he cherished were dwindling to a precious few. He refused to burden anyone with his struggle. To those who visited him, many for the last time, his quiet determination was embodied in words written by Sarah Churchill to her father, Winston, as he, too, was clinging to life:

Forgive me if I do not cry
The day you die
The simplest reason that I know
You said you'd rather have it so
That I hold my head serenely high
Remembering the good times that we knew
Forgive me if I do not cry
Forgive me
If I do.

During the final days, when even the simple act of breathing was difficult for Mark, there were questions still unanswered.

"We cried a lot together," said his father. "He would ask, 'When is it going to end? Why is God doing this to me?' When he was in extreme pain he wanted answers from God or from his dad. I didn't have them."

Mark Alcorn died peacefully one week ago and his family celebrated his death for what it represents. His spirit overcame the cancer his body could not defeat. Ultimately, he did what he set out to do 14 months ago. He won.

The Master's Cold, Hard Fist of Kindness

MARTIAL ARTS

By *MIKE D'ORSO*

From Commonwealth Magazine
Copyright © 1982, Cygnet Communications Company

More than 100 uppercuts sever the sweat-steamed air of a base-ment gymnasium. More than 100 legs kick in unison, 100 arms ex-tend in a single fist and 100 throats exhale together like a nest of angry snakes. The motions are those of an exotic Oriental dance, but the eyes that fill this room, burning with concentration on a midair point before them, are not almond. They are the rounded eyes of the Occident, and before them struts the short, Japanese source of their intensity.

Compact, solid as a slice of oak, Hiroshi Hamada weaves in and out of the white-robed columns of his students, wielding a bamboo *shinai* rod like a deadly scepter, whacking the calves and ankles of the slow or the distracted, guiding their movements with guttural grunts, preparing them for the test of a barefoot run over a rocky mountain trail or a mid-winter spar with the pounding surf of the Atlantic.

"Standing in the ice-cold ocean for one hour, punching away at it, the students come to realize swiftly that they are small and help-less," softly explains this man who would graft East to West. "In that process, they stop fighting the ocean, they forget their physical limi-tations, and they begin receiving energy from it. If they don't forget, they'll go into shock because of the bitter cold."

He is known simply as *Shihan*, or teacher, to the 20,000 men and women who have studied martial arts under him since he arrived in the United States 18 years ago. For the select 100 of those students who endured long enough to attain the rarefied realm of the black belt, the way of martial arts has become a way of life. Hamada, with the calm intensity he reserves for conversation, says it is the only way. There are few compromises on the path he follows, and he has traveled farther down that path than anyone outside his native Japan.

An 8th-degree black belt in karate-doh (The Way of the Empty Hand), a 5th-degree black belt in judo-jujutsu (The Gentle Way) and a 3rd-degree black belt in kendo-iaido (The Way of the Sword), Hamada is one of only three people to receive the title of *hanshi* (Master of Martial Arts) in karate-doh since World War II. The other two live in Japan.

But it is not titles or honors Hamada seeks. Nor is it prestige or recognition that has kept him in Tidewater for 14 years, teaching legions of men and women at the College of William and Mary and Old Dominion University. It is nothing less than a mission, what Hamada calls his "destiny," that brought him to Virginia and has kept him here. That destiny, he says, is aimed at linking the ancient spirit of his homeland to the modern soul of America—a soul he has tapped through his students—and taking that mixture back to Japan to help revitalize a nation that now is wallowing in purposelessness.

At a time when urban Americans, frightened by erupting crime statistics, are signing up for self-defense courses at the local YMCA, when a bastardized form of martial arts called "full contact karate" fills sports arenas, when Chuck Norris carries on the Bruce Lee box-office legacy to the tune of ringing cash registers, Hiroshi Hamada treats the martial arts with an intense reverence nurtured over thousands of years, kept alive in shadowed Zen temples, and taught to him as a young boy in the ravages of post-World War II Japan.

Hamada was only 9 years old when his father sent him to live in a Zen temple. For five years, he rose daily before dawn, cleaned the temple floor, worked in the temple graveyard and studied the spiritual and physical aspects of martial arts.

"There I saw discipline," he says. The temple priest became his mentor, his master. "I vividly recall him as the most gentle and at the same time the fiercest person I'd ever seen. His piercing eyes always gave me a lot of wisdom I couldn't receive in words. That's where I got the most training in seeing beyond the obvious."

When his master told him it was time to leave the temple and make his way in the outside world, Hamada turned to the West for education and perspective. He arrived in this country in the summer of 1964, hungry for a taste of an alien culture and clutching a scholarship to study at North Carolina's Greensboro College that fall.

Riding Greyhounds and hitchiking across the Midwest, sleeping in bus stations and working as a cowboy on an Oklahoma ranch, Hamada greeted America. Far from shy, he joined a folk group, singing for pocket money, and even spent some time driving dragsters at a North Carolina speedway.

"I was really into speed at that time, becoming one with it," he says, sitting in his closet-sized office on the ODU campus, an office diminished even more by the paper-filled boxes and dusty trophies stacked along its walls. He is officially the school's "Martial Artist in Residence," a title more imposing than the accommodations that come with it. In the academic setting, his voice is even-toned and earnest, scaled down several decibels from the one he uses to bark commands in the *dojo*, or training room. His eyes are expressive— sparkling with amusement or wincing at a painful memory as he talks about his first martial arts class at William and Mary. It was in 1968, when he arrived at the school to study for a master's degree in sociology. His was the first accredited martial arts course in the United States, and from the first day, he began planting the seeds of a reputation that has grown to near-epic proportions.

Hamada's first *dojo* at William and Mary was a damp, cavern- ous exercise room stuck deep in the college's oldest gymnasium. Its walls were lined with rotting mattresses and both ends were covered by wire screens, giving the room the appropriate feel of a cage. Sunk below ground level, the room's floor often was covered with mucky water, especially after a rain. To sop the water up, Hamada would have his students roll and crawl across the floor soaking up the liquid with their pajama-like *gis*. "To build discipline," he says.

It did not take long for the stories to spread beyond the walls of Hamada's basement cell. Stories of four-hour workouts followed by individual sparring with the master, bones cracked by the impact of a swinging *shinai*, ribs crushed by a violent kick, hour-long runs barefoot over gravel paths in the dead of winter. All, Hamada insists, in pursuit of an inner, spiritual strength, a reward that eluded the 80 percent of his students who dropped out after the first few days.

"Gradually I would introduce gentleness and the Way, but by that time I'd have lost most of the students, which didn't affect me because I thought they just could not overcome the physical chal- lenge.

"Outside the *dojo*, I have to adjust. When I am in the *dojo*, the Americans must adjust," he says with finality. "My early training was very physical, and at first, here in my classes, I was very physi- cal because I thought America was very physical. So I beat the stu- dents to a pulp."

Included among Hamada's dropouts were more than a few col- lege football players who could not understand that there are no huddles, no timeouts in the *dojo*. "In many sports you can pace your- self, but not in the martial arts. When you reach an impossible bar- rier, when you think you cannot go on, you have to create energy to pass that barrier. The transfer of power from the mind to the body is the key. Limitations of size, weight, height, blindness, physical hand- icap or sex are no matter of concern. I believe each human possesses this intrinsic power to break through the fundamental barrier of limitations set or preconditioned by the mind."

The term for this intrinsic power is *Ki*, and it was *Ki* Hamada sought, without compromise, in each of his students. "From the first day, my attitude was 'Here it is. Face it, take it or leave.' " Most left, but the few that stayed were, in their teacher's words, "trained like tanks." The best of them he took to Japan in 1972 for a historic, first-ever meeting between American and Japanese martial artists on the island nation. Hamada's intent was singular: "To show the martial spirit they had been following for four years." His "Iron-Hearted Friendship Team" became a martial arts machine.

"We shocked Japan," he says, without qualification. "They'd never seen that many martial arts athletes, a bunch of Caucasians, come to Japan, where martial arts originated, standing face-to-face and square-punching their way through, wiping them out.

"The old Japanese instructors saw Americans wearing black belts and annihilating their students, not just physically, but in etiquette and in their refined manner. You see, I had preserved many traditions as they were in Japan of old, but meanwhile Japan had changed. They'd become less disciplined and refined. Looking at us, they saw this, and that was a sad thing."

Hamada's sadness was coupled with a curious tension, a sense of separation from a newly industrialized Japan he didn't recognize, yet a nation to which he ultimately owed himself. "I'd come back to a different country, but I still felt pressure, the precisely prescribed form of role behavior as the first son, as a teacher, as someone linked to the 24th generation of the family, as the holder of the family's honor. I always feel pressure when I go back to Japan, always. I was looking at two countries, feeling myself in the middle of both."

Competitively, the Japan trip was a success. But the spiritual link Hamada had hoped to forge did not occur. "The students practiced the same art, but they kept their distance. There was no sharing." He returned to Virginia, his mission unfulfilled and his personal questions multiplied. Among these questions were doubts about his relentless approach to beginning students. Compounding his confusion was a painful marriage about which he has little to say except to call it "a time of personal anguish."

By 1975, when he moved to Old Dominion University as a one-man martial arts department, Hamada's once inflexible attitude toward his charges had softened . . . a bit. "I began to realize more the needs of the individual students. I tailored the program to accommodate different people with different objectives and limitations." He was still tough with the beginners, still unyielding with his advanced students, but Hamada found at ODU that his classes were growing steadily.

Among his first group of beginners were Janna Levinstein, an attorney with the Internal Revenue Service, and her husband, Irwin Levinstein, a professor at Old Dominion. Their motive was exercise.

"I was in absolutely no physical condition at all, and it was very, very physically difficult. But not harsh," says Janna Levinstein. "When he strikes people, it is to toughen them, and he gauges effectively where a student is and what he can take.

"It is different for a woman to train than a man. We're not at the

same physical level as a man. And the mental probelm—the idea of
sparring, of fighting—is very hard for a woman to overcome. It's
easy to take a punch, but it's very difficult to give a punch.

"It was the hardest thing I'd ever done in my life. But it started
the spark of the challenge."

The Challenge. Both Hamada and his students treat the phrase
almost with awe. It is the challenge that has taken Janna Levinstein
to the level of 3rd-degree black belt. It is the challenge that Ronald
Callahan sought when he wandered into Hamada's class that first
year.

"I'd already studied karate-doh for seven years when I heard
about Hamada while I was stationed overseas and again in New
York," says Callahan, a military computer consultant in Virginia
Beach and a major in the U.S. Army Reserve, through which he does
intelligence work with the National Security Agency. At 6-foot-3,
210 pounds, Callahan was offered 23 football scholarships when he
graduated from Virginia Beach's Kellam High School in 1968.
Sports, even karate, had always come easily to him, so he was intri-
gued when he got wind of Hamada.

"Word gets around pretty quick when a fanatic, someone into the
more rigorous teaching methods, comes on the scene. Although I'd
never attained my black belt, *Shihan* knew of my capabilities and
took me through, using the old way. It was like the death march of
Bataan, but in retrospect it was the most decisive period of my life.

"I was like many people, chasing two or three foxes at a time,"
says Callahan, who is now a 4th-degree black belt and Hamada's
right-hand man in the *dojo.* "The study here forced me to make com-
mitments I wanted to make but had always put off."

The same testimonial comes from Richard H. Brownley, a doctor
finishing his residency in internal medicine at the University of New
Mexico Medical School. A 2nd-degree black belt, he began studying
with Hamada seven years ago. His life before karate was a tangle of
personal problems, Brownley says. Now his workouts are as much
for mental therapy as physical exercise.

"If I go more than a couple of days without training hard and
busting a good sweat, really getting into it, my *Ki* gets down, and I
start getting down on things in general, letting problems get to me
and looking outside myself for a dog to kick.

"The problems are there, they don't go away, but through the
training I've learned to look inside myself to find them (answers). As
I used to feel in the *dojo,* if I don't push myself, *Shihan* will. If he
doesn't the world will."

Brownley recalls a drill in which Hamada would wrap his fore-
arm in a black bag, raising it while a chosen student kicked at it.
When the student became exhausted, Hamada would strike back.
"Once, my defenses were down and he side-kicked me into some
bleachers," remembers Brownley. "I figured this was a chance to
rest, having just been slammed. So when I got back up, my defenses

were still down, and he kicked me into the bleachers again. That's just the way it is in the world. If you get knocked down and don't pull yourself together, the world will roll over you."

It's a sticky concept, this idea of inner, spiritual discovery found through a journey soaked in sweat, bruises and blood. Hamada, echoing ancient Zen scripture, talks of "emptying the cup," exhausting the body and mind until they reach a point where they are able to receive a strength that flows from within. His teaching is rife with paradoxes he shares with his students through brief expressions. "The cold, hard fist of kindness," is his summary of reaching a gentle inner peace through harsh physical testing. "Crawl over your dead body" evokes the spirit of perseverance. "The gateless gate" is his description of the endless bounds of martial arts study.

"Even when they become black belts, there is still a gate to pass through, and there will always be gates until they cease to exist," Hamada says. "I tell them not to just funnel energy into martial arts training, but to go beyond and above. That is when they realize this isn't just physical."

To test that realization, even among his beginning students, Hamada conducts a "camp" at the end of each 16 weeks of training. Taking his group to the mountains or to the ocean, he devises a physical test that pushes his advanced students to the limits of their capabilities and gives his beginners a glimpse of what lies beyond should they continue their study. One of his more infamous tests is the mid-winter sparring session off the shore of Nags Head, N.C. No one has succumbed to the Atlantic chill, partly because they are prepared for the test, and partly because Hamada has a knack for weeding out the weak-willed.

On the face of it, his training is violent, but Hamada is quick to react to this charge. "People think martial arts is a violent form, but it is actually nothing but a defensive art. The Japanese character for 'martial' means literally, 'Stop the spear, quell the fire.' "

Hamada's argument for the integrity of his art is helped little by the proliferation of commercial karate studios, which, he says, often neglect the spiritual aspect of instruction. "Everything can be a commodity in America. If it's a good product, it shall sell. The consumer must simply become wise and be careful what he is purchasing."

One thing the American public has bought are the dozens of Bruce Lee genre films, in which *satori* (enlightenment) means a side-kick every second. "Those films are a Hollywood exaggeration," Hamada says. "They're an effort to feed an audience with what it wants to see—violence and sex. I think it's very sad. In our tradition, the martial artist will never fight, even if he is under the sword."

Hamada himself never has used his skills against an attack on a darkened street corner or in a barroom row. His feet and arms have been broken in training, along with several ribs, but his round, ruggedly attractive face never has been touched. "I use common sense and avoid places of trouble. And I look meek, really." Still, he is swamped by self-defense students, ranging from members of local rape-awareness agencies to police officers, who are seeking the power of swift kicks and lightning punches. He has developed programs in Tidewater and Peninsula high schools, YMCA's parks and recreation systems and on military bases. What he teaches all these students is the same inward-peering method he shares with his black belts.

"The best defense is to know the self. Then the job is done," he says. Avoiding confrontation is the first option in a dangerous situation. The next choice, says Hamada, is to "gracefully, yet effectively, defuse the opponent" through the right choice of words. Finally, comes force against force. In all cases, he says, the trigger for action is self-knowledge.

Skill and technical expertise are only part of the true martial artist's arsenal, emphasizes Hamada. "Just because a person can break three boards or six bricks doesn't mean he's a martial artist. And just because he can pay $1,000 to go to a Chuck Norris studio for a black belt doesn't mean he can get a black belt here. This is not for sale, this sense that my students are developing. It's not for everyone, only those who can endure."

Hamada points with satisfaction to a multi-page list of students spread across the country, a list studded with the names and addresses of Ph.D.'s, artists, architects, doctors, lawyers and teachers. "They are professionals," he says, vigorously spitting out the last word. "And I am proud of them."

Because their belts are black, each of these people shares an experience reserved only for the most advanced of Hamada's students. They have all tasted the blade of his family's Samurai sword. Upon passing from one stage of training to another, after their final "hardship exercises" are through, each of Hamada's black belts lies down on his back and, through breathing exercises and concentration, collects his Ki. Then Hamada pulls the heavy razor-edged sword from his sheath and holds its tip to either the throat or the stomach of the student. Gradually, he loosens his grip until the tension of sword on skin is controlled by gravity alone.

"If one has fear, the sword will penetrate the skin and cut," Hamada says. "With no fear, it will not."

Not once has the sword pierced a student's skin, says Hamada, who trusts his instinct to tell him who is ready and who is not. The test, he says, is not one of courage, but of collection. "The stomach, the sword and the person holding the sword must become one. It's all inclusive and cannot be separated by the mind. Separation is what creates conflict. This test establishes that all is one."

It is this sense of oneness that Hamada was taught as a child in post-World War II Japan. Born in 1941, he became the 24th generation of Japan's warrior class, inheriting his family's Samurai tradition. As the first-born son, the young boy felt the press of those two dozen generations squarely on his small shoulders. His father, a professional swordsman—a *hanshi* in kendo—and a real estate businessman, made his son's responsibilities clear. In the devastation of postwar Japan, when the young boy began skipping school to play war games with the gangs of street children who lived under the bridges near his home, the father wasted no time setting his son on the proper path. Hamada was sent to live in the Zen temple.

At 14, faced with the choice of continuing his physical and religious training or returning to the world, Hamada questioned his Zen teacher on what to do and was told, "The hardest thing is to find *satori* in the midst of chaos and confusion, not in a secluded temple." When he walked out of the temple's doors, he had only to turn the corner to find disquiet and uneasiness.

"All around me was tension and political unrest. Japan had grown economically, people had begun to get rich, but things were also very unstable. There was polticial unrest, and the youth was typically upset, feeling crushed between conservatism and reformism. Japan was headed for a turning point, and so was I. We were both seeking direction."

Surrounded by mounting turmoil, and his schooling suspended by Japan's nationwide student strikes in the mid-1960's, Hamada felt he had to climb out of Japan's raging emotional river to get a clear perspective on its course. A Methodist scholarship, arranged for him by an American woman missionary who had taught him English, was his ticket West. The move was not easy, especially for his tradition-steeped parents.

Knowing his son would never take over his business, Hamada's father folded his company, turning strictly to his swordsmanship, and gave his son the money he needed to come to America. But Hamada needed more than money to cope with the jolt of America in the 60's. Surrounded by flux, one thread of constancy ran through his indoctrination—the practice and study of the martial arts. He began teaching karate during his third year at Greensboro, formalized his instruction at William and Mary and humanized it when he arrived at ODU.

His lighter touch in the training room resulted in a growing oneness among his students that was reflected in the developing cohesion of his personal life. He married a Japanese woman named Mikiko Komparu in 1980, and after a great deal of persuasion was given her family's permission to bring her back to America. In early 1981, the two had a child, a daugther named Ayaka. The little spare time he had before his daughter's birth Hamada had spent on a mild addiction to sleek sportscars. He went through 16 Corvettes, Lotuses and Porsches in 10 years. "The workmanship and craftsmanship of those machines was something I wanted to talk to." Now the family cars are a Datsun station wagon and a black Plymonth Fury, and Hamada talks to Ayaka.

"Ever since I was born, I've accumulated many skins," he reflects. "I lost a lot of sincerity and purity along the way. I have long sought an opinion-free and totally intuitive instructor, and now I have found that teacher in my daughter."

Teaching 16 accredited martial arts and academic courses at Old Dominion and three classes at William and Mary, Hamada still has found time to write a book of poetry and two books on Zen and the martial arts. For pleasure, he reads Japanese poetry, especially the works of Sakutaro Hagiwara, a 19th-century romantic poet. To keep abreast of the news in Japan, he reads a daily Tokyo newspaper, and for American news, he faithfully watches ABC's *Nightline* television program and reads the Sunday *New York Times, Washington Post* and *Virginia Pilot*. Last spring's visit to Norfolk of the Japanese Classical Bamboo Flute and Koto Ensemble was arranged by Hamada, and this year, the mayor of the Japanese city of Kitakyushu has asked Hamada, who is on the board of Norfolk's Sister City Association, to make preparations for the visit of a Japanese delegation from that city to Norfolk in honor of Norfolk's Tricentennial celebration.

Occasionally Hamada will have a beer with his students at a group gathering, but his free time largely is devoted to his family in the traditionally Japanese furnished interior of his colonial American house in the suburban Kempsville area of Virginia Beach. His home life is a blend of West and East. He meditates in a room filled with relics, including a 150-year-old suit of Samurai armor. He eats meals with his wife and daughter in a den, where one wall is covered by a silk screen print and another by a color television, video tape deck and reel-to-reel audio system. He seems to have found a peace that long eluded him when he looked back to Japan.

Twice, in 1977 and 1979, he returned to his homeland with a corps of American students, but both times Hamada was left with the same gnawing sense of irresolution he felt after the first trip. On his frequent personal visits there, and when he hosted Japanese guests in Tidewater, Hamada would extol the virtues of America's heritage. Japan, with her freedom doled out in blueprint form by postwar occupation forces, does not know what that freedom means, says Hamada, but her people understand when they see its meaning in America. "When I bring Japanese visitors to Jamestown, and they see the first church standing there, built of clay, they are more impressed by that than by anything else they see. Many of them cry at that sight."

Hamada visits schools and colleges each time he returns to Japan, speaking to students and teachers about his experiences in this country. He also writes a correspondence column for a Japanese newspaper, labeling his pieces "News From America."

"The economic prosperity Japan now enjoys depends entirely on the stability of the outer world, but many Japanese people don't realize this. Japan has to become more dynamic, bold and sensitive to the world's needs, to learn what the outside world is like. Her youth must learn that Japan is not just an island nation producing automobiles and high technology equipment and making bucks. I am disappointed that the youth are not disciplined enough to see the world's needs, the bigger picture."

It was discipline he was trying to illustrate with his student traveling teams, but the tie Hamada sought was not made until his group's fourth visit in 1981. That journey, a whirlwind flight through schools and cities across Japan, was climaxed by a ceremony and exhibition at the seaport city of Kobe, in the Ikuta Shrine, a sanctuary into which no Westerner ever had stepped. There, following a demonstration of the martial arts before 400 Japanese dignitaries and business executives, the Americans were asked to show their feelings for their own country. A spontaneous chorus of "America the Beautiful" brought tears to both American and Japanese eyes.

That trip created a direction for many teachers in Japan, a move toward more self-awareness, Hamada says, admitting that he, too, has made that move, thanks in part, to his students. "At one time I would break 30 *shinais* a year on my students. Now I break maybe two, but they tell me my teaching is even stronger. They have taught me much. They were the challenge, because for a long time I did not think they could do it. And I never dreamed in the last 18 years that the American students, not I, would do this to the Japanese."

Hamada now sees the time he will return to Japan to stay. First, he plans to earn a Ph.D. in education from William and Mary, then he will go home to teach. But for the time being, he still spends nine hours a day in the *dojo*, splitting time between Williamsburg and Norfolk, and nine hours a week in the classroom, teaching ODU courses in the Japanese language, sociology and Zen philosophy. He gives almost 50 public demonstrations and exhibitions a year at events ranging from basketball games to outdoor festivals, and he still studies daily with his daughter, who he says teaches him "the grace of life."

"There will be no martial arts training for her, unless she desires. She'll learn to dance and skate if she likes. I'll not put her in a Zen temple by any means. That era is gone."

But not forgotten, at least not in the *dojo*.

"If all you want to do is train physically, you may as well go to Nautilus or pump a little iron," says Callahan. "The students in these classes are looking for spiritual enlightenment, learning about the self and the past and carrying it to the future."

For Hamada, the future always will contain the tinge of tension, of an incomplete mission. "To this date, if I search for what I've learned, I've missed everything. When I think I've seen enlightenment, something final, it's gone. I always feel I am on the tip of the sword, and I will feel that way until I cease to exist. It is a state of being, that feeling. If I'm on one side of the sword, I'll be cut. If I'm on the other side, I'll be cut also. So I stand right on the edge. That is the

way I attain peace, facing life by facing death. Facing both directions at once."

> *To tread the sharp edge of a sword,*
> *To run on smooth-frozen ice,*
> *One needs no footsteps to follow.*
> *Walk over the cliffs with hands free.*

13th-century Japanese *koan*

Out of Sight . . .

by Kurt Wilson of *The Daily News* in Longview, Wash. The ever-alert camera catches Jennifer Harrison, a member of a girls' high school softball team in Kelso, Wash., forgetting to follow that golden rule for hitting a baseball. Copyright © 1982, The Daily News, Longview, Wash.

Determination

by Richard A. Chapman of the *Daily Courier News* in Elgin, Ill. T-Ball, a pre-baseball program for children in which the ball is hit off a stationary rubber tee, was a little more than this youngster had bargained for. After several misses, he dug in and gave it his best shot with the help of a little facial English. Copyright © 1982, Daily Courier News.

Skull Sessions Are Old Stuff

GENERAL

By *BLACKIE SHERROD*

From the Dallas Times Herald
Copyright © 1982, Dallas Times Herald

The week past was not one for logic, not as us straightlaces learned it at the feet of our forefathers.

In Ohio, a politico paid a prostitute with a personal check. In New York, George Steinbrenner began his second month without strangling anyone. At Buckingham Palace, Prince Charles got his royal lip split in a polo match, and in Wisconsin a man did a mating dance with a whooping crane and it worked. In Pennsylvania, two Pitt students started a rugby game by rolling several human skulls on the field.

The last event interested some of us older professors as we chatted over tea at the faculty club. We are not much on fertility aspects of the whooping crane, and we have forgotten the nuances of credit with ladies of the street. But skulls on a rugby field struck a familiar chord somewhere in the dark reaches. (Familiar chords, you realize, seldom show up in the *light* reaches. It has something to do with astigmatism.)

These Pitt students, unnamed by authorities, resigned from the university after their prank. The skulls, said the university report, were seven in number and were stolen from the dental laboratory. The report referred to the stolen property as "anatomical materials," but witnesses to the match said the objects were pure and simple human skulls.

Pitt officials were most secretive about the entire caper, stressing that the Oakland Rugby Club involved students but was *not* affiliated with the school, and that the match was not a Pitt-sanctioned activity. Goodness knows why the university was so gun-shy, unless the dean and his associates feared any publicity might launch skull-rolling as a new campus fad, like swallowing goldfish and panty raids back in prehistoric days.

Back to the skull-rolling. The components rattled around fruitlessly in memory and finally led your addled prof to a history book.

Sure enough, there it was. The Pitt students, unrecognized by dean or opponents or even teammates, merely were commemorating. You have perhaps heard of re-enactment of buccaneer assaults in the Tampa Bay Gasparilla Festival each year. The battle of Bunker Hill is re-created as a part of some regional celebration. There is the Passion Play each Easter, staged on a thousand hillsides around the country.

These two students, by rolling the purloined skulls about the greensward, were celebrating the glorious start of soccer and/or rugby, and the eventual birth of American football. The dean wasn't up on his history; he probably thinks, like the Great Unwashed, that American football was invented by Grantland Rice and Earl Campbell, under a grant issued by Alvin Rozelle.

There have been attempts to tie football to both China and Greece in a couple centuries both preceding and after the birth of Christ. And surely the Russians will claim its origin, as soon as Roone Arledge signs the Moscow league to a summer contract and puts it on the tube.

But most researchers credit football to 11th century England. The Danes had occupied England for about 30 years, and they were rather rough on the Tommys, kicking them in the pants frequently and occasionally lopping off a British head or two. After the Danes went back to their own shores, some English workmen were digging in an old battlefield and unearthed a skull of a Dane. History doesn't say *how* the workmen knew the skull belonged to a Dane, so it is to be assumed that it had a sardine in its teeth or some other identifiable mark.

Anyway, the Briton gave a whoop and kicked the skull forthwith and it rolled merrily on the grass and another workman booted the thing, and soon the work project had halted and the employees were happily kicking the gong around. This later became known as the WPA.

Small lads, watching their elders at play, dug up a Danish skull of their own and began kicking it around. But small lads usually went barefoot or, at the most, wore some flimsy foot cover and the hard skull was not a comfortable target. Some innovative youth substituted a cow's bladder and the kicking proceeded at much the same fervor, because the object was still regarded as the head of a hated Dane.

Early in the 12th century, some basic rules were established and games were played between neighboring hamlets. Men would meet at a halfway point, the cow bladder was tossed down and the kicking commenced. The winner was the team that kicked the ball into the middle of the rival town.

Sometimes there were hundreds of players on each side and when a player couldn't get position for a swish at the old bladder, he simply kicked a player from the other town. This led to magnificent civic fun and many great bleeding welts. Players came charging through the streets of a small town, kicking at stray pedestrians and occasionally knocking over small buildings. At the time the game was still called "kicking the Dane's head."

Eventually, city dads wearied of having their property kicked full of dents, so they moved the activity to urban fields. And somebody even came up with the name of "futballe." It became so popular that King Henry II finally banned it because his subjects were spending too much time kicking that silly bladder, when they should have been practicing with their bows and arrows in case the Danes came back. After a couple centuries, futballe crept back into English culture. And there, of course, it remained until Knute Rockne brought the game to this country on a vessel captained by the late Leif Ericson and Tom Landry localized it with the Flex Defense. Those Pitt students should be lauded, not scolded, for recognizing history.

WBL: It Miss-Fired

WOMEN'S BASKETBALL

By *BILL BANKS*

From the Atlanta Journal
Copyright © 1982, Atlanta Journal-Constitution

"The last check I got was in January (1981), and that bounced. I had to work at a deli in Omaha a couple of months after the season so I could afford to come home."
—Carol Higginbottom, former player, Nebraska Wranglers.

"They did some strange things, like trying to sell sex appeal. Our owners definitely wanted players to do up their hair and to put on makeup. Listen, I like to go out with chicks as much as anybody. Maybe more. But I didn't see too many in the league I'd date."
—Butch van Breda Kolff, former coach, New Orleans Pride.

They wore red-and-white sweats and flip-flops, with tennis shoes slung over their shoulders. The colors shimmered in a late-afternoon sun, and it was like a troupe of psychedelic hobos. There were 12 women and this one guy wearing a coat and tie, their thumbs jerking toward the huge saucer a mile-and-a-half down the road. A truck from the electric company slowed down because, after all, it's not everyday you see 12 young ladies hitchhiking in New Orleans.

"Where you going?" said the driver.

The coat and tie shuffled to the front and said, "Superdome."

So they all piled into the back, with the steel wire and rusty poles and all that other paraphernalia electric company trucks carry. This was how the Nebraska Wranglers arrived for their game against the New Orleans Pride one evening last winter.

"I think they had about 500 people show up," said Carol Higginbottom, who averaged 13.3 points and 4.7 rebounds for the Wranglers last season. "Playing in there was like being lost."

Welcome to the Women's Basketball League (R.I.P. 1978-81); where basketballs ricocheted from a football stadium in New Orleans to a skating arena in New Jersey—where the lights hung so low they nearly singed your hair—"You didn't want to arch your shots too high in there," said New Orleans' Cindy Brogdon; where the Nebraska Wranglers, who beat the Dallas Diamonds for the 1981 WBL championship, still haven't been paid since last January; where an entire team of Minnesota Fillies walked off the floor before a game in Chicago; where coaches not only drove their players to perfection, but the team bus as well.

"The WBL was embarrassing," said Sherwin Fischer, who was league commissioner for eight months.

It is also extinct. At one time there were 14 teams (it finished with eight) scattered throughout its province, and each was a little more anonymous than the next. The whole melange was the brainchild of Bill Byrne, whose legacy would make any creditor cringe. He was once a scout for the old American Football League, worked for the now-defunct World Football League and helped establish a professional Slo-Pitch softball league.

Next would come women's professional basketball, which began play in December 1978. During a champagne party following the championship game of that initial season, Byrne clinked glasses with a sportwriter and said, "We're here to stay now. We've stabilized."

By October 1980, Byrne was relieved as commissioner, failing to maintain the shadowy fiction that were the league's financial reports. He tried to start a franchise in Tampa, Fla., signing among others, former Greater Atlanta Christian star Brogdon. But the franchise fell through, and Brogdon played in New Orleans.

"Somebody said he (Byrne) left the country," recalled Brogdon.

Byrne, no longer here to stay, was succeeded by Fischer, who was president of the Chicago Hustle. He lasted until May 22, 1981, and was succeeded by Dave Almstead, WBL cofounder and owner of the Dallas Diamonds. Meetings were called during the summer and, later in the fall, the Hustle began an exhibition schedule. By this time, however, the league's pulse rate was barely audible.

"I tried to resurrect it in December," said Fischer, "but nobody showed up to the meeting. I said, 'To hell with it.' "

"Each year, there's more and more better players coming up. That's kind of the shame of it, because it's pretty much accepted (by players) that after college there's nothing else. That's the end."
—Joyce Patterson, Georgia State women's basketball coach.

"I thought the girls played nice basketball. They tried to play the game the way I like to see it played. Some of 'em had some pretty fair moves. But face it, if you had seven bucks and a choice, who would you see—Julius Erving or Sybil Blalock?"
—Butch van Breda Kolff

It was one of those antiseptic park gyms, the kind where locker room toilets flush seven times out of 10. The gym floor was sliced by a million lines—white lines, black lines, green lines—so only a mystic could determine out of bounds.

It is 9:30 on a Monday night, and the Atlanta Tomboys are play-ing Omni Glass at Chastain Park. The Tomboys have a three-on-two break, the girl in the middle weaving through traffic and multicol-ored lines. They had said Cindy Brogdon could pass a watermelon through a keyhole, and now you see why. Her eyes dart right, her wrists snap and she whips a pass to a teammate on the left wing. Nobody in the joint is more surprised than the teammate, who fum-bles the pass away. The passer holds out her hands, palms up, and smiles sweetly. Cindy Brogdon, you see, is a long way from the Su-perdome.

A year ago she played for the New Orleans Pride, this 5-foot-10 dervish who can trip a light fandango on the break and shoot from the other side of the moon. She was second-team All-WBL, averag-ing 15.5 points and four assists in her only season as a pro.

Now Brogdon is 25 and plays one night a week. She isn't a preco-cious kid bouncing out of Mercer University and into the 1976 Olym-pics anymore, and she isn't queen of the court at Tennessee, either. During the two years in Knoxville, some considered her—along with the likes of Carol Blazejowski, Ann Meyers and Nancy Lieberman—one of the women's game nonpareils. Now she teaches physical edu-cation and coaches girls basketball and track at Parkview High School, limiting basketball to Monday nights.

"I still get satisfaction out of performing," Brogdon said. "I enjoy the rec leagues and all that, but it doesn't bring in two checks a month."

Brogdon was one of the few players in the WBL who received her entire salary. After her final season at Tennessee she sat out a year, completing her P.E. degree and waiting for the 1980 Olympics. The Olympics, of course, never came off, and Brogdon and Lieberman (the only two players left from the 1976 squad) walked out of tryout camp in Colorado before a team was chosen. In November she signed with New Orleans for $22,500.

"You work a couple of hours a day for six months a year," said Brogdon. "I really enjoyed it. It's an easy way to make a living."

The league's top players in its final season were New Jersey's Blazejowski, who led the league in scoring at 29.6, Nebraska's Rosie Walker (most valuable player) and Lieberman. Lady Magic herself. The Dallas Diamonds' guard was third in scoring (26.3), second in free-throw percentage (.811), third in assists (6.1), first in steals (3.6) and eighth in rebounding (8.6).

Even when it was over, when Fischer finally said, "To hell with it," Lady Magic remained her sport's most eloquent spokesperson. She is involved in clinics, and commercials—a national spot was for Johnson's Baby Powder—commentary for ESPN and ABC televi-sion's "Superstars" competition.

"I don't want women's pro basketball to be dead in this country," Lieberman told Ira Berkow of The New York Times several weeks ago. "I hope we can do something about it for next season. I'm trying. You know, a number of girls went to play in European leagues. I didn't. I thought it might hurt our chances of starting another league. It was all right for other girls to go, but I thought people might say, 'If Nancy Lieberman has decided to play outside the country, then there probably is no future for women's pro ball.' "

For most, the future is not in commercials or European leagues. More realistic is coaching basketball and track at Parkview High. Or, in the case of Carol Higginbottom, coaching at the University of Georgia. Or, in the case of former Georgia State star Terese Allen, finishing work on a P.E. degree so she can coach.

"I think a majority of girls are getting into coaching so they can stay close to the game," Allen said. "A lot of others are getting into sports medicine." Perhaps, more than inadequate financing or meager attendance, that is the WBL's most poignant lesson; that colleges are manufacturing more talent each year, that there are players worthy of such a forum, and now there is no forum.

Consider Brogdon. Growing up in Buford, she usually played basketball against boys. Day after day, she turned all those choice cuts of manhood into pillars of salt. Later she starred in high school and college, was an Olympian, and a professional, finally culling the ultimate compliment of male chauvinist piggery: The lady plays like a man.

"Sometimes it seems real frustrating," said Brogdon. "I have all my experience, all my knowledge and perception of the court. I feel I've played under some of the top coaches in the country. I feel I've acquired all that, but now I can't display it."

"If I see a woman in her panties, it's no big deal. It's not like there's candlelight and wine in the locker room."
—Rick Capistran, former trainer, New York Stars.

From the beginning, the coaches were men. Of the 14 teams which opened the 1979-80 season, 14 had men for coaches. Some of the more celebrated were van Breda Kolff, Dean Meminger (New York) and Larry Costello (briefly with Milwaukee).

It didn't take long for them to delineate between the WBL and the NBA. It wasn't uncommon, for instance, for a referee to stop action at the request of a player, blood dripping from her arm, who asked for an "earring check." And winners and losers would hug and kiss at midcourt after a game, or at least shake hands.

"Christ, I couldn't believe that," said van Breda Kolff. "I think they took losing better than men, you know, lining up and shaking each other's hands. It was like a damn hockey team."

There were graver, deep-seated problems that led to the league's demise: poor marketing, inadequate financing, lack of a television contract, extensive travel (there were teams from New York to San Francisco) and ludicrous selection of cities (Omaha, Nebraska?). The Chicago Hustle, the league's second-best draw, lost—according to Fischer—$350,000-to-$500,000 in the final season.

"I would say that was about average for the league," said Fischer, "but there's no way of knowing because all the receipts aren't in. But I know that three teams went bankrupt. I was also talking to one owner who said he personally lost $750,000 in two years, and he had several partners."

"The players weren't playing for peanuts, you know," said Claudette Simpson who, along with husband John W., owned the New Orleans Pride.

Some will debate the point. True, Lieberman was signed by Dallas for reportedly $100,000 a year for three years (although Brogdon believes it was closer to $50,000), the richest contract in the league by far. Fischer says the average salary was $15,000 or $16,000, although $10,000 is probably more accurate. One team, the short-lived New England Gulls, paid substitutes according to minutes played, dramatically reducing total minutes hugging and kissing among teammates.

Fischer admits very few teams paid off their players completely. For the Nebraska Wranglers, the checks stopped coming in January. Higginbottom and her husband Steve (the team's director of public relations), both found second jobs with Zaydas Deli in Omaha.

"For a while there," said Carol, "we ate plenty of peanut butter-and-jelly sandwiches."

Attendance figures were equally glum. Dallas drew an average of 3,300 in 1980-81, with Chicago second just above 3,000. Fischer is guessing when he sets the league average at around 1,200. Indeed, it is questionable how many of those were paid admissions.

"Our first year (1979-80) we played at Tulane, and the crowd control was not good," said Simpson. "We found that half the people were getting in for nothing."

"If there were some good things about the league," said van Breda Kolff, "it was the girls and the fans. The girls were fine, excellent learners. And the fans, the ones we had, were hard core. The male fans we had were the guys who played maybe 20 years ago, who liked ball-handling and patterns and team-oriented basketball. But face it, for the guy who likes the flair—the twisting and turning and dunking and hanging in the air—it wasn't for them.

"I don't know if women's pro ball will go or not," he said. "But my feeling is that, no matter the sport, people will support a winning team. I don't care if it's winning ants or turtles."

Maybe. But then you think of 12 girls hitchhiking to a game, or a husband and wife existing on peanut butter-and-jelly sandwiches, or a team spending five hours in an airport before a game because it couldn't afford a hotel. Sorry Bill Byrne, but three years of that is hardly stability.

"All the stuff that happened," Cindy Brogdon said, "left a bad taste in your mouth. It might take a long time for the women's league to get another chance."

Why Would Cheryl Tiegs Kiss The Scooter?

BASEBALL

By *BILL PENNINGTON*

From the Stamford (Conn.) Advocate
Copyright © 1982, The Advocate of Stamford,
Connecticut Newspapers Inc.

Cheryl Tiegs came to Yankee Stadium last weekend. Red satin pants, shining eyes and jewelry, she brought a little touch of Studio 54 to the Bronx.

Who did Supermodel want to meet in Yankeeland? When she arrived, she headed straight for the Yankee broadcast booth.

In heels she stood at least six inches taller than Phil Rizzuto, but she beamed as she held his hand, leaning over to give him a kiss on the cheek.

It was hard to tell who was more excited. If only she knew that more often than not Rizzuto goes to bed with his socks on and with a heavy woolen sweater over his pajamas.

Now that's not glamorous. So why would Cheryl Tiegs want to meet Rizzuto that badly?

Before you answer, ask the woman in Brooklyn why she sent Rizzuto a six-foot long piece of Italian bread in the shape of a golf club and another in the form of a baseball bat?

Or ask the thousands of fans who rise to their feet every Sept. 25 to give a long, loud standing ovation when the Stadium scoreboard announces Rizzuto's birthday? It is always the most heartfelt ovation of the year.

Or ask the hundreds who write him every week, mailing off more letters to "The Scooter" than most of the New York players?

Ask tri-state area fans high on "Holy Cow" why they tune in, indeed adore, a broadcaster who strays from the game before him like a politician diverting attention from a sticky issue?

The answer is as elusive as popularity itself. But it probably has something to do with Rizzuto's frailties, complaints and phobias. He is everybody's gabby, good-natured but sometimes cranky, old uncle watching the grand old game.

"I don't try to do the job like a professional," Rizzuto says in his usual more-than-honest fashion. "I'm just talking to the fan.

"I don't know if the fans like me because of the old underdog thing. You know, I'm little (5-foot-6) and the other guys in the booth are always kidding me. I don't try to figure it out, though. I just try to do an honest job."

Now that sounds normal enough. Except that to Phil Rizzuto, an honest job is something considerably different than it might be for announcers like Tony Kubek or Curt Gowdy.

For the Scooter (the nickname goes back to his days as a short-stop for the Yankees), an honest job means discussing his round of golf that afternoon, complaining about being cold, a couple of dozen "Holy Cows," a few more "Huckleberries," and really, most anything else.

Oh, yes, the Yankee game will get wedged in their somewhere.

Here's a piece of conversation during a game this past week in Milwaukee. Rizzuto is doing the play-by-play with colleague Bill White:

Rizzuto: Well, let's see. Bottom of the seventh, Yanks down 3-1... . Who's up anyway? Is that Charlie Moore?

White: Yes, that's him.

Rizzuto: I got confused.

White: Well, Scooter, the rain we had earlier has stopped completely.

Rizzuto: Boy, it rained during my golf game today. Thunder, lighting. (Rizzuto is terrified of electric storms and often leaves the broadcasting booth when such storms are in the area.) I'll tell you, it started raining and I ran to this hut on the course ... there's a ball to Moore. Anyway, I thought it was an outhouse, but the hut was bigger than that.

When I got there I took off everything I had on that was metal. . . . Moore takes strike two (who knows what happened to strike one?) . . . so I shove the caddy out into the rain because he had the clubs and they're metal. . . . Moore lines a single to right. . . . Boy, it kept raining. I was scared."

White: Who's up now, Scooter?

Rizzuto: Ah, let me see.

Now if you come from Detroit or Boston or most anywhere but within range of the Yankee broadcast network, all of this is appalling. From a technical and professional standpoint, Rizzuto can't be defended.

I mean, we're talking about an announcer who a few years ago stopped his broadcast to call down to the Yankee dugout to tell the manager that a television replay showed one of the baserunners from the opposing team had missed home plate on a tag play. Phil wanted them to try an appeal, but his call was too late.

That move even angered a lot of New York writers.

But it didn't affect Phil's popularity with the viewing Yankee fans. Nothing ever has. He's been losing his way in the lineup, talking about golf, leaving games early, and God knows what else, for 26 years now as a Yankee voice. And every year, people tell more Scooter stories and love every zany moment of his trip through nine innings of a slow-moving game.

"All my life, no matter what I'm doing I can only stay serious for a couple of minutes," Rizzuto said. "Then I've got to do something wacky, I guess. It's almost a challenge to see how far I can go."

How far has he gone?

Well, before this season when Fran Healy was dropped from the Yankee broadcast team, he went beyond the limits allowed any other baseball broadcaster.

Healy and Rizzuto worked on the radio side for a few innings every night. It was a unique treat; Healy the straight man pushing Rizzuto.

"That was 'Saturday Night Live' every night," Rizzuto says now. "I really miss that. That was wild."

Healy and Rizzuto are re-united occasionally when the cable network SportsChannel does Yankee games, but Phil says it's not the same.

"On TV, they won't let you get away with as much," he said.

But if Healy is gone, Rizzuto is carrying the torch.

There is plenty of zip left in his stride, even at 64. He is constant motion. For some home games, he will arrive at Yankee Stadium no more than 10 minutes before game time, blasting into the booth as he straightens his tie. Usually he completes the trip from his home in New Jersey by 6:30 p.m.

Sometimes a late round of golf will have him behind schedule and he'll shave in the men's room of the Yankee Stadium press room. It's quite a sight. The greatest shortstop in Yankee history—12 seasons and 11 pennant winning teams—jawing with whoever comes into the john.

Wherever he goes in the press area he is addressed every few seconds. One guy wants his wife's birthday announced on the air, another wants a picture, another wants a public service announcement read by the Scooter.

Rizzuto accommodates them all.

"There's no work attached to it," he says. "I love being at the park. It's the best thing next to playing. Except maybe managing, I guess."

The Scooter, you see, always wanted to manage.

"I dropped enough hints on the air for years," he said. "I wanted to work with a young club, like Seattle or Oakland before Billy Martin was there. But nobody ever took me up on it. Now I'm too old."

Maybe it's just as well. Think of all the "Holy Cows," that nobody would have heard. All the "Huckleberries," wasted on frustrated and uncaring ballplayers.

Where he'd get this "Holy Cow" anyway, you ask?

Tell 'em, Phil.

"My high school coach (in Brooklyn) taught me a lot of things—how to steal bases, how to bunt. He wanted me to get the most out of being little," he said. "So he wanted to make sure I knew everything I needed to get to the majors. So one day he tells me that I've got to have some kind of expression that I say when I get upset in games that won't get me thrown out. You've got to say something, he tells me. Something that can mean a lot of things.

"Well, I said 'Holy Cow' all the time, so I told him that. He said, 'That's good, use it.' And I certainly have. It's worked out, I think."

If that explanation seems too simple, you don't know Phil Rizzuto. He is as natural as he seems on the air.

He and his compatriots never discuss what they might talk about on the air before a game, and Rizzuto is as free-flowing and scattered in his casual conversation as he is on the air.

"I've always liked being different," he said, sitting over coffee before a game earlier this year. "I just go on and talk about what comes up. It's amazing the things that come up."

You don't have to tell us.

"Phil is very unpredictable," Frank Messer, who has broadcast the Yankees for 15 years, said. "His spontaneity is the appeal. I'm ready for anything. He'll say something crazy, and I'll say something and we'll both sit there and laugh like mad. I don't know if it's funny to the people at home, but we have fun."

"Phil's strong point is that he brings out other stuff during uninteresting games," said Yankee broadcaster Bill White, a 12-year veteran. "He says whatever he feels."

What he usually feels is cold. Rizzuto being cold is a daily topic on Yankee broadcasts.

"He'll get up and leave while I'm doing the play-by-play because he's cold," said White. "I'll just continue. If he's cold while he's doing the play-by-play, that's his problem."

Okay, Scooter, why are you always cold?

"I've got low blood pressure," he said. "I'm always cold."

It's no news to the regulars at the Yankee Stadium press room. April, May, September, October and any other rainy day is liable to bring Rizzuto into the Stadium with a raincoat on over a sweater, the collar turned up. He will wear gloves, and a woolen cap.

"Sometimes he comes in looking so ridiculous we just have to put him on camera." Messer said. But then, perhaps providing a glimpse of why Rizzuto is so well-liked, Messer added: "Hey, maybe the fan got cold on the way home and says, 'You're right, Phil, it is cold.' "

And yes, Cheryl, he does sleep in his socks.

But mostly, he's a regular guy. He and his wife, Cora, have three daughters who are all married, and a son who is completing his final year at the University of South Carolina.

It was his son who brought home a record album that would embarrass his father, but ultimately increase his notoriety.

It was the mid-1970s, and Rizzuto was asked to come to a recording studio in New York City.

"This guy, Meat Loaf, was there," Rizzuto explained. "There wasn't any orchestra or anything. They wanted me to read this script about a guy running the bases.

"I kept asking how this would fit in to the music. What was the music? They told me that they'd make it work. All I had to do was read this part. Well, you know he tricked me."

The song, called "Paradise by the Dashboard Light," became a huge international hit. Rizzuto's part was a fictional play-by-play of a runner reaching first, second and eventually stealing home. The rest of the lyrics followed roughly the same plot.

You get the idea.

Phil didn't.

"My son brought it home from college," Rizzuto said of the record last week. " 'Dad,' he says. 'You're a big star.' I listened to it about five times before I got the drift. But you know in every city I went to, the fans all knew me. Meat Loaf wanted me to tour with him."

When told that Meat Loaf is a Stamford resident who has maintained his interest in baseball by coaching Little League, Rizzuto said, "You tell him I'm after him."

No, rock stardom isn't in Scooter's future. In fact, one can't be sure how much longer broadcasting will be in Rizzuto's future.

Going back to 1941 when he broke in with the Yankees, he's been on the road for 41 years. There were all those years as a superlative shortstop—he was MVP of the American League in 1950—three years in the service, and then a broadcasting career when his playing career ended in 1957.

"You leave on Father's Day." Rizzuto said, lamenting the perils of the road. "You're not home for your wife's birthday, or your kids' birthdays. I'll be in Milwaukee for my wedding anniversary this year."

"I wouldn't be surprised if Phil retired soon." Messer said. "He's told me he's tired of the traveling."

"I hate traveling," is how Rizzuto put it. "I'm threatening to quit every other week because of it. I've always hated it, even when I was a player. I'd go on a road trip, and come home and my kids would all be two inches taller. For me, they grew up twice as fast."

An early riser, he plays golf nearly every day (his handicap is somewhere around 10-12). "It's mostly to get out of the hotel," he says. "I can't stand sitting around."

But soon, the Scooter may be frequenting his favorite New York area golf courses more than those in Toronto, Seattle, Texas.

"I made a promise to myself to quit after all my children were done with school," he said. "But now I don't know if I have the guts to quit."

And indeed, such a retirement wouldn't be easy—on Yankee fans.

He's the Scooter. Been with the team since Joe DiMaggio's 56-game hitting streak and on through Mickey Mantle, Roger Maris, Thurman Munson and Reggie Jackson.

Summer nights without the Scooter?

Holy Cow, you Huckleberry, who would be left for Cheryl Tiegs to visit?

Watson Big Shot at Open

GOLF

By *RON RAPOPORT*

From the Chicago Sun-Times
Copyright © 1982, Chicago Sun-Times

The shot goes straight from the golf course to the history books.

It goes directly from the rough over a rise and down a slope from the 17th green to the Hall of Fame.

It moves directly into the company of Ouimet's shot heard round the world and Sarazen's double-eagle at Augusta and Palmer's driving of the green at Cherry Hills and all the other moments that often make golf more interesting in the telling than in the playing.

There are some, in fact, who will say it moves ahead of them.

"You absolutely couldn't have sat there with a hundred balls in your hand and put one in," said Bill Rogers, who considered himself honored just to see what Watson had done from close up.

"Try about a thousand," said Jack Nicklaus, who failed to win a record fifth U.S. Open because of it.

The only person who did not doubt his chances of making the shot was Tom Watson, the man who won the Open.

"Now you get this close," Watson's caddy, Bruce Edwards, told him as they examined the precarious position Watson's ball was in on the 17th hole.

"I'm not trying to get this close," Watson replied. "I'm going to make it."

And he did, chipping the ball out of the grass, up over the rise, onto the green and down into the hole.

The shot that sent Watson to a round of 70 and a two-stroke victory over Nicklaus with a 6-under-par 72-hole score of 282 could not have come at a better time.

Watson had just bogeyed the 16th hole to fall into a tie with Nicklaus and had pushed his 2-iron off the tee at the par-3 17th to the left of the green. The ball came to rest in some three-inch-high grass two steps downhill from the green and about 16 feet from the pin.

Watson quickly set himself up and took his swing. The results will appear in the next edition of Golf's Greatest Shots.

"You talk about being in absolute shock," said Rogers, Watson's playing partner, who expected to see Watson's gamble slide at least 10 feet past the hole. "I'm amazed at what's just happened. It was a perfect golf shot. It's unbelievable to see something like this. I was on the ignorant end of it, but I'll remember it as long as I live."

Nicklaus, playing three groups ahead of Watson and already in the scorers' tent with a 69, missed seeing the shot on television. When he looked up he saw Watson dancing around the green and said, "I thought he lipped it out. I couldn't believe anyone would have holed it from there."

Poor Edwards was positively speechless as Watson pointed at him and said, "I told you so."

"He was choking," Watson said. "He couldn't utter anything."

But Watson thought he had a chance from the moment he approached the ball and saw it sitting up on the grass instead of embedded down into it.

"I've practiced that shot for hours and hours and hours," Watson said. "I had a good lie and I had 10 feet of green to work with. I got the leading edge of the club under the ball and it popped up softly. When it hit the green I said, 'That is in the hole.' "

Has he ever made a better shot?

"With the timing and the setting, it was the best shot of my life," Watson said. "It had more meaning than any other shot of my career."

When Watson proceeded to give his first Open victory a flourish by making a birdie on the 18th hole, Nicklaus greeted him on the green by saying, "You son of a bitch, you're something else."

Nicklaus, who now has four second-place Open finishes to go with his four championships, came into the tent thinking the very worst he could wind up was in an 18-hole playoff.

"I saw Tom's tee shot on 17 and I thought, 'He's going to have to birdie to tie me.' " Nicklaus said. "There was no way he could get the ball up and down from there unless it hit the pin."

When this Open is discussed in years to come, Watson's chip shot will be the focus of so much attention that it will overshadow the rest of his final Open nine. And that will be a shame because while what happened at 17 was the stuff of history, what took place on the preceeding holes was what championships are made of.

Before the tournament, Watson, whose inability to win an Open was a major black mark against his career, had spoken of what it would take to win. "People who have won it have achieved perfection or scrambled like a magician," he said. "I'm not a great prestidigitator, but as a magician around the greens I'm not bad."

There were no doubts about that Sunday when Watson put in three long pressure putts on the back nine, not to mention the one he didn't need at 18.

After hitting his second shot at 10 down in the rough near the ocean, he chipped up 25 feet from the pin and knocked the ball in to save par.

On 11, Watson rolled in a 20-foot putt to take a two-shot lead. He bogeyed 13 at a time when Nicklaus was birdieing 15 and tying him for the lead, but made a 35-foot birdie putt from the fringe at 14.

"Humans can only three-putt from where he was on 14," Rogers said.

Watson bogeyed 16 with a bad tee shot—it was the only fairway he missed all day—and fell back into a tie with Nicklaus, who was trying a 15-foot birdie putt at 18.

"I wanted to finish it right then and there," said Nicklaus. But he rolled the putt three feet past the hole and now the only man out on the course who mattered was Watson. Back in his college days, he had fantasized just such an event, going against Nicklaus for the U.S. Open title.

"I don't think you could have a better scenario than Pebble Beach and Jack Nicklaus, the greatest golfer of all time," Watson said. But he was far from intimidated.

Watson has won final-round duels with Nicklaus in two Masters and a British Open. "When it got down to Jack Nicklaus and Tom Watson, I drew upon some old memories and they were positive memories because I've won and I think that helped me," Watson said.

Though nervous and excited as he fought for the title he had come so close to before but never won, Watson said he never really lost a feeling of calm that started when he began his day relaxing over reports of earthquakes and budget confrontations in the newspapers.

And now that he has finally broken the jinx?

"It augments my other accomplishments," said Watson. "It makes me think I took my career one plateau higher."

Has Football Been Thrown for a Loss?

PRO FOOTBALL

By *GREG RAVER-LAMPMAN*

From Tampa Bay Magazine
Copyright © 1982, Greg Raver-Lampman

"I don't want you to kill yourself," Manny Rubio, a *Sports Illustrated* photographer, called across a pool of water to Lee Roy Selmon, defensive end for the Tampa Bay Buccaneers. "Run along the beach. Slowly. Just like you're working out."

Sunbathers lining Dunedin Beach in lawn chairs squinted beneath their visors to get a closer look at Selmon jogging along the water's edge, shirtless, wearing Buccaneer orange shorts. Multi-colored nylon sails fluttered in the background. Rubio let his motor drive run through roll after roll of 35-mm slides. This was a dream shot.

The NFL dream, a dream of rags-to-riches, the American anyone-can-make-it dream. The NFL consists of about 1,500 of the most talented players in the country, the one percent cream of each year's college crop. Being drafted into the NFL is something like being chose for the U.S. Olympic Team. Everyone knows your name. A tough kid from a desperate, dirt-poor background can become a sudden star.

Who can complain about living a dream?

Lee Roy Selmon, for one. Selmon—a quiet, articulate, levelheaded banker when he's not mutilating quarterbacks—is representing the NFL Players Association (NFLPA), a union that has threatened to shut down this year's football season.

Beneath the idyllic surface of the NFL dream reside some very real problems. As the first game of the season draws near, a bitter duel between NFL players and owners may end up tarnishing the football myth. On the field, players talk football. Off the field, they worry about a complex web of contractual technicalities, "deferred payments," and pathetically low wages.

The problems are many and have haunted NFL players for years. Many of the players, publicly treated like demigods, complain privately of being manipulated by team managers who use their superstar images to keep them in what amounts to wage slavery.

It's a complex numbers game with one consistent loser—the average player.

Take the case of Garry Puetz, who played offensive guard for the Bucs in 1978. For Puetz, the dream began in 1973 when he was drafted by the New York Jets—the perfect team at the perfect time. Joe Namath was quarterback. Puetz was a starter, huddling with Namath.

"When I was drafted," Puetz says now, "I was envisioning a $50,000 bonus and maybe $40,000 a year. When I got my contract, I was shocked." Garry Puetz, New York Jet, Joe Namath teammate, was offered an advance of $2,500 and a salary of $15,000. The second year, he let his option run out, hoping to bargain for more money. That year, he drew a salary of $13,500.

For most armchair football fans, Puetz's story must seem extraordinary. After all, whenever football players' salaries are quoted in the media, they have six figures. Usually they make people drool with envy.

Only $13,500 for a football player? Outrageous? Maybe. Unusual? Not really. Contrary to popular opinion, football is one of the lowest paying team sports in the country today. An average *hockey* player brings home almost $14,000 more per year than the average professional football player. Out of the entire 28-team National Football League—of over 1,500 players—only 32 make as much as the *average* baseball player. The majority make much less than half what a basketball bench warmer brings in.

The scope of the inequities between the salaries of the different sports is mind boggling at times. For example, Gary Carter, catcher for the Montreal Expos, is reportedly raking in $2.2 million this year. That is more than 50 percent of the combined salaries of every single player on the Tampa Bay Bucs 63-man roster. By comparison, Terry Bradshaw, one of the top quarterbacks in the NFL, makes only $329,000, less than one-sixth Carter's salary. Bradshaw's salary is also $4,000 shy of the average salary of a member of the Cleveland Cavaliers, a basketball team that lost two-thirds of its 1980 season games.

But Terry Bradshaw is not the biggest loser in the NFL numbers game. Those who really suffer are the players at the bottom of the NFL wage scales—thousands of players trying to make names for themselves, often earning salaries they are ashamed to admit.

The whole thing leaves some players and agents frustrated. "It's a sad commentary that a kid who grows up thinking he's going to make (big money) in sports, and who works his whole life toward getting into the NFL, finds out only then that the whole thing has been distorted," says Gene Burroughs, vice president of Argovitz and Associates, a business consulting firm representing players Hugh Green and Jerry Eckwood.

Yet, even as the private battle heats up, the NFL's public facade grows ever more oppressive. Mention salaries at One Buc Place and appointment books begin to fill up, players become intensely busy and PR people grow nervous.

"I'm not interested in discussing salaries in any phase or any manner," snapped Phil Krueger, the Bucs' chief contract negotiator. Krueger said inquiries about team earnings should be directed to the team owner, Jacksonville lawyer Hugh Culverhouse. Culverhouse was said to be salmon fishing in Vancouver. Coach John McKay refused to be interviewed regarding salaries. NFL commissioner Pete Rozelle's office in New York said any inquiries about comparative salaries should be addressed to the NFL Management Council, an organization representing NFL franchise owners. The Council also refused any comment on the various sports' comparative salaries.

The dispute is something the NFL and the team owners would rather keep under wraps. Even players are reluctant to become openly entangled in the conflict. Doing that could be the kiss of death, some say; doing that could end a career.

"Listen," said Bucs special teams player Billy Cesare, when asked about his own contract, "a lot of people want to play football, and the management doesn't take too kindly to . . . well, to people bad mouthing them. Anything else I'll talk about, but I don't want to talk about that. Who you should talk to are the ones making a lot of money. They aren't so expendable.

Actually, the expendable players, the players intimidated by fear of being cut from the team, are the ones with the most legitimate gripes—and have complaints least often aired in the sports pages. Although most of these players were reluctant to discuss their contracts, a handful of ex-Bucs and player agents are willing to fill in some of the missing pieces of the NFL's complex salary puzzle.

Things have changed somewhat since Garry Puetz signed with the Jets in 1973. The minimum wage for football players in 1981 was just over $20,000 per year.

That may sound like an awful lot to a school teacher or bus driver bringing home $16,000 or $17,000, but there are important differences. For one thing, people are often unaware of just how exclusive the NFL is. Even making the roster of a *college* football team requires tremendous talent and drive. To be one of the lucky ones out of 100 from the college teams to make it to the pros is an achievement of outstanding proportions. There is virtually no other career—law, medicine, economics, journalism—that weeds out so many potential candidates. It is cutthroat competition at its most intense.

Football is also the country's most dangerous team sport. Players often leave the league with broken bones, torn ligaments and crippled knees. Players, who have struggled and competed for as many as ten years to make the pros, can expect their careers to last an average of only 4.5 years—after which they must start a new career from scratch.

"If you work it out," says Burroughs, "a lot of players are making less than the average white collar worker. They've grown up with this image that they're supposed to be wealthy. They've been training for years for this. Then they find out that they're making less than the guy who's trying to sell them insurance—a guy with maybe 18 months training."

Who are those on the bottom of the wage scale? More often than not, they are players from small schools who were picked in the low rounds of the draft. Each year, every NFL team goes on a player shopping spree and drafts up to 15 players more than they will need. The players, anxious to prove themselves, often sign low-price contracts binding them for up to nine years—but leaving the owners free to fire them at any time. The majority are axed from the roster before the season begins.

The players who do prove themselves, on the other hand, are stuck with the original low-priced contracts. Even though they may outplay more expensive players, they are very rarely able to renegotiate their salaries.

George Ragsdale was one of those. Ragsdale was drafted by the Bucs in 1976 from North Carolina A&T, a relatively small school on the lush northeast flatlands of Greensboro. Ragsdale was in prime shape. He ran a 4.4-second 40-yard dash. He managed to make it through training camp. Before Ricky Bell arrived, "Rags" was one of the Bucs' top running backs. He was paid $22,000.

"People don't realize how rough it is," Ragsdale says now. "You keep hearing people chanting your name, telling you you're the greatest thing since Muhammad Ali. It really goes to your head." Ragsdale enjoyed the game. He had accomplished what tens of thousands envied. He figured he would play for a few years, earn some recognition, and finally start pulling down the huge salary people expect a professional football player to make.

In 1979, when the Bucs won the Central Division title, for the first time he and some of the other players sat around and discussed their own salaries. "I won't say any names," Ragsdale says, "But there were big name players who were making something like $40,000."

"People just aren't informed," says Puetz of the NFL wage scales. "The NFL Management Council has a great PR department, and they want people to know when someone is making good money. So when someone signs a $200,000-per-year contract, that'll get in the paper. Besides, nobody's interested in a 12th rounder making $15,000."

Before long, Ragsdale's dreams of hitting the big time began to fade. To someone fresh out of college, anxious to play, even $22,000 seemed like a lot. To someone approaching the end of a career and trying to stash enough money to make the end less traumatic for the family, it's not so much.

"All I wanted from football was a house," Ragsdale says now. "I wanted to be able to leave owning my own home." Ragsdale did manage to save enough for a down payment on a home. In 1980, his salary finally rose to $45,000—and he was cut from the team. No notice. No severance pay. No compensation for the wrist and collarbone he shattered during his tenure with the Bucs. "They just call and ask for your playbook, and that's the end," he says.

Why was Ragsdale cut? For one thing, his contract was running out and he was about to renegotiate. Although he did separate his shoulder, he was still in good shape. He could still run the 40-yard-dash in an impressive 4.5 seconds. But there were other players who could replace him.

At $45,000 he may have been too expensive to keep. The Bucs, often referred to as a "young" team, keep the team young by purging the more seasoned players about to renegotiate for higher salaries, some agents allege.

"I don't regret it," Ragsdale says of his five-year career. "I met a lot of wonderful people, some of the greatest. You can't hold a grudge. You just got to look ahead." But his wife tells a different story. "A lot of what happened with the Bucs left a bad taste in his mouth," she says. "He just doesn't want to talk about it."

Today, Ragsdale works as credit manager for Don Olson Firestone at 1000 East Bay Drive in Largo. Other ex-stars are selling cars, running trucking companies, working at phone companies—playing catch up.

"There are a lot of George Ragsdales out there, who would still make good solid players, but who are cut by various political or economic reasons," says Burroughs. "It's a sad story."

But complaints are not always limited to those on the lower end of the NFL wage scale. Many of the league's top players also complain about tremendously distorted public perceptions of their salaries—and the monopolistic stranglehold of NFL team owners that keeps their salaries depressed.

In many cases, star players are persuaded by agents and NFL management to sign seemingly enormous contracts that vastly distort their actual earnings.

"Let's say we're dealing with a top-notch first-round draft choice, one of the top players in the league," Burroughs says. "He gets a $600,000 signing bonus, plus $90,000 the first year, then $110,000 (the second year), $125,000 (the third), $150,000 (the fourth) and $175,000 (the fifth year). So the press reports that he got a great $1.2-million contract."

The problem, says Burroughs, is that the $600,000 might be "deferred" as much as 40 years, held by the club with no interest at all. All the player really sees is the yearly salary. By the time he gets the $600,000 bonus, its real value may have declined as much as 20-fold.

If we take the $600,000, for example, and project a modest 7%

rate of inflation, the relative worth would be $304,800 by the end of 10 years; $154,800 by the end of 20 years; $78,600 by the end of 30 years and $40,200 by the end of 40 years.

The club doesn't pay the players one penny of interest on the money and can invest it freely during the full deferred period. If the club invested the $600,000 bonus at a 10% rate of return, it would earn $1.5-million at the end of only ten years. After a 40-year deferral, the club would have over $27-million—all earned by collecting interest on the players' bonus. The club then pays the player in devalued dollars.

"It's definitely in the owners' interest to defer as much money as possible," says Robert Nies, president of R.J. Nies Financial Planning in St. Petersburg. Owners argue that the deferred money helps the players prepare for the future. Nies calls the argument a "cop out."

"It reminds me of the 20-year-old TV commericals about saving enough money so you could retire on $100-per-month—assuming that $100-a-month would be plenty," says Nies. With "a modicum of financial planning," he says, players would make far more money investing than deferring their salaries.

Sadly enough, some player agents agree to these multi-decade deferrals because they are paid a percentage of the gross contract. Thus, if the agent can negotiate a $600,000 bonus deferred 40 years he would get about $60,000. A smaller but more valuable bonus—say $300,000 after five years—would net the agent only $30,000.

The young, naive players are often confused by contract negotiations and caught in the crossfire between unscrupulous agents and NFL managers anxious to sign the cheapest contracts possible. They assume they are preparing themselves for the future with these huge deferred accounts, only to find that they've bargained away much of their earning power.

"When you sign the contract," says Lee Roy Selmon, "You think you've got enough to buy a Corvette. By the time you get the money, you can only afford an old Dodge."

Being caught in these contractual traps can leave players disillusioned. Ricky Bell, a fullback drafted by the Bucs in 1977 and now playing for the San Diego Chargers, had a substantial portion of his bonus deferred "between 20 and 40 years"—and ever since has watched as inflation has whittled his money away.

"You read about all these dollars you're supposed to be making," Bell says. "But you're not, and nobody believes you."

"Making it into the NFL was something I dreamed of," Bell added. "After accomplishing it, some of the things you thought as a kid aren't exactly true."

Most players have come to accept the perils of contract negotiations and the inevitability of an abbreviated career. Still, it bothers many that they make so little compared to players in other sports— sports with longer average careers and far more generous benefits.

Ironically, many of their complaints are actually the result of the NFL's stunning success in the past decade—and the bungling of the union purportedly representing player interests.

While baseball and basketball have languished, football has become the sport of the 1980s. Four of the top ten TV programs ever aired were Super Bowl games—and one minute of advertising during the game brings in almost $700,000. In almost every city, regardless of any team's records, football stadiums are jam-packed.

The Bucs, for example, will play 11 home games in 1982. The team has already sold 55,000 season tickets. It doesn't matter if they lose or win; the Bucs will more than likely come close to selling out every game. In addition, the NFL's television contract—$2.2 billion over the next five years—will be divided evenly between all 28 teams in the league regardless of any team's record or popularity. From the TV money alone, each football club will earn approximately $14 million per year even before the gates open.

"Football is one industry that doesn't have to worry about recession or inflation," says Burroughs.

It's a different story in baseball, hockey and basketball. All play more games per season and have thousands of empty seats in their stadiums each game. They require stars to draw fans—and they are willing to pay handsomely.

"Pete Rose could ask for $800,000," says Frank Woschitz, PR director for the NFLPA. "The Phils had 81 games and 55,000 seats to fill." Having Rose on the team caused fans to flock to the Phils. Local television stations alone paid an extra $600,000 because of the increased popularity of the team. Rose, in short, earned his keep.

In football, with the seats already full, and the TV money guaranteed, there really is very little incentive to engage in such costly bidding wars to recruit top players.

Moreover, under NFL commissioner Pete Rozelle, football owners have organized themselves into a tight, well-regulated family that not only shares the profits, but which also has demonstrated iron-fisted inflexibility toward player demands. Until 1977, for example, players were not allowed to have a lawyer present during contract negotiations. Free agency has been severely restricted by a number of rules that make it extremely costly to lure top players from rival teams.

"In baseball, you've got a lot of maverick owners," says *St. Petersburg Times* sports columnist Mike Tierney. "In football, the owners are together and they have a very strong commission."

One of the ground rules the owners have agreed upon is that high salaries and bidding wars will cut into all of their generous profit margins. Thus, even though the 1982 football season will gross a whopping $571 million, almost $200 million more than the revenues of baseball and well over three times the amount that pro basketball will bring in, pro football players continue to earn significantly less than their counterparts in the other sports.

In the case of the Bucs, the inequities are even more glaring. In 1981, for example, the Bucs earned more than all but four teams in the entire NFL—$17.04 million. Yet, according to the NFLPA, the club paid one of the lowest average salaries. The team's combined salaries totaled $4.3 million. The NFLPA estimates that the team's total operating expenses amounted to approximately $10.1 million. That leaves a tidy profit of just under $7 million.

"It's one of the stingiest teams in the league," grouses Jack Childers, a Skokie, Ill., agent representing linebacker Richard "Batman" Wood and tight end Jimmie Giles in a turbulent contract dispute.

Still, despite all the problems within the league, not all players are jumping on the union bandwagon. In fact, the NFLPA proposal that the teams divide 55 percent of their income according to a predetermined wage scale has angered as many players and agents as owners.

For one thing, many of those in the league believe that the NFL's problems resulted from a poorly negotiated settlement the union agreed to in 1977. At that time, players sued the NFL for antitrust violations over restrictive free agency rules—and won the case. The NFLPA, however, signed an agreement returning some of the free agency restrictions to the league in exchange for what now seem relatively minor concessions.

"What happened was that (NFLPA director Ed) Garvey botched the last contract," says Tierney. "He's desperately trying to make up for that this time around."

According to the NFLPA's latest proposal, 55 percent of the NFL's gross revenues would be collected by the union and distributed to the players according to a fixed wage scale: first-year players would receive $75,000, for example, second-year players $90,000, third-year $105,000—and so forth.

The problem, of course, is that top-round quarterbacks would make the same as 12th-round kickers. That, naturally, has offended many of the players' most visible spokesmen—the stars.

"I think the whole thing stinks," says Bucs quarterback Doug Williams. "I don't ever want to be a wage scale worker."

Williams is reportedly trying to negotiate a hefty new contract. The adoption of the wage scale could undermine his negotiations.

"I came into this world looking out for Doug," he says. "I went through school looking out for Doug, I made the team looking out for Doug, and I'm not about to quit now."

Conceivably, Lee Roy Selmon, the NFLPA's Bucs representative, could also lose money under the union proposal. But Selmon says he will support whatever will help the majority of his teammates.

"I'm a team guy," Selmon says. "I like to see all the guys do well."

Agents are almost unanimously against the contract. "For one thing," says Burroughs, "How are they going to figure out the gross? No team owner in his right mind would open his books to the unions. So let's say they decide to tie it to 55 percent of the TV income—something that's easy to trace. By the time they get it negotiated, they may get 40 percent of the TV income, and you'll have players making little more than they are now.

"And then what happens when you have a Doug Williams or a Terry Bradshaw go in and ask for more money? They won't have a leg to stand on. Management can say, 'Hey, we're paying you just what your union says. Now you want more?'

"We're supposed to be working on the same side, the side of the players, but I think the players would be better off if the union just folded."

How does the union feel about that?

"I don't know why you want to talk to agents," responded the NFLPA's Woschitz. "They're the flesh peddlers of the industry. They haven't done a damned thing for the sport, and we'd just as soon run them out of the business."

And players who disagree with the union?

"I guess they just don't know how to read," Woschitz snaps.

Selmon seems oddly cast in this angry battle. Selmon is painstakingly polite. He seems almost too gentlemanly to be an activist. He's supposed to be getting his troops ready for confrontation, threatening them with mayhem.

But then again, perhaps Selmon is the best player rep the team could hope for. After all, the battle between the union and the managers began in earnest when the NFLPA shot itself in the foot during the last duel. Selmon isn't likely to blindly accept any proposal the union dredges up this time around.

"We get a lot of figures thrown at us by both sides," Selmon says. "When the union says 55 percent, we have to know what that will mean in dollars and cents. There are also a lot more important things than the 55 percent deal."

Ricky Bell agrees. "With 55 percent, a player might make more in one year," he says. "So what? He may be cut the next year. Other things should be discussed. An insurance plan. A pension plan. Something that will be lasting, that'll help the player after his career has ended."

Although many players on the lower end of the salary range support the 55 percent-of-gross proposal because it would help them immediately, most see it as the best of two evils: They are either tied to a stingy management scale supported by the owners, or a more generous scale supported by the union. Both "scales" conflict with their own competitive spirits. For many, the formation of the United States Football League seems to offer more hope than the endless bickering between the union, the owners and the agents. Already, ex-players like George Ragsdale, players retired before their time, have been offered slots in the new league. Should it be successful, the

NFL's stranglehold on wages could relax considerably.

Whatever happens, though, players don't expect too much fan support for their plight. "People don't realize we all have families, we have pride, and we've worked hard," says Dewey Selmon, Lee Roy's older brother and a Bucs linebacker recently traded to San Diego. "You take off that helmet and you take off that number, and all you have underneath is a little bitty human being."

That may sound a bit trite, especially coming from Dewey Selmon, a 6'1", 240-pound bone crusher, but there's some truth to what he says. Regardless of what conditions they complain about, regardless of the fact that some Bucs may be making less than the plumber enjoying a Sunday morning game on TV, the myth of the iron-loined, barrel-chested, superhuman football hero is difficult to overcome.

As Lee Roy Selmon jogged along the sands of Dunedin Beach the sense of awe was palpable. Manny Rubio trained his camera on Lee Roy, trying to pull in the horizon and the sailboats for his *Sports Illustrated* dream shot. By 5:00 that evening Selmon—still shirtless and covered with trickling beads of sweat—started signing autographs, joking with his fans.

"He's a *moose*," said one of the beach lifeguards of the 6'3", 250-pound Selmon. "No, he's not that big," the lifeguard's friend answered. "Not for a football player."

As a crowd gathered, Sammy Shaw, a nine-year-old from Dunedin, worked his way toward Lee Roy and slowly, reluctantly, reached out to touch a scar on Selmon's knee.

Everyone laughed.

"He's real, Sammy," his mother reassured him as Sammy stroked Selmon's thigh. "He's real."

Ride 'Em, Cowboy Jack, Right to Winner's Circle

HORSE RACING

By *BILL CHRISTINE*

When Cowboy Jack Kaenel signed on with the Donald Dell athlete talent consultants in Washington, D.C., one of Dell's people figured the jockey would be a natural for the beer commercials.

For example, surround the 5-5, 113-pound Kaenel with end tables like Dick Butkus and Bubba Smith. *Voila!* A television spot that grabs you and doesn't let you go.

"There's only one problem with that," the Dell brainstormer was told. "Jack Kaenel's only 16 years old and a little young to be drinking beer."

So perhaps Jack Kaenel will start with peanut butter and work up to spirits. One thing he can't do is lie about his age. He's already tried that. After winning close to 40 races in Maryland last year, when he was only 15, a year beneath the legal minimum, he was exposed by a Washington newspaper and suspended by track stewards until his age caught up with his ability.

"Jack is 16 going on 50," says Kaenel's agent, Bill Vuotto, who was responsible for the teen-ager getting the mount on Aloma's Ruler, the colt who won the Preakness Stakes last month. Vuotto approached Butch Lenzini, trainer of Aloma's Ruler, after Angel Cordero, winner of four straight races with the colt, opted to ride another horse, Shimatoree, in the Withers Stakes at Aqueduct, two weeks before the Preakness.

Lenzini didn't give Kaenel the mount for the Withers until he called virtually every marquee jockey in the country, including Chris McCarron and Jeffrey Fell. Several jockeys were reluctant to ride Aloma's Ruler because Lenzini couldn't guarantee them that the horse would also run in the Preakness.

Kaenel won the Withers with Aloma's Ruler, but his Preakness status was still precarious. In the winner's circle, Cordero told Nathan Scherr of Baltimore, who owns the colt: "I'm loose for the Preakness."

"I told him no," Scherr said. "It ticked me off a little that he didn't want to ride our horse in the Withers."

Instead of returning to the telephone to obtain a name rider for the Preakness, Lenzini decided to stick with Kaenel. "I gave Jack tough orders in the Withers," Lenzini said. "I told him not to run with Shimatoree, but not to let him get too far off, either, and I also reminded him to try to save something with the colt. He did all those things perfectly."

But when Kaenel, four days before the Preakness, suffered a slight concussion in an automobile accident in which his $28,000 custom Cadillac Eldorado was demolished, Scherr had second thoughts.

"Butch," the owner said to his trainer, "this accident might be a mixed blessing. Maybe we should get back to Cordero. We're turning down the greatest riding talent in the country."

Lenzini wasn't having any. "No," he said, "I think Jack can do it. If he recovers from the accident, he should be our rider."

Kaenel showed that he had recovered by dancing the night away at a Preakness party on the eve of the race at a Baltimore country club. The last couple on the floor, just a little past midnight, was Kaenel and Miss Preakness.

In the Preakness, Kaenel and Aloma's Ruler held off the favored Linkage, with Bill Shoemaker, by a half-length at the wire. It is a Preakness that will be long remembered as a jockey's race. Kaenel did two things—he put Aloma's Ruler on the lead on a racing surface that had been favoring speed horses to the point of absurdity, and he kept his horse inside where the footing was better.

Kaenel, first jockey to appear in a Preakness winner's circle wearing a 10-gallon cowboy hat, had already appeared on the TV show "That's Incredible" after the flap over his phony age, but after becoming the youngest jockey to win the Preakness, his celebrity mushroomed: the "Today" show; People magazine; the contract with Donald Dell; and a "Good Morning America" appearance prior to the Belmont Stakes, in which Aloma's Ruler, unable to handle a quagmire of a track, finished ninth.

All the while, Kaenel has gained a reputation as the second coming of John Travolta in "Saturday Night Fever." After Miss Preakness in Baltimore, he moved on to an evening of gyrating with Karen Rogers, another jockey, at a Belmont party, then attended the Belmont ball at New York's Waldorf-Astoria with Sheila Kennedy, 20, who was Penthouse magazine's Pet of the Month last December.

Does Kaenel feel awkward dating older women such as Kennedy?

"Not as long as I'm taller than they are," he said.

How does he compare his social companions during the Triple

Crown weeks?

"Now, that would be incriminating if I answered that."

For her part, Rogers gives Kaenel high marks as a dancer. "Especially when the band is playing country-and-western music," she said.

Jack Kaenel's roots are country as well as Western. The son of a jockey who traveled bush tracks from Kansas to Colorado, he was born in Omaha, Neb., two blocks from the back stable gate at Ak-Sar-Ben Field. His first mount, at age 2, was the family coon dog.

"He'd climb up on that big old dog," says Dale Kaenel, Jack's father, "and he'd ride him all over the place."

Before he entered the first grade, young Kaenel was reading the Daily Racing Form. He started driving the family pickup truck at age 7. "Little House on the Prairie" was never like this.

Kaenel was an "A" student in school, but he has few of his report cards to prove it. After Dale Kaenel got too heavy to ride, he and his wife Kathy continued the bush-track circuit, training horses. They kept Jack and his younger sister, Jill, with them, so the children's grade reports often wound up at the dead-letter office.

The last grade Kaenel attended was the ninth. He had already been riding four years, starting at state fairs at 10 and moving on to unrecognized bullrings at outposts such as Rocky Ford, Colo., Anthony, Kan., and Woodward, Okla. Even without further learnin', Jack Kaenel was bound to be good at geography.

What did he ride? Anything with four legs that moved. Ponies, thoroughbreds, quarter horses, Appaloosas, bucking broncs in rodeos and—ready for this?—he had a mount in the Deer Trail Mule Derby.

"I think I was brought up the right way," Kaenel said. "My dad never pushed me to be a jockey. But when he saw I was inclined to ride, he spent four years teaching me how to do it."

Kaenel's fellow jockeys were as much as four times older than he was. Some were grizzled ne'er-do-wells, others were jockeys who had weight problems on the dignified circuits, or who had been ruled off for such things as fixing races and now were trying to eke out livings at the only business they knew.

In Anthony, Kan., Jack rode 53 horses in eight days, winning with 26. He got few handshakes.

"They didn't like it," Kaenel says. "It was a good lesson in defending myself. They'd shut me off when I tried to move with a horse; they'd hit me with their whips; they'd try to force me into the rail. Off the track, there were a lot of fights. I weighed about 65 pounds then."

Kaenel was asked about his record in fights.

"I haven't lost any fights," he said. "But there were some I didn't win, either, if you know what I mean. The ones you don't win, they go on forever. Those are the ones that are the killers."

Kaenel won over 400 races, by his reckoning, including a Triple Crown the Jockey Club never heard of—the Akron Derby, the Hugo

Derby and the Watermelon Derby, all held in Rocky Ford, Colo. The horse's name was Play with Rob and Kaenel earned $50, plus a watermelon that weighed almost as much as he did.

"Because the older riders resented me," Kaenel says, "I had to prove myself 200 percent every time I climbed on a horse."

The Kaenels' peregrinations took them to Winnipeg, Canada, and Assiniboine Downs in 1980, Jack riding his first winner at a track with parimutuel wagering on September 13.

A couple of months later Kaenel appeared at the jockey's room at Aqueduct in New York, having been licensed because he said his year of birth was 1964, instead of 1965.

Lenny Goodman, an established jockey agent whose only previous apprentice had been Steve Cauthen, began booking Kaenel's mounts.

"The kid looked like a rider," Goodman said. "He was no Cauthen. Cauthen was a natural from the word go. But I thought this kid might develop. And I had a trainer, P.G. Johnson, who was crazy about him."

Some trainers at Aqueduct questioned Kaenel's courage, believing he was reluctant to place a horse close to the rail, but Johnson disagreed.

"I thought Kaenel was the most natural rider to come along since Cauthen," Johnson said. "Horses ran for him. I thought he had the chance to become a super rider."

Johnson's support notwithstanding, other trainers weren't using Kaenel, even after he won with their horses. Twice he rode stakes winners out of town—Snow Plow at Laurel and Jameela at Oaklawn Park—only to be replaced by Angel Cordero the next time the horses started.

Kaenel moved to Maryland in the spring of 1981 and was Pimlico's leading jockey with purses totaling $897,000 when Betty Cuniberti, of the now-defunct Washington Star, discovered that his real birthday was July 27, 1965. Kaenel received a wrist slap from the stewards and was suspended until he really turned 16, which was a couple of months off.

"I wasn't legal," Kaenel says, "but I wasn't causing any trouble."

The day he returned, at Timonium Race Track on his 16th birthday, a camera crew from "That's Incredible" was there, and Kaenel was ready. "I wasn't born until 3:57 in the afternoon," Kaenel said, "but the stewards are still going to let me ride the races that start before that time."

Two days after his return, Kaenel was hospitalized for an appendicitis. By August, however, he was riding at Saratoga, where the mounts were scarce, and trying bareback contests in upstate New York on Friday nights.

"All kind of things happen to this kid," says Vuotto, Kaenel's agent. "After the auto accident before the Preakness, I was thinking about putting him in a rubber room and feeding him three times a day."

Before the Preakness, Kaenel watched a closed-circuit television program from the Pimlico jockey's room. The host of the show didn't mention Aloma's Ruler.

"What about Kaenel on the seven horse?" Kaenel shouted at the screen. "You haven't said a word about me. You'll be sorry."

Bill Shoemaker, sitting nearby, was asked about Kaenel's brashness.

"When I was that age," the 50-year-old Shoemaker said, "I didn't have a care in the world, either."

Scheduled to fly from Baltimore to New York to ride Aloma's Ruler in a workout prior to the Belmont Stakes, Kaenel missed his plane and hitched a ride aboard an executive's private jet. "I just saw this guy warming up his plane on the runway, and I went after him," Kaenel said. "He saw I wasn't kidding and told me to come along."

After the Belmont Stakes, Kaenel considered riding in New York. "This horse (Aloma's Ruler) has gotten my career in the right direction," he said. "If there's business in New York, I'll stay."

The business did not materialize and Kaenel returned to Maryland and Laurel, where there are signs that his weight could be a problem. Once 102 pounds, he has been riding lately at 113.

"I don't have to kill myself to keep my weight down," Kaenel said, "but if it happens, it happens. The only goals I have are to be happy and enjoy life. Those are the main things, no matter how much money you have. I've always just given it the best I could. I rode just as hard in the days when I'd make $20 on a horse as I did in the Preakness."

Kaenel has considered other avenues, however, should making weight be too much to overcome. He could always train horses, for one thing. While in Canada, he was once responsible for 15 head—seven quarter horses and eight thoroughbreds. It was a one-man stable, no grooms, no extra help, just Cowboy Jack. It's all part of going from age 16 to age 50, in a single bound.

Up and Over

by Kevin Kolczynski of *The Gainesville Sun*. With bodies crashing below him, Heisman Trophy winner Herschel Walker sails over teammates and Gator defenders for a touchdown during the Georgia-Florida game in Jacksonville, Fla. Copyright © 1982, Kevin Kolczynski.

Awe Americas

by Richard Darcey of *The Washington Post*. The much ballyhooed battle of the titans, Georgetown's Patrick Ewing and Virginia's Ralph Sampson, occurred on December 11 in Washington's Capital Centre. Although Ewing got the best of Sampson on this play, Sampson clearly won the battle and Virginia won the war. Copyright © 1982, The Washington Post.

Evans Fights Quiet Battle Off the Field

BASEBALL

By *JIM HODGES*

From The Day, New London, Conn.
Copyright © 1982, The Day Publishing Co.

By rights, given the time of year, this should be a baseball column. Well, forget that. Timmy and Justin are more important.

The winter of 1981 should have been a fiscal bonanza for Dwight Evans. Third in the American League's most valuable player voting; potential realized statistically; played right field in his accustomed exemplary manner; tied for the league lead in homers; played for the Red Sox, which automatically means demand in New England. That demand can be made into big bucks through endorsements and speaking engagements.

So Evans stayed home in Lynnfield with the family. Timmy and Justin are more important.

A winter which should have been relished in reflection became a nightmare of doctors and hospitals, a *deja vu* situation for the Evans household. Justin Dwight Evans, age 4, was found to have a tumor at the base of his brain.

It was a second strike for Dwight Evans, baseball player, all-star and picture of swarthy health. He had gone through the same shock in 1975. That time it was Timmy, then 18 months old.

Neurofibromatosis is perhaps the cruelest malady that the Almighty has been able to conjure up. To save you Medical Dictionary work, the play and movie "The Elephant Man" was the story of a man who had neurofibromatosis. It is a form of cancer which affects the nerve endings. It isn't usually fatal, but it is disfiguring. Its cruelty comes when people don't understand it and ask dumb questions. They ask a kid why he looks the way he looks. That's a dumb question.

"People are mean to him the way they look at him," says Dwight

Evans softly of Timmy. "He used to hide or say 'I ran into a tree.' Now he says 'I was born that way, and that's the way I am.' When I heard that I was so proud of him that I had to turn my head. I almost cried. It really hit me. I was so mad at that person for being an adult and asking that question I wanted to hit the guy. I just can't accept people's ignorance."

Particularly an adult's ignorance. Children can also be cruel, but Timmy Evans is learning to fight that on his own.

Dad fights, too. School systems have been one foe. Adults battle government-mandated programs for the handicapped because of their cost and the number of children they serve. They resent having money go for special teachers that could be spent for buildings and lower pupil-teacher ratios, and they particularly resent program cutbacks that stem from having to spend money for special teachers.

"Little things like that burn me up," says Evans, who can afford to send his offspring to special schools to learn to cope with life and education. But he's become increasingly aware that others aren't as financially fortunate.

As a member of Massachusetts Gov. Ed King's council on children, he's also become shaken by what he's seen. Again, it's the adults who are the targets of his wrath. "What bothers me is when people with normal children abuse those children," he says, the voice inflection rising in anger. "Child abuse is the worst thing I can think of. I can't understand how an adult can hit a child like that."

Dwight Evans' baseball career has been at once appealing and frustrating to Red Sox fans who aren't the most forgiving sort. They see talent, and apply goals that are at once unrealistic and unreachable. Their measure is statistical, and it is a daily aggregate. They're with you win or tie, but don't tie too many.

They accept nothing short of perfection, particularly where Dwight Evans is concerned. When a family man plays with family problems on the mind, perfection is out of the question. "Sometimes you can't leave it off the field," says Evans. "You do the best you can with what you have, but it affects me on the field. It's not easy."

Road trips are spent playing baseball and phoning Susan Evans, who has to play both the mother and father to the brood. Timmy Evans has been in hospitals 22 times in his nine years, and nine of those times have been for major operations. When the Red Sox are in New York, Susan Evans has to take young Timmy. "Have you ever put your son in the hospital?" Dwight asks. "I mean, have you ever put him in when he's been so many times before and knows what's happening? He's fantastic. He still has a problem, and he knows he's going to have it the rest of his life. But he's matured. He can handle it."

It's placed baseball and life in perspective for Dwight Evans. He's no stranger to medical problems himself, having survived a 1978 beaning by Seattle pitcher Mike Parrott and knee problems that were potentially crippling; having survived the slings and arrows of Red Sox fans that pierce to the core; having to survive the burden of potential.

"When I went through surgery, I put myself in his place," said Evans. "When I start feeling sorry for myself, I take a walk through the cancer ward of a children's hospital. Try it. When you come out, you see how fortunate you really are.

"Baseball can be very insignificant. Put everything in perspective. You just hit a white ball with a round bat. I can't take that as seriously as I used to."

It's a lesson in life's priorities. And, perhaps more important, it's a lesson in the capacity to handle life's trials. "We do everything we possibly can for the kids," says Evans. "I'm glad I have them . . . I don't look at them as a burden . . . what if they were in a family that couldn't take care of their individual needs? Physically, all this can't be explained. But I believe God never hands down more than you can handle."

You handle it by assigning priorities. Timmy and Justin are more important.

A Real Wonder on Just One Leg

GENERAL

By *BILL LYON*

From The Philadelphia Inquirer
Copyright © 1982, The Philadelphia Inquirer

There is an old saying that you don't miss what you never had.

What Carl Joseph has never had is a left leg. He was born without it. He has, however, never regarded its absence as anything but a minor inconvenience.

"Other people got something they can lean on when they get tired," he said without a trace of envy. "That's about the only difference."

Carl Joseph, the one-legged athlete who has high-jumped 5 feet 11 inches, who can dunk a basketball, who won a total of 13 high school letters in football, basketball and track, last night was named the Most Courageous Athlete by the Philadelphia Sports Writers Association.

"Am I courageous?" he asked, repeating the question that is inevitably asked of the winner, his face furrowed in concentration.

A soft voice floated from the back of the room, saying, "Blessed."

Carl Joseph's face brightened in recognition of that familiar voice. It belonged to his mother. He nodded his assent.

"Blessed," he said. "Yes, blessed."

And how can that be? wondered a man with two legs.

"God blessed me with one leg, and He blessed me to do all of this," he said. "What more can you ask for?"

What others regard as a handicap, Carl Joseph views as an advantage. One-legged people in a two-legged world can either go along for the ride or they can walk at the head of the pack Joseph chooses to walk.

"If I'd had two legs," he said, "I might be just layin' around, draggin' around. This way, you have to keep driving yourself. People see you, but they don't believe you, so you just continue and continue and continue."

He has been continuing ever since he first stood up and tried to walk.

"He was 3 years old then," his mother, Gladys Davis, remembered. "He had a peg leg at first, and then, later, he got crutches and an artificial leg. The nurses were always so proud of him, the way he'd learn so fast.

"You couldn't keep that child still. He was swift and always into things. I put up a barrier around the door so he couldn't get outside, but he'd just climb over it and go scooting off.

"He'd see other children outside, climbing trees, and the next thing you know, there he is, up there in the trees with them. They'd have races down the hill, and he'd throw away his crutches and go hopping off on that one leg, and, you know, there would be times he'd beat them all, and his face would just light up, he was so proud."

So was his mother.

She has 10 children, the rest of them healthy, normal, two-legged. She knew early that Carl was special. Not different, but special.

"I prayed a lot, but I pray for all my children," she said. "They told me it was very important that I didn't treat him any different, though. He might be special, but I shouldn't treat him special."

She balked, though, when he wanted to play sports.

"I was afraid he'd get hurt," she said.

Carl Joseph got around that.

"I had my older sister sign the papers so I could play football," he said, laughing.

He laughs often. He punctuates almost every sentence with laughter. It is a deep, rich, throaty laugh, and in it, you can hear the juices of life bubbling. Carl Joseph is full of the joy of living.

He is 6-foot-2, has bulked up to 220 pounds since enrolling at Bethune-Cookman College in Daytona Beach, Fla., where he blocked on the special teams and was a reserve inside linebacker last season. He saw more action than all but one other freshman on the squad.

But even that is not enough. He is driven to prove that he can do more, that he can play big-time college football.

He spent four weeks last August with the Pitt football team. It was suggested that he be a trainer. But Jackie Sherrill, the coach who has since moved to Texas A&M, knew that would not satisfy Carl Joseph.

"He said to me, 'You don't really want to be a trainer, do you?' " Joseph said. "And I told him I wanted to play. Now I think I'll transfer from Bethune-Cookman to Texas A&M."

He can play. He is not just an oddity. He blocked a punt in a high school game. He has made pursuit tackles, chasing down the ball-carrier on the other side of the field. He runs the 40-yard dash, on crutches, in 6.5 seconds. He can cover a mile in less than 6 minutes.

"I'm good at blitzing," he said, eyes twinkling, "because the blockers are going to miss one of my legs right off."

Joseph, you see, has a nice sense of humor.

Those who play against him are in awe at first.

"I can see them staring when we line up," he said. "I've tried to put myself in their position. I guess I'd forget the snap count and who I was supposed to block if I was looking at a guy who was standing on one leg. When I first played college football, they said they'd take it easy on me. I told them not to."

They found out the hard way that there was no need to. The one-legged player could hit. Hard.

"A lot of the guys were going to ease off him—until Carl started lighting them up," said Alvin Wyatt, the linebacker coach at Bethune-Cookman.

Joseph began playing football, on the sandlots in Madison, a town of 4,000 in northern Florida, with an artificial leg.

"But that leg was so hard and kids were getting hit with it on the head and complaining, so I just took it off and played without it," he said.

It never occurred to him that maybe everyone else should accommodate him, instead of the other way around.

"Well," he said, laughing, "I found out I played better without the artificial leg, so maybe they did me a favor."

On the high school track team, he threw the javelin and discus, but at one meet, the team was missing its regular high-jumper. Joseph got volunteered. He tried 5-4 twice and knocked off the crossbar.

"But I made it on my third try, like it wasn't even there," he said, the wonder and the pride still there in his voice, "and then I jumped 5-6 and then 5-8 and 5-10 and, finally, 5-11, and they stopped the meet right there and everyone started celebrating."

But, then, there has been a lot of celebrating of Carl Joseph. He has been on such TV shows as "That's Incredible," "To Tell the Truth" and "Today." There is a book about him, One of a Kind, and they are planning a TV movie about his life.

He is a reluctant hero.

"I'm just a natural person," he said. "I want what I earn. I don't want somebody to just give me something. If you're gonna be somebody, you've got to make it on your own."

He said he can never remember feeling sorry for himself.

"As long as I can remember, it's never been a problem for me," he said. "But I don't think about having one leg. If you start thinking too much, it makes you wonder what might have been, and that does you no good. I just always try to think positive."

A Tortuous Path to 500 Wins

COLLEGE BASEBALL

By *WOODY ANDERSON*

From The Hartford Courant
Copyright © 1982, The Hartford Courant

He is a tortured winner. He notched his 500th victory Saturday, but University of New Haven baseball coach Frank "Porky" Vieira still screams, throws things and can't sleep nights.

Now in his 20th season of discontent, the 47-year-old Vieira has the best winning percentage—better than 81%—of any baseball coach in the country, according to the 1982 NCAA Baseball guide, and is the first New England baseball coach to win 500 games.

He is consumed by winning, but finds the process agonizing. He can take college kids and turn them into pros, but he can also toss them aside, seemingly without a second thought. He has been called crazy and admits to being "wacky." He is both vilified and beatified.

He is a study in contrasts and in insecurity. "Either you win or you're garbage," he says. "I can't let up. There might be other Vieiras out there."

He chain smokes. During games he writhes with contortions over every pitch.

He has fits of temper. He throws anything he can get his hands on, including water coolers. He curses constantly.

He stalks angrily back and forth in his dugout. Someone once told him he walks 12 miles every game. His players give him room.

Porky Vieira says he has never met anyone as intense as he. "When I go into my act, well, it's not an act. It's real. I'm on a kid every play. That's how you develop players. I'm like this every game, every practice. Other coaches tell me they can sit back and just let 'em play. That's bull. You've got to keep them up."

He said he's never had a baseball player that wanted to play as badly as he did as a kid. "I tell them, 'if you want it one-quarter or one-half as much as me, you'll be OK.' "

Vieira's baseball intensity has boiled over to his home life. "He used to be unbearable," said his wife, Barbara. "No one (the Vieiras have three daughters) wanted to come home to face him, especially if he lost. It was as if his best friend had died. He's the kind who can win and still not be satisfied. He has to feel his team deserved to win."

She also said, "He has mellowed in the last five years."

Once this season, a small boy sitting in front of Barbara in the bleachers said of Porky's dugout madness, "That man's crazy." Barbara said she can laugh now at comments about her husband. "Comments like that used to bother me. I used to cringe at what people were saying about him. But not now. That's how Porky is. He doesn't care what he looks like or what people say about him."

Vieira believes there is a thin line that separates average players from the best players. "I make them come over that line. The key is how much heart does he have? What's inside? I have to reach in and find out what kind of a person he is. That's why it's a war, because I'll grab you by the throat and pull it out of you."

During the season, Vieira keeps his distance from his players.

Dave Caiazzo, who pitched for Vieira in 1977 and '78, said Vieira is strictly business. "On a Florida trip he once said to us, 'You don't talk to me and I won't talk to you.' Of all the players he's had, maybe he's close to only five or 10. Still, you can't help but respect the guy," Caiazzo said.

Said Vieira, "No one in 20 years has called me Frank. It's always 'coach.' No one gets that close. I make a commitment to a kid until he gets where he's going. Then they're on their way and everything stops."

Said Barbara Vieira: "Out of a team, he'll get about one player he likes and they'll be friends for life. He cuts the cord except for a select few."

What does this man who has won five times as many games as he has lost think about winning? "It's absolute torture. I hate it," Vieira said. "It's no game to me. It's war. If it's a game, it's a game of life," he says. "At least I tell my players, die for a 'W.' Die in a war like Vietnam? For what? Who coached that game? That was an 'L.' Life is bull but games are real. It seems like I'm fighting for my life every game. It means that much to me.

"And if my players don't think that way, they can't last with me."

Many don't last. He estimates he's lost more than 100 players, some of whom couldn't make it through the first day. Last year he recruited five junior college players. Only one remains.

Tony Notorino pitched for Vieira in the late '70s. He was kicked off the team his junior season but came back for more the next year.

Notorino missed eight or nine games his junior year after he was jumped and beaten up. He remembers the day he came back to play and Vieira said "how I hadn't done anything for three years."

"Do it today or you're all done," the coach said to the kid.

In the third inning Notorino allowed a run. Vieira came out of the dugout to replace him. He told Notorino not to bother stopping by the dugout. "Keep walking," Vieira said.

"I gave him the ball and it took all the will power in the world not to throw it at him," Notorino said. "I kept walking off the field and didn't come back the rest of the season. We could have won the national title that year and I guess I cheated myself and my teammates," he said.

But he came back in his senior year, posted a 14-1 record, earned All-America honors and signed a contract with the Pittsburgh organization.

"I believe because of what I did to him," Vieira said, "he came back a better person. If he hadn't come back he'd be one of the ifs at the local bar."

Notorino says he likes Vieira. "I wish I could play for him again. I'd do it the same way. I guess I needed that kind of a coach. He probably made a man out of me."

Making men out of boys.

He was fired from his first coaching job—a Little League team. "We never lost a game," Vieira said. "But every parent signed a petition to get rid of me. They said their kids were having nightmares."

When he recruits for his college, he often does everything possible to discourage the player from coming to New Haven. "That way when the kid shows up, he knows what he's in for and I know what I'm getting."

When he was recruiting Notorino he told the kid in front of his parents, "If you ever blow your top at me, I'll knock your teeth out."

Vieira recruited Gary Zavatkay, his junior captain, by saying, "I'm a sick son of a bitch. If you want to play for me, I'll do the best I can for you."

Second baseman Joel Grampietro, the only starting senior this season, said "I heard some good stories about coach before I got here. I knew what I was in for." Grampietro said he went to New Haven because, "I knew he was the best coach in the East. I don't care how much he yells at me. He's making us men. It's like the Marines. I would never question his tactics."

Once Vieira had a "bad feeling" about his right fielder and used three in one inning. Another time he pulled his starting pitcher out of a game after one batter because he saw a hesitation in the pitcher's arm.

A typical Vieira rule is no uniform pants with a waist larger than 36. He said one player lost 55 pounds so he could fit into the pants. Vieira does not allow beards, only trimmed mustaches.

One player said he "got caught" blowing bubbles. "He'd let you chew gum, but he wouldn't allow bubbles. I quit chewing gum," said the player.

And you had better be on time for the team bus. Once, when the bus was about to leave for a game, a player hollered that someone was missing. Without missing a beat, Vieira said, "Let's have a minute of silence." The player was at that moment no longer on the team. Vieira never even saw him again.

His competitiveness flows over into everything he does, whether it is playing racquetball or officiating at basketball games. He stopped playing cards because when he lost, he would tear up the deck.

He said he can't help the way he is. "I'm a victim of what happened to me growing up. I envy the coaches who can sit in the dugout and cross their legs. I pray I wouldn't take it as seriously as I do. But I worry if I ever let up I'd be taking something away from the kids."

If Vieira does get any enjoyment from winning, it is after the season when he sees how far his team has come. His team has been in a post-season tourney every one of his 19 years. Thirty of his players have signed pro contracts. Porky's older brother, Gus, travels on the team bus and sees nearly every New Haven baseball game. "Frank always had a fire in him," Gus said. "We grew up in a tough Bridgeport neighborhood in The Depression. If someone wanted to fight, you fought. Frank was always tough. We all were."

Frank Vieira can't remember when people didn't call him Porky. One of his Bridgeport neighbors called him the "Little Portuguese" and that was shortened to Porky.

He said there were only five Portuguese families in Bridgeport when he was growing up. "I was never totally accepted by the Italians, Irish or blacks," he said. "Being Portuguese made you different. It was always that I was different. I was always behind the eight ball. I fought every day."

In school, nuns used to break yardsticks over Vieira's legs and then charge his father 26 cents for each broken stick. "One day my father came in with a log. He told the nuns to use it instead of a yardstick. 'I don't want to come up here again,' he told them. He never had to pay for another yardstick."

One day Gus told Porky to put his energy to better use, that fighting wouldn't get him anywhere. "He took me to the Boys Club, where I got my first taste of being accepted—in sports."

At first, he fought for acceptance at the Boys Club. But soon he just let his play do the talking.

At age 10, Vieira played basketball in Madison Square Garden; at age 11, in Boston Garden. At 12, winning already was in his bones. He said his coaches were "heartless . . . if you lost, they told you to jump off a bridge."

He scored 41 points in a basketball game—a ridiculous total for the early '50s when dunking and jump shots were almost unheard of—and got some fanfare for the first time. "From then on I was sick with winning," he said.

Vieira was only 13, but he had already learned there was no such thing as a game. "It was survival. It's been that way ever since," he said. "Practice, practice, practice. Survive, survive, survive."

When he was 15, his Bridgeport Central High School team won

the New England basketball title. "When we got home there were 12,000 people waiting for us. There was no prejudice. You weren't Italian, Irish, black or Portuguese. You were just good."

He practiced six hours a day during basketball season and six hours a day during baseball season. "What fun?" he says sarcastically. "If I scored 30. I wanted to score 50." He once scored 89 points in a local semi-pro game. "I wanted to score 100," Vieira said.

He doesn't remember having fun and he misses it. "When I was 15, I was 35. I was never a kid. What is it like being a kid 9 to 15?"

In high school, Vieira also ran on the track team. One day while the baseball team was playing he ran—and won—a half-mile race in his baseball uniform. "When I finished I ran to center field. I didn't miss a thing." He said he was one of the first high schoolers in the state to run a mile under 5 minutes. He ran a 4:48.

Vieira was one of the first in Connecticut to use the jump shot in basketball. He had to. At only 5-6¾, he knew his set shot could be blocked. So he jumped before shooting. At Quinnipiac College in Hamden, he led the nation in scoring one year, and finished with 3,154 career points, then the New England record. He also batted .400 on the Quinnipiac baseball team and was given a look by the St. Louis Cardinals.

Porky Vieira sits in an empty dugout watching his team take batting practice. His cap is hung up. He wears sunglasses. He studies the batting cage where one of his players is taking his turn. Suddenly Vieira shouts, "Swing down you son of a bitch."

Quietly, he says, "If I can get them over the hump of messing in their pants this year. . . . I'm like a drill sergeant with recruits who have never been in the fire. I'm still wacky as ever," he says, taking a puff on an ever-present cigarette, "but I have more compassion with these younger kids. I'll have to be more patient."

The batter takes another uppercut. "Swing down," Vieira shouts. "What are you gonna do? Give us a pep rally?"

Another puff on the cigarette. "Either they'll learn from me this year or send me to Portugal with a one-way ticket. It never gets easier."

It's the second inning and his team trails, 5-1. He says to no one in particular, "Long way to go, long way to go."

His pitcher can't find the strike zone. Vieira paces back and forth on the skids in front of the dugout. Mud oozes up between the skids. It is early April and it is windy and cold.

One of his players is doubled off second, taking the Chargers out of a scoring situation. Vieira kicks over a garbage can.

Eric McDowell is a senior and the sports information director at New Haven. Once, as a freshman, he was keeping the scorebook in the dugout when five bats suddenly flew over his head. "Somebody made an error of some sort," McDowell said.

McDowell said he's sure that at one time or another Vieira has swallowed a couple of cigarettes.

Vieira's style "makes his players play above their abilities. But a lot of kids can't hack him," said McDowell.

One of those was Joe Lahoud, who began his 11-year major league career with the Boston Red Sox.

"I have nothing nice to say about Porky Vieira," said Lahoud, who played at New Haven in 1965. "It's a year I'd like to forget."

Lahoud remembers an incident that occurred that season. Lahoud said he missed all of the first game of a doubleheader because his father had undergone open heart surgery.

"I got to the field about the third inning of the second game and Porky says to me, 'Where have you been?' " Lahoud said. "I told him about my father and he told me, 'That's no excuse.'

"I took off my uniform right there and walked off the field in my jock and shorts. I lost all respect for the man.

"After I quit and was signed by the Red Sox, I read a quote by Porky saying I was a dog. Well, tell him I barked for 10 years."

Vieira's version of that day does not include surgery to Lahoud's father. He said Lahoud played in the first game. "When he went 0-for-4 in the first game, I replaced him in the second game," Vieira said. "When he saw his name wasn't on the lineup card, he threw his glove on the field. I told him, 'pick it up and leave my dugout, you SOB.' "

Vieira said Lahoud came back the next day. "I told him he had to beat out another player. When he told me he wanted to start, I told him to get out."

Vieira said that later that season, Lahoud asked him to sign a waiver that was necessary in those days when a college player wanted to sign with a major league team. "He said he had a chance to go with the Red Sox. So I signed the waiver," Vieira said. "He told me when he got to the majors he'd send me tickets. The SOB never did.

"He had more ability than any player I've ever had," Vieira said. "But he never got the right reading of where I was coming from. If he could have taken me for a few years he would have played 15 years in the major leagues and he would have been a star. He would have made $100,000.

Joe Tonelli has been Vieira's assistant coach for 13 years. "He's one of the most misunderstood people I know," Tonelli said of Vieira. "They say he wins at all cost and is a renegade. No way. You'll never see his players argue with an umpire. They win with class. They say he's a maniac and doesn't give anybody else credit. That's not true.

"I don't think there's a coach who does as much for his players once they leave," Tonelli said. "After last season he spent three or four weeks getting players (four) signed to pro contracts or coaching jobs instead of recruiting for this year."

Tonelli says no one can "read" a player like Vieira can. "He knows when to challenge a kid, when to get the most out of him."

Former players, by a large majority, feel they were helped by

Vieira.

"He did nothing but help me," said Steve Bedrosian, a pitcher on the Atlanta Braves. "When I first came to the campus he drove me around, helping me look for an apartment. He told me, 'Kid, I'm gonna make you a pro.' "

Bedrosian admitted that Vieira's style isn't for everybody. "He keeps his teams well-disciplined and in good shape. Scouts told me if I could run for Porky, I could run for any team in the majors."

He said pro coaches treat the players the same as Vieira. "They're all business."

Caiazzo, who signed with the Philadelphia organization but is no longer in baseball, drove 2½ hours from his home in Malden, Mass., to see New Haven play a game this season.

"He's my idol," Caiazzo said of Vieira. "There's something about him that separates him from everybody else. He's a step or two ahead of everyone else."

Opposing coaches generally respect Vieira. "You can't criticize his success," said Bill Holowaty, coach at Eastern Connecticut State College. "He makes his players play to their potential. He does a really good job."

Coach Dan Gooley, whose Quinnipiac baseball team usually loses to New Haven, has nothing but praise for Vieira.

"My relationship with Porky has been fabulous," Gooley said. "He helped keep my head on straight when we went 9-16 one year. He called me and told me to be myself and not to change. He's a pro."

Gooley said not all coaches share his view of Vieira. "There are a lot of coaches who are envious of him," Gooley said, "because he wins so much."

"When you're on top, they want to bring you down to them," said Vieira. "My act is solo. I'm not a 'them.' Other than myself, there aren't many Vieira fans. I view myself as the very best. I'm what it's all about."

Strike Force

BASEBALL

By *PAUL FROILAND*

From TWA Ambassador
Copyright © 1982, Trans World Airlines, Inc.

It is midwinter just north of San Bernardino, California, and 44 mostly young men are clustered around home plate at the Bill Kinnamon Umpire School (as of March 8, the Joe Brinkman Umpire School), listening to John McSherry, a 37-year-old umpire in the National League, explain to them in sometimes brilliant rhetoric how it is properly done.

"On a swipe tag from here," McSherry says, pointing several feet up the third-base line, "the one thing you will *not* do is you will *not* head for third base. In other words, if the tag's coming up the line, you will not move up here to see the tag: all this does is compound your problems. By coming this way, you're making it tougher to see home plate."

McSherry draws up his considerable bulk and pushes his forefinger into the air.

"Don't get the idea that there's no big deal about seeing home plate," he continues. "Guys will miss bases out there all their lives, and no one will call them on it. Here, if he even *looks* like he might have missed home plate, they'll *all* freakin' start yelling. In the first place there's a pitcher hopefully backing up the play; he can see whether the guy misses it. Also, there's an on-deck hitter supposedly helping the guy score. You don't want to be the only guy in the park that missed the play, all right? You will not come up the third-base line. You will stay back on top of home plate.

"You gotta realize," McSherry goes on, "that they try and score people they would never send to another base. I don't know how many of you watched the World Series last year, but Burt Hooton scored from second base against the best arm on the Yankees on a play that should never have happened. He wasn't at third base yet when Winfield came up with the ball, he rounded third base like an old lady chasing a purse snatcher, he got halfway down and stumbled, he ran out of breath fourteen feet from home plate, and he still scored. Why? Cause Winfield thought it was shuffleboard or something and wheeled the ball in, and it took 72 hops, my point being that if Hooton was rounding second, going for third, he wouldn't have even thought about it. He would have stopped at second base. But there were two out, he was going on the hit—bizarre kind of running right from the gun, and they got lucky.

"They will score. They will run. Plays will happen up here, up the line. Throws will be up here. That outfielder comes up *firing*. He comes up *firing*. So the ball will go up there. The freakin' play will be all over the place. So you've got to be ready to move. Standing set, ready to move."

There is something about McSherry that belies the umpire mold. He is overweight, true; but it somehow adds to his overall presence rather than detracting from it. You could see him playing Falstaff in a Shakespearean Company. You could envision him creating the definitive role of Mycroft Holmes, Sherlock's older, smarter brother, in a film. He could certainly do stand-up comedy. But these are his lesser gifts. Add to these an uncommon perceptiveness, a sense of spatial awareness perhaps the equal of the NBA's Larry Bird, and an ability to make split-second judgments flawlessly, simultaneously selling them to an oftentimes hostile crowd through sheer drama, and you have some measure of a man who was good enough to break into the majors at the age of 26, while many other umpires toiled thanklessly through their thirties in the minors.

But chief among the possible pleasures of a brisk morning in the low fifties in southern California is that of watching John McSherry tell the young men in the umpire school how to work the plate.

"At home plate," he says, "if the guy has the ball, or is about to receive the ball, he can block the plate; it's not obstruction. Understand that. He *has* the ball, or is *about to receive* the ball. Now *about to receive* the ball does not mean that the ball is just being played home. It means it's so damn close that you can't tell.

"Now there's a lot of difference between having the ball in the position to tag a man out, and just having the ball in your possession. To illustrate this play, here's a situation I was in: you've got Morrison on third base for the Phillies against Los Angeles, and you've got a half-assed bunt down the first-base line, like a little chopper, from McBride. Garvey charges the ball, picks it up, and he's got no play on McBride at all. McBride's gone. So he comes in and flips the ball to home, to Yeager. Yeager went from here straight out like a first baseman"—he illustrates by blocking home plate with his foot and stretching forward the entire length of his body—"and he caught the ball way out here, seven feet from home plate, from tagging the guy. Morrison came in standing up, because he was in. *He was in!* Yeager caught the ball out here; not even able to turn around, Morrison hit Yeager's foot and went flying. Yeager turned around, looked at me; I'm giving no sign whatsoever, because the play isn't done yet: he's not safe and he's not out. So Yeager ran over and tagged Morrison out. Why could he do that? Because he had the ball in his glove. He had possession of the ball.

"Obviously, you're not going to see that kind of play too often. You've got to have Yeager's kind of mind: Yeager would run through a brick wall to win a ball game. Yeager is just a hard player. So Yeager stuck his leg out there to be *crippled,* all right? But he did it, got the out, made the play, and the inning's over.

"This is the place, I tell you," McSherry continues. "Guys come to watch you work; guys see you work. And here, home plate, is where you win or lose. We had a slide play one night, and my partner's working the plate. The ball comes in, hits the catcher's glove, pops out of the glove and comes right back into the glove. Up—boom. Safe. Nobody in the park knows that ball's come up. So you could stand at home plate and go, 'Safe,' in a tiny little voice. But what does my partner do, he goes, 'SAFE! NO! YOU BOBBLED IT! SAFE!' It's a great play. You can do that at home plate. It looks lousy out there on the bases, but here it sells. The biggest plays of the game, right here. They can make you or break you."

At this point McSherry could have sold five-gallon jugs of snake oil for $100 each. The 44 students, most of them wearing blue jeans or dark pants of some variety, and nearly all of them presuming upon the discipline enough to wear the official black, short-billed cap of the major league professionals, stand in rapt attention. The two minor league umpires assisting at the school, Danny Powers from Triple A and Al Kaplon from Double A, kneel on the ground behind McSherry, Powers in frank admiration, Kaplon in even-tempered enjoyment at the stories. American League umpire Joe Brinkman, 37, who just weeks ago bought the school from Bill Kinnamon, a retired American League umpire, turns to a visitor standing near first base, and says in masterful understatement, "John is an excellent instructor."

McSherry goes on: "Okay, again I go back from my experience. We've got a play, a guy from Atlanta is trying to score about the eighth inning in Dodger Stadium. Scioscia is up the line a few feet and in foul territory. He has to go up the line about 25 feet to catch the ball, and the runner—it was the young kid who led the International League—Butler, a little guy named Butler—he's coming around third base and trying to score, and Scioscia is catching the ball as Butler gets to him. Butler hits into him—and I mean the whole body into him—and goes up on Scioscia's back as Scioscia's bending over catching the ball. Scioscia catches the ball and swings up at him, and, as he swings, Butler goes flying off the other side of his back and literally bounces three times into home plate. All right? Safe. Contact was made, but the tag was never made. He never tagged him with the ball. He tagged him with every freakin' thing else, but never with the ball. Lasorda and I had a big argument about it, and Scioscia was upset with me, and I says, 'No problem.'

And the next day, 25 guys say, 'Hey, I saw the replay of that. He *did* miss him, didn't he?' 'Yeah,' I said. 'That's what I was freakin' tellin' ya when I was waving my arms safe.' "

There is a murmur of approval and delight from the students as McSherry concludes the lecture. Within a few minutes he and Brinkman distribute the students across the field for practice drills. Nine men go out to play fielders, and the rest form two queues, one behind home plate and one at the foul line just beyond first base. The students behind the plate call three pitches, and then become baserunners. The students beyond first come dashing out on a hit ball, pivot in the basepath several feet to the left of the first-base bag, and look into the play to make the safe or out call. They also get three chances to make calls, and then they return to the queue behind home plate.

Simultaneously with the pitch, Joe Brinkman tosses a ball into the air and hits it with an outfield fungo bat (a long, thin bat used in fielding practice because it's easier to control than a normal bat). So regardless of the pitch thrown being a ball or a strike, there is a fielding play on every pitch.

Looking at the students as they assemble at their appointed stations, it is difficult to define a typical umpire-student type. Brinkman says later that the average age is 24. Out of 44 students, 19 have college degrees, something Brinkman encourages. Very few are overweight, and you can count the number wearing eyeglasses on one hand. All of them are courting a possible future profession in the field for themselves seriously enough that they are willing to pay the $880 tuition, endure the five strenuous weeks of intensive lecture and practice drills, and spend their nights in a barracks on the grounds with their compatriots.

As the drill begins, McSherry establishes an arbitrary ground rule to add to the complexity of the situation: any ball thrown past the first baseman that hits the chain-link fence is an automatic time out, and the students will need to call time.

The first pitch is thrown. The student behind the plate screams "Ball!" Brinkman hits a chopper to the shortstop, and the first student in the first-base queue comes streaking into the infield, pivots inside first, watches the ball beat the runner to first, and stabs his thumb into the air, yelling, "He-e-e-e-e-e's out!" McSherry nods.

The drill continues, and all the students in the first-base queue come dashing into the infield, yelling, "He-e-e-e-e-e's out!" with varying degrees of inflection and accuracy. This happens about twelve straight times. When the thirteenth ball is hit, the fourth student comes flying out to make the thirteenth replication of the out call, except the first baseman drops the ball, and the student finds himself holding his arms at a 45-degree angle and looking stupidly at his errant thumb, saying, "He-e-e-e-e-e's ... uh ... safe," concluding in a very small voice. McSherry gives him a sarcastic look, and Danny Powers, the minor league umpire assisting at first, inadvertently completes the humiliation by saying, "You just say 'safe!' not 'he's safe!" The student dies a little bit, then returns to foul territory beyond first to get ready for his second call.

The drill heats up and goes faster. The infielders, either by design or through lack of ability, begin throwing the ball over the first baseman's head, so that it hits the fence on the fly, and the students have to call time. One student timorously extends one arm and yells, "Time!" McSherry stops him in midfield. "What's that?" he says. "You have to go to the bathroom? If you're going to call time, use two hands and belt it out: TIME! All right?"

There are also, among the 44 students, three Japanese umpires, all of them professionals in Japan's Central League. Only one of them speaks English, and he interprets for the other two. Then there are three Koreans, two of them umpiring at the amateur level and the third, considerably older, the chief of all amateur umpires in Korea. His name is Min, JunGi, and, like the Japanese, he interprets for the two younger Koreans. The Koreans are always smiling; the Japanese are thin and intense, seeming to hold great charges of energy within them ready to be released at any second.

On the first call at first base by the first Japanese, the ball is hit to third and the Japanese bursts onto the field like a Roman candle, pivots, concentrates his energy on the ball, and shouts, "He's o-u-u-u-u-u-t!" blasting the air with an out sign. His mastery of the play is such that you would know it was perfectly executed even if you'd never seen a baseball game. Of this student Joe Brinkman would say later, "He can barely speak a word of English, and he's probably the best umpire in the class." After each play, the three Japanese chatter excitedly to each other in their native language.

When the Koreans come up behind first base, Min gets into the first-base coaching box and yells a few thousand encouraging words at them in Korean. The first student charges out, pivots, sees the play, and jerks his thumb into the air: "Hesho!" On the second play the same student rushes out, sees the first baseman drop the ball, and yells, "Have!" McSherry doesn't know quite what to say. The school doesn't have the time to teach them English.

Min pulls out the world's tiniest camera and starts taking pictures.

Back at home plate, there is less activity, because the students there are basically just calling balls and strikes. When they discover they won't have to do a lot of running, one of them goes off to the dugout and comes back with a packet of Red Man chewing tobacco. "Oh, can I borrow some?" asks another student. "I'm just dying." Soon several cheeks are bulging with the stuff, and all you can hear behind home plate is "squeet . . . squeet . . . squeet." They always spit neatly through their teeth. They never go "patooie!" with their lips.

Joe Brinkman is gently advising the young umpires behind the plate. Brinkman is quite nearly the opposite of McSherry. He is quiet, introspective, supportive and warm. He takes things very seriously. (Actually, McSherry does too, but he doesn't show it.)

Above all he has gold-plated integrity that just exudes from him.

On one play, in which Brinkman spins a little bunt down the third-base line, the student umpire behind the plate charges after the ball so quickly that he beats the catcher and prevents him from fielding the ball. Rather than broadcasting the error to the entire group, Brinkman just says, "You got the play wrong, but if there's such a thing as overhustle, that was it."

Brinkman continues to hit fungos, talking all the while in a low, calm voice: exhorting with restraint, correcting with compassion. He delivers an instruction on what to do when a ground ball is hit. The Japanese interpreter, standing a few feet away, keeps pace with him, explaining it all to his two charges. "Grunder, grunder . . ." he says, imitating the motion of a bouncing ball with his hand.

Brinkman hits a grounder to short. The shortstop picks the ball up and throws it wildly over the first baseman's glove. The home-plate umpire and the first-base umpire run toward each other, watch the ball sail into the chain-link fence, and scream in almost perfect unison in their McSherry-instructed voices, "TIME! YOU!" pointing to the baserunner, "SECOND BASE!" McSherry chuckles. They are actually beginning to sound like umpires.

The drills go on for another hour or so, and then the group breaks for lunch. McSherry comes up to Brinkman and says, "It's a good time to break; they're getting on each other a little. There's a chill in the air, if you know what I mean."

Brinkman nods and smiles, and follows the boisterous procession up to the mess hall.

Brinkman eats lunch with his wife of less than a year, Karen. Umpires take marriage seriously. They don't talk about chicks and broads. They talk about relationships. They actually use the word *relationships* to describe their marriages, and they talk about sacrifice and commitment. One of the first things you perceive about umpires is that they are very different from ball players, and the differences are mostly positive. The worst thing about umpires is that they have a big stake in being right and in being the authority. But the best things about umpires are their maturity, their self-control, their considered judgments, their sense of order and their integrity.

It is not easy to become a major league umpire. Only one percent of all the umpire school graduates make it all the way to the majors, and they make it only after a minor-league apprenticeship that averages eight years. Most of the candidates wash out in the minors, where they are paid a pittance, where they have to drive twelve hours on travel days from one tumbleweed Texas town to another, and where, if they might perhaps one day blow a call, they are roundly abused by at least one manager and probably several players. After incidents like this they will return to a motel to spend the night perspiring and hating themselves until they reach such utter shoals of despair that they will just pack up their things and leave without telling anyone.

The ones that don't leave become crystallized and hardened into persons so indomitable, so acquainted with defeat and harsh use that no indignity, no hardship, no popular disapproval can ever significantly affect them again. They can stand impassive before the boos rising from 50,000 throats and hold to the truth that they know to be so, even when the hometown fans hate them for it.

Such a person is Joe Brinkman, and his attractive and perceptive wife Karen is rapidly learning her role in this complex scenario of justice and psychology.

"One of the hardest adjustments for me," she says over lunch, "is having to sit through an entire baseball game and not cheer. I can't act like I want one team to win, because that would reflect back on Joe, so I have to say things like, 'Interesting play! Very interesting!' And people notice. One time I was in Texas at a game, and there was a row of men in front of me who were really drunk and were betting on everything—big bets: fifties and hundreds were changing hands. Then all of a sudden they noticed me behind them, not particularly cheering. So they started placing bets on who I was married to or related to that was on the field. They finally narrowed it down to umpires, and finally they were betting on which umpire. Then they asked me who it was. Large sums of money changed hands. It was unbelievable."

After lunch, Brinkman talks about some of the singularities of his career as an umpire. "The hardest part of the job is when you kick a play," he says, "You just have to live with it—or die with it, which is umpires' talk. You live and die with it. You can't change your mind and reverse the call to be right, or else the other team's going to say, 'Well, you changed a call for him; now you've got to change one for me.' And you say, 'Well, that one I blew, and this one I didn't.' And they will say," he laughs, " 'No, no; you blew this one too.' So you just can't do that. If you miss a pitch, you can't call the next one a strike to get it even, because by the end of the game you'll owe so many people that you'll need a chart: now I owe you one, and I owe you one, and I owe you half a one. If you make a mistake, you just have to live with it.

"A couple of years back I knew an umpire who tried admitting his mistakes. Every time he'd make a mistake, he'd tell the player. At first they said, 'Well, that's great. Why, he's a hell of an umpire. When he makes a mistake, he tells me; when you do, you never tell me. You're so hardheaded.' Well, that caught up with him. And you can see how it would. Every time you get a tough play you can't say, 'Well, all right, I made a mistake on this one,' because now, when it gets tough, he's going to want that same answer. I'm not always going to be wrong because you think I'm wrong. So your best way to be is this: what it is is what it is, and you go from there.

"You can't let it get you," he continues. "There are managers like (Billy) Martin and (Earl) Weaver that are just *waiting* to jump on you. They holler all the time. They holler because of what they think they might get. They think that maybe they'll get a pitch in the ninth inning. If I holler all night, they think, I'll get a pitch or a call when I may really need it—and a lot of games come down to a pitch or a play. So that's the way they think, and their thinking is all screwed up. And if they've ever gotten one, that just gives them more fuel, you see. They think, I got that; now if I holler a little more, maybe I'll get two. They're not going to be satisfied with something happening; they want more, want more, want more. And that's the reason they holler: they aren't hollering for the play that's just happened. They're hollering for the play that's *going to* happen.

"So that's why you get arguments. You have managers like Martin and Weaver who think they're right because they're successful, and umpires who think they're right because they're always right. In fact, one of the problems we have at our Umpires Association meetings is that you have an entire room full of people who are always right, and when everyone in the room is always right, you end up having very long meetings where nothing much gets accomplished. But in arguments on the field, you are often dealing with a successful manager and an umpire: the two rightest men on the field.

"I used to have problems with Billy," Brinkman goes on, "but Weaver was the real problem for me. I didn't speak to Weaver for the last three years until a couple of months ago. I just refused to speak to him. I have run him out of ball games and wouldn't speak to him. I ran him out of a game in Florida in spring training last year. He says, 'Why are you running me out of the game?' So I told my partner, a guy named Johnson, 'Johnson, tell Earl that I ran him out of the game because of what he said.' So Johnson says, 'Joe says he ran you out of the game because of what you said.' And Weaver just went on and on: 'You're crazy!' he says, and then as he walked away he said, 'There's something wrong with you, Brinkman.'

"So anyway, a couple months ago I was playing in a golf tournament in Vegas, and I saw Earl sitting at a table a little ways away, so I came over and said, 'Earl! How ya doing?' and he almost fell over. It was the first word I'd said to him in three years. So when I saw him at the winter meetings in Miami, it was just like old home week. He was making jokes like it had never happened, so I'm sure our dispute is going to go by the wayside."

One of the aspects of umpiring that Brinkman finds particularly difficult is the degree and amount of abuse an umpire has to take. Another aspect that he finds unnecessary, and detrimental to the entire game, is the way that umpires coming up through the minor league system are kept in continual mystery about their status, and are kept hanging on, year after year, without any assessment being given of their probable chances of making it all the way to the majors. This latter problem Brinkman is correcting to the degree he is able to within the parameters of the school: he always tells the students the truth. He fosters no illusions in the hearts of those who are truly unsuited to be professional umpires, and he encourages all the students to keep their options open, chief among which is the attaining of a college degree. He also would like to see the day when umpires can be paid a living wage in the minor leagues, instead of having to depend, as he did, on the kindness of strangers and munificence of parents. Brinkman always used to tell his father, "I'm going to make it. I'm going to make it." And his father, sending the monthly subsidy check, would write "Well, when?" across it.

"The minors are tough," Brinkman continues. "You drive all night, work a game, get in the car and drive all night to get to the next city. The reason you drive all night is to save a night's rent. You check out of one hotel, go to the game, drive all night, and get to the next hotel at seven in the morning. So you check in and sleep, and then you've got a game that night. And you end up sleeping in the car. I remember my first year I slept in the car and gave people the phone number of the phone booth outside the car. Then you'd sleep in the car, and the phone would ring, and you would get up and answer it and then go back to sleep in the car. We just didn't have any money. I remember my partner and I, we would go to breakfast and we'd *split* it. It's funny now; it wasn't funny then."

With regard to the abuse an umpire must take, Brinkman says this: "The league office asks us a lot of times to take a lot of abuse. I say, pay me for the abuse I have to take, and I'll take it. Pay me enough that when a guy calls me an obscenity I won't feel so bad. But instead they sit you down and tell you that if a player calls you a dirty name you're supposed to turn the other way. Well, hell! That's easy to *say*. But when it happens to you, it's completely different. For instance, a few years ago, the president of one of the minor leagues was talking to the umpires in that league in his office, and he said, 'Now when those players call you an obscenity or something, just turn away, and remember that they're really talking to me.' And one of the umpires comes up to his desk, leans over, and says in a slow voice, 'I know you're a no-good obscenity!' and the president was furious. He just went nuts. And the umpire said, 'That's what you want me to take out there. And not just one-on-one in an office, but in front of thousands of people.' And the league president fired him right there."

Brinkman talks some more, about his plans for the school, about the inequity of baseball's salary structure, with star players earning easily half a million dollars a year and more, and umpires breaking in at $22,500, with a ceiling of $50,000 for veterans. The game has rewarded Brinkman with many intangible benefits, but he cannot look back on it without regret.

"When I think back," he says, "if I had to start again, I wouldn't. I honestly wouldn't, because there's not enough of a guarantee; there just isn't. Like I say, if you hit .300 or you win twenty games, you can move up, but there's no guarantee in umpiring. Youth is what keeps you going. Everybody thinks they can make it. Thank God for that."

The next day the school is ravaged by 80-mile-an-hour winds,

Santa Ana winds, as they are known. The banner headline of the *Los Angeles Times* the next morning reads, "Wind Flips Trucks, Rips Roofs." The story notes that wind gusts overturned the trailer units of nine trucks on Interstate 15 through the Cajon Pass. The umpire school is situated about three wild pitches from the Cajon Pass, and things are hectic that morning. Practice on the field is canceled when Joe Brinkman comes back to the classroom building after surveying the diamond, walking bent over into the wind at nearly a 90-degree angle. Once inside, he says, "That's ridiculous out there. You couldn't get a curveball to break in that wind."

The students go out to check their cars. Two of them are piled into each other, having been blown sideways in the night. The windows on seven or eight others have been blown entirely out, or cracked into multifaceted spider-web patterns. When one of the students opens a door of the building, it comes off at the hinges, the wind pulling the screws and the hinge plate right out of the jamb. It takes several students to recover it and prop it back into the door frame. By turning its lock, they get it fixed in a shut position. Someone puts a sign on it to warn others off.

Brinkman, McSherry and Bill Kinnamon, the previous owner of the school, who is still helping out this year, decided to conduct class all day in the classroom. Minor league umpires Danny Powers, 35, from the Pacific Coast League, and Al Kaplon, 24, from the Texas League, give up their time to be interviewed in a room down the hall. Talk turns from the weather to the hardest part of being an umpire. Powers tells a story.

"I had a beanball incident last year in the Coast League," he begins. "What happened was a guy stole second base with an 8-0 lead, which is taboo, because in baseball there are as many unwritten rules, rules of etiquette, so to speak, as there are rules in the book. So this guy violated one of them by stealing with an eight-run lead.

"So the other team took offense at it, and when he comes to bat, the pitcher knocked him down, and I thought, well, you've got that coming. So I didn't issue any warnings or anything. Also, it's hard to interpret intent. You can't assume that it was a head throw; it was just a little brush-back, high and tight. So he now takes his bat and stands across the top of home plate, and yells at the pitcher, 'Throw it again. Throw it right here!' At this point I thought, okay, here we go. So he throws the next pitch at him again, and I thought, well, you've got that one coming, too. So now I'm one pitch too late in warning someone. I should have handled it.

"So now the next pitch he throws behind his head, and at this point I *did* go out and warn him, but I was one pitch too late. So the pitcher says—it was Chris Knapp, who pitched for California for quite some time—he says, 'Danny, what are you going to do when I hit him with the next one?' I said, 'Chris, I just told you. I'll throw you out of the game.'

"So by now I have warned both managers, and done all the little things you're supposed to do. So Knapp gets back on the mound, and I get behind the plate, and he throws the next one for a strike. And I think now that the situation's handled. But he fools me. He throws the next one behind the guy's head for ball four. So the guy runs toward first base and he pops off: 'Hey, that's okay; you don't have a fastball anyway. It won't hurt me if you *do* hit me.' So Knapp shouts an obscenity back, and this guy, who still has that bat in his hand, charges the mound and hits him with the bat.

"So all the responsibility came down on my shoulders because I didn't stop it. The umpiring crew talked about the situation for days and weeks, and I truly believe we could not have stopped it from happening, because both teams were egging the two players on the whole time. But I was working the plate, so I took the responsibility. That's what you have to do when you're the umpire. But when that kind of thing happens, you live with it for a long time.

"I asked John (McSherry) one day, 'Do you live with a bad plate job, or a play that you didn't feel good about, for a couple of days afterwards?' And he says, 'Pal, I live with them for life.' And that's the way it is for a lot of us."

Kaplon's worst-incident story also involves an ejection that should have taken place. "It was my first year in baseball," he begins. "I was only 19, and I was umpiring in the now-defunct Lone Star League. I had a game in which there was a player-manager who was also a catcher. Now catchers are bad enough to handle, and managers are bad enough to handle, but when you have a player-manager who's also a catcher, that's *real bad.* So my thinking at the time was, I guess I have to take a little more guff off of this guy, because, my God, he's the manager, and he's sitting right in front of me, and he *knows* whether it's a ball or a strike.

"Well, I missed a couple pitches in a row, and he turned around on me and said a few choice words, and I didn't eject him. And I should have. And when I got back to my room, my God, I was drunk that night, and I was so upset with myself that I couldn't live with myself until the next day, when I finally woke up. And I was upset until the next night when I went out to the ball park. I never did eject him. It wasn't a thing where it was appropriate to get revenge. I just got out there and said to myself, well, if you're going to be a professional, you'd better put that aside and just start from scratch.

"You know," he concludes, "I really didn't know how well I did that year until after the season. It's just like a relationship: you don't know what went wrong until six months after it's over."

And what are the satisfactions of being an umpire? Though Powers and Kaplon are distinctly unalike as individuals—Kaplon is cool and takes life as it comes, and Powers is intense, conscientious and highly self-critical—their answers are quite similar.

Says Powers, "The rewards are self-satisfaction. If you go back there and have a great plate job, you know it in your heart. You come off the field and you've got a high that—I don't know what you can compare it to: it's probably like a heart surgeon putting a new heart in someone."

Says Kaplon, "It's the self-satisfaction: knowing you can do this and that you can compete on a high level where there's really more pressure than in any other kind of business. If I walk off the field, and it's been a fantastic game, and I've been a part of that game because I did a fantastic job—like having an interference call and getting it right—then that's the greatest high in the world."

Powers and Kaplon relate some more experiences. When you are an umpire in the minor leagues, they say, you grow up very fast. You learn to absorb abuse without retaliating. You confront managers that are twice your age. It is a hard existence.

After a while the two return to the classroom to hear the end of a McSherry lecture. At this point in the morning, everyone's cars have been moved to the playing field and are parked in the shelter of an eight-foot-high retaining wall running along the third-base line. A house trailer that one student brought with him to the school has crashed on its side and has partially brought down a chain-link fence with it. Two doors that open from the classroom to the outside have been propped open six inches to keep the wind pressure from blowing the building's windows out. The swimming pool just outside the classroom has whitecaps on it, where the water splashes against the leeward end. There is a 50-yard-long river of water streaming down the concrete apron beyond the pool, water that has been dashed out of the pool by the wind.

All of this is happening, but the ebullient McSherry rolls on, pausing only occasionally to deliver an incredulous comment about the wind. "Another thing to watch for in the low minors," he says, "is bat boys. They will come running out in the middle of—you can not be*lieve* where bat boys will come from. You got a slide play, and there comes junior grabbing the freakin' bat. Get rid of them. Throw them out of there. Grab 'em. Yell at 'em. They'll move. On some plays you will have wild pitches and passed balls, and the ball boy over there is five years old. And he's been taught (he breaks into a singsong falsetto), 'If the ball comes back here, get the ball.' Well, here he comes. Do not be afraid to *blast* him—'LEAVE THE BALL ALONE!' Stop him. Later, if you like to, you can go over and pat him on the head, and say, 'You're a nice little guy,' you know. Don't be kind to children at this point. Be kind to the players. 'Cause if a little child picks up the ball, he goes into the dugout and you go into the doghouse."

You just had to be there.

Bewitched, Bothered, Beaten

COLLEGE FOOTBALL

By *ART SPANDER*

From the San Francisco Examiner
Copyright © 1982, San Francisco Examiner

The twilight zone has descended upon Memorial Stadium. Scoreboard lights flicker with the miraculous news. California has beaten Stanford, 25-20, and standards by which games are judged have been blasphemed.

Reality dictates it could not happen. But reality exists no more. Fantasy has strangled truth. The impossible has become ordinary. The descriptions of mortals are rendered useless.

This was a game for the ages, perhaps of all time, a game which ended in a manner so preposterous it had to be the work of witchcraft. This was the only Big Game they'll recall, whether in triumph, or in the case of Stanford, anger and helplessness.

Stanford had this game, or God doesn't make little green apples and it don't snow in Minneapolis in the winter time. Stanford had this game on a 35-yard field goal by reliable Mark Harmon with four seconds left.

Stanford had this game, 20-19, and it also had a bid from the Hall of Fame Bowl, whose representatives were expectedly grateful when Harmon's kick flew over the crossbar of the northern goalpost.

And then, unbelievably, Stanford had nothing.

The game was stolen from the Cardinal on the most unusual kickoff return in memory, a play of total implausibility, a play that made the Immaculate Reception seem like a trifle and Bobby Thomson's pennant-winning homer run-of-the-mill.

It was something out of a Disney movie, the sort where the ball carrier leaps tall buildings, soars over tacklers and finally lands in the middle of the Sousaphone section. OK, the script was changed slightly. When Cal's Kevin Moen finished the play, he was not only in the end zone but in the lap of a trombonist from the Stanford band.

Football evolved from the English game of rugby, a sport where the ball is lateraled from one player to another each time a tackle is made. Yesterday on the final play, football regressed.

What do you do when there's only four seconds left, you're in front and required to kick off? Squib the ball, naturally, kick it on the top half so it bounces crazily, especially on AstroTurf, and becomes impossible to return.

Then you celebrate the victory.

Harmon did kick the bouncer, and when the ball landed in the arms of Moen, a defensive back, it seemed he would be swarmed under.

But as he was about to be tackled, he lateraled to Richard Rodgers. And as Rodgers was about to be hit, he lateraled to Dwight Garner. And now time had ended, but the play was still alive. Or was it?

Garner, stubby (5-foot-9, 185) and mischievous, was engulfed by numerous white-shirted Stanford players about midfield and started to fall. Impetuously, the Stanford band, an irreverent group if ever there was one, surged into the south end zone, to celebrate the victory.

"We thought the play was dead," a contrite musician would say later. "We would never do anything to hurt our team." The play wasn't dead. If there would be epitaphs written this day, they would be for Stanford, not Cal.

"I swear, my knee never hit the ground," said Garner. "I was just about to fall, and then I saw Rodgers."

And for the second time on this play, Richard Rodgers was off and running. Along with seemingly everyone else in the stadium, band members, fans and even a couple of Stanford players coming off the bench onto the playing surface. It looked like Times Square on New Year's Eve. But the game hadn't ended.

Rodgers pitched the ball to Mariet Ford who headed for the right, or western sideline. In front of him was, yes, the Stanford band.

Ford got the ball to the man who started the entire chain reaction, flipping it over his shoulder to Moen about the 25 or next to the woodwinds. And with musicians fleeing in all directions, Moen scored.

Surely this was a joke. This didn't happen. In the press box, journalists stood with mouths open. On the Stanford sideline coach Paul Wiggin waited for an official to call back the play. But the only call that was made was for a touchdown. Cal had won. And now the field was choked with humanity.

Fans poured from the seats. Stanford players wandered aimlessly, as if to appeal to some higher authority. Wiggin was aghast, demanding a recount. This was chaos. This was history.

The result would have to stand. No official would have the fortitude to order this one replayed. Hell, they couldn't even clear the field to try the extra point. If you wanted to see it again, you'd have to watch the videotape.

That's exactly what Paul Wiggin did. And then he went after the officials again. But the bitterness would have to be accepted. Stanford would never end up ahead if Wiggin argued until the year 2000.

Dwight Garner may have been stopped, but he never went down. And it was the Stanford band that made the mistake of screening off Stanford defenders. The game was over.

"Whatever happened on the last play," said Cal athletic director Dave Maggard, "we deserved to win this game. We outplayed them. And no matter what anybody says from now on, the score will stand. Cal will always be the winner."

Stanford simply finished second. In this game, the only loser was reality.

Quincy Basketball Is Devilishly Good

HIGH SCHOOL BASKETBALL

By *MICHAEL DAVIS*

From the Chicago Sun-Times
Copyright © 1982, Chicago Sun-Times

There is a shrine in this Mississippi River town where they worship The Devil.

Townsfolk come out on Friday and Saturday nights for a rejuvenation of the spirit, a bolstering of faith for those who trust in him. It is a sight to behold.

Even on frost-sheared winter nights, when a hateful wind whistles across the river from Missouri, his believers come without fail. They forge over snow-caked roads to partake in the ritual, 5,000 unrelenting souls conquering every obstacle that stands in the way of seeing him emerge from the darkness, his pitchfork spewing hellfire and his frenzied eyes ablaze.

"I've gone with a 102-degree temperature, I've gone with the flu, and I've even gone with diarrhea," says Dick Wentura, owner of the Volkswagen dealership on the edge of town. "Nothing could keep me away from seeing that Devil." Wentura hasn't missed an appearance for 30 years.

The very sight of him strikes terror in the hearts of first-time visitors. Some run to an adjoining dressing room and hide. Others merely turn their heads. Only the bravest look at him squarely and return his savage taunts with angry words of their own.

The men from Collinsville did. And they paid dearly for it.

It is 11 minutes past 7 on a Saturday night, 49 minutes from showtime, and Brad Schrader is having a devil of a time straightening his costume so that everything is wrinkle-free and satin perfect. That is the way it must be when you are mascot of the Quincy High School Blue Devils. After all, you are the second-most-important person in town.

Jerry Leggett, the basketball coach, is the most important.

For Leggett is the silver-haired basketball evangelist who has made believers of all those Devil-worshipers chanting outside the locker room. After four decades of near-misses in the state tournament, Leggett finally brought a championship back from Champaign last year with a crack team that was 33-0. Despite losing its indomitable center, Michael Payne, to graduation and the University of Iowa, Quincy's unbeaten string remains intact, 55 straight games after Saturday night's victory over Jacksonville. The Blue Devils are four games away from tying the Illinois record of 58 consecutive victories, set in 1972 by Thornridge High School, the team by which standards for greatness are measured in this basketball-rich state.

"When was the last time we lost at home?" Leggett asks the team in a down-to-business pre-game briefing. "The 1977-78 season," he hears in reply. "And who beat us that night?" he asks. "Collinsville," they say.

"It's a six-hurdle race until the end of the regular season, gentlemen, before we start worrying about the state playoffs," Leggett says. "There are six hurdles in the race, but two of them are just a little bit bigger than the others. Collinsville tonight and Galesburg later on. Now if you were running a race and you came to a taller hurdle, what do you do? You'd put out a little more energy, a little more effort. And that's what we're asking for tonight. Quincy plays its best in big games, and this is one of them."

The starting five, including all-state guard Bruce Douglas and his brother, Dennis, a 6-5 junior forward, are sitting in the front row, the reserves directly behind them, and all eyes are affixed to Leggett and the blackboard behind him. To the left is the Devil's Graveyard, a collection of cutout tombstones that represent every team Quincy has snuffed this season. To the right is a meticulously detailed chart chronicling every Blue Devil's offensive and defensive performance. There are symbols and artifacts everywhere in the locker room, a handsomely equipped facility by most college standards. In addition to the weight-training equipment, the wall-to-wall carpeting and the piped-in stereo rock, the players have a videotape screening room where they can drop in and replay any game from this season or last. This seeming luxury is all part of Leggett's "system" for winning, an all-encompassing philosophy of coaching that starts in Quincy's elementary schools and comes to full flower in the secondary grades.

"The kids in this town will do anything to grow up to be a Blue Devil," Leggett says. "And all the coaches in the lower grades know my plays and how I want drills run in practice, so that by the time these kids reach high school, there's no time lost teaching them the fundamentals. When I stand up from the bench and hold four fingers in the air for an out-of-bounds play, nearly every kid in the gym will know what's going to happen."

On this night, as always, the youngest Blue Devil fans are sitting in their own section, high above the sidelines. The high school student section is filled to overflow in the stands directly behind the Quincy bench on both levels of the 5,200-seat gym. The rest of the seats are sold to adults on a season-ticket basis, and there are more than 200 people on a waiting list, hoping against hope they will someday own season seats to the Blue Devils.

"It's crazy," says Leo Henning, a former Chicagoan who moved to Quincy in 1973 to work at WGEM-TV and its AM and FM radio stations, all of which broadcast Blue Devil basketball. "Ever since I came here I've been trying to figure out this mania for basketball. And now, after all these years, I think I've got it. A basketball game in this town is our Picasso, our Sears Tower," he says. "When you ask people about Quincy, the biggest source of pride is its basketball teams. The biggest status symbol among the most prosperous and influential people in town is to have season tickets to all three games in town: Quincy High School, Notre Dame High School and Quincy College. And the best way for any newcomer in town to know who is and who isn't a big shot is to see how close the person is sitting to the floor."

Many of the wealthy of Quincy reside on Maine Street, in homes with handcarved filigree and rounded dormers, touches of elegance that German immigrant craftsmen gave to homes built during a post-Civil War boom. The stone-mortared homes are as sturdy now as they were then.

In the sweet used-to-be, Quincy was a convenient stop between Rock Island and St. Louis, a welcome outpost on the winding way downriver. Now, it is merely an isolated dot on the map, just a town across the water from Hannibal, Mo., and not the center of commerce and commotion it once was. Though hundreds of day-workers still punch in at the calcium carbonate mines and the Gardner-Denver compressor factory, the list of unemployed grows each week. Like so many smaller Midwestern manufacturing centers, Quincy is a town in transition.

Though the mill wheels have slowed and the train doesn't stop as frequently any more, Quincy's heart beats strong and steady.

"We're isolated from the mainstream of metropolitanism in our own corner of the world, without a doubt," says Dick Wentura. "But our people have a lot of pride in everything we do. And because of that, we feel we have a great community."

No greater moment in the lives of the citizenry has come than on a Saturday night last March, when the Blue Devils obliterated Proviso East 68-39 for the Class AA championship. "It was the culmination of a community's pride," says principal Richard Heitholt, a forward on the 1945 Quincy team that finished third in the state. "There was something unfulfilled in our community until we won that championship. It wasn't anything that was ever demanded, never a do-or-die situation. But in the minds of people it was a goal that the community deserved; a kind of community prize.

"It was uncanny at Champaign that night. Since we were able to buy about twice as many tickets as we were allotted, with thanks from other schools, the Quincy contingent literally made a ring around the Assembly Hall. And a tremendous thing happened in the middle of the third quarter, when it was evident we were going to win the championship. The adult fans on one side of the gym started a yell: 'Q-U-I.' Then on the other side, spontaneously, they began answering 'N-C-Y.' It just went on and on like that, rocking the gymnasium. . . ."

The fans were already on their feet at 7:59 as coach Leggett and his team wound its way in a snake dance through the locker room to the entrance of the gymnasium. The players were clapping in unison and singing a capella. "Q . . . Q City . . . uh huh . . . Q . . . Q City."

Leggett spots the peanut gallery, where the children are squealing in eager anticipation of the blackout, the spotlight introduction of the visiting team, and the arrival of the Blue Devil himself. "That's the reason Quincy is going to keep winning," Leggett says, pointing to the Class of 1990. "There's the future."

At precisely 8 the lights go down and it's bedlam. "I've never seen anything like this anywhere I've ever been," says Leo Henning, overseeing the production of the radio broadcast and delayed-TV broadcast of the Quincy-Collinsville game. "When the devil runs out on the court with that pitchfork aflame, it scares the living hell out of the opposition before they even throw the ball up."

Though the 10th-ranked Collinsville Kahoks scoffed in the Devil's face, the No. 1-ranked Blue Devils vaulted to a 17-2 lead and never looked back, winning 75-46.

The Quincy Blue Devil got his due.

Follow the Bouncing Ball

by Ricardo Ferro of the *St. Petersburg Times.* St. Louis Cardinals reserve catcher Glenn Brummer took his lumps on this play during a spring training game against the Minnesota Twins in St. Petersburg, Fla. Brummer collided with Twins catcher Butch Wynegar on a close play at the plate and then took a shot to the head when Wynegar missed connections with the ball. Copyright © 1982, St. Petersburg Times.

Earning Her Stripes

by William Meyer of the *Milwaukee Journal.* With a large American flag forming a patriotic backdrop, Tristan Baker performs a dive during competition in the U.S. Indoor Diving Championships at the Schroeder Aquatic Center in Brown Deer, Wisc. This was one of several dives that qualified her for the finals. Copyright © 1982, Milwaukee Journal.

Hogan vs. Nicklaus vs. Watson

GOLF

By *JERRY TARDE*

From Golf Digest
Copyright © 1982, Golf Digest/Tennis, Inc.

Ben Hogan and Jack Nicklaus are widely considered the greatest players of the past two generations. Hogan, the man who was "never away" on the golf course, is remembered as the game's ultimate technician. Nicklaus is regarded as its consummate competitor and record-holder of major championships. The two have been compared for years, and each has his supporters.

The Nicklaus camp was buoyed in 1980 by its leader's complete overhaul of his short and long games and by his 18th and 19th victories in the majors. Some argue that, at last, Nicklaus has "gone around" Hogan and is history's greatest golfer. The Hogan camp remains unconvinced.

Tom Watson, the heir apparent to Nicklaus, has steadily built a reputation for greatness in his decade on tour. As the leading money winner four of the last five years, as a two-time Masters champion and a three-time British Open champion, at age 32 Watson is the premier player of the present generation.

With this continued interest in the Hogan-Nicklaus rivalry and the emergence of Watson as a player of historical significance, Golf Digest asked its Professional Instruction Staff to compare and evaluate Hogan, Nicklaus and Watson—their backgrounds, their full swings, their short games, their tactical approaches, their personalities. Our purpose was two-fold: (1) to gain an insight into what makes a great player stand above the rest, and (2) to learn from their techniques and strategies and become better golfers, too.

Our Professional Instruction Staff, whose comments formed the basis of this article, is composed of some of the game's best players, teachers and analysts: Sam Snead, Cary Middlecoff, Paul Runyan,

Bob Toski, Jim Flick, Peter Kostis, Davis Love, Gary Wiren and DeDe Owens. Byron Nelson, also a member of the staff, writes an additional opinion accompanying this article, reflecting on his personal experiences with the three subjects.

Although their playing techniques are quite different, Ben Hogan, Jack Nicklaus and Tom Watson share one inarguable quality: "Whether by trial and error or by design or by coaching, they have made the absolute best possible use of their physical assets while covering up their liabilities," says Kostis. "When people look at their swings, I hope they realize that a great player consists of more than a great swing. It takes intelligence and inner strength to be a winner. That's what helps a great player develop a swing that works."

While Nicklaus and Watson continue to consult with the instructors who taught them the game, they have become their own best teachers. Hogan was always his own best teacher.

"It seems the weaker the player is mentally, the more he looks to teaching methodologies and teachers to improve his game," says Toski. "Taking lessons will help to some degree, but many players never are able to handle the stress and strain of competitive play, because their basic problem is themselves and the inability to become their own best teachers. Hogan, Nicklaus and Watson have learned to teach themselves. They know what their mental and physical shortcomings are, and they've learned to cope. Too many good players are running around the country today analyzing different teacher's methods, when they should be learning to perform and execute and concentrate and believe in what they already have."

Their upbringing and environment

Ben Hogan came from modest beginnings in Fort Worth, Tex., and started in golf as a caddie. "He was self-taught," says Toski. "He built a swing as he went along in his career. It wasn't productive for the first 10 years he played the tour, but gradually he changed it so it became productive. He never had the advantage of going to a Jack Grout."

Grout is the teacher who has worked with Nicklaus since his introduction to the game at age 10. He was the professional at Nicklaus' home course, Scioto Country Club in Columbus, Ohio. Similarly, Tom Watson was tutored as a youngster by Stan Thirsk, the professional at the Kansas City Country Club, where Tom's father is a member. "This is important to keep in mind," says Toski. "Good instruction at an early age made their development so much easier than Hogan's."

Hogan had to work harder than either Nicklaus or Watson, perhaps harder than anyone ever did, to develop his swing. "It's my honest opinion that Hogan had to strike three practice balls for every one that Nicklaus hit," says Paul Runyan. "He was the most dedicated practicer of all time. His tenacity had no equal."

Hogan's swing originally was loose and wild, almost the very antithesis of what it eventually became. Says Snead: "He swung the club so far around on the backswing that the shaft pointed down at the ground. He could whack the ball out of sight with a big hook, but he didn't know where it was going. Most people don't realize he started on tour in the early '30s and didn't win a tournament until 1940. But in that time he worked longer and harder than anybody else, trying to find a swing that would repeat. Then all of a sudden he started putting red gravy on the scoreboards."

When Hogan's game matured in the early '40s, World War II soon followed. He spent three years in the Army, away from competition. He returned to the tour in 1945 and won his first major championship, the PGA, the next season at the advanced age of 34.

The change he made in his swing became known as "Hogan's secret," because he did not reveal it until his retirement in 1955 in an exclusive story in Life magazine. The "secret" consisted of two swing adjustments: First, he moved his left hand slightly to the left so his thumb rested directly on top of the grip. Second, he cupped his left hand gradually upward and inward on the backswing so it formed a slight V at the top.

Hogan contended his swing was then hook-proof: "No matter how much wrist I put into the downswing, no matter how hard I swung or how hard I tried to roll into and through the ball (pronate), the face of the club could not close fast enough to become absolutely square at the moment of impact. The result was that lovely, long-fading ball which is a highly effective weapon on any golf course."

Says Middlecoff: "In 1946 and '47, Hogan evidently had a different swing, but 1948 was really the first year he made it work. He was the worst-looking banana-ball slicer you ever saw that summer, but he kept it in play and made every putt he looked at. He won the Open and the PGA that year and seemed to have the world by the tail."

The following year, Hogan was seriously injured in a car accident, and there was doubt that he would play tournament golf again. Slowly and painfully, he came back. In 1950 and '51, he won the U.S. Open. In 1953, he entered only six tournaments and won five of them, including the Masters, U.S. Open and British Open.

"It took Hogan a lot longer to reach the top than Nicklaus," says Snead. "And it all stems from the fact that he never had somebody to tutor him right in the beginning." Adds Toski, "Hogan's attitude today reflects all the adversity he suffered to succeed. He's known for not being very helpful to players when they ask advice, probably because he figures nobody helped him along the way." In all fairness, Hogan probably feels his thoughts on the golf swing are explained in his 1957 book, Five Lessons: The Modern Fundamentals of Golf.

On the other hand, Nicklaus was an accomplished player when he turned professional in 1961, twice having won the U.S. Amateur. His first victory as a tour rookie was the 1962 U.S. Open, in a playoff with Arnold Palmer, at the height of Palmer's popularity. Nicklaus won the Masters and the PGA the next year and never had to look back. He's collected 68 tour titles in two decades on tour.

"Jack never had to stop like Hogan and go into the service," says Middlecoff. "From the time he was 16 years old until he went on tour at 22, nothing ever stopped Jack. The prize money jumped dramatically about that time, too. I've always thought how nice it would've been to have my own private airplane on tour, because that's what Jack had. Hogan drove a car 50,000 miles a year on tour."

Watson's incubation period was longer than Nicklaus' but shorter than Hogan's. He arrived on tour in 1971, won his first tournament in 1974, collected his first major in 1975 and was leading money winner for the first time in 1977. Watson also had the advantages of a well-to-do family and a college education; he is a psychology graduate of Stanford University. Nicklaus majored in business at Ohio State, but didn't graduate.

The types of golf courses on which a player learns the game have a significant influence on his later development, according to our instruction staff. "Nicklaus learned to play at Scioto, which demands long drives and high approach shots," says Flick, also an Ohio native. "Nicklaus directed himself to competing in major championships, which require higher, softer ball flight. Conversely, Hogan grew up in Texas, where the wind was more of a factor and the courses were flatter. He learned to play hooking the ball low into the wind. Watson grew up on a lush, private course. His trajectory and shot patterns are more like Nicklaus.' "

Their address positions

While different in the particulars of technique, Hogan, Nicklaus and Watson all set up to the ball with similar machine-like precision. It has been written of Hogan that he gave the clear impression a shot was 9/10ths over when he addressed the ball; the same can be said of Nicklaus and Watson.

Says Runyan: "I've always felt that if you extended a straight line perpendicular from their clubfaces at address, it would come within an inch of the target itself." Actually, both Nicklaus and Hogan deliberately play with a slightly open clubface at address.

Says Davis Love: "These players never took for granted golf's three dullest jobs—gripping the club the same every time, aiming the clubface the same way and assuming the proper posture. It contributed to their ability to repeat their swings. From what I've observed, I'd have to rate Jack a shade above Hogan and Watson in this category."

All three golfers play with a relatively neutral grip—palm facing palm and the V's formed by the bases of the thumbs and forefingers pointing toward the right eye at address. Our instruction staff recommends a slightly stronger grip for the average golfer—palm still facing palm, but with the V's pointing toward the right shoulder.

"Hogan experimented with a very, very strong grip early in his career and then shifted to a much weaker position later," says Runyan. "He went through an evolution of putting his hands on the club every way he could think of until finally he found the best combination for power and control."

Hogan's posture at address was military-erect, his spine almost vertical, causing him to swing more around his body in a relatively flat plane. Nicklaus and Watson bend more from the hips and swing in relatively upright planes, with the hands much higher at the top of the swing. Jack Grout taught Nicklaus to "reach for the sky" on his backswing, contributing to his uprightness and the high trajectory of his shots. In the last couple of years, Nicklaus has stood more erect and flattened his plane by a few degrees to achieve a shallower arc and recapture waning distance, but his swing is still quite upright relative to Hogan's standards. Our panel recommends a posture closer to Watson's, with sufficient bend at the hips to allow the arms to swing freely.

Their swings

Hogan, Nicklaus and Watson each developed a technique that maximized their physical strengths. While Nicklaus has relatively small and weak hands, Hogan had strong hands, wrists and forearms. If Hogan was more of an upper-body player and Nicklaus more of a lower-body player, the instruction staff generally agrees Watson is a whole-body player, his strength being more balanced. He has strong forearms and legs, so his swing uses both advantages.

"Hogan was more of a hands-and-hips player," says Kostis. "He moved his upper body with a tremendous amount of flash speed through the ball. He retained the angle of the clubshaft and his left arm far into the forward swing, resulting in one hell of a lot of catching up in the last two or three feet before impact.

"Nicklaus' swing has a much more uniform rate of acceleration, because he's more of an arms-and-legs player. He moves his feet more freely in the swing. Hogan used his legs as a platform on which to swing his upper body. Hogan's swing is the result of his using longer-than-standard clubs to generate more distance."

Flick explains that every golf swing has three dimensions: "A rotary motion, a vertical motion and a lateral motion. Because of his erect posture and longer clubs, Hogan's swing had more rotary action. Nicklaus, using a more upright plane, has more vertical motion."

Nicklaus' upright swing arc makes him a better player out of the rough than Hogan, contends the panel, because his clubface strikes the ball at a steeper angle with less interference from the grass. Both players swing the club from inside to along the target line through impact to back inside again, but Kostis says Nicklaus' greater vertical action keeps the clubface on the target line longer.

Kostis further argues that Hogan was a hitter of the ball and Nicklaus is a swinger of the club, causing several members of the panel to disagree. "My understanding of the terms 'hitter' versus 'swinger' is that hit relates more to hand action and swing relates more to arm action. Hogan's swing requires a more active release through the ball with the hands. Nicklaus has a more passive release with the arms doing a lot of work, though he has emphasized more hand action in recent years."

Middlecoff contends that Hogan was a "lasher," who let the ball simply get in the way of the club. Adds Snead: "When I played with Hogan, it really upset my timing if I watched him swing. I had to look away. He took the club away so fast and, swoosh-swoosh, the shot was over. It wasn't smooth at all, just effective."

On the subject of Watson's potential, there is no disagreement. "Watson has a chance to be the best ball-striker of the three," says Kostis, "because he has the physical attributes of Hogan's upper body and Nicklaus' lower body. His hand-wrist-and-arm action is impeccable. His leg movement is superb. Now if he could just incorporate Sam Snead's footwork to control the pace of his swing, he would reach his potential. He's got tremendous strength in his upper body and tremendous suppleness in his lower body—the best of both worlds."

Their tempos

The instruction staff agrees that Watson's swing may have the greatest potential, but at present Nicklaus' swing is rated the best. Putting it in quantitative terms, Runyan scored Nicklaus' swing a 98 on a scale of 100, Hogan's a 97 and Watson's a 96. "It is that close," he says, "but golf is a game of inches."

Watson loses points in this comparison because his fast swing tempo tends to get faster under pressure. "I think Watson has a better technique than either Nicklaus or Hogan," summarizes Snead. "But sometimes he gets quick and then he doesn't know where the ball is going."

Says Toski: "When I watch Tom and Jack, I pay close attention to the left heel. The faster Tom swings back, the quicker the left heel comes off the ground. Jack's left heel lifts much more gradually. Therefore, he keeps the tempo of his swing slower and more in control."

High-speed photography seems to substantiate the differece in swing tempo. Photographed at 60 frames per second, Nicklaus' swing takes 46 frames from the start of the takeaway to the top of the backswing; Watson's takes 34. Both players require exactly 10 frames from the top to impact. Nicklaus takes 24 frames more to the completion of his follow-through, Watson only 18, which indicates that Jack's arms are "softer" and more relaxed throughout the swing. In all, Nicklaus' swing requires 80 frames to Watson's 62. A similar test of Hogan's swing speed isn't possible, because comparative photography from his prime doesn't exist. Panel members who played with Hogan estimate that his swing was somewhat faster than Nicklaus', but slower than Watson's.

Their short games
    The instruction staff rates Watson the best off-green player inside 100 yards, Hogan second and Nicklaus third. The consensus also is that Hogan, Nicklaus and Watson have been the finest putters in the game in their eras.
    Says Toski: "Watson has a marvelous touch around the greens. He is well-rounded in every department of the short game. And he is a terrific bunker player, which was Hogan's only deficiency. Watson may drive the ball spasmodically off the tee, but he has the ability to recover no matter where it comes to rest."
    Middlecoff agrees that Hogan was no better than an adequate bunker player. "He really could pitch the ball well from 80 or 90 yards out, but he was only average from the sand. However, he was a lot better than Nicklaus in most facets of the short game. Jack could practice around the green for two months ahead of a major and still hit the worst bunch of short shots you ever saw."
    Kostis traces Nicklaus' short-game deficiencies to his long-game technique. "Jack has short, stubby fingers and not a lot of hand strength, so he developed a swing that didn't use much hand-and-wrist action. That's fine for full shots, but around the green his type of swing gives him trouble. I personally think the reason he's not been a good short-game player is that he hadn't developed a sense of feel and control of the club in his fingers, hands and wrist."
    This theory seems to explain Nicklaus' success with chipping since he converted to the firm-wristed technique pioneered by Paul Runyan. Before the 1980 season, Nicklaus took a series of short-game lessons from Runyan-disciple Phil Rodgers, who taught him to play certain chip shots like putts—with an arm-and-shoulder motion and no wrist break. Rodgers also taught Nicklaus to use more hand action on lob and pitch shots, always considered the weakest part of Jack's repertoire. While still not satisfied entirely with his short game, Nicklaus has made strides. Soon after he overhauled his chipping and pitching, he won his fourth U.S. Open and fifth PGA Championship.
    Hogan apparently had been a better short-game player and scrambler earlier than later in his career. "He had more imagination when he played badly than later when he played well," says Runyan. "There was a time Hogan could quickly size up the right thing to do in any situation—whether to chip with the 7- or the 8-iron, or when to run the ball instead of lobbing it. But as he improved his swing and missed fewer greens, the decisions became harder for him."
    Says Middlecoff: "I think it got to the point when his tee-to-green game improved that he was almost embarrassed to play the result of a bad shot. It wasn't his nerves as much as the embarrassment of chasing down a bad shot in the woods. There was some overlap, however, between the time he was wild and when he was super accurate;

then he was as good as anybody I ever saw at getting the ball up and down."

On the greens, the panel judges it a draw among the three as putters. "You can't imagine how good they were on the putting green," says Snead. "You don't win tournaments and not putt well. In their times they were the best putters in the field."

While Hogan is not especially known as a good putter, Snead, Middlecoff and Runyan agree he was the deadliest putter in the game inside 12 feet. Middlecoff recalls Hogan's final putt on the 72nd green in the 1950 U.S. Open at Merion. "Ben hit that 1-iron shot 50 feet from the last hole and had to two-putt to tie. He rolled the first putt six feet past the hole. I was playing with him. I had missed the green, chipped up close and tapped in. Then I looked his putt over, walked off the green and sat down. I told my caddie, 'There ain't no way he's gonna make that thing.' He stood over the ball I guess 40 seconds without moving a muscle and then he made the purest stroke you ever saw."

Their mental approaches

Beyond technique, the quality that sets Hogan, Nicklaus and Watson apart from their contemporaries is an immeasurable mental toughness, according to the panel. "Their dispositions are in some ways very similar," says Runyan. "They're highly motivated, if for different reasons. I was kidding Snead the other day that he has the greatest motivation of all, and he asked me what it is. I said, 'Greed!' But seriously, Snead's motivation is pride, just as it's the factor that drives these great players. I see a tenacious disposition in all three. Sometimes Jack vacillates; he'd rather play football with his kids, or fish. But Hogan never had any children or business distractions. He kept exclusively to the purpose."

Runyan rates Hogan as the best concentrator of the three. "But at a great price," he adds. "Even one of Hogan's closest friends wouldn't dare go up to him during a round. It'd break Ben's concentration and Hogan would bite his head off. Ben couldn't fraternize between shots. In the end, I think it shortened his career—having to concentrate so hard."

Nicklaus possesses an easier manner of concentration, but even he has been known to play in a trance. Says Middlecoff: "Bob Hoag, a good friend of Jack's from Columbus, once told me about the time he and Jack went to Palm Springs for a tournament and shared a suite together. Jack was about to win the tournament when he came across Hoag on the back nine the last day. 'Hey, Hoagy, how are you, boy? I haven't seen you in ages,' he said. He truthfully didn't remember he was rooming with the guy. Now that's concentration. But on the other hand, I've seen Jack able to walk down the fairway and talk to somebody and then quickly get his concentration back."

Middlecoff says Nicklaus has always displayed a maturity beyond his years. "Once, when Jack was in his 20s, Gardner Dickinson and I flew with him in his plane to a fall tournament," he says. "The only reason Jack went out there was to become leading money winner, and he had to win the tournament to do that. Anyway, Jack didn't win. Flying back home on Monday, Nicklaus said: 'You know, I wanted it so badly my legs locked up. It didn't dawn on me until the middle of the last round that I was trying too hard.'

"Now imagine being able to recognize that in yourself at that age. I seriously doubt Jack allowed it to happen to him again."

Watson likewise is seen as a player of exceptional maturity, undoubtedly aided by his education in psychology. Says Middlecoff, "For instance, we have been critical of his fast swing pace, but the fact is Watson plays every shot fast. I'd wager that no matter how difficult the shot, he plays it within a split second of his normal pace. And I think he does this consciously. His mind performs best at a certain speed and he knows it.

"This quick tempo enables him to play well so often. He plays 25 tournaments a year, more than Nicklaus ever did. Hogan may have played that many before the War, but not after he became successful. Jack and Ben, you know, went through years when they were very slow players, but later they speeded up some. But at their fastest, they couldn't keep up with Tom. He's one, two, three, hit."

Hogan, Nicklaus and Watson each share a lack of emotion. While they may emote in victory with the best of them, it is only after the last putt drops. "They never get excited or flustered," says Snead. "You never know whether they're making a bogey or a birdie. They might grin a little, but their actions don't change. They play the game on an even keel."

Snead warns, however, that some of their physical and mental abilities may be exaggerated with the passing of time. "Take Hogan, for instance," he says. "They're now saying of him what they used to say of Harry Vardon—Ben couldn't play the same course twice in one day, because he'd be playing out of his divot holes the second time around. If he were that accurate, why didn't he put it a little bit to the right or a little bit to the left?"

Legends indeed spread about these great players, and some may be apocryphal. But what cannot be denied is that in their times Hogan, Nicklaus and Watson were or are the very best in the world at their chosen profession. They have entertained and inspired the people who have watched them. No higher compliment can be paid.

The Miracles Ended at Lake Placid

HOCKEY

By *STAN HOCHMAN*

From the Philadelphia Daily News
Copyright © 1982, Philadelphia Daily News

America saw him scanning the screeching spectators, mouthing the words, "Where's my father? Where's my father?" And then they saw him wrapped in a flag. And America took goalie Jim Craig to its bosom, because you've gotta love fatherhood and brotherhood and the grand old flag and what those kids did to the Russians on the ice.

How was America to know that inside that flag, inside that lumpy body, there was an ego fragile as glass? How could America guess that Jimmy Craig could never come down off that Lake Placid mountain without shattering into jagged pieces?

His teammates knew. They had an idea of what Jimmy Craig really was like. But America was throwing a party for its Olympic hockey team and none of the guys would spit in the champagne punch. Hey, nobody would have listened, there were so many people hollering with love.

Craig got sent down and then he got traded. And then he started busting things. His finger, his leg, a phone booth in New England, other people's hearts. And now he's up on a vehicular homicide charge.

"The headlines make him sound like a murderer," Mike Eruzione said, "I've talked to Jimmy. He says it wasn't even his fault. That kind of thing, that could have happened to anybody."

But it happened to Jimmy Craig, the Olympic gold medal-winning goalie. And it happened after he'd failed with two pro teams, and kept busting things, including hearts. Couldn't someone have helped Jimmy Craig down off that mountain?

"I don't know," Eruzione said. "Me, I relied on what I was taught as a kid. My parents told me about winning and losing. Score a touchdown and everyone likes you. Next game, fumble, and where are they?

"I'm not saying Jimmy wasn't brought up correctly. But something *was* lost after we won."

Eruzione is here, at the National Sports Festival, as an assistant coach of the East hockey squad. Bill Baker is on the South staff, Dave Christian on the West and Mark Wells on the North. Gold medalists all.

Eruzione, captain of that 1980 bunch, is making it as a television commentator. The other three are in the NHL. They may not be as glib, as earthy, as open as Eruzione, but they took a run at the grim topic.

"If someone there at the time," Wells said, "Had said, 'Hey, this is what you're in for, people asking the same questions over and over, people wanting to shake your hand day in and day out,' it might have helped."

"If you knew the type of kids we had on our team, that wasn't necessary," Baker said. "Most of the kids were brought up where they were taught certain things.

"It wasn't hard to handle. I don't think anyone has changed. None of us consider ourselves better people just because we won the gold. That was two weeks out of our lives."

They weren't going to kick Jimmy Craig in the teeth while he was sprawled on the jagged glass of his shattered ego, but they wanted America to know that a guy's character is formed long before he ever steps up to that Olympic victory stand.

"Why don't they write about Dave Christian being captain of the Winnipeg Jets?" Eruzione muttered. "Why don't they write about Ken Morrow winning three Stanley Cups? Buzzy Schneider's wife had a baby boy, why don't they write about that?

"The thing that happened to Jimmy could have happened to anybody in this room. And, as far as his career, maybe he just doesn't have the skills."

They were young and tough and white and they skated across America's television screens and into its heart at a time when the world was spinning crazily.

"We beat the Communists," Eruzione said bluntly. "There was Afghanistan, and Iran, and the economy in trouble, and who was gonna be the next president. We came along at the right time."

"We didn't even have any idea of the impact on the public," Baker said. "We didn't realize it 'til we got to Plattsburg, a little town, and we saw the crowds waiting for the team.

"And then we got to Andrews Air Force Base and a couple of thousand people were there, and everybody was going crazy. It kind of grew from there."

They didn't know they were satisfying America's desperate hunger for heroes in a muddled time. They didn't hear the clamor because the coach, Herb Brooks, kept them isolated in the harsh igloo he created with his haughty manner.

"He never was close to his players," Baker said. "I respect him for what he did in hockey, but I have a tough time talking to him, even now."

"Discipline, that's the most important thing in coaching," Wells said. "Vince Lombardi, all the great coaches are disciplinarians. That's the best approach."

"Honesty," Eruzione added. "The coaches who are most honest, are the ones I worked hardest for.

"Brooks was honest. He told you if you were playing lousy. The fear is still there. I go in to talk to him before a game I'm broadcasting, and I still feel the fear. I don't think we'd have won without Herb, but I don't think Herb would have won without us."

Brooks coaches the Rangers now. Maybe eight of the 20 gold medalists still are playing hockey. A whole new bunch will represent America in Sarajevo in '84. Maybe.

Maybe? Only in America. First, the U.S. team must finish in the top four of an eight-team B pool tournament in Japan next March, which is college time, which is junior hockey league time. Which means scrambling for players.

Lou Vairo will coach the players they find for him. He's got a pebbles-in-a-can voice, and he calls asphalt 'ash-fault," as in, "You play street hockey in Brooklyn on ash-fault."

He grew up playing street hockey in Brooklyn, on roller skates, with a roll of black electric tape for a puck. He says it is the same game.

"Different puck, different skates, different surface, but it's the same game as ice hockey," Vairo said yesterday at a press conference to introduce his assistant coaches (two high school guys and the Yale coach).

"I don't feel any pressure," Vairo said. "Everybody says, 'You've got a tough act to follow.' Hey, I'd rather be coaching the Olympic team than installing air conditioners, which is what I used to do.

"I love hockey. I love America. I've got the best job in the world."

He surely will do it differently than Brooks. Style-wise. "We'll play a style I introduced 12 years ago," he said. "It's an American style and it suits our players. It combines the North American style of physical confrontations, one player against another.

"Plus the European style, where the players are better skilled and good conditioning is emphasized."

Warmth-wise? "I'm different, I'm me," Vairo said. "I'm not aloof. I love to live. I love life. I like people, the camaraderie of the team. I like to mix with the players, the staff."

Player-wise? "You ever see Willie Shoemaker win on a donkey?" Vairo asked. "If you don't have the players, you're not gonna win.

"We want players of high skill. We want players that are brave, that have courage. That doesn't mean guys who fight. There's different ways to be brave.

"Character? Everybody is different. We want good people, good human beings, not machines."

Machines can make it back down the side of a mountain no matter how many people are cheering and spraying champagne around. America thought Jimmy Craig was some flag-draped, dutiful-son, kid-next-door kind of machine, and he came unglued, scattering busted parts all over the landscape as people gasped.

None of the other guys came apart, and some have handled the descent to sea level better than others. Eruzione has learned a terrific answer to the inevitable question about maybe never feeling that high again.

"You don't stop living," he said. "It's nice when you're down in the dumps, to look back on it. But, hey, you win a Nobel Prize, you don't stop. You keep going.

"The best thing that happened is that we never had to play again."

An Unsung Hero

PRO FOOTBALL

By *MARK PURDY*

From Ohio Magazine
Copyright © 1982, by Mark Purdy

If Ken Anderson were forced to write a theme on how he spent his winter vacation, the paper would be splattered with gravy stains. Let's see, where was the prime rib dinner? Miami? Yes, Miami. Great prime rib in Miami. The hardware was decent, too. A simple, tasteful trophy. No silly chromed wings or tacky accessories. Just basic metal and wood. Elegant, but restrained. Miami was worth the trip. Buffalo, too. A $10,000 silver trophy in Buffalo. But don't forget Fort Wayne. Now, there was a deal. A gourmet dinner, vintage wines. For Fort Wayne, that was really something. But it wasn't unusual. They threw a lot of fine parties for Ken Anderson last winter, in every zip code on the map.

So he made a rule, and followed it strictly. Only one appearance a week that required a night away from home. An organization in Alabama called. The trip would take two days, and he turned them down. They raised the speaker's fee. "No," he said, politely, "you don't understand . . ."

Anderson exhales a bemused sigh. Imagine. People in Alabama bidding serious money for him. Cash money. And meanwhile, hungry children throughout the country are nibbling away at their father's unemployment checks. Anderson contemplates this irony as he sips coffee on the deck behind his suburban Cincinnati house.

The house sits, California-style rustic, at the end of a wooded street in the Northern Kentucky community of Lakeside Park. It is not the biggest on the street, but it is not the smallest, either. Three cars are in the driveway. Two of them are courtesy cars from a local Chevy dealer. The other is a Datsun 280-Z. Anderson often drives the Z to work at his new off-season job in a Cincinnati law firm. After five years of part-time study, he received his law degree last year from Northern Kentucky University. He was to take the Ohio bar exam in late July, but he's already set up in an office overlooking downtown. The firm of Strauss, Troy and Ruehlmann hired him in the futures market. Anderson won't occupy his office year-round until he finishes playing football, which could be another three or four years, at a salary somewhere on the high side of $175,000 per. Off-season speaking engagements probably add another $30,000 or $40,000 to his bank account. He has a pretty wife and two cute children. He's respected for his charity work. He can have a seat at the Kentucky Derby any time he wants. He can get a preferred tee time at any golf course in town.

And there are the new trophies, relics of the Cincinnati Bengals' Super Bowl season, and testaments to his own considerable achievements. Most of the trophies are stashed away in the basement recreation room, awaiting more display space. But this morning, two trophies are also standing on the kitchen table. They are recent arrivals. One is a stylized pewter sculpture. The other is the "Spark Plug of the Year" award from the Mutual Radio Network. This trophy is not so simple and elegant. It features two immense spark plugs embedded in Lucite. It is, quite possibly, the most spectacular trophy ever made out of spark plugs. Anderson shrugs and laughs.

It is difficult to discuss football with Anderson because when you talk about football, you have to talk about him. He doesn't warm easily to the subject. His modesty is no rumor. In Cincinnati for many years, he has had the reputation of being too nice a guy to win. A better phrase would be "a regular guy." They say nice guys finish last. Regular guys may also finish last sometimes, but they never go down nicely, the way nice guys are required to do. Nice guys have fan clubs. Regular guys have a beer. They shake off their disappointments and dive back into the storm. Regular guys can take a joke. Regular guys curse once in a while, but are careful not to do it around women and children. Regular guys, often, are not cut out to be NFL quarterbacks. But Anderson is the exception.

He is the son of a high school custodian, and grew up in Batavia, Illinois, population 12,000. Batavia is stocked with the standard American scenery: A Moose Lodge, a roller rink, a high school team called the Bulldogs and a main street named Main Street. Anderson will always be a child of Batavia, a pro football delegate of the regular citizens who work hard, try to raise their kids properly, but aren't above doing something silly once in a while to relieve the tremors of modern living. He is probably the best pure passer and best pure beer drinker in the NFL, but both facts are a well-kept secret. He is not a self-promoter. When NBC offered to send a limousine to pick him up for a *Today Show* appearance, Anderson declined politely and said he'd drive his own car. This year when he was asked to play in the nationally-televised Bing Crosby Clambake, the most prestigious Pro-Am golf tournament in the country, Anderson turned down the invitation because he'd already been on the road two weeks, too long away from his family.

"What can you say about Kenny?" says Bob Trumpy, a former

teammate and a friend. "He likes his family, likes to play his game and likes to drink beer. He should have been a hockey player."

Kenny's proud of what he's doing, but I don't think he wants to let anybody know it. The time he'll show it is maybe a few hours after a game at home when he'll sit down, open up a beer and say, "Dad, I think I had a good game today."

—Erik Anderson, Ken's father

In the American psyche, the professional football quarterback occupies a significant, almost frightening niche. Pop quiz: Name the mayors of Cincinnati, Cleveland, Pittsburgh, San Diego and Denver. Now, name their quarterbacks. What does that tell you about you, and about this country? We make symbols of our quarterbacks. We embrace them, hold them up as icons, cast them out as devils and ponder their every move, every Sunday, every autumn. If they make one bad play out of four, we don't forget it. We dwell on it. And since, even in a good season, a National Football League team will lose five or six games, we blame the quarterbacks for every loss. They touch the ball every play, don't they? Bradshaw? What a hick. Stabler? Ought to stop drinking so hard. Sipe? Just a beach bum. And after a touchdown pass, we love them all for at least two seconds.

Anderson's theory on this is simple. The public, he guesses, never really thinks of football players as real people. Pro football is exposed largely to the masses through television, which never really humanizes the players. Instead, it either shows them in instant replay with an announcer talking about zip patterns or flex defenses. And if a player actually makes it on camera with his helmet off, they give him half a minute to describe his feelings. If you're in the stadium watching a game, what do you see? No faces, just numbers. There is a doctoral thesis waiting to be written about the social psychology of the pro football customer.

Ken Anderson was never groomed to be a public figure. Main Street in Batavia didn't prepare him for it, and neither did Augustana College in Rock Island, Illinois, his alma mater. At neither of those places did people cheer when their quarterback got hurt. Ken himself certainly never booed anyone as a kid. Billy Wade of the Bears was the first quarterback he liked. The Packers' Bart Starr was a favorite, too, but Billy Wade played for the Bears. Batavia, a town of twelve thousand people forty miles west of Chicago, was a Bears' town. To this day, Anderson's family friends say his biggest football disappointment is that in 1972, when the Bengals played the Bears in Chicago, Paul Brown decided to start Virgil Carter and Ken didn't play a single down.

In 1963, when Ken was fourteen years old, the Bears won the NFL championship. Anderson's uncle took him to a few games at Soldier Field. Ken can still recall the first sports autograph he got: Harlon Hill, a Bears' offensive end. Truth to be told, though, Ken was more hooked on basketball.

"We're basically a basketball town," explains Erik Anderson, sitting in his Batavia living room. "Football was secondary. In 1912, Batavia High won the state basketball championship. The old-timers still talk about that."

Erik Anderson and his wife, Jean, still live in the house where they raised Ken. It is a small frame structure with a big back yard, built thirty years ago on Republic Road, in a development northwest of downtown. Erik constructed much of the house himself. When that was finished, he put up a basketball hoop on the garage, for Ken.

"I can remember seeing him out there when he was small," says Erik, "throwing a tennis ball up there through the basket."

When Ken Anderson remembers Batavia, he always mentions that he liked the place because, as a kid, he could ride his bicycle all over town and not get into trouble, or have his parents worry about him. You can still do that in Batavia. It has resisted the suburban sprawl admirably. The town is a tree-splotched postcard, a community of old big homes with old big porches, slashed in half by the Fox River, which flows right through downtown. During the early years of this century, the Germans and Irish lived on the east side of the Fox. The Swedes lived on the west side.

Erik Anderson was born on the west side in 1918. His father—Ken's grandfather—was a Swedish immigrant.

In small towns, a social caste system is almost non-existent. There aren't enough rich kids to be snobs. It hardly makes a difference if you're a janitor's son or a banker's son. Ken Anderson is a janitor's son, a job his father held with the Batavia School System for 25 years, and when people hear this, they automatically assume he had a hungry, sad upbringing.

"I laugh at that," Ken says. "When I was a kid, I thought it was neat my dad was a custodian, because he could get me and my friends into the gym any time we wanted."

Erik was happy to oblige. He's not hard to get along with. He has white hair, a comfortably wrinkled face and the manner of a man who could deal with students, teachers and principals for all those years. After he returned from the war, Erik never bothered to get a driver's license. Didn't see the need for one. The Anderson house was seven blocks from the high school, six blocks from the church, eight blocks from the barber shop.

It was also one block from the town playground, a huge park at the end of Republic Street. The playground, with its ball diamonds and basketball courts, is where Ken Anderson became an athlete.

Ken matured quickly and played baseball with the bigger kids. One of those bigger kids was Dan Issel, who lived on Harrison Street, directly behind Ken's house. Issel was a year older than Ken, bigger than Ken, and a better athlete in most respects. When the two of them reached high school, Issel was 6'9", still bigger, still better. He was the star of the school, not Anderson. That, plus a standard teen-age complexion problem, apparently made Ken shy around girls.

Says his mother, "Dad used to tell him, 'Kenny, the girls are out there cheering for you, and the least you can do is ask a gal to go for a dance.' But Ken just didn't care to take them out. He'd go to the proms because he thought he should."

Sports filled any void that existed in Anderson's love life. When he was a junior and Issel was a senior, the Batavia Battling Bulldogs had a 28-2 record and nearly reached the state finals.

Batavia wasn't as excited about football. In seventh grade, when the coach called his troops together and asked who wanted to play quarterback, Ken was the only one who raised his hand. However, he didn't start at quarterback in high school until his senior year, because his coach liked an upperclassman better. When Anderson made All-Conference, it was as a defensive back, not a quarterback. The football Bulldogs had a 6-2 record his senior year, ran the ball more than passed it, and no major colleges made scholarship offers to Ken, either in football or basketball. Issel was at the University of Kentucky, and would go on to play pro basketball, but no school wanted to take a chance on a 6'1" kid.

He wound up at Augustana College, enrollment 1,845, in Rock Island, Illinois. The basketball coach there thought he could use a playmaker. Anderson decided to write the Augustana football coach a letter, requesting a tryout. The coach agreed to give Anderson a look, but reminded him that the starting quarterback was returning from a team that had won the league championship the previous season. Breaking into the lineup, the coach noted, wouldn't be easy.

It took Anderson two games to become a starter. His first touchdown pass went for 62 yards. Fifty-five yards in the air. That's in the history books at Augustana. He started four years there, set nine school records and, as a senior, led the NCAA College Division in passing. He also kicked field goals, played varsity basketball and graduated with a 3.4 grade point average in mathematics. Today, Augustana College has no cinematic record of the Anderson years. Over the seasons, players have stolen the game films as keepsakes.

If there's one thing I guess I regret, it's that I didn't open up to the media more, and sooner.   —Ken Anderson

When the Bengals took Ken Anderson in the third round of the 1971 college draft, no one in Cincinnati knew who he was, and so the skinny, small-college kid walks into training camp and the reporters ask him who he is and why he went to Augustana and he says, "Because I just wanted to go there."

And the reporters look at each other and snicker and kiss him off as another in a long line of jocks with nothing to say.

The problem was that he had no clue how to cope. In high school, he'd been second banana to Issel. In college, he'd been covered by *The Argus* in Rock Island. He'd never seen a mini-cam. Now, he was being smothered by them, and he clammed up. He started a few games as a rookie, and the reporters joked that his best quotes were when he was calling signals. That was fine with his coach, Paul Brown, who each year issued these instructions to his players with regard to media: "When you lose, say little. When you win, say less."

And so Anderson's image in Cincinnati was set. Dull, square kid from small Illinois town. It was the Woodstock Age, and Anderson had short hair with no sideburns. He also seemed to have no flair, unlike the town's baseball heroes: Bench, Rose, Perez.

As soon as Anderson was drafted in 1971, he made two good decisions. He immediately moved to Cincinnati and began working with the Bengals' quarterback coach, and he took an apartment with a policeman as a roommate. The cop kept Anderson out of trouble, and the quarterback coach made him a pro. The coach's name was Bill Walsh. Ten years later, he would direct the San Francisco 49ers to their Super Bowl victory over the Bengals. But in 1971, Walsh's project was the kid from Augustana. Walsh took Anderson through the pro dropback and passing offense, step-by-step, coverage by coverage. Paul Brown, watching from the side, approved. He called Anderson's plays for him. And so Ken gained another component of his image, that of a mechanical man, a robot.

But he was hardly that. Bonnie Ziegler was probably the first to realize it. She was his first Cincinnati girlfriend, and eventually his wife. Blonde, petite and full of what was formerly called perkiness, Bonnie grew up in the Northern Kentucky suburb of Fort Wright and met Ken at a party.

Today, he and she make perfect bookends. During a joint interview, if Ken is reticent, Bonnie will jump in. If Bonnie could have done Ken's interviews during his rookie year, his image would never have been a problem. She conducts an exercise class in Kentucky to work off all her energy. When people want to talk about Ken's image, she rolls her eyes. "This guy isn't a saint."

Okay, so let's destroy Anderson's drab image once and for all with some of the best stories about him.

KEN, THE DESEGREGATIONIST: Every year at the Bengals' training camp, the veteran players throw a party for the rookies. Usually, the party includes several rounds of cold ones. This particular year after the party, receivers Issac Curtis and Don Bass are sleeping off the celebration when Anderson skulks into their room. Slowly, methodically, he covers them with shaving cream from head to toe. Then, with a flourish, Anderson dusts them off with talcum powder. When Curtis and Bass awake the next morning, they discover they are no longer the team's two leading black receivers. Instead, they have been transformed into the team's two leading white receivers.

KEN MEETS HIS MATCH, AND IT HAS A SPANISH ACCENT: The traditional Bengal hangout during training camp is a bowling alley lounge on the east edge of Wilmington. One night, Bob Brown, a huge tackle, issues a Tequila-drinking challenge to anyone in the room. Anderson takes him up. (Once, on a golfing expedition to Florida, Anderson drank thirty-two beers before staggering off to bed.) After six shots, with beer chasers, Anderson is still standing but retreats to his dorm room where he becomes sick in the trash can, and collapses. "As he's lying there passed out," says Bob Trumpy, "I'm thinking to myself, 'Well, here he is—the quarterback who's supposed to take us to the Super Bowl.' " The next day, Anderson has a great practice.

KEN GOES UNDERCOVER: At training camp last season, Anderson decides it is time to pull the famous claw trick on Dan Ross, the Bengals' tight end. While Ross is in the dorm bathroom, Anderson crawls under Ross' bed. After four or five minutes, just as Ross is drifting off to sleep, Anderson reaches up from beneath the bed and clutches his hand to Ross' chest, nearly sending him through the ceiling. A few days later, Ross retaliates by releasing a live turkey in Anderson's room.

It's fairly evident why, for five straight seasons, the Bengal veterans gave Anderson their unofficial Rookie Of The Year award.

When things are going good, Ken likes to keep it low-key. When things are going bad, he likes to keep it low-key. And when things are neither good nor bad, he likes to keep it low-key. I guess, all in all, you'd have to say Ken's a low-key guy.

—Dave Lapham, Bengals offensive lineman

It is easy to recognize one of Ken Anderson's passes. The spiral is not too tight nor is it too loose. The height is not too high and not too low. The speed is not too fast and not slow. Says Bengals receiver Steve Kreider, in as eloquent a testimony to a quarterback as can be made: "When Ken puts a little air under the ball, I run for it; I know he's leading me to open space, not to a collision."

Statistics are boring, but there are few you have to know about Anderson. Among quarterbacks currently playing the game, he ranks the highest in the league's rating system, which uses a formula involving completions, interceptions and touchdowns. That's supposed to mean he's the best man throwing the ball today. Anderson's pass interception percentage is the best of all time, better than Starr or Unitas or Staubach.

None of which explains why Anderson threw the ball like Ethel Merman in the Bengals' first game of the 1981 season, against Seattle. The black comedy began calmly enough. The temperature was 70 degrees at Riverfront Stadium on September 6, and the sky was partly cloudy. The Bengals took the kickoff, ran six plays and punted. The Seahawks took the punt and did the same thing.

The next eighteen plays were the worst of Anderson's Bengal career. In those eighteen plays, he threw the ball fourteen times. Only four of the fourteen were completed successfully. Seven of the passes were incomplete, most by several miles. One pass was complete, but was fumbled away. The other two passes were intercepted. On one of them, it appeared as if Anderson meant to throw the ball at Seattle's

John Harris, who easily ran the ball in for a touchdown. At the end of those eighteen plays, Seattle was leading 21-0. The crowd booed him. Seven-year-old Matt Anderson told his mother he wanted to go home.

On the sidelines, Cincinnati coach Forrest Gregg pondered his choices, and decided to yank Anderson. It was the first time in his career that Anderson had been replaced as a quarterback while healthy. What followed was even more bizzare: Turk Schonert, the Bengals' third-string quarterback, brought the team back from the 21-0 deficit to a 27-21 victory.

In the locker room afterward, Anderson said there was nothing wrong with him physically. He couldn't explain what had occurred, except to suggest he might have been trying too hard. Across the room, Gregg, the coach, was besieged by questions about whether Anderson would start the following week's game in New York against the Jets. At first, he was non-committal. Then he said Schonert would be the likely choice.

Anderson didn't find out until the next day. He was at a Labor Day picnic with Bonnie's relatives when someone asked him how it would feel to be sitting on the bench against the Jets. Anderson left his potato salad and phoned Lindy Infante, the Bengals' quarterback coach. Infante called Gregg, Gregg called Anderson.

"We talked about a lot of things," Anderson says. "We talked that maybe it would be better to have Turk start and have me come off the bench if I was needed, that it would be the best way to handle it. But at the end of it all, Forrest asked me what I wanted to do. And I told him I wanted to start."

It was on to New York, and Bonnie Anderson thanked the Lord it was an away game. She would later tell a reporter that if her husband would have had to face another week of Riverfront Stadium's booing fans after the Seattle debacle, it might have "broken him."

The week before the New York game was definitely no lark in the Anderson household. In addition to Ken's woes, Matt developed bad bruises all over his body. It turned out to be a blood condition, a low platelet count, but until that was confirmed, Bonnie and Ken had fears of leukemia. When the Bengals' charter plane landed at LaGuardia on Saturday afternoon, Anderson was in no mood to joke.

But before the first play of the game, he entered the huddle, called a screen pass, and he reminded the offensive line the play was going to the right, in case they wanted to get in position to cover an interception. The Bengals cracked up. Then they cracked down and beat the Jets, 31-30. Anderson had a good day. Two weeks later against Buffalo, he had a better one, in what he regards as the watershed game of the season, because it proved the Bengals could beat anybody, and it proved he could still throw the ball a little.

Against the Bills at Riverfront Stadium, Anderson attempted 40 passes without being intercepted, and led one memorable 90-yard touchdown drive. Cincinnati won in overtime. Anderson ran off the field with his index finger in the air. Matt, taking treatment for his blood problem, was in the locker room. He was not talkative when someone wondered if it was good to hear his dad being cheered again.

"I don't care if they boo him or not," Matt said. "I just want him to have a good game."

The enmity in Cincinnati for Anderson is largely inexplicable. He has never done anything off the field to create enemies, and on the field, his sins have been few. In 1974, he completed twenty of twenty-two passes against the Steelers, an all-time NFL record for completion percentage. In 1975 and 1976, he led the NFL in passing percentages. In 1977, with the temperature two degrees above zero, he threw for 303 yards against the Steelers. And still, they had booed him, even in his best years. The jeers began in 1974, when Anderson took over the quarterback job from Virgil Carter, a flamboyant soul who had become a popular character in the Cincinnati area despite his inability to throw a football farther than ten yards. Before Carter, the Bengal quarterback had been Greg Cook, a dashing blond wunderkind who set the town on its ear before he developed arm problems. After Cook and Carter, the fans weren't ready for a pure passer with bowlegs and no sideburns.

Against the Browns in 1974, he was sacked by Walter Johnson, and the fans cheered when he was removed from the game. The incident would be repeated six years later, when Anderson was tackled against San Diego, and didn't get up. Before the trainer even arrived on the field to diagnose his condition, the stands erupted in applause. By then, however, he had become immune to the treatment.

"There are some funny people out there," he said.

Even during the Super Bowl season, there were skeptics. One letter writer suggested that Anderson was purposely throwing interceptions to help the gamblers. Anderson had ten interceptions all year, only eight in the last fifteen games of the season. Ask the people in the $11 seats why they don't like Anderson and they mention two things. First, they say, he's not a leader. Second, they say, he's not durable, and can't play hurt.

The leadership charge is the more irksome, because leadership is a nebulous thing. Some of Anderson's friends, Trumpy among them, encouraged Anderson to raise a little hell in the huddle if a lineman misses a block or a receiver runs a wrong pass route.

"Be a little bit of an egotist," Trumpy told Anderson when they were still teammates.

"I believe a quarterback has to keep an even keel," Anderson says, holding his ground. "Cris Collinsworth says he can't tell in the huddle if we're thirty points behind or thirty points ahead. I like that. Nothing bugs me more than to see a quarterback chewing out a lineman after he gets sacked. If I were the lineman, I'd be damned if I would want to play for the quarterback after that. I won't complete every throw, either."

The leadership critics were silent last season until, of course, after the Super Bowl. When the Bengals failed to score on four plays at the San Francisco goal line. The final Bengal running attempt was an off-tackle blast by Pete Johnson, who was stopped inches short of a touchdown. In the huddle before the run, it was learned later, Anderson said nothing except the name of the play, and the snap count: "Forty-six M Lead. On first sound."

"I wish," says one of Anderson's teammates, "that Kenny had maybe said a little something to get us fired up. We took a timeout before the play, and we're standing on the field a long time waiting to see what's going to be called. He comes back and just says the name of the play. He could have said something like, 'Okay guys, this is the whole game on the line,' but he didn't."

Anderson says he can't remember exactly what went on in the huddle before the play, but implies that if a team can't get excited about fourth and goal at the Super Bowl, it doesn't belong there. "It's kind of tough," he says, "to respond to that subject."

Once again, you see, he is talking about himself, about his ego, and that makes the discussion a difficult journey. He hates to talk about his injuries, too. He took the most heat about them during the Bengals' nightmare seasons of 1978 through 1980, when Cincinnati won only 14 games in 48 attempts. On many of those Sundays, Anderson's offensive linemen came disguised as invisible men. The most telling comment came from an opponent, Houston defensive back Willie Alexander, who after a 1978 Bengal loss in the Astrodome, said of Anderson: "A quarterback can't throw when he's looking at the ceiling."

The arrival of some solid linemen in the draft have eased that problem, though not totally. Anderson's toe is currently sore from being hyperextended last season, and his left shoulder makes a clicking noise now and then. His back also occasionally reminds him of 1979. In the home opener against New England, he was badly speared in the back, then came back to throw 16 touchdown passes that year. Anyone who says he can't play with pain needs a doctor himself.

"I've thought a lot about retirement," Anderson says on his patio, finishing his coffee on this spring day. "But I've come to the conclusion that I really enjoy what I'm doing. In a certain sadistic way, I enjoy feeling sore on a Monday morning."

Actually, the sore Mondays are only part of the answer. For a regular guy, football is the best sport. It is a chance to prove you can take it, a chance to keep playing the game you learned on a small-town playground. After all the grief Anderson has taken from fans in the past, some observers wondered last season why he didn't shout, "I told you so." They didn't understand. The cheers are only a small part of Anderson's football fix. He never learned to depend on fans for affection, because in high school the fans were usually cheering someone else—Issel—and in college there were only a few thousand fans cheering at each game. Anderson has his family and his respect and his clicking shoulder to remind him of what he can accomplish.

Besides, he knows it will happen again. He knows he's bound to throw another interception, and when he does, someone will boo him. It would be nice if they don't applaud his injuries, but that probably won't happen for a while, at least. He and the Bengals should receive a waiver of sorts this season. After the electroshock thrills of last year, no Bengals' fans can rightfully complain. During a series of team workouts on Memorial Day weekend, the mood was light. When Anderson's shoulder, rusty from inactivity, caused him to throw a few passes that dipped and weaved, a chorus of quacks erupted from the other players.

"Boy, my arm sure feels great," Lapham, the lineman, teased his friend in the locker room. "Your arm feel pretty good, Kenny?"

Anderson pretended not to hear, but he had. He was sitting on the floor, taking off his socks. He had his back to Lapham. In a terrific move, without turning around, or looking, Anderson flipped one of his socks over his head and scored a direct hit on Lapham's nose. Another completion for Ken Anderson. The season is off to a pretty good start.

Dean Smith Finally Is No. 1

COLLEGE BASKETBALL

By _MIKE LITTWIN_

From the Los Angeles Times
Copyright © 1982, Los Angeles Times
Reprinted by permission.

The monkey is finally off Dean Smith's back. But it had to be wrenched off. All but dynamited off. The monkey, which after 16 years with Smith figured he had found a home, was seen leaving the Superdome Monday night, by the back door.

Smith, after seven Final Four appearances, is for once the Final One. He coached North Carolina to a 63-62 win over Georgetown and an NCAA championship in a game that gave the monkey hope until its final moment. A desperation shot at the buzzer by Eric (Sleepy) Floyd from 45 feet traveled maybe 40.

And so the Tar Heels (32-2) were NCAA champions. Smith was vindicated. And 61,612 fans at the Superdome joined a national television audience—most of whom had a better seat—in watching a championship game that was worthy of the name.

Worthy was the name. James Worthy, the Tar Heels' All-America, led all scorers with 28 points and was chosen the tournament's outstanding player. But the biggest play he made, someone else actually made for him.

Freshman Michael Jordan's clutch 16-foot jump shot with 15 seconds to play had returned the lead to the Tar Heels. Georgetown's Fred Brown had the ball at the top of the circle, looking desperately for someone to pass it to. He looked for Sleepy Floyd but couldn't find him. He looked for Eric Smith and thought he saw him out of the corner of his right eye. Worthy, who does slam dunks pretty well, apparently also does imitations. For Brown, thinking he saw Smith, actually saw Worthy and shot him a neat little chest pass. The only question was who was more surprised—Brown or Worthy?

"I was shocked," said Worthy, who took the pass off his chest and then dribbled the ball into the corner, dribbling away all but the last two seconds of the game. Eric Smith, the real Eric Smith, finally found Worthy and fouled him. Worthy missed both free throws, but at that point it didn't matter. The monkey was done for.

"I picked Eric out of the corner of my eye," Brown said. "It was James Worthy."

Brown said he wanted the pass back. You don't get takebacks in this game, no more than Dean Smith can take back those six times Carolina left the Final Four a loser. The word was out: Dean Smith couldn't win the big ones.

Jimmy Black, the lone senior in the Tar Heels' starting lineup, had called a team meeting last Thursday to impress upon his team-mates the importance of winning this one for Coach Smith.

"If we had lost, the media would have jumped on him again," Black told a group of writers. "We wanted to get you off his back."

Black talked a better game than he played. Carolina's point guard couldn't handle Sleepy Floyd and he couldn't find his jump shot. Meanwhile, Georgetown center Pat Ewing (23 points, 11 rebounds) was as dominating as any freshman has ever been in an NCAA championship, completely outplaying a very good player in Sam Perkins. Ewing was so pumped up that Carolina's first four baskets were all goaltending calls on the 7-footer.

Anyway, Smith, whose first Final Four team was in 1966, seemed to take the win in stride. He doesn't experience either highs or lows, he said. This one was for the seniors, he said. Oh, he said just everything you expect Smith to say, even that his good friend John Thompson had outcoached him.

"This was the only year it would have bothered me," Smith was finally forced to concede. "We had the best basketball team, I thought. We were ranked No. 1 in the country in preseason and post-season . . . (but) I'm not sure we were the best team tonight."

It was left to Worthy and Jordan to prove that the Tar Heels were.

Worthy was inside, outside, all around the court. He made five dunks that were somewhere between Jammin' James and Dr. J. He took the ball inside Georgetown's zone so readily that Coach Thompson had to try a man-to-man. Worthy had 16 of Carolina's first 22 points and missed only 4 of 17 shots all night from the field. His weakness was at the foul line, where he was 2 for 7.

Foul shooting almost cost the Tar Heels, who, of course, went to their delay game at the end. With 1:19 to play and Carolina leading, 61-60, Matt Doherty was on the line, shooting one-and-one. But he missed the first shot badly and Floyd, on the other end, slithered into the lane and snaked in a 10-footer to give Georgetown a 62-61 lead.

Smith called time out and then called young Jordan's number. You might think the ball would go to Worthy, but Georgetown's zone was so packed that even Fred Brown couldn't have gotten the ball to

Worthy. Instead, Smith figured Jordan, who scored 16 points and grabbed 9 rebounds, could get an open shot.

"It felt real good," Jordan said of the shot, a wide-open 16-footer from the left side. "I could feel it going in. I'll remember this one from here to eternity."

So will Smith. He had faith enough in Jordan to get him the ball and faith, too, that the shot would fall. But some will remember it differently. Floyd called the shot a 23-footer. It must have taken an eternity to drop, from Floyd's point of view.

Jordan had given Carolina a three-point lead, a momentous lead in this game, with 3:15 to play when he drove the baseline out of the Tar Heels' delay game to drop a bank shot over Ewing himself, *left-handed.*

"That was one I wasn't sure I wanted him to take," Smith said.

Said Jordan: "I knew something bad could happen."

What did happen was that Ewing, who couldn't block it, came back to hit a jumper. Doherty missed his foul shot and Georgetown got back the lead, setting up Jordan's final shot and Fred Brown's final embarrassment.

This game didn't figure to end on a mistake, though. It was a game mostly of big plays, of grand moments, of Ewing blocks and Worthy drives. It was a game between friends—Smith and Thompson—and friendly enemies—Floyd and Black, who exchanged words. It was the closest final since the 1963 overtime game between Loyola of Chicago and Cincinnati.

It might not have been that close and Smith might still be frustrated if Floyd, who played so well, hadn't missed a breakaway layup with Georgetown leading, 47-43. A minute later, a would-be six-point lead was reduced to one on a high-flying dunk by—who else? Worthy. There would never be more than three points separating the teams thereafter.

But Georgetown held the lead until a Worthy free throw put Carolina ahead, 57-56. He missed the second, but Perkins, stymied most of the night, tapped the ball back out. Black would eventually hit two free throws and Carolina remained in the lead until Floyd's basket with 55 seconds left returned the advantage to the Hoyas.

Carolina had never been this close, not last year when it lost to Indiana in the final or any other year since it won the championship in 1957, four years before the Dean Smith era began.

Jordan's classy jump shot and Worthy's lucky steal put Smith on top of the college basketball world. It's the only part he'd never seen.

Thompson, his good friend, was happy for Smith. Not so happy for himself. It was a difficult match for Thompson, set against his teacher.

"There were double problems in my mind, which caused me to be more emotional . . . because of my great affection for the guy who was sitting on the other bench," said Thompson, who was in his first Final Four. "I made up my mind that I wasn't going to be a nice guy.

In a sense, I felt like the student wanting to show the teacher he knew something about the game of basketball."

Thompson did his job well and, with Ewing, certainly could be back. Smith loses only one starter, and with seven Final Four appearances in 21 years and two in two years, it's safe to say he'll be back.

But if Smith returns, he won't be back with the monkey.

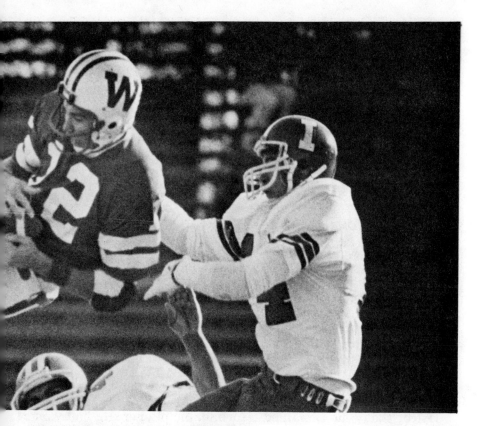

Wright in the Middle

by Gary Weber of the *United Press International*. Wisconsin quarter-back Randy Wright, whose normal job is to throw the ball, found himself on the receiving end against Indiana University—and the Hoosier defenders were ready. Wright caught the ball in the second quarter but suffered a mild concussion that forced him to sit out the third quarter. Copyright © 1982, United Press International.

Net Results

by Richard Pilling, a free-lance photographer whose photo appeared in *Hockey Illustrated.* A quick skate count illustrates the plight of the unknown New York Ranger who ended up in goal under the visible Andre Dore (left) and Philadelphia Flyers goalie Pete Peeters during a National Hockey League game. Copyright © 1982, Richard Pilling.

The Ancient Mariner

BASEBALL

By *JOHN McDONALD*

From the Everett (Wash.) Herald
Copyright © 1982, Everett (Wash.) Herald

Only Gaylord Perry's calling card remained.

The man was long gone. He wasted no time in vacating the Kingdome that summer evening in 1979 after he pitched briefly and ineffectively for the National League in the annual All-Star game. He had faced three batters and given up three hits, including a go-ahead, pinch hit single by Seattle's Bruce Bochte.

The rocky outing was out of character for the big righthander, then toiling for the San Diego Padres. Even in 1979, as he neared his 41st birthday, he remained a formidable pitcher. He had won 21 games for the Padres the season before and thus became the first pitcher to win the Cy Young award in both leagues.

Perry had no time to wait for reporters that night, though. He showered, dressed and was gone. His locker was cleaned out. Almost.

Sitting on the top shelf of the otherwise bare locker was an unopened, quart-sized jar of Vaseline. Petroleum jelly can be a pitcher's best friend, and not just to soothe his chapped lips. Some say pitchers —especially those who have lost a little zip off their fastball—use Vaseline to doctor the baseball. Some say Gaylord Perry is the Marcus Welby of baseball doctors.

None of that has ever been proven, of course. They've focused cameras on him. They've analyzed his fidgeting on the mound. Is he really tugging on his cap or is he picking up a little dab that will do him some good? They've stopped the game and checked the ball. But they've never caught him.

The spitball and its many variations have been illegal since 1920. When the pitch was outlawed, each team designated two pitchers as spitball pitchers. Those pitchers were allowed to load it up for the rest of their career.

Although the spitball is illegal now, it is not extinct. From Whitey Ford's belt buckle to Rick Honeycutt's thumb tack, pitchers still try to deface the ball so it will defy the laws of gravity and organized baseball. Or they moisten it, grease it—everything except baste it—so it will drop suddenly as if it were reentering the atmosphere.

Perry watchers say he fits into the second category. He is a baseball greaser, so they say. Yet he is also baseball's equivalent of the daring cat burglar no one can catch. Does he or doesn't he?

Whether Perry left the jar of Vaseline there in 1979—and that would be in keeping with his sense of humor—or some prankster put it there after his departure doesn't matter. The point is Perry was then and always will be associated with the spitball.

And that's unfortunate because there is much more to this man, who sometime this season figures to become the 15th pitcher in major league history to win 300 games and also may become baseball's all-time strikeout leader. No one survives 20 years in the major leagues on one pitch. They survive by being strong, smart and staying one step ahead of the competition and their own diminishing capabilities.

"I stay fit the year 'round," said Perry, who operates a farm near Williamston, N.C., during the offseason. "I use my entire body when pitching and not just my arm. And I've stayed away from injuries.

"I've improved my pitches, developed new ones and done a great deal more studying of the hitters and what their weaknesses and strong points are."

Those abilities have enabled Perry to stay in the major leagues well beyond the normal age of retirement. Even after being released by the Atlanta Braves at the age of 43 following the '81 season, Perry was able to get a tryout with Seattle and make the Mariners' ballclub.

Since then the 6-foot-4, 220-pound righthander has pitched two complete-game losses and his 298th career victory, recording 23 strikeouts in the process to pull within 149 of Walter Johnson's all-time record of 3,336.

On the mound he is ageless, pitching with the same craft and determination he brought with him to professional baseball 24 years ago.

"Throughout his career, anytime that something physical changes with him—maybe he loses a little bit off his fastball or whatever the case may be—he has always been prepared with an adjustment," said Dave Duncan, the Mariners' pitching coach and Perry's catcher with the Cleveland Indians during the 1973 and '74 seasons. "It seems like he forsees the possibility of things changing in his physical abilities two to three years ahead of time and starts preparing for when that occurs. And when it does occur, he's ready to accept it and make an adjustment in his style of pitching. I believe that's why he has been so successful."

Perhaps the most effective adjustment Perry made was the development of a forkball.

"In 1974 I caught him and he was 21-13," Duncan said. "That

was the year he won 15 in a row (falling one victory short of the American League record for consecutive wins in a season). He was absolutely awesome that year.

"That was the first year that he really started using the forkball and it became the best pitch he had. His fastball was a little better than it had been the previous year plus the forkball was so good. It was a new pitch for him and a pitch that the hitters hadn't seen before."

Some members of the Mariners pitching staff think Perry is still pretty awesome.

"I think all our pitchers and catchers are prospering from Gaylord being here," Duncan said. "They can watch him work and see how he prepares himself between starts for a start and how he prepares himself on the day of the game to go out there and give maximum effort.

"He gears himself up so that he peaks at the time the game starts and he's ready to start that game with full concentration. It takes a lot of years to develop that type of a routine and if our pitchers pay attention to him, they can pick up things along the line. At the same time, there's a lot to be learned from the way he goes about pitching a game."

Perry's non-pitching teammates will benefit from his presence, as well, according to Duncan. First, they'll learn how to win from him.

"His competitive nature has always been extremely high," Duncan said. "You've heard the phrase, 'burning desire to win?' He has always had it."

Second, they won't have to bat against him.

"It's frustrating," said M's hitting instructor and first base coach Vada Pinson, who faced Perry many times during his career as an outfielder for the Cincinnati Reds, St. Louis Cardinals, Cleveland Indians, California Angels and Kansas City Royals, "especially for the guys that have the big swing like Reggie Jackson. All of a sudden he just takes something off the ball and it takes away the hitter's timing.

"I wasn't a big swinger, I had a short, choppy type swing and I'd go to the opposite field on him so it wasn't as frustrating for me. I think we evened out somewhere along the way. He got to me and I got to him.

"But he's the type of individual who moves the ball around and keeps it down. And you don't know where he's going to throw it.

"Everybody says he has an unsanitary pitch, but they haven't proved anything, either, so . . .

"He's hard to hit. That's all there is to it."

He was then, is now and may be for some time to come.

"It seems like he can go on forever," Duncan said.

The Glitter Has Gone

TENNIS

By *BARRY McDERMOTT*

From Sports Illustrated
The article, "The Glitter Has Gone" by Barry McDermott,
is reprinted courtesy of Sports Illustrated © Time Inc., November 8, 1982.

It's a typical teen-ager's room, a refuge as much as anything else. In the satisfying, comforting clutter are a pushbutton phone, a stack of 45s, a Mickey Mouse wall clock and a poster promising love. Lori Kosten is sitting on her bed, sifting absentmindedly through crimped photographs and yellowed newspaper clippings, evidence that she was special. She's playing *The Way We Were* on her stereo. She has tears in her eyes. If she had it to do all over again, would she? Could she?

Five years ago, at age 12, Lori told her hometown newspaper in Memphis, "I want to be like Chris Evert, or maybe better." Now, lying on the bed in front of her is a poem she has written, *I Had This Dream:*

> The dream didn't come true. . . .
> So I threw away all the fame,
> All that's left is memories of the
>   past. . . .
> Once I was the big shot, I was so hot,
> But now it's no longer to be.

Trying to explain what happened to Lori, tennis folks say, "She had too much too soon." Eventually, her precociousness played havoc with her. She contemplated suicide. Her health deteriorated. Life became chaotic. Three years ago Lori said, "Tennis is everything. I wouldn't want to live without tennis." A year later she walked away from the game.

Lori didn't quit tennis because she wasn't improving, but because others were getting better faster. She quit because she made one too many trips to hospital emergency rooms, because she lay awake one night too many, worrying, because she finally listened to herself. "It used to make me mad that no one would ever say the word 'quit,'" says Lori. "Everyone just kept putting on more and more pressure to be better. No one would say it. They were so gung-ho about my being a winner."

Even now, a lot of people in tennis can't believe she could give up the sport. In 1981, after Zina Garrison won the Wimbledon junior championship she said to Lori, "I still wonder if I could get a game off of you."

Lori *was* good. At seven she was a phenom. By eight she had won seven trophies. In an early tournament she lost a set and her opponent's father screamed, "Ten thousand dollars worth of lessons finally paid off." At 12, she was ranked No. 2 in the U.S. in her age division. At 14 her picture was in *Life* magazine. She went out with Leif Garrett, the young Hollywood star. "I woke up to a world of all these super things happening," she says. "Headlines, traveling from state to state, missing school, meeting people, winning, being a fighter, wanting things and never being satisfied. Almost from the beginning of my life I was a star. Then when it ended, when I couldn't take it anymore, I said, 'I'm sick of fighting, I want to live.'"

Often in the early rounds of junior tournaments, the kids score their own matches, and the winner returns the balls and reports the outcome. Lori was always eager to return the balls.

"Score please."

"Kosten 6-0, 6-0."

The next day, Lori would be there again.

"Score please."

"Kosten 6-0, 6-0."

The officials would look up curiously. Lori could see them thinking: Is this girl special?

The first time she played Andrea Jaeger, in the 12-and-under division at the Southern Open, when they both were 10, Lori lost one game in two sets. She practiced with members of the Memphis State University men's team. Crowds would gather. Lori knew people were watching, and talking about her.

That same year, at the Orange Bowl tournament, she was leading Jaeger 3-0 in the second set after having lost the first. On the changeover, Andrea, a friend, said to Lori, "You're fat. You're ugly. And nobody likes you." Lori lost the next six games.

Altogether, some 90,000 boys and girls play in local, sectional and national age-group tennis tournaments in the U.S., and for the vast majority of them the game is a healthy endeavor. But for the elite, those with national rankings and aspirations of playing professionally, tennis often isn't a game but a way of life. As a result, perhaps no other sport adversely affects so many youngsters or demands so much of them mentally and emotionally. It can destroy as much as build, not only the participants, but families and friendships as well.

"I've never felt the pressure, not at Wimbledon, not at the U.S.

Open, nowhere, that I went through in junior tennis," says Chris Evert Lloyd. "I still get chills thinking about it. Every match was life or death. I remember playing one of my best friends. We must have played 100 times. And before each match, I would almost get physically ill. I beat her every time. And the next time, I would get sick again."

A few months ago, Lori's mother, Marilyn, asked her daughter if she missed playing the Easter Bowl, a major junior event. "I miss the tournament," said Lori. "I don't miss throwing up before the matches."

In 1969 the fathers of Dick Stockton and Harold Solomon got into a fistfight at the Orange Bowl tournament during a match between their sons. Since then, with more and more professional players making immense sums of money, the competition on the junior level has become even stiffer, the pressure on the kids more intense—and parental striving more acute. "They're out of control," says Nick Bollettieri, who runs a tennis academy for junior players in Longboat Key, Fla. "In other sports, if your coach yells at you, you still have your parents to turn to. Your parents yell, who do you turn to?"

But leaning on a kid too heavily for sloppy footwork isn't the only problem with many of today's tennis parents. At just about any major junior tournament one can see moms and dads allowing their children to cheat, argue with opponents, insult officials and throw tantrums. Some won't hesitate to instruct their kids to default a match if playing and losing could jeopardize their ranking. Anything goes to protect a ranking.

Compounding parents' anxiety over whether their children will "make it" is the fact that in tennis, unlike most other sports, which have established methods for producing champions, no one knows for sure what to do. Parents face a myriad of decisions: Big racket or small? Wood or composite? Two hands or one? Top spin or flat? Train at home or at a camp? Compete in the proper age group or play up? College or the circuit? Tracy Austin did it one way, Jaeger another, John McEnroe another.

Bill Amend has a 16-year-old son, Eric, who has won seven national titles. His 12-year-old daughter, Krista, is one of the best in the country in her age division. When Eric was 10, Bill built an indoor tennis club in Chicago so Eric could practice year round. Later, Bill, a research engineer, quit his job and moved his family to California, where the competition is better and Eric could be coached by Robert Lansdorp, until 1980 Tracy Austin's mentor. One day Krista was playing one of the nation's best 12-year-olds. After a disputed call went her opponent's way, Bill yelled, "She cheats! She always has cheated! Maybe I should teach my kids to cheat!" The people at the tournament were shocked, but as tennis parents, they understood.

"These parents look at these kids as the financial salvation of the family,"says Toronto film and sports mogul John Bassett. His daughter, Carling, 15, is one of the top-ranked girls in the world and a student at Bollettieri's. When Bassett, a former Davis Cup player for Canada, attended his first junior tournament in the U.S., he was startled. "Here were kids coming off the court in tears," he says, "and their parents were yelling at them."

The father of one top junior player is renowned for heckling his son from the sidelines. If the boy double-faults, the man yells, "That's one." If he does it again, the father yells, "That's two."

The prevailing opinion among tennis parents is that the pressure is good, that it steels young players for the pro tour. "You've got to learn to handle the pressure," says Dr. Herb Krickstein of Grosse Pointe, Mich. His son, Aaron, won the national 16s this summer. "The better kids handle it. You think not many crack, but talking about it, I guess there are quite a few.

"Yet, these tennis prodigies don't come out of nowhere. The parents have to give them guidance. I don't *want* to say push. But Roland Jaeger would admit he pushed Andrea. I'll admit I push, too. If I don't think my kid is doing the right thing, I'll tell him about it." Or see to it that someone else does. Twice a month Aaron flies to Florida to work out at Bollettieri's academy for four or five days at a time.

Chris Green, a sophomore at Foothill College in Los Altos Hills, Calif., was ranked in the Top 25 nationally for much of his junior career. Once he watched a friend jump in a river and swim across it after he had lost a match in St. Louis. "Back then I never realized how many guys were going bonkers," he says. "We just laughed about it. The parents push the kids, force them to play, criticize them. You come home and it's the worst when you have to say, 'I didn't do well.' It's almost like the kid has no say. Those are the ones that crack."

The Kostens became involved in tennis accidentally, innocently, as is so frequently the case. Herb, Lori's father, was an athlete. He and Marilyn met at the University of Alabama, where Herb was All-Southeastern Conference in baseball for three years. In 1970, after 12 years of marriage and a struggle through hard times, things were looking up for Herb and Marilyn. He was successful in the construction business in Memphis. They belonged to a country club. They had a maid. Their older daughter, Julie, was 9, and Lori was 5.

As Marilyn was sitting by the country club pool one day that summer, the club pro came up to her and said, "Did you know that your daughter can really hit a tennis ball?" Marilyn asked if he would move a bit; he was blocking her sun. But being a dutiful mother, she took Julie to Tommy Buford, the Memphis State coach. After hitting a few balls, Buford jumped the net and told Julie, "You're going to win the state tournament!" Two years later, she did.

While Julie played, Lori banged balls against the house, occasionally breaking a window. She hit alone for hours. "We used to play mini-tennis out in the garage," Julie recalls. "Lori wanted to win so bad. She'd beg me to play. It was ridiculous. The racket was as big as she was."

Lori tagged along to Julie's tournaments. Pretty soon she was telling her father, "I can beat all of them." Finally, Herb and Marilyn entered her in a tournament. A man took one look at the half-pint and quipped, "She ought to be in diapers." Lori won.

In the summer of 1973 she faced Julie in the Memphis City girls' 12-and-under finals. Julie was so nervous she fainted during the match and defaulted. Immediately afterward, Lori, proud as she could be, ran up to the tournament director and asked him, "Can I have my trophy now?" Lori got so good so fast that before long Julie had to offer her sister $5 just to get her to hit with her. The Kostens had a prodigy.

As an 11-year-old Lori was short and a bit pudgy, but while the other girls just pushed the ball back, Lori blasted away and went for the lines. "I beat almost everybody 0 and 0," she says. "I didn't just beat them. I destroyed them."

She won the national 12-and-under indoor title and the Orange Bowl 12s in 1976 and the Orange Bowl 14s in '78. "I used to be into every point," says Lori. "People said, 'She plays every point like it's match point at Wimbledon. I was never comfortable unless I was up 6-0, 5-0, 40-love."

Roland Jaeger remembers a final between Andrea and Lori when they were 12. Andrea seemed distracted. Later, Roland wanted to know why. Andrea shrugged. "I didn't think I could have won," she said. "Lori's still too good for me." But Andrea could forget her losses. As it developed, Lori never could.

Of course, her downfall didn't happen all at once. Just as it takes time to build champions, their unraveling doesn't occur overnight. Through her 12th, 13th and most of her 14th years, Lori's titles piled up. During the 1976 Sugar Bowl tournament, Lori was introduced at halftime at a New Orleans Jazz basketball game in the Superdome. Two years later Eddie Sapir, a Kosten family friend, Billy Martin's lawyer and a confidant of Joe Namath's introduced Lori to Leif Garrett when the teen idol was grand marshal at a "parade of champions" in New Orleans before the Ali-Spinks fight. She and Garrett became good buddies. One teen magazine captioned a picture of Lori "Women's Tennis Star." Namath wrote her letters of encouragement. She met other celebrities.

But Lori grew uncomfortable being at the top, at having—rather than simply trying—to win. After she won the national 12-and-under indoor title, she stayed in her room for two days, refusing interviews with local newspapers. Once friends at school asked about an article on her in the morning paper. After class Lori went home, found the story, ripped it into little pieces and threw the scraps on the floor of her parents' bedroom. She was starting to come apart.

Friends now talk about Lori's sensitivity, and it's true that any slight, real or imagined, brings a stricken look to her face. "Lori gets hurt easily," says Julie. "To me she was like a Brooke Shields. How can you lead a normal life? It was so competitive, sort of like who is going to break first. And it's worse with girls. They put more pressure on themselves than the guys."

Julie became accustomed to people asking, "Are you the good one or the bad one?" But she stuck with tennis, crying after every loss. Then one day she didn't cry. "That's when I knew I didn't care anymore," she says. From then on, if she and Lori were playing the same event, Julie couldn't wait to get off the court so she could watch her sister.

Though she worked hard, Lori started playing with less confidence. New names were challenging her. Jaeger was making phenomenal progress. "It always seemed people were looking at me," says Lori. " 'Oh, there's Lori Kosten.' Always judging you, watching you. I'd go to a tournament and I'd hope for rain. Here I was, seeded No. 1, and I couldn't stand the thought of playing."

A significant turn in Lori's career came at the U.S. Open when she was 13. Her father had brought her there to watch the matches as a reward for a fine summer. He believed, with good reason, that his daughter could hold her own with 60% of the women in the tournament. He, Lori, Marilyn and Jaeger were walking out of the stadium after a match when Bollettieri came up to them and said he was opening a tennis academy in Florida. Would Lori come? She could live in his house. Two other top juniors, Anne White and Jimmy Arias, would be among the students.

"Please let me go," Lori said to her father. "Please, please, please."

It sounded great. Tennis every day, against the country's best, with expert instruction, in Florida no less. The Kostens said yes. At the time Buford was working with Lori on her strokes. Herb provided moral, and tactical support. Whenever Lori played, she knew where daddy was standing. By enrolling at Bollettieri's, Lori was losing the two most important influences in her life.

Now everyone agrees that going to Florida was a mistake. Says Buford, "It bothered me because I knew it would end up with her either making it, or it would kill her." Adds Herb, "It was wrong because, especially in women's tennis, all the ones who make it have a close relationship with someone. Lori wound up missing that. There's no question I let her make too many decisions when she was young, but that doesn't mean I was wrong. That's how I am with everybody in my family." While Herb is talking he's driving his wife's white Eldorado. Beside him Marilyn sits rigidly, staring straight ahead. Back when Lori was struggling with tennis, Marilyn had decisions to make about her own life.

Herb and Marilyn are opposites in almost every way, from looks to temperament. He is a patient, low-key everyday kind of guy. She's petrified by hospitals, doctors, failing and messy confrontations. Marilyn has a youthful figure, Herb's hair is thinning, and his athlete's body has swelled. Marilyn wears fashionable clothes and diets fastidiously. Herb is a walking rummage sale.

As the girls became more and more involved in tennis, so did Herb. He played. He worked with the state tennis association. He became an umpire. (Herb called the Jimmy Connors-Guillermo Vilas semifinal match at this year's U.S. Open.) He helped coach his daughters. "Herb's an athlete, and athletes understand other athletes," says Marilyn. "He would say to me, 'Just take care of Lori's clothes and her hair, and I'll take care of the rest.' That's hard, mentally, to be left out. It was: 'Don't get in the way.' My feelings were hurt. I wanted so much to help. But they were athletes. Just keep her pretty, they said." Marilyn reacted by staying away when Lori played. "The fences around the court started to look like prison walls to me," she says.

At the Sugar Bowl tournament in 1975, while Lori played in the finals, Marilyn drove her car around the park adjacent to the courts, returning occasionally to ask Herb the score. She could do so without getting out of the car. Finally, he became exasperated. "Listen, either stay or leave," he said. Marilyn thought for a moment and then stepped on the gas. The car rammed into the fence alongside Lori's court. Marilyn says she thought the car was in reverse.

At one tournament Marilyn saw a father smash his son's head against a tree after the boy lost. She watched as parents fought. She saw children cheat. It never made sense. "I thought it was degrading," Marilyn says. "Everybody was concerned about Lori. She was running the show. No one was saying, 'What about Marilyn?' I was proud to be Lori's mother, but people thought I was a nobody. I said, 'I'm not a tennis mother. And I'm not going to do what I'm *supposed* to do.'"

Marilyn started taking art classes. She began talking about "honesty," a marriage alarm signal if ever there was one. She discovered the passionate films of the Italian director, Lina Wertmuller. Sports bored her, she told friends. She fantasized about running away to Greenwich Village. Instead, she designed a tennis dress. At a tournament she showed it to Tracy Austin, who loved it. Marilyn started a company, Little Miss Tennis, and designed its dresses. When Austin burst onto the national scene, she wore Marilyn's dresses. The company took off. Marilyn had her own business. She was a person, too.

Howard Schoenfield, now 24, won virtually every tournament he entered in 1975, including the national 18-and-under championship. Later that year he had a breakdown and entered a mental hospital for several months. Howard currently lives in a halfway house on the outskirts of Jacksonville, suffering from a mental illness his psychiatrists have been unable to diagnose with any certainty. Twice a month he has to take an injection of Prolixin, a drug to relieve severe anxiety, agitation and psychotic behavior. Residents with zombie-like stares shuffle around the grounds outside the converted whitewashed motel, and teen-agers driving by scream cruel epithets at them. A tennis-court construction company is next door.

The Schoenfields were a tennis family through and through. Howard's father, Leslie, was a renowned physician at the Mayo Clinic in Rochester, Minn. When Howard was 13, Jack Kramer evaluated his game in Los Angeles. Shortly thereafter, the Schoenfields moved to Beverly Hills, largely so that Howard could play with the best. "It was a classic case of the tail wagging the dog, rather than the dog wagging the tail," says Dr. Simon Levit, Howard's uncle. "Of course, tennis affected Howard. There's no question about it."

When Howard was 16, his mother killed herself. He was shattered by her death. Levit says Howard's mother couldn't cope with the tremendous change in her life. According to him, the family had been happy in Minnesota. Suddenly they were living a vastly different life style in California.

After his hospitalization ended in 1976, Howard practiced tennis for five days and then told his coach, Paul Cohen, that he wanted to defend his national title. In the semifinals Howard lost a two-hour match to Larry Gottfried, Brian's brother. Following the match, Cohen carried Howard back to the hotel. He couldn't walk because his feet were so blistered. Cohen says Howard's performance that day was the most courageous thing he had ever witnessed.

Soon afterward, Jane and Winder Hughes of Ponte Vedra Beach, Fla. met him at a tournament, befriended him and sponsored him on the pro tour for two years. "It was junior tennis that affected Howard," says Jane. "That did it. There was nothing else wrong with him. He thought so, too. He was worn out from the pressure. He always said, "Why don't they let me rest? That's what I need—rest.""

Today Howard has nothing but rest. His hair is bushy, and he wears the same shirt, shorts and sandals every day. "I felt pressure as a kid," he says. "Expectations were pretty high, and you had to succeed. It kind of gets to you. But I loved the pressure. It felt good. Right now I don't feel a damn thing, I'm just a vegetable."

Two years ago Howard seemed to be making progress. He won a $50,000 pro tournament in Tulsa, beating Bob Lutz along the way. But seven months later he was back in a hospital. "I don't care if people know about me," says Howard. "Everybody in tennis knows anyway. I just don't have anything to protect anymore—no self-pride, nothing. People say I look fine, that I act fine, but I still feel rotten. It's really depressing here. I can't sleep. Nothing can hurt me because I don't have anything left."

Howard would like to begin playing tennis again, but, he says, "It would surprise me if I could come back." He pauses and then adds, "My father pushed me, but maybe you shouldn't write that. It might upset him." Howard's father, now the head of the gastroenterology department at Cedars-Sinai Medical Center in Los Angeles, hesitates to connect his son's illness with tennis, although he admits he cannot rule it out. Both of Howard's brothers have made it through adolescence unscathed. Mark, 23, was graduated from Yale and was a member of the varsity wrestling team, and Steve, 21, attends Cal

State-Northridge. Neither played serious tennis.

Howard's father and a psychiatrist who treated Howard believe the death of his mother—not tennis—precipitated his illness. Moreover, the mother had a history of mental illness. Two of Howard's most steadfast supporters during his ordeal have been his paternal grandparents, Harriet and Morey Schoenfield of Davie, Fla. The grandparents still have hope he will some day get back into tennis. They have told him that if he demonstrates a show of good faith by jogging 10 miles a day for a month, they will take him in, oversee his training and accompany him on the pro circuit.

While Marilyn Kosten was coping with the problems of being a tennis mother, her daughter's world was disintegrating. At Bollettieri's academy, where Lori lived from September 1978 until January 1979 and from January through May of 1980, she was in an environment in which everyone had talent. Frequently she'd telephone home, her voice tight with anxiety. "I lost to a girl today who's a nobody," she would wail. Recalls Bollettieri. "Lori would win the first set, be 1-1 in the second and get sick. She was afraid of losing. Then the injuries would start."

Always it was something. At one tournament her eyes bothered her, and she had to take out her contact lenses, which left her almost blind. On another occasion, after winning a match, she suddenly felt as if she couldn't breathe, and she collapsed. A bystander gave her mouth-to-mouth resuscitation. In Miami she suffered leg cramps and was rushed to the hospital. The doctors phoned her parents for permission to administer revitalizing injections. In the background Marilyn could hear Lori yelling, "Not in my tennis arm."

People started gossiping. In Mission Viejo, Calif., Lori got sick and threw up all over her rackets. In Dallas, playing in blistering heat, she fainted. An ambulance was called. Lori was adamant about not going to the hospital. Tournament officials insisted. Lori became hysterical. She couldn't stand losing. She couldn't stand getting sick. She couldn't stand people talking about her.

In Chattanooga, facing a state rival, Lori began hallucinating. She thought she was at Wimbledon. Watching her sister suffer, Julie burst into tears. But no one said quit. Lori won the match. Winners don't quit. Quitters don't win.

"If I did win a tournament, I'd be happy for a day," says Lori, "but then it would start all over. It made me so mad because I couldn't stand the people talking like I was nuts or something. I felt abandoned."

At Bollettieri's, the competition was intense, and all the students were affected by it. One of the stars, another young girl, who's now on the pro tour, became more and more manic. She was running a low-grade fever and complained that the instructors didn't work her enough. Suddenly she would dash outside and start skipping rope furiously. One afternoon she picked up 10 rackets and threw them out the door. Lori asked why. "I told them," the girl shrieked, "to string them at 80 (pounds), not 70." Finally, the girl started experiencing what must have been delusions of grandeur. She said to another student, "Get out of here. You're not good enough to be in the same room with me."

About this time Herb told Marilyn to take down a plaque that was hanging in the kitchen. On it were inscribed the words attributed to Vince Lombardi: WINNING ISN'T EVERYTHING: IT'S THE ONLY THING.

"Why take it down?" Marilyn asked.

"Because Lori has read it enough," replied Herb. Bollettieri, too, sensed Lori's deterioration. "Lori definitely had the physical equipment to be a top pro," he says. "But she had always felt so much pressure to win that she got to the point where she couldn't cope with the losses to girls she had beaten. When she couldn't adjust the bottom fell out." One day Bollettieri told Lori that being No. 1 wasn't the most important thing in the world. Lori was horrified by such blasphemy. "If I couldn't become number one," she said, "I wouldn't want to play." Then she walked away.

"I couldn't figure out what was happening," says Lori. "I knew I had the talent. Tennis meant everything because I always wanted to be different, not just a school kid. Maybe it would have helped not to be so good. I had so much so young. Seven years old, and they were already making me into something. Then I took the fall I never expected."

By the time she began her second stint at Bollettieri's, Lori's star had begun to wane. She was 15 and was coming off a No. 3 national ranking in the 14s, a disappointment. More and more good players were enrolling at the academy. "It hurt so bad," says Lori. "It bothered me when the press would interview kids and I wouldn't be the one." Some students teased her. "Oh Lori," they would say, thumbing through old tennis books, "did you win the Orange Bowl?"

"Before, I was always better than them," she says. "Now I was being looked down on. Oh yeah, they improved. They got good. But they had areas to improve on. Nothing was satisfying, because I had already done it. My world had reversed." She was No. 3 in the country, and she was failure. She started telling people, "I feel like killing myself." Says Lori now, "I didn't think about it once; I thought about it a million times."

Jennifer Amdur and Lori hit it off right away. Lori called her "Bambi"; Jennifer dubbed Lori "Cutie." Jennifer was the youngest child of a Miami eye surgeon, Dr. Joseph Amdur, and his wife, Phyllis, and she enjoyed the benefits of an upper middle-class environment, loving parents and an exceptional talent for tennis. The Amdurs are a tennis family. Jennifer's brother Bobby, 23, was a Division III All-America at Swarthmore. Her sister Libby, 21, is captain of the women's team at Tulane. But Joseph and Phyllis didn't let tennis dominate their lives. Their home is filled with happy, effervescent pictures of family outings: fishing in the Keys, water skiing, rafting, windsurfing. Jennifer took many of the snapshots.

Over the years Jennifer and Lori suffered similar despair as their rankings slipped. In July 1981, Jennifer, 17 at the time, played the national girls' 18-and-under clay-court championships. After almost every point she would whisper to Lori through the fence, "Do I look fat?" Jennifer was in the first stages of anorexia nervosa, a disease that leaves victims so obsessed with their weight that they have been known to starve themselves to death. The malady usually strikes goal-oriented teen-age girls who are struggling with their identities. It frequently afflicts tennis players. In fact, when Jennifer told college coaches about her ailment, they weren't surprised. More than one had already had an anorexic girl on his team.

"I understand how Jenny felt," says Lori. "She replaced one obsession, tennis, with another. I went through the same thing—losing weight. People would say, 'Lori, you're losing too much weight.' I would say, 'Oh no, I've got to lose more.' "

Within a few months after the national clay courts, Jennifer's weight dropped to 81 pounds, 50 below normal. She grew more despondent. Twice she tried to kill herself with pills. She entered a hospital for three months, and was under the care of psychiatrists. Last May, while alone in the house, Jennifer patiently searched for the bolt and shells to an old deer-hunting shotgun. After she found them she carefully assembled the gun. Then she went into a closet in her room and shot herself in the head.

When her father returned home he changed into his tennis clothes. He had a game with a friend on the family's backyard court. Before long, Amdur began feeling uneasy. Jennifer usually came out to watch, to kibitz, to kid him about his lack of grace. He went inside. But no sign of his daughter. Apprehensive, Amdur searched the rooms until he saw the closet door ajar. Inside Jennifer lay dead.

Amdur has wracked his brain. Did tennis help kill his daughter? Amdur never pushed Jennifer. If she practiced, fine. If not, he was disappointed but never said anything. When she lost, he never chastised her. Instead he said, "It's OK. If you'd practice, you would have won."

Jennifer's psychiatrist doesn't think the game had anything to do with her death, but many of the family's tennis friends are convinced that it did. "Only Jennifer and God know," says Amdur. "If tennis did it, that's a terrible thing for me to live with. Jenny's life was tennis and success. Maybe when she lost that identity, she had nothing left."

Lori cried for days when she heard about Jennifer's suicide. She understood better than the others. Says Lori, "If you keep reaching back for your past, it'll drive you crazy."

In 1966 Jake Warde of Denver was ranked No. 1 in the U.S. in the boys 12s for the second straight year. Warde walked away from tennis at 16. "One day I couldn't serve," he says. "The nerves, this time they wouldn't go away." Shortly thereafter he lost in the first round of the nationals. Dazed, he started trying to thumb a ride, no destination in mind. He just had to get away. Friends found him sitting on a curb, staring. It was his last junior tournament.

Warde's story is especially germane because his wife, Eliza Pande, also was a junior tennis player who quit the game. They met at Stanford. Eliza, like Lori, had been a phenom. In 1969 she defeated Evert Lloyd in the finals of the U.S. Girls 16-and-under Championships. At 18 Eliza won a pro tournament and two rounds at Wimbledon. Then, while playing for the women's team in college her freshman year, she realized "there were other things besides tennis in the world. Winning was all tied into being the perfect person. I had no choices. To get a different perspective, I had to quit and almost go through a deprogramming. I always saw myself as a championship tennis player. That was my identity and I lost it."

The Wardes, who live in Palo Alto, Calif., have both returned to tennis, though on a much lower level. They play a few local tournaments each year, and Eliza is coach of the women's team at Santa Clara University. Jake works as a sales and marketing representative for a publishing company. They have a 10-month-old son, Eben. Jake has fantasized about the boy becoming a pro tennis player.

One day in August 1980, while riding on a bus to the national girls 18s in Middlebury, Conn., Lori made her decision to quit tennis. This would be her last tournament. She was tired of living on yesterdays. Her father was waiting for her in Middlebury, and she told him what she had decided.

Still she had a tournament to play. In the second round, Lori, who was unseeded, faced one of the best players in the tournament, and a remarkable thing happened. Her game returned. It was the old Lori, the fighter with the punishing ground strokes. She cruised through the first set and led 4-2 in the second. "It was scary," she recalls. "And then I went to hit a serve and I couldn't even put my arm up. I served *underhanded.* I went to hit a backhand, and the ball went about a foot. It was like my muscles had gone."

After losing the second set 7-6, Lori retired at 0-2 in the third. "I walked to the sidelines and threw up in a towel." she says. "I couldn't believe it. The old Lori had come back for a time, but did I really want to keep on going? Or did I want to go home and be set free from all of this? To be normal? I walked off the court and said to my dad, 'Let's go.' What had happened, not being able to serve, the feeble backhand, the throwing up, proved it. I didn't want this anymore. It was over."

For nearly two years Lori barely touched a racket. Through her sophomore and junior years in high school she was an everyday kid. She went on a school trip to Washington, she attended the prom, she ran cross-country. "You've quit tennis," her father said. "What are you going to replace it with?"

"I didn't quit tennis to replace it with anything," Lori said. "I quit for me."

Last year Lori said, "I realize now there is so much more to living. I don't ever have to play again to be happy. Who cares what the rest of the world thinks? That used to be my whole life."

One afternoon in 1981 Lori walked into the living room, where her father was watching Jaeger play Bettina Bunge on TV. "I've beaten both of them," Lori announced with a smile, and then walked out of the room. Another day, Lori sat in her bedroom, the scrapbook and pictures in front of her. As she thumbed through the articles, Lori sounded like an adult recalling her youth. "Here they called me a child prodigy," she said, holding up a story. "Back then I was a chubby little girl with all the guts in the world. Here's me and Bettina at the Orange Bowl. Here's Andrea. I guess people wouldn't have written this stuff if I wasn't something." Once a junior champion.

Last May—21 months after she had left tennis and nine days before Jennifer killed herself—Lori was sitting in psychology class at Ridgeway High in Memphis when it came to her. "All of a sudden I had all the confidence in the world," she says. "I can still play. Once I wanted to die, but now I know living can be wonderful. I've proven I can live without tennis. Why fight it? My talent is tennis. Now I want a challenge."

Lori was going back, this time as an underdog—unranked, unseeded and, she says, unafraid. Over the last five months she has played several local and national tournaments, winning a round here and there, slowly regaining her form. Her father is hopeful. Her mother says Lori's outlook has never been better. Bollettieri thinks if she returned to him with a new attitude, she could be on the pro tour within two years. Listen closely, and you may be able to hear the whistling in the dark.

Football Religion Has Its Doubters

GENERAL

By *BILL KNIGHT*

From the El Paso Times
Copyright © 1982, El Paso Times

Fall Fridays are magic.

The special flavor in the air as the day's excitement builds to tension in the evening. Bands, cheerleaders, fans.

It was almost a religion at our house. Now the pages on the calendar of my life fly away so quickly. One second I was a burr-headed kid, enviously watching high school two-a-days. The next second I'm watching a six-year-old of my own.

I have a suspicion about her, though. When it comes to Friday night religion, she is at best agnostic. More likely, she is a downright atheist.

Little things clued me in. Like when she turns briefly to a televised football game, utters "Sick," then turns quickly again.

"Come on, now Kiki," I said. "Football is fun. Let's watch it, whaddya say?"

"It's sick."

But dads always get the last word.

"Communist," I said.

Now, both my daughters know strong discipline. I mean, I'm practically a Vince Lombardi of fathers. Witness:

"Dad, I really need those doll clothes."

"Now Kiki, we've been over and over this. If you bring it up again, I'm going to break all your arms and legs and leave you in the desert for the wolves."

"But Dad, I really need 'em."

"Well, O.K."

Dads always get the last word.

In that spirit, it came time to escape the press box and introduce my daughters to the fun of Friday religion. Now my two-year-old is no concern to me. Courtney seems to enjoy the games and shows all the instincts of a linebacker.

So, last Friday night we bundled up, had some hot dogs and headed for the Coronado-Bowie game. As we neared the stands, we stopped to let the Bowie squad pass. Were any of us ever that young, that thin? My mind began to drift:

We were watching our high school heroes work, sweat, collide. Coaches were yelling. None of us was too eager to approach one of those gruff coaches, but I was shoved forward. "Excuse me, sir, when do y'all practice again?"

He looked way down, wondering where the timid voice came from, then bent down and put his arm around me. "Right out there at 6:30 in the morning, son."

We were there. Ten years later, that man was yelling at me on the same field. And he was a fine man.

This reminiscing intensified my urge to translate fall Fridays to my daughters and as we settled into our seats, I thought I was ready for all questions.

Coronado kicked off, Bowie intercepted, Bowie punted and Coronado ran two more plays.

My agnostic was looking around when I quipped, "Did you know the game had started?"

"Where?"

"Down there."

"Well, why aren't they playing down here where we are?"

The questions got tougher: "Dad, why aren't the cheerleaders using their pom-pons?"

It was one of those nights.

As we were driving home, she came up with one more question: "Did you ever play football?"

After answering, I awaited other questions. What was it like? Was it fun?

But she just sat there, red stoplight reflecting on her tiny blonde head. I imagined all the things running through her mind:

My dad, the guy who cracks an egg on his forehead just to get a laugh at breakfast, who does a bellyflop in a backyard mudpuddle to liven up a dull afternoon, who let a Junebug fly out of his mouth at Mom's class reunion, is crazier than I thought.

When she wrapped those little arms around my neck for a good-night hug, my mind began to race again.

Fall Fridays are great. Football is fun. But nothing is more fun than having a couple of goofy little girls.

Even if one of them is a Communist.

All the Pieces Fall Into Place for Cardinals

BASEBALL

By JACK ETKIN

From the Kansas City Star
Copyright © 1982, Kansas City Star

All the you-play-my-game-and-I'll-play-yours masquerading finally ended Wednesday night as the World Series wound its way to a form-following conclusion. The Cardinals, masters at scratching and clawing, used their phony-turf game to the fullest, overcame a two-run Milwaukee lead and beat the Brewers 6-3 for the ninth World Series championship in St. Louis' history.

Before scoring three go-ahead runs in the sixth inning, the Cardinals managed to make base hits as devalued as the Mexican peso. They collected eight hits and stranded nine baserunners through the first five innings, scored one run and created a cluttered scorecard that resembled the note pad of a trading specialist on a 130-million share day on the Big Board.

"We had a lot of AstroTurf hits," Manager Whitey Herzog said. "But we couldn't get a two-out hit. That worries me when we can't get a two-out hit."

St. Louis opportunities seemed to increase by the inning as they nicked away at Pete Vuckovich. But squandered rallies that were increasing with an inning-by-inning morbidity were all that resulted. The Cardinals failed to score in the second with runners on first and second and two out. They came away empty in the third after moving runners to first and second and one out. And by cashing in one run in the fourth after having runners on first and third and no outs they experienced all the joys of winning at a slot machine after being humbled at craps.

Keith Hernandez, who emerged from a zero for 15 performance in the first four games, did a midgame turnaround that was his Series in microcosm. Hernandez, who was to go seven for 12 in the final three games, struck out in the fourth and stranded two runners. Then with one out in the sixth, he hit a three-and-one pitch from Bob McClure with the bases loaded that tied the game 3-3.

"I wasn't going to let that zero for 15 and all the press bother me," Hernandez said. "If I make a mistake that costs the ballgame, I expect it in the paper. That's the key, when you're having bad days not to let it bother you.

"I don't know what's going to happen. I can hit a ball right at someone. My task is to get a hit. Sacrifice fly and we're still down one run. I haven't felt a lot of pressure offensively. I pride myself on being an RBI man (he had 94 this year and a team-leading eight in the Series). I'm a better hitter with men on base."

During that sixth-inning rally, the Busch Stadium crowd rose to its feet to cheer. No prodding was needed from the unctuous public address announcer or the organist. Like their raucous counterparts in Milwaukee, the St. Louis fans finally had plunged deep into the game. Their behavior didn't go unnoticed.

"I honestly feel if the seventh game had been played in Milwaukee, we would've lost it," Hernandez said.

Before rallying to win, the Cardinals had come close to pushing their margin for error to its limits before George Hendrick followed Hernandez's hit by skidding a single through the right side for what proved to be the game-winning run.

"I knew we were two down and not the kind of club that comes back from big deficits," Cardinals pitcher Jim Kaat said. "We finally came back with a Cardinal type of rally. It's like it took us seven games to finally play our game."

The victory meant different things to different players, although savoring the experience, it seemed, would come later in quiet moments and not in the champagne-drenched clubhouse. Willie McGee said he'd believe the Cardinals had won when he received his winner's share.

"That's Willie," Bruce Sutter said. "I want the ring."

"I think what the Series does," Kaat said, "is give us bragging rights and a little bigger ring. I have a feeling for Julius Erving. Great player that he is, he's never worn that ring. The little bit of extra money and things are secondary to saying you beat everybody."

Herzog was extremely low-keyed about the team's championship. "I'm not that excited about it," he said. "The World Series is kind of anticlimactic. The big thing is to get to the World Series. Losing the playoffs is the toughest thing."

The Milwaukee loss marked the end of their win-or-else scenario that had carried them past the Baltimore Orioles into the playoffs and past the California Angels into the Series. "Maybe the third time is not a charm," first baseman Cecil Cooper said.

Ted Simmons saw it differently. He thought any talk of a negative residue from past drama was folly. "If you want to say that we went to the well once too often that's your business," he said. "I'm not going to say that. It came down to one game, and they won. I thought we were going to win when we were ahead 3-1. I still thought we could come back in the eighth (before the Cardinals scored their final two runs). You know you're down to three outs, and you've got to get three off Sutter. That's not easy."

Before striking out Gorman Thomas at the end of the game, Sutter had to step off the pitching rubber for a mental spotcheck. His five seasons with the lowly Chicago Cubs were about to culminate in baseball's most glorious moment. "I had to back up a little bit to relax," said Sutter, who came to the Cards last season. "It's hard to believe. I know it probably won't sink in for a while. I imagine I'll be hunting deer this winter and all of a sudden it will sink in and I'll let out a great big yell."

Artistically the Series was nothing to bellow about. Two games were blow-outs. The first Cardinals victory came on a rub-two-sticks-together rally that featured three walks and a single. St. Louis lost Game 4 when Pitcher Dave LaPoint muffed an easy toss from Hernandez that led to a two-out six-run Milwaukee eruption. Jim Gantner, despite his reputation at turning the double play, looked adrift from the bag and made five errors. Bob Forsch, so sharp against Atlanta in the playoffs, lost his two starts and was hit hard.

Still, enough autumn magic lingers to form a pleasant montage. The pudgy Mike Caldwell winning two games with grit and guile. Joaquin Andujar writhing on the County Stadium grass and winning two games with excellent pitching. Ted Simmons' triumphant return to St. Louis in Game 1. Robin Yount's two four-hit games and genuine embarrassment at the "MVP, MVP," chant of the Brewer fans. Willie McGee's surprising power. John Stuper waiting out a rain delay and pitching superbly in Game 6. Darrell Porter's opposite-field double off Don Sutton that tied the score in Game 2.

In the end, Herzog, the master builder whom Hernandez called, "the first manager I've met who can communicate with 25 different personalities," guided the Cardinals to their first championship since 1967. This Series seemed to swerve through alleys, backroads and other misdirected avenues before resuming a final-game course. Turf hits—the Cardinals ended up with 13 singles and two doubles—and Bruce Sutter, neither element a surprise, meant the difference Wednesday night.

"It all worked out," said shortstop Ozzie Smith, who was realizing the good fortune of both himself—he had spent four years with the San Diego Padres—and the way Game 7 unfolded. "Just a beautiful script. I couldn't have written it any better myself."

In Pursuit of Patrice

TRACK

By *SUSAN BRENNEMAN*

From Women's Sports
Copyright © 1982, Women's Sports

Eyes straight ahead, feet pivoting for purchase and position, Patrice Donnelly crouches at the bar of a 127-pound barbell. She lifts it—"cleans" it—to her chin, shoulders rotating smoothly, neck muscles tensed, every part of her body straining toward the weight. Then her arms drop and the weight hits the platform with a sound like the wrath of God.

Three reps and she turns and steps off the platform. She sits down, gulps a little water from a plastic bottle and bends to adjust one of the ace bandages wrapped around her knees. Her dark hair angles across her face.

It's Monday night at the gym, a place about the size of two basketball courts set down amid the parking lots and fast-food franchises that crowd the valley at the south end of the San Francisco Bay. Donnelly has what amounts to the only seat in the house—a bench pushed up against the back wall—and the scene being played out in front of her looks and sounds like it might have been written by the Marquis de Sade. Every four feet in all directions there is a piece of clanging metal apparatus with a sweating, grimacing, sometimes shrieking, nearly naked man in its embrace. The place is full of men, and a few women, flexing, stretching, groaning.

Suddenly one of them pauses, does a double take and steps out of the scene toward Donnelly. He is young, perhaps 18 or 19. His neck is about the size of one of his thighs, and his thighs are elephantine. He is flushed an incongruous pink, his blond hair spiking up a little from sweat. Not quite knowing what to do, but committed now, he leans toward Patrice, hand outstretched, face open. It is a courtly motion.

"I saw you in that movie," he begins. "I was sitting there in the dark, watching, and I said to myself, 'Hey, that's the girl who works out in the gym!'" He is warming to this now and he mimes his movie-theater surprise with a backward jerk of his head and widened eyes. "That was your first movie, right?"

Patrice, who has taken his hand and is smiling at him, nods.

He straightens up and makes a circle with his forefinger and thumb, lifting the other fingers in salute. Then he backs away grinning, brandishing that physical gesture of appreciation—his version of the fanny pat, the high fives, the cheer.

There are a lot of fans who want to tell 32-year-old Patrice Donnelly just how much they liked her as Tory Skinner in Robert Towne's film *Personal Best.* An entire girls' softball team cornered her at a restaurant one night, an amateur agent in Oregon sends presents and career advice, a young woman with MS writes that she owes her new determination to get well to Donnelly. Legions of in- and out-of-the-closet lesbians are at the least appreciative, at the most, madly in love. In return for their devotion, these fans want to know all about Patrice Donnelly by return mail, collect call, personal appearance.

Donnelly is a little bemused. "Robert told me this would happen," she says. "I didn't really think about it much. I was too busy just trying to do the movie."

So far Donnelly's admirers have had precious little to go on. There is the film itself ("I've just seen *Personal Best* for the fifth time," begins a typical letter) in which Donnelly portrays a top U.S. pentathlete who befriends, nurtures and falls in love with a younger athlete, Chris Cahill, played by Mariel Hemingway. There are the rave reviews of Donnelly's performance ("astonishing," "beautiful," "absolutely compelling") and a few other published pieces with some biographical clues ("former world-class hurdler Patrice Donnelly . . . fed parts of her own life into the Chris Cahill character when she worked with Towne on the script"). And there is the *Newsweek* write-up that revealed to the careful reader that Donnelly is not gay.

Maybe her fans missed some of that; maybe they just want to know more. At any rate, the letters and the fans keep coming, and they all seem to ask the same questions: Is Patrice Donnelly really Tory Skinner? Is she Chris Cahill? Or is she someone else entirely?

The answer, of course, is the same for all the questions: Yes.

In the spring of 1980, Robert Towne had a serious problem. With little more than a month before the cameras were set to roll, the writer, producer and director of *Personal Best* was minus one out of two leading ladies. In the end, with no time to spare, Towne followed a gut feeling. He cast Patrice Donnelly in the role of Tory Skinner.

Towne and Donnelly had met in 1978. She was in Los Angeles visiting friends—penthathlete Jane Frederick and javelin specialist Kate Schmidt—who turned out to be Towne's friends as well. Patrice was on leave from an unhappy life in San Diego. Just one week after the 1976 Montreal Olympics, she had married shot-putter and fellow Olympian Pete Shmock. He was heavily into training and Patrice was back in school, with a scholarship and coaching position at San Diego State. She was training too but feeling a definite letdown after the Olympics and, at the same time, holding down a series of make-ends-meet jobs—cocktail waitress, electrician's helper, paint-sealant seller, free-lance high school coach. By 1978 the marriage was failing and Patrice was floundering, trying to figure out what to do with her life.

About the same time that Patrice was meeting her husband to be, Robert Towne encountered Jane Frederick at the UCLA weight room. She was bench pressing 150 pounds, and Towne was impressed. With Frederick as an inspiration and advisor, Towne began to work on an old film idea about women athletes, an outgrowth of his longtime fascination with women in general and women athletes in particular. Along the way, they added Kate Schmidt to their informal team, and then a year or so later, Patrice. "Kate and Jane and myself were like reference books for him," says Donnelly.

Towne had the film's basic story in mind. He had two characters, Chris Cahill and Tory Skinner; he had their love affair; and he had his central drama: How do you compete against someone you love? The "reference books" added tone and texture and true-life adventures.

"We talked for months," says Donnelly. "And then the writing went very fast. It took only six weeks, working day and night. Waiting for a page to read was like waiting for cookies in the oven."

Towne finished the script in 1979 and began a year of planning for the filming. Casting *Personal Best* was a major hurdle. Towne wanted realism—no doubles. He was looking for the same quality of movement that had attracted him to women athletes in the first place. Donnelly was tested, initially with the Chris Cahill role in mind—after all, many of the details that brought that character to life came directly from Donnelly's history. But the test wasn't impressive, and Mariel Hemingway was hired to play Chris.

That left Tory. After Towne considered and rejected a host of actresses, dancers and athletes for the role, he went back to Patrice. He was almost sure that the qualities he had observed over the past year could be made to serve the character of Tory.

"At first," says Towne, "Patrice was quiet and very, very tentative. But as she became more at ease, you could see that she had a diabolical wit and a wonderfully cunning eye for detail." It was the kind of eye that Towne associated with artists, with "anyone who in any way, shape or form tries to represent life." And on the track Patrice Donnelly was totally at home—"an uncommonly graceful human being."

He said to Patrice, "Look, we tried this before. If you want to do this, I'll work with you, but you won't like what I'm going to ask you to do."

"A director," says Towne, "must convince an actor to be ashamed of nothing. Because if he is ashamed, he'll hide things. And he can't hide anything, not his anger, not his jealously, not his pettiness."

For Donnelly it was a 45-day process, learning to act—learning not to be ashamed—by way of cruel, constant analysis. It was "a little bit like Abraham and Issac," says Towne. "The hardest thing I ever had to do." At the end of the rehearsal he called for screen tests —not just for Patrice, but four or five actresses as well.

"About a day and a half before testing," he admits, "I finally became convinced that she was going to be able to do it. I told no one. The tests were made, I let other people 'decide.' Clearly, she was the best."

Donnelly will confess that she had wanted a part in the movie from the beginning. It was just a fantasy, then. But when fantasy moved closer to reality, she began to want it fiercely. "She is a competitive person," says Towne. "She'd felt slighted by people saying she couldn't do it. I think there was a great rage in her because she felt she could."

Donnelly puts it this way: "I thought, 'Hell, if I can make the Olympic team, I can do anything.' "

Patrice Donnelly grew up in Tucson, Ariz., in the sort of family that always eats dinner together. She remembers a "strict, sheltered upbringing," Catholic schools, troubles with the multiplication tables. Donnelly traces her competitive instincts to a "tough" mom and life with three brothers. She attributes her cheekbones to her maternal grandmother, who was part Indian. And she tracks her ten-year athletic career to a school fitness test at Salpointe High when she was 16.

"I long-jumped the farthest of 300 girls, so I went home and bragged about it." Her mother, however, was not impressed. With her husband holding the tape Dorothy Donnelly beat her daughter's PE record by two inches. But Patrice came back. "I was *not* going to let my mother beat me," she says. In the end it was Patrice over Dorothy by "an inch or so."

After the living room exhibition Mike Donnelly, who had been a pole vaulter, high jumper, hurdler, football player and PE major in college, began to coach his daughter. They started, naturally, with the long jump, but soon switched to the hurdles. In three years Patrice ranked among America's top four women in the 100-meter hurdles. "I had basic speed," she says, "and good balance. And oh, God, I *loved* the hurdles."

Actually, in high school, it appears that it was more of a love-hate relationship. Donnelly lived, ate and breathed track, and sometimes she just about suffocated. "I dreaded workouts for a while. I would get scared weeks before a meet." Describing it now she mimes a self-strangled athlete, a choke artist, one hand clutching her throat and the other trying to lift off a shot put.

By the time she graduated, though, her prospects were bright enough for her father to pack up the family—at this point consisting of Patrice, her still-at-home younger brother, Patrick, and her mom —and move to Southern California, where the real track and field action was.

Patrice enrolled in Grossmont College, essentially pursuing a hurdling major. Her dad was still her coach and she was still the only girl at the school track, training alongside the boys. In 1971 she decided to go for a little equality and battled the Grossmont student senate for funds to get to the qualifying meet of the World University Games.

"I made my plea," says Donnelly. " 'Can I go?' 'May I have the money?' 'I'm going to represent the school and I *know* I can make the team.' " They gave her the money and she not only made the team, she won.

It was a particularly sweet victory for Patrice. She made her first international team, and her dad was with her when she did it. "I was so excited," she remembers. "My dad was standing close to the track, and he had tears in his eyes and I had tears . . . me and my dad. That was really neat."

The following year, after she'd finished junior college, Donnelly began training with coach Chuck DeBus and the Naturite Track Club. He quickly picked her to begin a crash program in the pentathlon. She trained hard for six months—her shotput distance went from 26 feet to 46 feet, and she did so many long jumps and high jumps she got shinsplints. At the 1972 Olympic trials, the focus of all her efforts, she came in ninth in the pentathlon and a heartbreaking fourth in the hurdles, a finger snap away from qualifying.

Donnelly was invited to the Olympic training camp anyway, but she said no thanks, she didn't want to wave goodbye when the others left for Munich. Instead she headed for Europe and three months of competition and traveling. When she returned she joined the women's track program, then in its first year, at California Polytechnic University in San Luis Obispo.

Donnelly doesn't like to talk about 1972 "for many, many reasons." She alludes to minor skirmishes in a kind of cold war with DeBus, as well as dissatisfaction with the program at Cal Poly, and her losses at the trials still rankle. Then she comes to 1973 and it's almost as if she has fast-forwarded everything up to this point—now she wants to push the "play" button and relive every minute.

"My coach and I made the commitment," she says. "My training was a three-year project and I dedicated myself totally. I was ready to do that."

The coach this time was Dave Rodda at the Lakewood International Track Club near Long Beach. The commitment was to the hurdles, again, and to making the 1976 Olympic team.

Donnelly moved to Long Beach in order to train with Rodda, and she wrangled a job teaching at a nearby high school in about the same way she convinced the Grossmont student senate to send her to the World University Games trials. This time she made her plea to the school's principal.

"It was a Catholic school, a really big athletic school. I didn't have a degree, but I was training for the Olympics and I had PE credits from Cal Poly and Grossmont. They needed a teacher, and I needed a job."

Donnelly coached the girls' track team and taught physical education, typing, health and first aid at St. Paul High for the same three years she trained for the Olympics. "I was standing all day teaching, standing coaching till five. I'd go home, rest for half an hour, then go to my own workout at night at a high school in Lakewood."

Under the lights in Lakewood, Rodda and Patrice worked on combining her hurdling technique—"excellent," according to Rodda, "Mike Donnelly had done a great job"—with sprinting skills. She ran the 100 meters and the 200 meters in local competitions. It was a quest for speed.

The first year was disastrous. "For the first time in I don't know how long," says Rodda, "she didn't make the finals at the national championships."

At the beginning of the 1974-75 season, he saw things take off. Patrice made the AAU international touring team and the Pan Am team in quick succession. She had false-started out of the Pan Ams in 1971; she came in fourth in 1975. "She was stronger; the speed was coming."

"The big breakthrough for me was at a Phoenix meet early in 1976," explains Donnelly. "At the start of the race the block slipped and I fell, but the starter didn't call the race back. I was so pissed, I got up and started passing people. I hardly remember hurdling, except bodies were going by me and I ended up second or third out of nine.

"I finished the race and was so mad I went up to Dave and I said, 'My block slipped and I fell and the goddamned starter didn't call the race back . . .' He said, 'Patrice, Patrice, do you know what you did?' And then I realized I had really shifted gears, I really could do it. It was like something clicked."

What had clicked was confidence and the Donnelly version of the killer instinct: " 'I'm gonna do it' instead of 'Oh, God, can I do it?' "

The next big meet, the San Jose Invitational, provided more proof. Patrice came north by herself. "I was psyched," she says. "I had been running well—13.5, 13.5, 13.5—and I wanted a breakthrough. But then I realized I forgot my sweats. All I had was my raingear—that sh-sh-sh kind of material. I thought, How STUPID of me. I mean, I had always done stuff like that and it made me nervous, being a dingbat.

"Then I said, 'Okay, I'm not going to let this bother me.' I went off by myself and started self-hypnosis and programming the race, seeing it in my mind, feeling myself run. I warmed up, felt great—I was feeling almost cocky."

Donnelly won with a time below the Olympic qualifying standard of 13.4. Unfortunately it didn't count—it was "wind aided." She was sure, however, that she could do it for the books, and in the next few weeks she did, at a meet in Irvine, Calif.

Then came the U.S. Olympic trials—in any year, says Dave Rodda, "the world's greatest track meet." For Patrice, everything hung on this one meet, on making the Olympics. Anything that would come after that, she thought, would be icing on the cake.

In 1976, for the first time, the women and men competed for berths on the team together; for the first time the women walked out on the track to the sound of 16,000 people screaming. "Through all of this," Rodda remarks, "she was just moving through the trials, doing her thing. She was so self-confident. It came down to the last day, and there she was, in the finals.

"I'll never forget it. We were staying at the New Oregon Hotel, and Patrice came to get me. As we walked across the street to the track I felt like I was going into a bullfight. She looked at me and said, 'Relax. Everything's going to be great.'

"Then, God as my witness, the gun went off, she went—she really went—and my knees gave out."

Donnelly came in third, separated from the competition by just hundredths of a second. She ran the hurdles in 13.36 seconds, faster than she ever had before or ever would again.

"I ran a great race from start to finish," she declares. "Not only did I make the team, I ran my personal best.

"To be an actor," says Donnelly, "you have to face things in yourself that you don't want to face. I was kind of a timid person. I forced myself to do things, like hurdling, but that was all external. In acting you have to open yourself up, expose the nerve."

When the shooting began on *Personal Best*, Patrice proved just how good she was at this new, self-revelatory craft. She even won over Scott Glenn, who portrayed coach Terry Tingloff and who came into the enterprise worried that he was about to be "stuck with a stiff that can't act." "It was a bitch to get her out of the blocks," Towne says, "but once she was out she was gone."

The first time Donnelly saw herself on the screen she was surprised. "Hell, I *liked* myself. I was impressed," she hoots. Now she'll tell you quietly, "I'm good." Still, below the confidence is a remnant of surprise and she repeats her self-assessment like a charm: saying it aloud makes it so.

For most critics, Donnelly's screen debut was plenty of proof of her acting abilities. In *Newsweek* Jack Kroll enthused, "Most astonishing is the performance of Patrice Donnelly. She not only has a ravishing physical grace but in her first acting role plays with unerring emotional truth and sensitivity." And Towne's own critical overview of his discovery is simple: "Her potential as an actress is greater than she realizes. It is as great," he says, "as her desire."

Nowhere was Donnelly's acting more convincing, her potential more apparent than in the difficult and passionate portrayal of Tory Skinner in love with Chris Cahill. It was a performance fueled by the feelings it reflects. "How much of Tory Skinner is me?" asks Donnelly. She repeats the question. "A lot. All those emotions are mine."

But Patrice Donnelly says she is neither homosexual nor bisexual, as she suspects her movie character is. "Don't get me wrong," she says, "I love women, but I'm in love with men." The feelings she projects on the screen come from what Donnelly defines as a basic human need—the desire to be loved, to hold, to touch. They also come from her experiences as an athlete.

"When times are really rough, you're thrown together with this group of women and you have to support each other, and you do *love* each other—and that doesn't mean you're lesbians.

"I know that a lot of people who are gay want so badly for me to be gay, and when they know that I'm not, it's like, oh, God, they feel betrayed. I don't want them to feel like that.

"Part of me wishes I could sit down with every one of them and say, 'Hey, it's okay, be what you want to be, love who you want to love.' But I really do feel the movie made that statement."

Patrice Donnelly has earned herself a closet full of hurdling trophies and a drawerful of great reviews, and right now she is taking a break—resting, you might say, on her laurels. "For so long I worried about the future, I worried about the past. Now I love living moment by moment, day by day."

In real life, just as in the movie, Donnelly lives in gym shorts, faded T-shirts and flipflops. ("I was heavily involved in wardrobe on the film," she laughs. "But the Hawaiian shirts are all Robert's.") There is, however, one new detail. On the ring finger of her left hand a large, clear, white diamond flashes. It is a birthday present *cum* engagement ring from Richard Marks, the man she has been sharing her "moment by moment, day by day" life with.

Marks is a 38-year-old baby-faced titan—a former title holder in the sport of Olympic weight lifting and a shot-put contender as well. He did eight years as a computer engineer in California's Silicon Valley before corporate life got the better of him and he walked out. Now he pursues his avocations—mostly athletic—and on the side manages investments and business interests that keep him in Porsches, tropical fish and handguns.

He has his eye on a return to competitive shot-putting, an occupation that was interrupted two years ago by a knee injury. He also has his eye on the training regimens of a half dozen or so local athletes for whom he is something between a coach and a guru. Shot-putters wake him up in the morning so they can tell him exactly how they think they strained a muscle; athletes call him on the phone to discuss yesterday's performance in detail.

Marks seems to dispense about as much encouragement as he does substantive advice. He has designed—engineered—training programs for the likes of Ben Plucknett, American record holder in the discus, and Carol Cady, a promising Stanford discus thrower. And, like most of the important men in her life, Marks is also Patrice

Donnelly's coach.

Donnelly moved in with Marks about a year ago, before *Personal Best* was finished. They had been track and field acquaintances for years, but when they met again in 1981, Patrice ended up four days late getting back to the set. Initially she commuted from northern California to L.A., finishing last-minute details on the film right up until it opened in February.

Since then her life, and Richard's as well, has taken on its own idiosyncratic pace. They get up late and stay up late, a particularly gratifying self-indulgence for Donnelly, who ascribes her 19th-place finish in the '76 Olympics in part to the fact that her race was scheduled for nine a.m.

"I am not a morning person," she says with some chagrin.

Three times a week in the middle of their day—about the time the rest of us are contemplating a glass of wine and the evening news —they head for the track and the gym and a two- or three-hour workout. The track is her bailiwick; she supervises the routine through jogging and stretching to paced strides. Marks works on the shot put; Donnelly offers advice.

It takes about 15 minutes to get to the gym—his domain—and along the way they continue the dialogue they began at the track, a running commentary on how things feel, an analysis of motion, speed, strength, pain. They will keep this up, in hushed conferences, between reps with the barbells, between squats, between presses.

The weight training has satisfied Donnelly's ever-present need for a challenge. The workouts in general have been a way to maintain her body the way that she likes it and close to its old competitive edge. For her, training is like breathing—it is just what she does.

She toys with the idea of returning to competition, curious about the effects of the Marks-directed weight program on Patrice the hurdler. She knows she is lighter and stronger—at 5'8½" and 126 pounds, she can clean 135, squat 235. And she certainly wants to do another movie, a comedy perhaps. Her agent is looking out for her, she says, and when a good part comes along . . .

But she is not in any hurry. If she never does another movie, *Personal Best*—her "baby," she calls it—will have been enough.

The fact of the matter is that Donnelly is waiting for the payoff, waiting for her due. She has pursued two goals and succeeded spectacularly at both. In the process she has lived two American fantasies, realized two durable American dreams. Now, like a true heroine of such tales, she looks out on the future and will not speculate on what it holds. She is content, expectant, hoping to live happily ever after.

Table Talk

by Paul F. Gero of the *Milwaukee Journal.* Marquette University's Terry Reason made a perfect landing after saving a loose ball, much to the surprise of those seated at the scorer's table during a game against Florida A&M. Copyright © 1982, Paul F. Gero.

Lost in Space

by Anacleto Rapping of *The Hartford Courant.* The overhead view of Czechoslovakia's Ivan Lendl serving during a World Championship Tennis tournament in Hartford, Conn., distorts the WCT logo on the floor behind Lendl. Copyright © 1982, The Hartford Courant.

Verdi May Be Small, But It Sure Wins Big

HIGH SCHOOL FOOTBALL

By *HOWARD SINKER*

From the Minneapolis Star and Tribune
Copyright © 1982, Minneapolis Star and Tribune Company

It's really that small.

Somehow, though, Verdi High School has survived talk of consolidation and closing for longer than some folks can remember. And this year, which may really be the school's last, the boys on the football team are providing another reason for people to take pride in their town.

Verdi is 6-0 and one win away from qualifying for the Minnesota nine-man playoffs. After beating Waverly, S.D., 38-0 Friday night, the Trojans had scored 309 points while giving up 24.

"A lot of sports programs put their towns on the map," said Coach Joel Determan. "No one heard of Lake City until Randy Breuer played there. The recognition for these people by going to the playoffs would really be tremendous, it would really prove a point. Nobody has it worse than Verdi as far as having kids come out for sports—and look what they're doing."

How bad does Verdi have it?

Fifteen of the 25 high-schoolers are seniors. Thirteen, though, are senior boys. Ten play football. They are good. Two juniors also play and three younger kids—an eighth-grader and two seventh-graders, including 4-foot-8, 88-pound Torey Rosenboom—suit up to give the appearance of a bench. Verdi is the smallest school in Minnesota with a football team. The entire system, kindergarten through high school, has only 93 kids.

Next year, with only five players returning, there won't be a Verdi football team. "Next year," said junior lineman Allen Trigg, "it's going to be a lot different."

"The seniors have been together as a group since first grade and they know what they have to do," Determan said. "As an independent, our only real chance of making the playoffs is going undefeated. They don't want to blow it. I'm not sleeping well at night."

The school is so small that

Donna Kuehl is 50 percent of Verdi's sophomore class; Merle Parsley is the other half. They have two classes, English and social studies, by themselves and join other students for the rest of the day.

Recently, Kuehl and Parsley got into a bit of trouble over a sign they made for Verdi's homecoming game. It urged the Trojans to "Can the Flyers." Trouble was, they tacked a beer can to the sign and social studies teacher Alan Steinhoff took offense.

The sophomore "class" discussed the incident and the beer can was replaced.

Parsley is class president and secretary; Kuehl is vice president and treasurer. "We just switched from last year," Kuehl said.

She added that friends from elsewhere "know better than to make fun of our school when I'm around. We're really proud of this place."

Every so often, a Southwest State University professor brings a class to Verdi (pronounced VER-die) to examine life at a tiny rural school. The two sophomores are feature attractions and repeatedly are asked the same questions—What's it like? Do you like it here? Would you rather go to a bigger school? What's there to do?

"But they don't know it any other way," Steinhoff said.
What Kuehl knows is this: "In a bigger school, you always have drug or alcohol problems. Even in a school that's not much bigger than this. Here, we wouldn't know where to find it even if we wanted some."

The school is so small that

Alumni suit up for practice on Wednesday night.

"They have to," said quarterback Deven Houselog. "Otherwise, we don't get any hitting in."

The 15-man roster means there aren't enough bodies for a full scrimmage and Wednesday practice is the only time when workouts include contact. Determan and Bob Plueger, the assistant coach, also don uniforms and line up across from their team.

"You find out a lot about your players this way," Determan said. "Hey, I'm 25 years old and I just want to come out in one piece. You find out who the players are; it's like being able to scrimmage with them in basketball. There are some vicious hits out there. Two weeks ago I almost got killed on the first two plays. I had black and blue marks and was sore for a week."

"It's great," said Jim Ripley, a 230-pound tight end and linebacker. "He doesn't lip off too much during practice because he knows he's going to get it on Wednesday night."

Ripley, fortunately for Determan, was laughing when he said it.

The school is so small that

Homecoming 1982 had touches that made Verdi's celebration different from any other homecoming in the free world. Thursday night, after the volleyball team won its first match in two seasons, the gym was cleared and a stage quickly assembled.

Verdi's gym is a Quonset hut that was trucked into town in 1966 from Ruthton, 14 miles east, where it had been used for storing grain. The basketball court is about 15 feet too narrow and the out-of-bounds lines are almost flush against the wall. Because of those problems, the basketball team plays home games seven miles away in Elkton, S.D.

"You just take things in stride," said Determan, who grew up in Wheaton, Minn., and also coaches basketball. "We make do. You can have bad facilities or would you rather have bad athletes? I take bad facilities."

After the final nail was pounded in the homecoming stage and 100 or so people seated, the king and queen candidates entered—four boys and both senior girls, Janelle Otkin and Vicky Selken.

"I kind of wish we had more women around here," complained Randy Hunter, a senior wingback and king candidate.

Before the coronation, however, the freshmen had to be initiated. Last year, Kuehl and Parsley had to sit on a block of ice and sing eight verses of "Old McDonald," down to the rabbit. This year's freshmen had their hands tied behind them and were forced to eat pie tins full of chocolate pudding followed by a pickle.

Then, the big moment came. Houselog, the quarterback, was select-ed king; Otkin defeated Selken in balloting for queen. The royalty held court at a receiving line and were the featured attraction in the next afternoon's homecoming parade.

The entire school, kindergarten and up, participated in the parade. Still the event didn't force the Lincoln County sheriff's office to close down the main drag, a tar strip barely two blocks long.

First came the band, a dozen or so strong, followed by kinder-gartners with heads encircled by construction-paper stars. Older kids carried signs and the royalty trailed. Some teachers dressed as clowns. Earlier, in the school hallway, the king and queen held a sheepish conversation during which they opted for wearing their ceremonial robes while riding atop an old Pontiac. Houselog carried a trophy, Otkin a bouquet of roses.

Everything stopped in front of Kit's Corner—Verdi's restaurant, grocery, gas station and center of gossip. There were pep talks and cheers and more tunes from the band. About half of Verdi Town-ship's 325 residents (all but about 60 of whom live outside on the rectangle called "town") either watched or participated in the 15-minute spectacle, which ended with another tradition—dousing the coach with a bucket of water.

"We don't drag it out," Determan said before getting soaked.

Many of those who didn't have to be elsewhere ended the afternoon with coffee at Kit's.

The school is so small that

"We have a fairly good turnout for everything," said Ann Peterson, whose son, Doug, is a 275-pound lineman. "Our Christmas program, Veterans Day program, spring concert, anything else we have dur-ing the year."

School board Chairman Leo Wagner, Verdi class of 1937 and son of the original school janitor, added that students "have to be active in a lot of things in a small school because it wouldn't work if they didn't. We used to have a wrestling team and a lot of basketball players would wrestle too, just to keep the program going. That was a long time ago."

It's also been a long time since they first talked about locking the doors of the one-story brick school. "They've always said they were going to close it," said Houselog. "They were saying that when I was in first grade."

"I didn't think I'd graduate from here," said Dale Lambert, class of '57. "I had a year to go and the school was so small I didn't think I'd make it. You don't want to guess about it anymore."

School janitor Don Kuehl, class of '55, recalled "right around then they were talking about how it wouldn't last much longer. But it has. Of course, the way the economy is makes things that much worse."

Recently, the school board discussed a half-dozen options, from keeping the status quo to consolidation with a nearby district. Currently, several students take some classes at Ruthton and most have gone to a vocational cooperative at Tyler. Children with learning disabilities attend school in Pipestone or Lake Benton. There is strong sentiment for at least keeping kindergarten through sixth grade at Verdi. "We're biting the bullet of Reaganomics funding," said Walter Lauer, assistant superintendent and principal.

Wagner said the entire school could stay open. "But is it feasible when you'll only have 40 kids in the top six grades? It's not easy." Because of his position, he won't elaborate. "It's kind of like going to the polls to vote. You don't want someone standing around outside telling you what to do."

The school is so small that

The one small, wooden bleacher by the football field is reserved for the band and there isn't a scoreboard to be found. The goalposts wobble when hit. Yard-line markers are old tires with white-painted numbers. Fans crowd the east sideline and scurry away when play moves their way.

Florence, S.D., was the homecoming opponent. Verdi's seven-game regular season schedule is made up entirely of South Dakota schools. "Last year we had an option to go into a (Minnesota) conference," Lauer said. "But we saw that some of the schools, like Hills-Beaver Creek, are six times our size and others were four or five times as big. We felt we'd sooner play schools more our size, like two or three times bigger. Teams that are three or four players deep could wear us down over a season. We felt this would be best for the kids."

"I've got to make sure there are three or four kids who can play any position in case someone gets hurt," Determan said.

The game was a rout. Verdi scored on 10 of its first 11 possessions and was stopped on the other by the halftime whistle. In the third quarter, Determan allowed Doug Peterson, the 275-pound tackle, to play halfback and he dragged several Florence players into the end zone for a 4-yard touchdown. Jim Ripley and Dayle Grooters, two other linemen, were moved into the backfield with similar results during the fourth quarter. Houselog returned a punt for a touchdown, threw a touchdown pass and ran 29 yards for another score on a broken play. Randy Hunter also scored on a punt return and caught a touchdown pass. Scott Hager, who really plays halfback and is the team's leading rusher, gained 150 yards and scored two touchdowns as well. Florence (enrollment 45) had just three first downs, two by penalty.

Final score: Verdi 70, Florence 0. The offense was basic, with up-the-middle and off-tackle plays predominating. There was no need for much else. Both teams—Florence brought 20 players—used their starters throughout the game.

"I don't believe in running up the score," Determan said. "The first couple of games we were close to scoring late in the game and I had Deven just down the ball. If you tell the guys not to go 100 percent, they'll get hurt. I don't have the answer. But I wouldn't mind having that problem every game."

Against Waverly (enrollment 62 and the only loss in Verdi's 5-1 1981 season), Houselog threw two touchdown passes to Hunter and returned an interception 63 yards for another score. Hager added a 66-yard run for the final touchdown and carried 19 times for 171 yards despite playing on a rain-soaked field. Dan Schoonhoven, whose older brother Dave brought fleeting fame to Verdi by winning the Class A pole vault title in 1980, scored the other touchdown.

If Verdi wins October 22 at Ramona, S.D., it will meet the Pheasant-North Conference champion, probably Starbuck. The game is tentatively scheduled for October 28 at Starbuck, which is tied with Westbrook for No. 1 in the state nine-man poll. Verdi is unranked but has been receiving votes.

"We can smell it now," Determan said after the Waverly win.

"I'll tell you one thing," Leo Wagner said. "People are talking about going to the playoffs no matter where the games are played. They're really excited. It's good for the kids, too. Sports mean an awful lot to the community.

The ultimate—however improbable—would be for Verdi's players and partisans to make the 200-mile trip to Minneapolis for next month's Prep Bowl.

"We've kind of been fantasizing about that," Hunter said.

"Anything can happen in a tournament," Determan said. "I know that's a stereotype. But each team has only nine players on the field at a time and I'll take our nine anytime."

Chacon Lives With Dream, Relives Nightmare

BOXING

By *RICHARD HOFFER*

From the Los Angeles Times
Copyright © 1982, Los Angeles Times
Reprinted by permission.

Bobby Chacon, one-time street-gang fighter, must now travel some 10 miles to find a street, about 60 more to find a fight. This is a long way from Pacoima, any way you look at it. From the San Fernando Valley to the Big Valley, from urban guerrilla to boxer to gentleman farmer.

Chacon has lived here two years, in a handsome "double-wide" mobile home. Palermo, no metropolis, is really just a four-way stop an hour's drive north of Sacramento. The Once-in-a-While barber shop, Engasser's Market, a Peacock service station and the Palermo Hardware constitute the downtown area. Chacon's home, at the end of several miles of twisting dirt road, may be said to constitute the suburbs.

He lives bounded by 20 acres of grassy meadows, some of it just now afire with purple wildflowers, some of it cooled by a rock-strewn, pool-pocked stream. Stands of oak populate the softly hilled horizon. There is a rabbit hutch some 100 yards from the home, a pig pen a bit farther. An aggressive goose, a turkey and two yapping dogs—a squat boxer and a chihuahua—form a kind of rural street gang. Or would, were there a street.

This is Chacon's landscape, a tranquil one with laughing kids—who produce the only sounds—and contented animals. It's a leafy playground is what it is, on this day alternately cooled by gentle breezes, warmed by unobstructed sunshine.

Yet it is not now an altogether happy picture, the Walden-like backdrop notwithstanding. For Chacon's interior landscape has been ravaged, the once-tranquil scenery within now a chaos of loss and guilt, personal rubble. And the most terrible landmark of all, the horror of a young wife, waiting for a call that never came, shooting herself in the head with a .22 caliber bullet, the record, "You Could Have Been With Me," spinning to a silent conclusion on the turntable.

Chacon has just completed the day's training at the Butte County Police Athletic League gym in nearby Oroville. He's working toward a May 4 fight with Rosendo Ramirez, a headliner on one of Babe Griffin's cards in Sacramento. Chacon, the featherweight champion in 1974 but an unpredictable fighter since losing the title in his first defense, hopes to be working for a title shot as well. He's 31 now and if time hasn't already run out, it is certainly running short.

At the gym he spars six rounds with some local amateurs, offering them as much instruction as he is deriving preparation ("You've got to keep your hands up—look how easy it is to get through—boom"). He uses the speed bag, jumps rope, does pushups, then finishes with 100 situps. By then the little gym is empty, the sparring partners and their wives, girlfriends and kids having left.

On his way to his own kids, he mounts the last hill in his gray-primer-painted '48 Chevy, a roostertail of dust hanging in the air behind him. This is still home to him and his three young children. Home, too, to memories both happy and horrible. He settles onto a couch and his two youngest, 6-year-old James and 8-year-old Chico, drape themselves around him, almost like the wedding rings he now wears on a gold chain around his neck.

A reporter who has been spending the day with Chacon asks questions about Chacon's grief and the story of his wife's suicide spills out, along, in time, with tears. A photographer records them—a wipe of the eye, a click of the camera. Good journalism, maybe. As human behavior goes, it's a bit shaky.

It All Came Down to Boxing.

It is not a new story, anyway. Chacon told it to reporters the day after his wife Valorie's self-inflicted death more than a month ago. He had sat in a Sacramento motel room and had said that his 13-year marriage, a loving one by all accounts, had degenerated into a kind of war over boxing. She had gotten him off the streets and into boxing, long ago. But now she wanted him out of the ring.

It may have begun with the beating an out-of-shape Chacon took several years ago at the hands of David Sotelo. Valorie, who had never seen her husband hurt, was as devastated by the damage as he was. She began insisting that he retire. Chacon resisted, but was haunted by her doubts about his future. He became an unpredictable performer, postponing important fights for vague reasons. He folded one show saying he wanted to leave camp to see his kids at play.

In the ring, he was still unpredictable. His manager, Jackie Barnett, remembers that Chacon, between rounds, would scan the ringside for his wife. Once or twice during a round, Chacon would clinch, spin his opponent, just to locate Valorie in the crowd.

Chacon either could not or would not give up boxing. His promises, even in their retelling, sound vague. He would stop after this fight, or that fight. At the end of this year, at the beginning of that. Or once he won the title. Or something.

There were these broken promises then. And other things—her loneliness, her low self-esteem. Who knows what? Early in the year, while Chacon was in Sacramento preparing for a fight, she attempted suicide with sleeping pills. Her brother had to break the door down to reach her. In the hospital she awoke in a rage at having failed. She tore the tubes from her arm, returned home and tore that apart. Chacon wasn't told until after his fight.

Doctors told Chacon she would try again. Chacon says it's funny that you can be told a thing like that and yet not really hear it. He didn't find out until later but Valorie was telling friends—everyone but him—of her desperation. The phone bills mounted as Valorie reached out. She told one friend that Bobby would fight again, but over her dead body. She told another that her husband would be better off in boxing without her. She told Barnett that she had a million-dollar ending for the Bobby Chacon story he was then trying to produce. "I'm going to kill myself," she told him.

Valorie took a trip to Hawaii, apparently looking for a job. Finding nothing but rejection, she returned. She was found wandering in the San Francisco airport. Chacon went and got her from a hospital in San Mateo. That night, back home, he lay with her on the floor, hugging her. He thought everything was all right.

But several days later he had to leave for Sacramento for yet another fight camp, and she couldn't believe it, that he was leaving so soon after her return. There were phone conversations in which Chacon promised to quit. But there were not enough phone calls, apparently. Valorie's mother was in the mobile home that day and she remembers Valorie waiting tensely by the phone. Late that morning, just as Chacon would have been going to train, Valorie abandoned her vigil, placed the record, "You Could Have Been With Me," on the turntable and went into her room and killed herself.

When Chacon reached her, she was still lying on the floor. "There she was," he says, "that little cutie. All that terrible blood. The blood just ran off. She looked pretty. I loved her so long—I only had love for her. I always loved her but I lost her . . ."

The next night Chacon climbed into the ring in Sacramento to fight Salvador Ugalde.

There is no explaining that, not even now, a month later. "All I know," he says, "is that it would keep me right for another day." For another day it did keep him right. But, having smashed Ugalde for a third-round knockout, there was little immediate redemption to be found in boxing. He returned to their home and cried for two weeks.

"She got tangled up in the web and the spider got her," Chacon says quietly, still haunted by her presence, still trying to locate her. "She was trying to figure out a lot of things those last few days but I didn't realize how she was slipping. It's funny—13 years, we knew each other to the bone, all the truths. She was my best friend. There was real love there. But you just don't hear things."

Chacon is at times furious with the inadequacy of his grief. At times he is just furious. "I was trying to make a good life for us," he says, recognizing his wife's suicide as an accusation, a blow he could neither fend nor return. "What was I going to be? A fireman? I wanted to make something out of my boxing . . ."

He trails off, as he must do often during these awful recollections. "Now it's all too late and it doesn't really matter," he finally says. "Except late at night."

Chacon says he was visited by Valorie's spirit two days after her death. His account: He walked into the bedroom and he was blinded. "Val, I can't see," he said. But Chacon said she guided him to the bed, not saying a thing, and placed her arm around him. "It was a good feeling," he said "a warm feeling. It was as if she was saying, 'You've got a tough road ahead of you.' "

And it is a tough road. He comes home from his training for a fight and walks into his house to see another woman, a married friend, taking care of his children. It seems to him he should be able to hug that person. There is that hole in his life.

But he still has those children. The youngest two sleep with him at night, crowding him into a far corner of his queen-size bed. Eleven-year-old Jahna sometimes joins them. They do everything together, although, on this day they are doing it without Jahna, who has yet to return from play practice at school. Jahna plays the part of the bear who sings "The Bear Blues." Chacon and his two younger children know the "Bear Blues" by heart and, for the reporter and photographer, they sing together, "I'm not a very happy bear . . ."

He has his boxing. He says he was rededicated himself anew to that difficult and demanding sport. He says he threw his youth away on the game, doing it without reason. He won the title in spite of himself, he says. He'll win it again. In spite of everybody else.

Mostly, though, he has his grief, which is a kind of comfort after all, maybe the last available to him. "You wanted to see me cry," he says to the reporter. "It's all right: it's good to cry. I hadn't talked about these things since the night it happened. I hadn't thought about them. It felt good to talk about them and I'm glad we did. I never want to forget her."

Veni, Vidi, Vindication

PRO FOOTBALL

By *TONY KORNHEISER*

From Inside Sports
Copyright © 1982, Active Markets, Inc.

Bill Walsh does with the passing game what Vince Lombardi did with the running game.

There—in the same breath, in the same sentence, on the same level with St. Vincent. Such a narrow ledge to walk. Such a long drop down.

As odd a coupling as it may appear, it is threaded on the needles of right time, right place, right man. Both men, well into their 40s when they became head coaches, were given wrecks to salvage. The early '60s matched a cold, demanding foreman, Lombardi, with a small, working-class town, Green Bay, and produced the concept of the invincible dog-soldier infantry. The early '80s match the pearl-handled theorist, Walsh, with an androgynous sophisticate, San Francisco, and produce the concept of intelligently negotiated victory.

Walsh, the Lombardi of the '80s.

So what took him so long to become a head coach?

For a week in the dead of winter, in the despair of Detroit, a meticulously seamless package of style and substance was handed an open microphone and a captive audience—an opportunity to cement the first brick in the wall of his legend. Full faith and credit reached out for Bill Walsh at 50 and found him joyful and absolutely in his prime, as if all his life he was only waiting for this moment to arrive.

Walsh popped out of the pack as Most Visible Personality of this Super Bowl in the tradition of Hank Stram (1970) and George Allen (1973). A Super Bowl is an annual Write of Hype, and in this one—where both teams Bob Beamoned from 6-10 to Super Sunday—the excessive praise justifiably landed on the coaches. And who would the media rather identify with: Forrest Gregg, the Thunder from the Tundra, or Walsh, the understatedly elegant San Francisco Savant?

Walsh was called "urbane," "refined," "sophisticated," "cerebral," "professorial"—not to mention, "a genius." (OUR MAN INTER-VIEWS GRIDIRON GENIUS!!! FILM AT 11) He was Frank Lloyd Wright of quarterbacks. You wondered how anyone completed a pass before Walsh came into the league. (SAMMY BAUGH ON WALSH: "HE COULD'VE HELPED ME." SEE SPORTS) After so many years of watching Landry, Noll, Shula and Grant advertise Facials by Mount Rushmore, Walsh's look was delicate in comparison. And he was so approachable. First of all, he laughed; he has a good, quick, mischievous sense of humor. Who can forget him greeting his team in Detroit disguised as a bellhop? And Walsh's body language—last seen on Jack Benny—gave him an intriguingly feline ambience on the sidelines. A cultured pearl with silver hair and steel rims. Put away that play book—get this man Gentlemen's Quarterly (COMING NEXT MONTH: BILL WALSH'S FASHION SECRETS —A PHOTO ESSAY)

Consider how he started: born in The Great Depression, the only son of a factory worker who, in 1931, was lucky to find work for 35 cents an hour in an automobile plant. Consider how the times shrink the dreams: "There weren't any big plans for me; we weren't from a family that was destined for all that much." Consider how so much of his adult life was spent working for someone else, frustrated by the belief that he'd never get the chance to be a head coach and the lingering doubt that he'd chosen his profession unwisely.

Considering all that, you'd think it couldn't have worked out better for Bill Walsh. Sooner, maybe. But not better.

The Walsh profile inevitably poses the question: What is he doing here? Football seems far too violent, to base—too plebian—for one as cultured and gentle as Walsh.

Intellectual because he reads about ethology, political science and the philosophy of strategy rather than Jack Tatum's epic auto-biography, *They Call Me Assassin.*

Sophisticated because he is fond of art and classical music—although color blindness severely restricts his appreciation of painting, and he'd rather play guitar behind Willie Nelson than oboe behind Wolfie Mozart.

Refined because his clothes match and they aren't all polyester, his fingernails are clean, his tone is soft and he doesn't chew, dip, spit or have a gun rack in his car.

Without fail, Walsh is presented as classier than his milieu. And let it be said that Walsh does not go out of his way to discourage this perception. Has the media simply skewered him on its double-edge sword, puffing him up now just to make him a bigger target later? Or is Bill Walsh a genius? *Buffalo Evening News* columnist Larry Felser laughs at the notion: "Anyone in the NFL who subscribes to *National Geographic* is considered a genius."

There's a story about this very question. It seems a bunch of so-called coaching geniuses once got together at a convention and found a room with a blackboard. Hour after hour they put those X's and O's up on the board. And every time an offensive genius diagramed something "unstoppable," a defensive genius came back with something "impenetrable." Until finally only one of them was left awake, and it was he who uttered the famous last words on being a coaching genius: "Last guy with the chalk wins."

Even if stretching the most subjective definition of genius—great and original creative ability in some art, science, etc.—opens an umbrella that shades Walsh, it is craft-related, not unilateral. Would you ask Einstein to do body-and-fender work? Dropping "genius" into the same sentence with "football coach" seems to be asking for trouble. Any coach who takes a team from last to first in three years will be called a genius. If Brian Sipe completes that pass two years ago, Sam Rutigliano's a genius.

Certainly the blue smoke of mystique already wafts about Walsh, and he no longer has to fan it, since "it tends to work without my adding fuel to it." Part of the mystique stems from Walsh's image as Leonardo da Vinci in cleats. And part stems from his offense, which is the state of the art in the NFL, and apparently so conceptually advanced that it unnerves opponents. Nolan Cromwell of the Rams told Randy Cross of the 49ers, "It drives me nuts." Dwight Hicks and Willie Harper, 49ers who know how it functions, admit they can't design a defense to stop it.

But could the cosmopolitan aspect of the Walsh mystique be artificially flavored? One of Walsh's former players, Bob Trumpy, says that when Walsh became coach and general manager of the 49ers, he decided to do everything he could to deflect attention from how bad the team really was. And so he played what Trumpy admiringly calls The Stanford Card: "To buy some time for the team, he painted a picture of himself as a Renaissance Man who was just stopping off for a while on his way to better things. For the rest of his career he'll be known as a quasi-sophisticate. In reality, Bill's life is football." Although Walsh dismisses the means of Trumpy's theory, as a former quarterback he believes in the ends.

He may look unlike the others. Not that Pete Rozelle, Mr. PR himself, would mind that the winning Super Bowl coach, the symbol of football leadership, has a scholarly, pastoral look. Finally, a coach without Football Forehead—that Cro-Magnon shelf resulting from too many head-ons.

He may think unlike the others. John Madden says of Walsh: "The rest of us react to situation, down and distance. Walsh doesn't. He'll dive on second-and-10. You have no idea what's coming."

He may be ahead of the others. After analyzing the defense of the upcoming opponent, Walsh will decide on his first 20 or 25 plays a few days before the game, explaining he'd "rather make decisions—as the British admirals used to say—in a watertight compartment than on the deck or in the lifeboats." Although this advance scripting seems arrogant and egotistical in that it dismisses the reality of the game and assumes the predictability of the defense, it has impressed many football people. John Brodie, former star quarterback with the 49ers, says of Walsh: "He's at least a step ahead of everyone in the game offensively. There's no downside to calling the plays beforehand. He tells his offensive people what the plays will be, so they can practice them and never make a mistake executing them. And he doesn't just draw up plays and say: 'We'll throw some stuff on the wall and see what sticks.' These first 20 tell Walsh what he needs to know about the defense."

He may even be better than the others.

But he isn't different from the others. He's a football coach. The range just isn't that wide.

He's put a lifetime into this. He started coaching in 1955 and spent 18 years as somebody's assistant. During the season, he gets to work by 7:30 in the morning and as often as not stays until 11 at night. He watches a lot of game films alone. His wife, Geri, says, "Sometimes I go in and watch with him, and when I ask a question I get no answer, so I leave." He's physical. To get away from football he plays tennis. He believes in consolidating power and exercising control. Everyone in the organization except the owner was hired by and is responsible to Walsh. "Basically there's only one way of doing things—his way," says Cross. He loves the game, but hates what it does to him: "As soon as I leave my driveway and head to training camp, my whole life changes. I revert to the football part and it consumes me for months—more than it should, more than it should—it consumes me and it takes my life."

Close your eyes and tell me you don't see Tom Landry.

Most of what you need to know about Bill Walsh is this: He's a 50-year-old native Californian.

If there is indeed any culture in California, it is physical. While much of the rest of the country has to spend between two and four months every year worrying about staying warm, California's top priority 12 months a year is fun, fun, fun till your daddy takes the T-bird away. Californians advise you to "Go for it," because Californians never have to worry about apportioning their time to take care of anything other than going for it. Geography is destiny. You can't go for it in Cincinnati; you have to shovel out of it first. Being a native Californian means never having to say, "It's snowing."

Being a 50-year-old native Californian also means that as you were growing up, your sport was football. Hockey is meaningless to Californians, basketball was an Eastern and Midwestern game, and until 1958 the only baseball west of Missouri was minor league. Walsh grew up near the Los Angeles Coliseum, and part of his Saturday routine was to work mornings for his father in the body-and-fender shop, then take a streetcar to the USC or UCLA game. On Sunday he would see the Rams. In a state in which football was king, Walsh played the kingly position—quarterback (until his college coach said lefthanders don't play there and moved him to end). And unlike in the Midwest, where quarterbacks hand the ball off to somebody named Bronco, in California the priority of the quarterback is to throw. California has always attracted the coaches with a passing fancy, from the NFL's aerial guru, Sid Gillman, through Al Davis, Don Coryell, Joe Gibbs and Doug Scovil. Looking back on his own high school and college days as a California quarterback, Brodie says, "All I wanted to do was throw the ball. The only time I thought we should run was when my receivers got tired. Every quarterback in the state felt the same way."

So we have a California kid who likes football. And what he likes most is the passing and catching. Not the protracted trench warfare, but the go-for-it stuff—the stuff that *looks good*. And when he thinks about what he'd really like to be if he had the talent—it's an artist. And although he's a bright kid, he doesn't have the right courses to qualify for Cal. And he doesn't have the money for Stanford, so he goes to San Mateo Junior College and then San Jose State—and not to knock those places, but he knows they're not Cal or Stanford. And because he's ambitious—"I wasn't going to let my life pass in a journeyman's role"—he wants to prove he's as creative and innovative as the Cal and Stanford kids. Now, add eight years in Cincinnati where a California kid learns to respect what real weather can do and why you can build a conceptual attack based on passing anywhere, but if you do it in the Midwest, you're stalled by November.

Mid-morning in Redwood City and the clouds are still low over the peninsula, a layer of cotton camouflage on the mountain not unlike the layer of blue smoke between Bill Walsh and his public image. Under his easy manner, his casual attire and his quick wit breathes a formal man. Friendly, but not familiar. Cooperative, but not cloying. Responsive, but not introspective. He is always fastidiously clean, as if he has just scrubbed up. He is so clean, so precise, so strategic. He may long to be an artist, but he was born to be an architect.

In his disarmingly civilized way, Walsh calls any extended chat a "visit," and this is a visit in his office about his theoretical principle of coaching. He slips into the royal "we" so often that it seems more an invasion than an incursion. He is flanked by his books, his stereo speakers and his metal sculptures. The tiny photo posters of the San Francisco skyline and a fog-shrouded Golden Gate Bridge were selected by his assistant, Nicole, who also selected the beige-and-brown office furniture not just because she sees Walsh as white-wine-and-earth tones but also because if left to his own color-blind devices he might pick screaming-salmon chairs and an air-raid-red couch.

He is speaking about a violent game and purposefully keeping the volume on soft. The more time you spend with Walsh, the more you become convinced that he loathes violence and the contemporary macho notions of acceptable violence. But here he is working in the combat zone. To watch him trying to keep clean is to hear the sound of whistling in the graveyard.

"A given coach will say, 'We lost because we were out-hit.' Or, 'We lost because Jones missed a block.' Or, 'We lost because we weren't tough enough.' That coaching rhetoric explains away defeat and minimizes the coach's role in it. We don't have that luxury to hide behind. We do our research. We do our statistical analyses. We make decisions as to how to defeat our opponent. If we lose, we can hardly say that we lost because of some macho things.

"You have to have a formula for winning an evenly matched game. You prefer the purely physical overpowering of the opponent. It's more consistent, more dependable. You can use it in any weather. But it doesn't happen much anymore. So you look for a sustained drive early, to demonstrate what you're capable of doing—or at least create the image in your opponent's mind. You see some teams in the NFL that throw for tremendous yardage but cannot hold a lead because they've never developed a running game and they're forced to throw for first downs. You have to practice and develop the rigors and discipline to run the football. We will run the ball. We ran it the last 14 plays in the Super Bowl. But we don't go out to *prove* we can run the football. We don't go out to *prove* we can dominate the other team physically.

"At some point we expect to, and we hope the other teams come to that conclusion. But we don't go out to see who is the most courageous, toughest team in the league. It's unfortunate language, but we know it's taught that football is a game for men, and that to be a man you must dominate at the line of scrimmage. Well, at some point we will test them at the line of scrimmage. But we're not going out on the field to *prove our masculinity.*"

Maybe real men do eat quiche.

In 1978, responding to the growl that defense had become oppressive in its dominance and threatened to numb the public tastebud to the NFL, new rules were written to spice the passing game. One rule guaranteed receivers downfield freedom by restricting a defensive player's contact to within five yards of scrimmage. Another increased the quarterback's time to throw by allowing pass blockers to extend their arms and open their hands.

In 1979, responding to the growl that his team had become oppressive in its foulness and threatened to offend the public nose if not disinfected, Edward DeBartolo Jr., the 32-year-old owner of the recently 2-14 49ers, fired his coaches and general manager and brought in Walsh from Stanford, asking him to reverse the misfortune of the worst team in pro football.

That season the 49ers again finished 2-14, but team offense shot from 27th (of 28 overall) to sixth, and Steve DeBerg, a quarterback of whom little had been heard before—or since—led the NFC in passing yardage. "Walsh should have been coach of the year," says Jerry Glanville, Atlanta's defensive coordinator. "I started bragging on him then, telling people he had the offense of the '80s. They said I was crazy. But I wasn't, was I?" And Glanville wasn't the only one who felt it. Stram, who tried to hire Walsh as his offensive coordinator in New Orleans, says, "Even when Bill was losing, you could see he was going to win big."

The next season the 49ers improved to 6-10 and again increased their point total even as DeBerg was gradually displaced by Joe Montana. Montana's arm had never been deemed praiseworthy, and his success was as instructive as DeBerg's had been. "I have the impression that Bill Walsh never has his quarterbacks in a bad situation. They always have someone to throw to," says Lynn Dickey, Green Bay's quarterback. "And every place he goes his quarterbacks are 60 percent passers. Under his system, they blossom. He magnifies them." The mere listing of the quarterbacks who credit Walsh with making them what they are (or were when he had them)—DeBerg, Montana, Greg Cook, Ken Anderson, Dan Fouts and his two NCAA passing leaders in two years at Stanford, Guy Benjamin and Steve Dils—prompts Glanville to claim, "Bill Walsh's system could make me a good quarterback, and I can't throw the ball in the ocean from the beach."

Q. *Joe Montana, how do you feel about Bill Walsh's system?*
A. I fit in and I'm glad I'm here.
Q. *How important are you to it?*
A. Well, it's his system, but someone has to run it.
Q. *But do you think that Walsh could do it with any quarter-back?*
A. Probably.

1981 was the fourth season for the new rules. Passing yardage was up 115 per game and scoring was up seven points per game.

1981 was the third season for Walsh. The 49ers won the Super Bowl.

Stram says: "Walsh understood the rule changes and how to take advantage of them better than anybody. He did as fine a coaching job as I've ever seen." But, as Gil Brandt, vice-president of personnel for the Cowboys, points out, "Walsh was fortunate there were so many defensive backs in the 1981 draft" and was able to reconstruct a secondary that ranked 27th the year before. "Everyone knew Ronnie Lott would be good but he became dominant as a rookie; Montana and Dwight Clark panned out better than anybody thought; Lenvil Elliott was thought to be washed up; no one even wanted Hicks, but he got nine interceptions. Bill Walsh did an outstanding job; he kept people no one wanted, and they all worked out." (Walsh's reply? Rather testy. "Tony Hill was a third-round pick. No one felt he'd be that good. Dallas was fortunate to get him. There's a certain arrogance about Dallas. You can't say, 'We're brilliant, they're fortunate.' ")

"The rest of the NFL ought to be in awe of Bill Walsh, but I really don't think they realize how good he is," Randy Cross says with some amusement. "They would never let him get people like Russ Francis and Renaldo Nehemiah if they understood the extent of what he's doing."

And what he is doing is synthesizing into an offensive system the product of an assiduous Midwestern work ethic and an unfettered California play ethic as they clash along the fault line of his soul.

The trademarks of that system are its complexity and comprehensiveness; its continual burden to be innovative, because, says quarterback coach Sam Wyche, "What you did last week can be defensed this week;" its 60 percent completion rate for the quarterback, whoever he is; its advance scripting and overwhelming number of plays. "Most teams go into a game with about 12 passes and 12 runs," Wyche says. "We went into one last year with 89 passes and 31 runs." Walsh's offense is a movable feast. "Walsh is sort of like a kid at the park; he calls plays with so many options," says Jack Reilly, the coach at El Camino Community College and a devoted student of passing offense. "His ability to consistently get people *wide open* amazes everyone." (Last guy with the chalk wins.)

But where Walsh has actually advanced the game itself is in the joining of the conservative doctrine of ball control with the radically liberal concept of controlling the ball through passing.

"Walsh has always believed that passing is as safe as running and that no matter what you do on defense, he'll have a receiver open and his quarterback will find him," says Dick Steinberg, director of player development for the Patriots. Trumpy says Walsh tells his quarterback, "Don't throw the pass away. Complete it, even if it's only for six inches. Make the defense make the tackle." Glanville, who prides himself on an obsessive study of Walsh's offense, concludes: "It's like eating an elephant. You can't put it all in your mouth at once. It's nibble, nibble, nibble. We chart Walsh's passing game as long handoffs. They don't want to score in a hurry. They'd just as soon take eight minutes. Against the 49ers there's a lot of thirds-and-short. Against San Diego and Oakland there's no such thing. And he's a great defensive coach because he keeps his defense off the field. The philosophy is, don't turn it over and eat up the clock. All of a sudden they're up 14-0 and you discover that there's no time left."

Walsh began his coaching career as a graduate assistant at San Jose State and then at Monterey Peninsula College. He got his first head-coaching job in 1957 at Washington Union High School in Fremont. When Walsh arrived, the school had 2,100 students and three years' worth of 1-26 in football. Three years later when he left, the Freeway had been completed, there were 4,000 students and he'd posted a 9-1.

From there he went to Cal, as an assistant coach under Marv Levy, and then to Stanford, to assist John Ralston. Cal and Stanford are the two best academic institutions in the state, and Walsh not only felt proud working there, but he felt a certain vindication—the concept plays a large part in his life—when he found out he "was capable of dealing with that group of people." Walsh used the same recruiting pitch at both schools, emphasizing the academic reputation and telling students that by attending Cal (or Stanford) they could be "better" than they were. On a number of levels, it was a class pitch.

Walsh went to the Oakland Raiders in 1966 as an assistant. He stayed only one year, but says it had the biggest impact on his career because he learned the Raider offense as created in San Diego by Gillman and improved by Davis when he moved on to Oakland. Walsh calls Gillman and Davis "brilliant football minds" and their system "the most complicated offensive system the game has ever known." One year to learn the most complicated offensive system the game has ever known? "To be honest I think I was capable of learning it in a year, where a lot of people would have come out shaking their heads."

The following year Walsh had a midlife crisis of sorts. "I was probably a little overly ambitious about becoming a head coach," he says. "But it didn't seem to be working out. I didn't want to let my life slip by. I wasn't that old, but I felt I could do more with my life."

He decided to go to graduate school at Stanford and study business. But to cushion the culture shock, he would coach the Continental Football League San Jose Apaches, "and then step out of coaching altogether." On the once-a-coach-always-a-coach theory, most people figured Walsh went to San Jose to have his own team. Madden, who was an assistant at Oakland with Walsh, says Walsh "always wanted to be a head coach. But I think he went too far down for it. You don't go to the San Jose Apaches to coach in the AFL or NFL."

After one season Walsh didn't go to the San Jose Apaches at all. There were no San Jose Apaches. The team went belly-up. And so, apparently, did Walsh's career change because the next year he was assisting Paul Brown in the first year of the Cincinnati Bengals. He must have gotten tired of packing and unpacking because he stayed eight years developing and refining one of the best offenses in football. "He built Ken Anderson from the ground up," says Trumpy.

As well as the Bengals did, making the playoffs three times, you'd think Walsh would have received some coaching offers. And he might well have received offers to coordinate the offenses of other teams had Brown not denied teams permission to talk to him. Gillman says he tried to hire Walsh at Houston (to spend a year learning the system before becoming head coach) but Brown denied him permission. Trumpy says, "Paul denied several teams and never even told Bill." Walsh declines to accuse Brown of that, but says, "I was caught up in a syndrome where you become too valuable to someone and they can't afford to lose you."

Still, nobody but Gillman ever inquired about making Walsh a head coach. "I think I might have scared people off," Walsh says. "I think my style may have been too penetrating. I wasn't your typical comfort-zone coach. The people who'd recommend me couldn't pat me on the head and feel good privately that I'd fail. And the people who'd hire me couldn't feel comfortable thinking they'd be in full control. The years would pass, and we became more established in Cincinnati. I became less aggressive in pursuit of jobs. And lurking behind the scenes somewhere was the thought: 'What if Paul Brown retired?' You didn't want to damage your relationship with Paul. There was always the good possibility I would become the coach."

Q: *Did Brown ever tell you that you would become the coach?*

A: I wouldn't want to remark on that; it wouldn't be in good taste.

Q: *But you thought you would become the coach?*

A: Oh, sure.

On January 1, 1976, without advance warning, Brown retired and named Bill Johnson, for eight years the Cincinnati offensive line coach, as his successor. Walsh says he was "devastated" by the announcement.

Gil Brandt says, "The question you have to ask is: Why didn't Brown make Walsh the head coach?" Brown's biographer, Jack Clary, maintains that Johnson was always the heir apparent to Brown. Clary is no fan of Walsh; he calls him "a California con man" and "a snake-oil salesman." But Clary and Walsh agree that Brown thought Johnson would be more apt to continue Brown's program in Brown's style than Walsh, who might have tried to make the Bengals his own. Johnson, a gruff, aggressive disciplinarian nicknamed "Tiger," was obviously more in Brown's comfort zone. One man's tinker is another man's damn.

"For years I was in the booth calling the plays," Walsh says, "and Bill was down on the field, wearing the headset, next to Paul. Paul steps away. Bill stays on the field. I stay in the booth. Paul probably felt it was simple and convenient that way and that I'd remain in Cincinnati. But after the decision I felt I was obliged to leave."

As soon as they heard that Johnson was their new coach, Trumpy, Anderson, Chip Myers and Bruce Coslet visited with Walsh. "We went over and said: 'Don't leave,' " Trumpy says. "But he said, 'I've got to go where I can get some credit for what I've done.' What really pisses me off is, if Bill Walsh had been given his reign, I'd be wearing a Super Bowl ring."

Q: *Bill, did you feel you weren't given enough credit?*

A: There isn't any question that at that stage of Paul's life the credit was to go to one person.

Q: *John Madden says, "The Cincinnati thing hurt. The way people saw it was—If he didn't get the head job at the place he worked, then why should anybody hire him?" Do you think it hurt your reputation around the league?*

A: No question about it.

The San Diego Chargers were coming off 2-12. Gene Klein, the owner, and Tommy Prothro, the coach, needed a new offense. And Prothro had often talked about retiring. Walsh went to San Diego as offensive coordinator with a clear understanding from Klein and Prothro that he had the opportunity to become the next coach of the Chargers. The Chargers improved their record to 6-8, and Dan Fouts, in his only year with Walsh, threw for 12 more touchdowns and 1,139 more yards than he had the year before.

But the next year, 1977, the Stanford job opened up, and Walsh became a head coach. "I was going home, going to a great school, and getting a chance to have a won-lost record," Walsh says. "It wasn't a difficult decision. As far as I was concerned, Stanford was the ultimate."

Q: *Could the Chargers have kept you by promising you the head job?*

A: It would have had to have been in contractural terms.

Walsh inherited the remains of a 6-5 team, and brought them in at 9-3, including a victory in the Sun Bowl, Stanford's first bowl game in six years. The next year Walsh's team finished 8-4, including a victory in the Bluebonnet Bowl. "Once we'd established a track record at Stanford, I think it became rather clear that I was a very good football coach," Walsh says. "Very few people become head coaches for the first time at 45. Major colleges wonder: Why weren't you a head coach before? Can you do the hard work? Stanford proved my vindication."

Although it is not clear who called whom, it was reported that at least the Giants, Jets, Bears and Rams spoke with Walsh about possible head-coaching jobs while he was at Stanford. But no offers were made. Walsh says the first team actually to offer him an NFL head job was San Francisco. Walsh was disposed to the 49ers because it was pro, it was home and they were lousy. "You couldn't do anything but improve it." Walsh felt he had "good leverage in terms of the contract" because he was a local hero with a good image, "and the owner was a little beside himself as to where to turn." So Walsh began to visit with DeBartolo. "Ed wasn't interested in running the club. He wanted a coach. I was ideally suited for it. And I was a natural to be general manager. I felt, and Ed immediately agreed, that I had to have control over personnel." Al LoCasale, Al Davis' executive assistant, calls it a "perfect" relationship: "The owner is invisible, and Walsh never calls him, 'Hey, kid.' "

So, at 47, Walsh took virtual control of the San Francisco 49ers. And, at 50, won the Super Bowl. And again felt vindicated.

Of all the words you might pick if you won the Super Bowl and someone asked you to describe your feelings, how many would you go through before you got to "vindicated" and "justified"? Bill Walsh carries them around for openers. And then says: "There were some remarks made about me as an assistant coach. The cast was that I was the kind of person you'd put in a think tank and pass the food under the door, and I'd slip out the magic formula. The more acceptance I got as an offensive coach, the more people said: He's a specialist, not a head coach. Is he really tough enough to command people? Or is he more a teacher that you isolate with a player to teach him the *Scheherazade*? All along I felt I had the talent. I knew I had the training. Once I stepped into it, it felt rather natural. And I think I dealt with it very well."

He is proof that what he told his recruits is possible. He has made himself *better*.

There are no rough edges anymore. He has buffed the outside smooth. In so doing he may have buffed out the passion, but that is a small price to pay for the luster.

He is a rich man now. The house has a pool, and if the Cadillac— the one with so much digital equipment that the guarantee has to be co-signed by GM and Seiko—is in the shop, he can drive the Porsche to work. He is a cultivated man. He has a piano for his wife and daughter; he doesn't play, but he listens. He sketches; his wife paints. He no longer talks about his days as an amateur light-heavyweight boxer. "Boxing is brutal and a dead end," he says. Case closed. He is a successful man. He is at the very top of his profession. He doesn't have to consider leaving football for the corporate world anymore. He doesn't have to worry about being a journeyman, about settling. San Mateo Junior College is just part of the mystique. "At some point we are forced to accept our fate," Walsh says. At this point he doesn't mind being forced.

Part of his fate is to be respected, but not loved. ("You don't want to be too common," Walsh says of his relationship with his players. "It's not like one big Eastern European family.") And part of the reason may be his attitude toward sharing credit. Walsh says he pays people well and he works hard seeking jobs for them, but is "cautious about continuous accolades to people, about heaping trumped-up remarks on people in the hopes of pacifying them." No wonder his coaches and players do not hold their breath waiting for Walsh to praise them. Dwight Hicks says Walsh "isn't the kind of man who'll come up to you personally and stress his satisfaction." Sam Wyche says compliments from Walsh "come in private, and sometimes they are belated." Go around the league and the knock you'll hear on Walsh is, as one source puts it, "He crowns himself like Napoleon." One of Walsh's players says, "Bill likes the spotlight, enough to where sharing it might not seem important." In Walsh's defense comes Trumpy. "He suffered for years with no credit. I don't blame him for not giving any. He's not up for Humanitarian of the Year. He's a football coach."

Part of his fate (and/or his bargaining strategy) also may be that he's not long for coaching. He has a new four-year contract to coach and general manage the 49ers, but says, "I'm not sure I'll coach out the length of it." It seems incomprehensible after waiting for so many years to get a head job that he would give it up so quickly. Yet Walsh admits he has felt like quitting in the middle of each season he has coached. "I'm not as calloused and toughened to the stress and the time it takes. I put more pressure on myself than I should. I don't explain our losses by saying a guard missed a block or we didn't try hard enough. I personally am a little more vulnerable, a little more precarious all the time. It takes its toll."

Q: *Fear? Are you saying there's fear?*

A: I've never had a strong sense of confidence. I've always had a certain fear, a certain uneasiness. I've always accounted for the worst.

Q: *Did the Super Bowl win come too soon?*

A: When it's there, you'd better take it.

"He's always been nervous, and now he's more frightened than ever," says Greg Cook. "He accomplished the ultimate in football, and he knows it. Fear sets in on your ass. Where you going to go from there?"

One antidote to fear is detail. A person can submerge himself in attention to detail and not have time for fear: Walsh is sensitive to appearance, i.e,, stylishness, demeanor, neatness and trimness. "I'm not trying to *prove* I'm a coach by wearing some baggy outfit," he says. That the 49ers are an uncommonly trim and attractive football team may not be coincidental. "We like to be considered a class organization, to have a certain attention to detail. How can you be a detail man with your shirttail hanging out? Your shoes untied? Your socks down around your ankles?" And as he attaches personality traits to dress, he attaches behavioral traits to demeanor. He is careful to separate his practice from his game bearing. "In practice, you're demonstrative because you're orchestrating toward a performance. But in the performance, you don't berate people, you don't run up and down shaking your fist at people. You then are on display yourself. If anyone has command during the game, it's the coach. If he appears disheveled and distraught—emotionally broken—who do the players then look to?"

Who indeed? As he leans back to consider it, Walsh's face tightens in concentration, then gradually relaxes as he comes forward and says, "I came into head coaching too late to ever be The Grand Master. I'll never dominate the game like a Bear Bryant. I'll never own it. But I'd like to have pushed it a little. I'd like to be thought of as creative and having impact on football in an artistic sense. My feeling was always around the artistic part of football."

Last guy with the chalk wins.

Alcorn's Battle Over

COLLEGE BASKETBALL

By *RAY DIDINGER*

From the Philadelphia Daily News
Copyright © 1982, Philadelphia Daily News

Mark Alcorn died Sunday afternoon. The wire service story said he died "peacefully." Obviously, the man who wrote the obituary never met Mark Alcorn.

Mark died quietly, perhaps. He died in his sleep in his St. Louis home, his father and his best friend at his bedside. But, peacefully? No, that description will never do.

It suggests giving in, letting go. Mark Alcorn never did that, not once in his whole life. He surely didn't do it in his final hours when the fate he had defied for 14 months closed in on him at last.

The former LSU guard went down fighting, damn it. If this was a basketball game, he would have kicked open the locker-room door. He would have rolled up his sweaty jersey and splattered it against the wall. Mark Alcorn was many things, but a quitter was not one of them.

He was a competitor, a battler, a kid who never believed a cause was lost until the stands were empty and the gym lights turned off. Ten points down with a minute to go? Mark would figure things were just getting interesting. That's the way he was.

The doctor found the cancer in his lymph nodes in December 1980. They said he had 90 days to live. When he survived the 90 days, they gave him six months. Alcorn laughed and said he'd prove them wrong again. He did, though to this day no one knows how.

The will to live, like the will to win, ran deep in Mark Alcorn. It kept him going through a year of constant pain. It kept him sane through four operations and months of chemotherapy. It gave him strength when nothing else could.

He had to quit school when the disease was discovered, but he stayed close to the LSU basketball program. Last year, when the Tigers defeated Wichita State in the finals of the NCAA Midwest Regional, Alcorn was fidgeting at the end of the bench, chewing on his fingernails, just as always.

When the game ended, they brought a ladder onto the floor of the New Orleans Superdome. The LSU players and fans gathered around the basket and cheered while Mark Alcorn, resplendent in a blue, three-piece suit, snipped away the nets.

He handed the prize to assistant coach Ron Abernathy. Abernathy handed it back. Then freshman guard Johnny Jones took the net and draped it royally around Alcorn's neck.

"The guys want you to keep it," Jones said.

An hour later, standing outside the Superdome, shaking hands, Alcorn still was wearing the net over his open-neck shirt. There were tears in his eyes.

"This is the happiest day of my life," he said. "People keep asking me how I feel. Geez, I never felt better."

The Tigers came to the Spectrum for the Final Four and Mark came with them. It wasn't easy. First, he had to talk his doctor into postponing surgery to remove tumors behind his spleen and breastbone. No one thought the kid could pull it off, but he did.

"I just kept bugging him until he gave in," Alcorn explained. Persistence, that was his trademark.

LSU lost to Indiana in the semifinals, then lost to Virginia in the consolation game. Afterward, Alcorn sat in the locker room, forcing a smile.

"Wait 'til next year," he said. "We'll be back."

Eleven months later, Mark Alcorn was gone, dead at age 23.

Darren Sneed and Mark Alcorn grew up together in St. Louis. They met when they were teenagers and they fell in love with the same dame, namely basketball.

Darren was 14, a freshman at Oakville High. Mark was 15, a sophomore at DeSmet High, the local Catholic school. They were hot-shots on their respective teams when, one day, Darren dropped by Mark's house to get acquainted.

"We only lived a mile apart," Sneed recalled yesterday, "so I thought, 'Why not get together?' I introduced myself. We went around back where he had his basket set up and we started playing.

"We didn't stop for five years. In the summer, we'd play all day long. In the winter, we'd play until it was dark. We went after each other like you wouldn't believe.

"I pushed Mark, he pushed me. I don't know if either of us were super-talented, but we made each other better. His dad (Harold) worked with us quite a bit. He was a big star at St. Louis University in the '50s. Great teacher of fundamentals.

"I had a pretty good high school career," Sneed said, "and I owe it all to Mark and his father. I scored 30 points once as a senior and I was only 6-foot, 160 pounds. I didn't overpower anybody. I just kept digging. That was Mark's game."

Mark Alcorn was the playmaking 6-1 guard on a DeSmet team that had Steve Stipanovich and Mark Dressler, two University of

Missouri stars, in the frontcourt. Alcorn was quick, smart and handled the ball, Sneed said, "like a yo-yo."

He made all-state and accepted a scholarship to St. Louis U. After one year, he transferred to LSU, partly to escape the inevitable comparisons to his father, partly to follow in the sneaker prints of his idol, Pete Maravich.

"That was Mark's dream . . . to play at LSU," Sneed said. "The Pistol was his man. When we played one-on-one, he'd drive past me, throw in a wild, off-balance shot and he'd say, 'Pistol Pete strikes again.'

"Mark went to Maravich's summer camp one year. He came back with this photograph of him with the Pistol. He had it hanging in his room. He talked about playing at LSU a lot."

Mark Alcorn did not have a great career at LSU. In fact, he hardly had a career at all. He sat out the year after his transfer, played in only 10 games as a sophomore, then became ill early last season.

"I'm sure Mark would have worked his way into the program if he had stayed healthy," said Sneed, who played two seasons at the University of Wyoming.

"He could run an offense as well as any guard around. He'd give you a fake, then take off for the basket, make a play. An unselfish player, a born leader.

"We talked a couple times a week and last fall he started telling me about these stomach pains he was having. They'd wake him up in the middle of the night. They'd hit him during practice and make him double over.

"He thought he was getting an ulcer. He said he was taking some pills and they were helping. The next thing I knew, I heard he got real sick when the team was up in Alaska and they sent him home.

"I went to see him," Sneed said, "and his father took me aside. He told me what the doctors had found (tumors). I felt numb. I couldn't believe it.

"Mark was such a vital guy. Always in great shape. Never smoked, never drank, never did drugs. It didn't seem possible. But he took it in stride. He said, 'I'm gonna beat this thing.' He had that attitude right to the end."

In June, it appeared Mark Alcorn had, indeed, beaten the odds. The tumors had shrunk significantly and the doctors felt his cancer was in remission.

There was a brief celebration, followed by a crushing reversal. The cancer flared up again, but this time it spread more swiftly, more savagely. Alcorn was rushed to a special clinic in Houston for treatment.

His condition deteriorated steadily. He lost his hair. His weight dropped from 185 pounds to 110. The pain grew more intense. Still, he refused to complain, he refused to give up.

"They brought Mark home around Christmas time," Sneed said,

"and I would sit with him every afternoon. We'd play backgammon and chess. We'd play video games and talk basketball. Anything to pass the time.

"I could see how much he was suffering . . . I could see it in his eyes. But he never once said a word about it. He never once said, 'Why me?' You know the one thing he kept talking about? Going back to LSU. That was his goal."

Mark Alcorn went back to campus in the fall for the LSU-Alabama football game. Then, several weeks ago, he flew to College Station, Texas, to visit the Tiger basketball team when it played Texas A & M.

"I couldn't believe it when I saw him," said guard Joe Costello, Alcorn's old dorm roommate. "He didn't look like the same person. He seemed so weak, so frail. . . .

"Then I called him on his birthday, January 28th. I had a few of the guys here in the room waiting to talk to him. We had trouble hearing him, his voice was so faint.

"But, as sick as he was, he was still really into the team," Costello said. "He knew our record, he knew who we had just beaten and by how much. He was asking me about our freshmen and our next game.

"He had just received a postcard from Willie Sims (an old LSU teammate). Willie's playing pro ball in Israel now. And Rudy Macklin (now with the Atlanta Hawks) had called. We talked about that. . . ."

During the weekend, Mark Alcorn's condition worsened. His left lung was riddled with cancer. His right lung was functioning at only 50 percent. He literally struggled for every breath.

At 1 p.m., he took one last, shallow gasp and he was gone. Harold Alcorn and Darren Sneed were there.

That night, Joe Costello received the news at the dorm. He sat up 'til dawn, staring at the bunk where Mark Alcorn used to stretch out, play cards and listen to his Bruce Springsteen albums.

He recalled the winter day he had to help Alcorn pack his belongings in a cardboard box for the drive back to Missouri. He recalled sitting on the curb, crying, for an hour after the Alcorn family pulled away.

The LSU basketball team practiced yesterday. Joe Costello said it was their worst workout of the year. No one was concentrating, no one was talking.

The Auburn game is coming up tomorrow night. It just doesn't seem that important somehow.

Deafening Defense

by Bruce Bisping of the *Minneapolis Tribune.* DePaul University's Janine Douglas makes absolutely sure that Minnesota's Barb Meredith knows of her presence, just in case she has any ideas of shooting the ball. Copyright © 1982, Minneapolis Star and Tribune.

PRIZE-WINNING WRITERS IN
BEST SPORTS STORIES 1983

Thomas Boswell (On the Threshold of a Dream) is a reporter for the *Washington Post* with special affections for baseball and golf. The 1969 Amherst College graduate contributes to such magazines as *Golf Digest, Esquire, Playboy* and often appeared in the now-defunct *Inside Sports*. Boswell's first book, *How Life Imitates the World Series*, was published in 1982. This is the second news coverage winner for Boswell, who is making his sixth appearance overall in *Best Sports Stories*. Boswell also won the American Society of Newspaper Editors first prize for sportswriting in 1981.

Armen Keteyian (Julie Moss Found Ecstasy After Losing to Agony) is a reporter for *Sports Illustrated*. Keteyian, a 1976 graduate of San Diego State University, began his career as a writer for the *Times Advocate* in Escondido, Calif., and later worked as a free-lancer for two years in San Diego. His feature winner in *Best Sports Stories 1983* was a free-lance effort written for the *San Diego Union*. Keteyian moved to New York in June of 1982 after being hired by *Sports Illustrated* to do feature work with some emphasis on college basketball.

John Schulian (Dailey Is a Sorry Character In Deed) writes a nationally syndicated sports column for the *Chicago Sun-Times*. His first-place award in the commentary category of *Best Sports Stories 1983* adds to a glowing list of credits that include a National Headliner Award, two first-place finishes in the Associated Press Sports Editors column-writing contest, three Newspaper Guild Stick-O-Type awards and two nominations for a Pulitzer Prize. Schulian has free-lanced for a number of magazines, including *Playboy, American Film* and the now-defunct *Inside Sports*. His first book, *Writers' Fighters and Other Sweet Scientists*, is scheduled for publication in June.

John Underwood ("I'm Not Worth a Damn") is a Senior Writer for *Sports Illustrated*. His award-winning magazine story, written with former National Football League player Don Reese, is an investigative piece dealing with drugs in sports based on Reese's experiences during his pro football career. The 47-year-old Underwood has spent the last 18 years of his illustrious writing career with *Sports Illustrated* after early stops at the *Miami News* and the *Miami Herald*. He has won numerous writing awards, the latest coming in 1981 when he captured the J.C. Penney-Missouri Journalism Award in the consumerism category for his piece *The Writing Is on the Wall*, an investigative report on the failures of colleges to educate their athletes. Underwood has written seven books with another scheduled to appear in the fall. *Spoiled Sport* will deal with the writer's personal interpretations of what is happening to sports.

OTHER WRITERS IN
BEST SPORTS STORIES 1983

Sherwood (Woody) Anderson (A Tortuous Path to 500 Wins) has spent the last 13 years writing sports for *The Hartford Courant*. The 1970 University of Connecticut graduate has won four writing awards in state and national competitions. The 36-year-old Anderson, who also served two years on the board of directors for the United States Basketball Writers' Association, is making his first appearance in *Best Sports Stories.*

Bill Banks (WBL: It Miss-Fired) began working in 1981 as a sportswriter for the *Atlanta Constitution.* After graduation from the University of Louisville in 1979, Banks worked one year for the *Shreveport Journal* before moving to Atlanta. He is making his first appearance in *Best Sports Stories.*

Furman Bisher (Just Plain Red) is sports editor of the *Atlanta Journal.* He has been honored by *Time* magazine as one of the outstanding sports columnists in the country. After attending Furman University and graduating from the University of North Carolina, Bisher took his first journalism job as editor of the *Lumberton Voice,* a weekly newspaper. From there he went to *High Point Enterprise* and the *Charlotte News* before a three-year stint in the U.S. Navy Air Corps. He joined the sports staff at Charlotte in 1946 and eventually became sports editor. Bisher later became sports editor of the *Atlanta Constitution* and *Atlanta Journal,* the latter a position he has held since 1957. He has written more than 500 magazine stories and seven books, the latest of which is *The Masters—Augusta Revisited.* Bisher, who has been included in *Best Sports Stories* a record 22 times, is a weekly columnist for *The Sporting News.*

Susan Brenneman (In Pursuit of Patrice) is a consulting editor of *Women's Sports* magazine and a free-lance book editor and writer. Her previous credits include stints as assistant editor of *Rolling Stone* and *Outside,* and managing editor of *Rocky Mountain Magazine.* Brenneman's most recent book project is *Grateful Dead: The Official Book of the Dead Heads.* This is her first appearance in *Best Sports Stories.*

Bill Christine (Ride 'Em, Cowboy Jack, Right to Winner's Circle) covers horse racing for the *Los Angeles Times.* The 1960 Southern Illinois University graduate started his career as a sportswriter for the *Chicago Daily News* and moved to the *Pittsburgh Post-Gazette* in 1973. Christine became public relations director at Commodore Downs in Fairview, Pa., in 1976 and joined the Thoroughbred Racing Association as vice president of public relations in 1978 before moving to Los Angeles in '82. Christine has written three books, including *Roberto,* a biography of the late Hall of Famer Roberto Clemente.

Michael Davis (Quincy Basketball Is Devilishly Good) is deputy sports editor of the *Chicago Sun-Times,* a position he took in October of 1982 after serving as assistant sports editor since joining the paper in 1980. Davis holds a bachelor's degree in psychology from the University of North Carolina and a master's in journalism from Northwestern University, where he now teaches a writing course. Before moving to Chicago, Davis worked for the *Clearwater (Fla.) Sun,* holding such positions as assistant city editor, sports editor and managing editor. He received a third-place award in the 1982 Illinois UPI Newspaper Awards competition for feature writing and was a 1979 first-place winner in the Associated Press Sports Editors competition.

Ken Denlinger (Sue Stadler: Alone in a Crowd Through Tears and Triumph) is a columnist for the *Washington Post.* Denlinger, a 1964 graduate of Penn State University, began his career with the *Pittsburgh Press.* He worked there for two years before joining the *Post,* where he has worked since. Denlinger and Len Shapiro are co-authors of a book, *Athletes For Sale,* about college recruiting.

Ray Didinger (Alcorn's Battle Over) is a sports columnist for the *Philadelphia Daily News.* The 1968 Temple University graduate spent one year as a news reporter for the *Delaware County Daily Times* before joining the sports department of the *Philadelphia Bulletin* in 1969. He joined the *Daily News* in 1980.

Didinger, who is making his sixth appearance in *Best Sports Stories,* has won four Pennsylvania Keystone Awards and four Philadelphia Press Association Awards for writing.

Dave Dorr (Mark Alcorn) is a member of the sports staff at the *St. Louis Post-Dispatch.* He was born in Colorado, raised in Iowa and was a 1962 graduate of the University of Missouri. His writing career began at the *Des Moines Register,* where he worked until 1966. His specialties are college sports, with an emphasis on football, basketball and track and field. He is a former president of the U.S. Basketball Writers Association and has covered three Olympic Games. He was selected Sports Writer of the Year in Missouri in 1981 and 1982 and is the author of a non-fiction book, *Running Back.* This is his third appearance in *Best Sports Stories.*

Mike D'Orso (The Master's Cold, Hard Fist of Kindness) is a staff writer for *Commonwealth* magazine in Norfolk, Va. Before joining *Commonwealth,* D'Orso was sports editor at the *Virginia Beach Sun* and a sports columnist at the *Virginia Gazette.* D'Orso, who holds a bachelor's degree in philosophy and a master's in English from William and Mary, is making his first appearance in *Best Sports Stories.*

Jack Etkin (All the Pieces Fall Into Place for the Cardinals) is a sports feature writer for the *Kansas City Star.* Etkin received an economics degree from Union College in Schenectady, N.Y., in 1968 and a master's degree in business from the University of Pennsylvania three years later. After working for an advertising agency in New York City and the New York City Welfare Department, Etkin moved to Colorado and began doing free-lance writing. He was hired in Kansas City in 1978 as a general assignment reporter and worked on the police beat and the financial desk before moving into the sports department in 1981. This is his first appearance in *Best Sports Stories.*

Joe Fitzgerald (Henderson's Joke on Us) writes four columns a week for the *Boston Herald American.* The 38-year-old Fitzgerald has written five books, including *El Tiante: The Luis Tiant Story* and *Red Auerbach: An Autobiography.* He is married and has three children.

Paul Froiland (Strike Force) is a senior writer for *TWA Ambassador* magazine and the managing editor of *Northwest Orient* magazine. Born in Minneapolis, Froiland attended St. Olaf College in Northfield, Minn., receiving an English degree, and later obtained his master's degree in journalism from the University of Minnesota, where he now teaches journalism courses. After graduation, Froiland free-lanced for a year before going to work for the Webb Company in St. Paul. This is his first appearance in *Best Sports Stories.*

Joe Gergen (Gritty Connors a Two-Timer) is in his 15th year at Long Island-based *Newsday.* He has spent the last eight of those years writing a sports column. Gergen was graduated from Boston College in 1963 and spent five years on the sports desk of United Press International in New York before moving to *Newsday.* He was the 1971 winner of the National Headliners Award for sportswriting. Gergen, the 1982 winner in the news-feature category of *Best Sports Stories,* is making is ninth appearance in the anthology.

Lee Green (The Masochists' Marathon) is a free-lance writer who works out of Ventura, Calif. The 1972 UCLA graduate worked as publicity director for women's athletics at the university from 1974 to 1978 after a stint as a television news and sportswriter for Metromedia in Los Angeles, for which he also worked part-time while in school. Green has free-lanced for the last five years with his work appearing in such publications as *TV Guide, Los Angeles, Pro, Outside,* numerous running magazines and *Playboy,* in which his *Best Sports Stories* entry appeared. He also was the associate producer on a documentary about UCLA basketball which appeared on cable television's *Dynasty* series in 1981. This is Green's first appearance in *Best Sports Stories.*

Alan Greenberg (He Didn't Ask to Be a Hero) writes features and covers the National Football League Raiders for the *Los Angeles Times.* He came to Los Angeles four years ago, after a two-year stint with the *Atlanta Constitution.* The 1973 Syracuse University graduate's story on Norm Standlee, the late former Stanford football great, captured first-place honors in the 1982 Associated Press Sports Editors national awards.

Stan Hochman (The Miracles Ended at Lake Placid) has been writing about sports at the *Philadelphia Daily News* for 24 years. Before going to Philadelphia, Hochman worked for newspapers in Texas and California. The Brooklyn native, who holds a master's degree from New York University, is not the only member of the Hochman family with journalistic abilities. Hochman's wife is an award-winning medical writer and his daughter is editor-in-chief of the *Yale Daily News.*

Jim Hodges (Evans Fights Quiet Battle Off the Field) is the 35-year-old sports editor of *The Day* in New London, Conn. He writes three columns a week on topics ranging from high school football to major league sports. The 1969 graduate of Elon College in North Carolina is making his first appearance in *Best Sports Stories.*

Richard Hoffer (Chacon Lives With Dream, Relives Nightmare) has been writing features and covering boxing events at the *Los Angeles Times* for the last four years. He previously wrote for the *Riverside (Calif.) Press-Enterprise* and *The Cincinnati Post.* The Miami (Ohio) University graduate also holds a master's degree from Stanford University.

Pat Jordan (Going Nowhere, FAST) is a free-lance writer and author. His work has appeared in such magazines as *Sports Illustrated* and the now-defunct *Inside Sports,* for which he wrote the story that appears in *Best Sports Stories 1983.* Jordan, a former professional baseball pitcher who spent most of his three years in the Atlanta Braves organization, is a graduate of Fairfield University in Fairfield, Conn. Among the books he has written are *Broken Patterns, A False Spring* and *The Suitors of Spring.*

Bill Knight (Football Religion Has Its Doubters) has covered sports events for the last 3½ years for the *El Paso Times.* After a short stint in the Texas Panhandle town of Childress, Knight spent four years covering high school sports in Temple, Tex. His El Paso assignments have included minor league baseball and college football and basketball. Knight, a University of Texas at Arlington graduate, has won the Texas Associated Press Sweepstakes award and a first place in the Texas Associated Press column competition.

Tony Kornheiser (Veni, Vidi, Vindication) has been with the *Washington Post* for the last four years after stints at *Newsday* and the *New York Times.* His work has appeared in such publications as *Esquire, New York, Rolling Stone, Sports Illustrated, New Times, Cosmopolitan* and the now-defunct *Inside Sports,* in which his *Best Spots Stories 1983* entry appeared. He won the feature competitions sponsored by the Associated Press in 1977 and 1981 and his 1978 story on Reggie Jackson captured news-feature honors in *Best Sports Stories.* Kornheiser's new book, *The Baby Chase,* is a non-fiction work about adoption, scheduled for publication in October. This is his 10th straight appearance in the anthology.

Mike Littwin (Dean Smith Finally *Is* No. 1) is a sports feature writer for the *Los*

Angeles Times. Before coming to Los Angeles in 1979 to cover the Dodgers, the University of Virginia graduate worked for the *Newport News Times-Herald* and the *Norfolk Virginian-Pilot.* Littwin's biography of Fernando Valenzuela, *Fernando,* was published in 1981. He is making his second appearance in *Best Sports Stories.*

Bill Lyon (A Real Wonder on Just One Leg) is a sports columnist for the *Philadelphia Inquirer,* where he has worked since 1972. Lyon, who has won 27 state and national writing awards and been named Pennsylvania's sportswriter of the year four times, was born in Carmi, Ill. He worked his way through the University of Illinois as a reporter for the *Champaign-Urbana News-Gazette* and later became a columnist and news editor for the East St. Louis, Ill., *Journal.* After working again in Champaign as managing editor, Lyon went to Philadelphia as business editor before moving into sports.

Steve Marantz (Why Suicide?) is a sportswriter for the *Boston Globe.* Born in Weirton, W. Va., Marantz grew up in Weirton and Omaha, Neb., and attended the University of Missouri. After graduation in 1973, he worked four years as a sports reporter for the *Kansas City Star.* After a short stint with the *Trenton Times* in 1977, he was hired in Boston.

Barry McDermott (The Glitter Has Gone) is an Associate Writer for *Sports Illustrated,* specializing in golf and tennis coverage. Born in Covington, Ky., McDermott won a golf scholarship to the University of Cincinnati, where he "made a cameo appearance." He later worked for *The Cincinnati Enquirer,* based just across the Ohio River from his native Covington, before getting the call from *Sports Illustrated* in 1971.

John McDonald (The Ancient Mariner) has worked as a sportswriter since 1973 for *The Everett Herald* in Everett, Wash. Since 1978, he has covered the Seattle Mariners. The 35-year-old from Portland, Ore., is married and has a 2-year-old son named Andy. He is making his first appearance in *Best Sports Stories.*

Bill Pennington (Why Would Cheryl Tiegs Kiss The Scooter?) is a staff writer and twice-a-week sports columnist for *The Advocate of Stamford,* a daily newspaper in lower Fairfield County, Connecticut. Pennington, a graduate of Boston University, covers the New York Yankees and University of Connecticut football and basketball. The Hartford, Conn., native, who has been with *The Advocate* five years, is making his first appearance in *Best Sports Stories.*

Mark Purdy (An Unsung Hero) is sports editor and columnist for the *Cincinnati Enquirer* and a frequent contributor to *Ohio* magazine. Purdy, a native of Celina, Ohio, was a sportswriter for the *Los Angeles Times* before moving to Cincinnati. He is making his first appearance in *Best Sports Stories.*

Ron Rapoport (Watson Big Shot at Open) is a sports columnist for the *Chicago Sun-Times.* Before moving to Chicago, Rapoport worked for the *Los Angeles Times* and the Associated Press. Rapoport, who won a 1982 award for best column in a Chicago newspaper, has written three books. He is making his third appearance in *Best Sports Stories.*

Greg Raver-Lampman (Has Football Been Thrown for a Loss?) is a free-lance writer who has had more than 100 stories published in newspapers and magazines. The 28-year-old Raver-Lampman, a 1979 University of California at Berkeley graduate, spent two years with the *St. Petersburg Times* before opting for free-lance work. After graduation in 1979, he spent a year in both Jamaica and Equador as a communications consultant with the Peace Corps. Raver-Lampman is making his first appearance in *Best Sports Stories.*

Howard Sinker (Verdi May Be Small, But It Sure Wins Big) is a sports feature writer for the *Minneapolis Star and Tribune.* The 26-year-old Sinker has worked at newspapers in Indianapolis, Grand Forks, N.D., and Brainerd, Minn. The Macalester College graduate has won awards for investigative reporting and for his contribution to a series on the Twins' last opening day at Metropolitan Stadium.

Blackie Sherrod (Skull Sessions Are Old Stuff) is the executive sports editor of the *Dallas Times Herald.* Sherrod has captured most of the important sportswriting prizes in the country. To name a few: The National Headliners Award, seven citations as the outstanding sportswriter by newspaper, radio and television colleagues, and many inclusions in *Best Sports Stories.* He also has made a big reputation as a master of ceremonies and banquet speaker and has his own radio and television programs.

Art Spander (Bewitched, Bothered, Beaten) has been the lead columnist for the *San Francisco Examiner* since 1979. After graduation from UCLA in 1960 with a degree in political science, Spander went to work for United Press International in Los Angeles. A later stint at the *Santa Monica Evening Outlook* was followed by a 14½-year hitch with the *San Francisco Chronicle* covering golf, pro basketball, football and baseball. Spander, a frequent contributor to *The Sporting News* and several other magazines, also writes a wine column for *San Francisco Magazine.* He was voted 1980 California Sportswriter of the Year, won the top prize in the 1982 San Francisco Press Club competition and has been honored several times by the Golf Writers Association of America. Spander captured first place for reporting in the 1971 edition of *Best Sports Stories.*

Jerry Tarde (Hogan vs. Nicklaus vs. Watson) is an associate editor of *Golf Digest* and the author of many instructional articles with leading tour players and teaching professionals. He has worked for the magazine since graduation from Northwestern University in 1978. The 8-handicapper plays out of the Winged Foot Golf Club in New York and Juniata Golf Course in Philadelphia.

Prize-Winning Photographers In
Best Sports Stories 1983

Glenn S. Capers (Envy in Stride), a photographer for the *Tucson Citizen*, is making his debut in *Best Sports Stories* with the winning feature photo. Capers, born and raised in New York City, attended Los Angeles City College and did his first professional work as a stringer for the *Associated Press* in Los Angeles. His biggest break was a free-lance assignment for Long Island-based *Newsday* from the Soviet Union. Capers worked for *The Sun* in San Bernardino, Calif., before moving to Tucson.

Jay Hector (Didier Pironi/Ferrari) is a 31-year-old photographer-writer whose winning color picture appeared in *Road & Track* magazine. Hector, a graduate of the California State Northridge school of journalism, was a child actor who lists *The Twilight Zone* among his television credits. Hector, who lives in Canoga Park, Calif., is making his first appearance in *Best Sports Stories*.

Robert B. Stinnett (Cal Beats the Band) is making his first appearance in *Best Sports Stories* a triumphant one with the action photo winner. Stinnett, a member of the National Press Photographers Association and San Francisco Press Photographers Association, has been a staff photographer for the *Oakland Tribune* since 1950. Stinnett lives in Oakland with wife Peggy and children James and Colleen.

Other Photographers In
Best Sports Stories 1983

Bruce Bisping (Deafening Defense) has worked as a staff photographer at the *Minneapolis Star and Tribune* since his graduation from the University of Missouri in 1975. Bisping, who does free-lance work for *The Sporting News*, was named National Photographer of the Year in 1976 by the National Press Photographers Association, Regional Photographer of the Year the same year and recently was elected regional director of the NPPA. He is making his second appearance in *Best Sports Stories*.

Terry Bochatey (Super Block) began his career with United Press International *Newspictures* in New York after graduating from Colorado State University in 1972. Bochatey transferred to Columbus, Ohio, as *Newspictures* Bureau Manager in 1973 and currently works out of Cincinnati.

Richard A. Chapman (Determination) is a staff photographer for *The Daily Courier News* in Elgin, Ill. After attending College of DuPage in Glen Ellyn, Ill., Chapman served a four-year stint at *Press Publications* in Elmhurst, Ill., and worked for a year at *The Daily Journal* in Wheaton, Ill., before moving to Elgin. The 29-year-old Chapman, who is making his first appearance in *Best Sports Stories*, won a National Press Photographers Association first-place prize in 1979 and a first place in the 1980 National Newspapers Association contest.

Curtis Chatelain (Horsing Around) is a lab technician in Ogden, Utah, who spends weekends shooting rodeo events for the Professional Rodeo Cowboys Association. The 24-year-old Chatelain, a first-timer in *Best Sports Stories*, freelances his material to the *Pro Rodeo Sports Newspaper* and the cowboys that participate in rodeo events.

Richard Darcey (Awe Americas) has been photographing sports events for the *Washington Post* for 35 years. Darcey, a three-time winner in *Best Sports Stories* competition (including 1982), also is a former winner in the old *Look* magazine Best Picture of the Year contest and is a four-time winner in the White House News Photographers Association competition.

Ricardo Ferro (Follow the Bouncing Ball) is a staff photographer for the *St. Petersburg Times* whose wide-ranging assignments have taken him to such places as Nicaragua, Honduras, Nassau and Mexico and led to his pictures appearing in publications abroad and throughout the United States. The 42-year-old Ferro was born in Pinar del Rio, Cuba, and attended the Havana branch of Villanova University from 1958 to 1961. He came to the United States in 1961 and received his first photography training in a photo lab in Tampa, Fla. Three years later, he became a lab technician for the *Tampa Tribune* and two years later became a staff photographer. Ferro was named the Florida West Coast Press Photographers Association's Photographer of the Year in 1965 and captured the same award in 1966, 1968 and 1969 while working in St. Petersburg. He is a four-time winner of the NPPA's Southeastern United States Photographer of the Year Award and a five-time winner in the Florida Society of Newspaper Editors' contest.

Paul F. Gero (Table-Top Advantage) is a 22-year-old senior at Marquette University. His first appearance in *Best Stories Stories* is the result of a 1982 internship with the *Milwaukee Journal*. Gero, who started working in photography at age 12 and has worked for newspapers and a photography studio at various times since, plans a May graduation at which time he will seek newspaper employment.

Kevin Kolczynski (Up and Over) is a staff photographer for *The Gainesville Sun* in Gainesville, Fla. After graduation from the University of Florida, Kolczynski worked briefly for the *Miami Herald* before moving to Gainesville, where he has worked for the last year and a half. The 24-year-old Melbourne, Fla., native is making his first appearance in *Best Sports Stories*.

Eric Mencher (Armed and Dangerous) is a staff photographer for the *St. Petersburg Times*. He was born in Enid, Okla., but grew up in Tampa, Fla. After earning a political science degree from the University of South Florida in Tampa, Mencher began working at the *Tampa Tribune*. He moved across the bay three years later. This is his second appearance in *Best Sports Stories*.

William Meyer (Earning Her Stripes) is a staff photographer for the *Milwaukee Journal*, where he has worked since his graduation from the University of Wisconsin-Milwaukee in 1971. He has been named Wisconsin News Photographer of the Year twice and is making his ninth consecutive appearance in *Best Sports Stories*.

Richard Pilling (Close Encounter) is a free-lance photographer based in Fair Lawn, N.J. After graduation from Curry College in Milton, Mass., Pilling began his career with an advertising firm. He gave up advertising six years ago to concentrate on photography and has had his work published in such publications as *Newsweek, Life, Sport Magazine, Football Digest, Basketball Digest, Hockey Digest* and *Hockey Illustrated*, the publication in which his *Best Sports Stories 1983* entry appeared. Pilling also is a regular contributor to *The Sporting News*.

Anacleto Rapping (Lost in Space) is a staff photographer and weekend picture editor for *The Hartford Courant*. Before moving to Hartford, Rapping worked as chief photographer for the *Thousand Oaks News Chronicle* in Thousand Oaks, Calif. He received a journalism degree from San Jose State University in 1978 and has free-lanced for such magazines as *Soccer World, Soccer America, Soccer Corner* and *California Today*.

Bill Serne (Hard Right) is making his sixth appearance in *Best Sports Stories*. Serne, who was graduated from Kent State University in 1974 with a photo-journalism degree, worked for 10 years at the *Tampa Tribune*. The 32-year-old Serne currently is a staff photographer for the *St. Petersburg Times* and was an action photo winner in *Best Sports Stories* in 1974, his first appearance in the anthology.

Gary Weber (Wright On) is *Newspictures* bureau manager for United Press International in Des Moines, Ia. The 22-year-old Weber was graduated from the University of Wisconsin-Milwaukee in 1982. While going to school, he worked part-time for the *Milwaukee Journal* and was a stringer for UPI. Weber is making his first appearance in *Best Sports Stories*.

Kurt Wilson (Out of Sight. . .) is a staff photographer for *The Daily News* in Longview, Wash. He was born and raised in Missoula, Mont., and continued living there until February of 1982. He attended the University of Montana. The 24-year-old Wilson is making his first appearance in *Best Sports Stories*.

The Panel of Judges for Best Sports Stories 1983

Brian Brooks is an associate professor at the University of Missouri and news editor of the *Columbia Missourian*. The former reporter and editor of the *Memphis Press-Scimitar* is co-author of *News Reporting and Writing* and *The Art of Editing*, best-selling text books in their fields.

George Kennedy is an associate professor at the University of Missouri and chairman of the Editorial Department. Before moving to Columbia, Kennedy spent 7½ years as a reporter and editor with the *Miami Herald* and two summers as a writing coach for the *San Jose Mercury*. He is co-author of *News Reporting and Writing* and *The Writing Book*, two college and professional text books.

Ken Kobre is an associate professor and the head of the photo-journalism sequence at the University of Missouri. The former *St. Petersburg Times* and *Boston Phoenix* staff photographer is the author of two leading books on photography and director of the national Pictures of the Year competition.

Daryl Moen is a professor at the University of Missouri and news editor of the *Columbia Missourian*. Before moving to Columbia, he was the editor of two other dailies. Moen is an active member of the Associated Press Managing Editors and a regular judge of such national writing competitions as J. C. Penney-Missouri and Business Journalism. He is co-author of *News Reporting and Writing* and *The Writing Book*.

George Pica is an instructor at the University of Missouri and city editor of the *Columbia Missourian*. He is a former prize-winning editor of the feature and magazine sections of the *Eugene (Ore.) Register-Guard* and the assistant managing editor of the *Seattle Post-Intelligencer*. Pica is a regular judge for other national writing competitions, including J.C. Penney-Missouri.